I0578008

Danielle Ackley-McPhail
Tomorrow's Memories

Book Two in the Eternal Cycle Series

PAPER PHOENIX PRESS

Pennsville, NJ

PUBLISHED BY
Paper Phoenix Press
A division of eSpec Books
PO Box 242
Pennsville, NJ 08070
www.especbooks.com

Copyright © 2009, 2012, 2020 Danielle Ackley-McPhail

ISBN: 978-1-942990-57-4
ISBN (ebook): 978-1-942990-58-1

Originally published by Mundania Press (2009) and subsequently
re-released by Dark Quest Books (2012).

Earlier versions of the Prelude previously appeared in print as *The Birth of the
Tuatha de Danaan* in the following publications: Sabledrake Magazine,
www.sabledrake.com; *Through a Glass Darkly* ©2002 Lite Circle Books;
Children of Morpheus ©2004 Lite Circle Books.)

All rights reserved. No part of the contents of this book may be
reproduced or transmitted in any form or by any means without
the written permission of the publisher.

All persons, places, and events in this book are fictitious, and any
resemblance to actual persons, places, or events is purely coincidental.

Interior Design: Danielle McPhail
www.*sidhe*nadaire.com

Interior Art: vector musical composition ©BuketGvozdey
http://www.shutterstock.com

Cover Art: L.W. Perkins and Christina Yoder
Cover Design: Christina Yoder

Copyediting: Wrenn Simms and Greg Schauer

Praise for the Eternal Cycle Series

ON YESTERDAY'S DREAMS
[Danielle Ackley-McPhail] certainly seems to know
her Celtic mythology...a solid story.
— Piers Anthony, bestselling author of the *Xanth* series

A powerful, poignant tale...a writer of talent, imagination,
and superb storytelling ability. — The Midwest Book Review

Yesterday's Dreams is an interesting mix of Celtic myth, women's
empowerment literature, and urban fantasy...The story, though set in a
modern period, is imbued with all the details and richness
that readers expect from Celtic lore.
— John Ottinger III, Grasping For The Wind Reviews

This novel will appeal to fans of Charles DeLint with its urban approach
to Irish mythology. At times I was mesmerized while at other times...
I had to get up and turn the lights on... — Bitten By Books Reviews

ON TOMORROW'S MEMORIES
The artist in me itches to have a crack at some of the vivid images that
are filling my brain after reading this book. I am eagerly awaiting another
installment. Please make it soon! — Helen Fleischer, artist

Danielle Ackley-McPhail seems to get better with every book...I didn't
want [*Tomorrow's Memories*] to end, and I'm looking forward to reading
the third novel of the trilogy. — Douglas Cobb, BookspotCentral

ON TODAY'S PROMISE
A solid end to the trilogy, well-paced and with a satisfying ending.
Everything came together nicely.
— Keith R.A. DeCandido, author of *Dragon Precinct*

Ackley-McPhail delivers the goods once again in the final book of
her Eternal Cycle series. [*Today's Promise*] is a must-read.
— Jan Nerenberg, Right, Write, and Word-Wright

Other titles by
Danielle Ackley-McPhail

The Eternal Cycle Series
Yesterday's Dreams
Today's Promise

The Eternal Wanderings Series
Eternal Wanderings

The Bad-Ass Faerie Tale Series
The Halfling's Court
The Redcap's Queen

Baba Ali and the Clockwork Djinn
(with Day Al-Mohamed)

The Literary Handyman
The Literary Handyman: Build-A-Book-Workshop

The Ginger KICK! Cookbook

Short Fiction
A Legacy of Stars
Transcendence
Consigned to the Sea
Flash in the Can
The Die Is Cast
(with Mike McPhail)

To Mike,
For giving up so much of my time.

A Note of Thanks

Tomorrow's Memories would not be the book it is today without the selfless, dedicated efforts of David Goldstein, Lee C. Hillman, Wrenn Simms, and my husband, Mike McPhail. All sacrificed their time and effort to the cause.

I have the best friends in the world!

Thank you,
Danielle

Prelude

 death's relentless pursuit. The faithful wind whipped behind them, blurring the signs of their passage, and in its newness, the moon betrayed them not.

Graceful, even in their panic, Anu and Danu locked away their grief to fight for their survival. Anu stumbled, tangled by the tall, wind-plaited grass. Locks of shimmering red hair escaped from her travel braids. The tresses mingled with the grass, giving the illusion that the meadow was pulling Anu under, consuming her.

Danu frantically reached back for the reassurance of her sister's hand. She could not allow Anu to fall behind. From the very womb, their fingers had intertwined, and, if they were to leave this life, she wanted it to be in the same way.

As their hands clasped, Danu nearly faltered. She drew her focus away from what stalked them and settled her senses on her sister. Both love and determination filled Anu's brown eyes to brimming as they met hers. The pain and despair she saw there also nearly brought Danu down. Death did not follow in their footsteps; it ran stride by stride beside them.

"Do not do it, *Lhiannon*." *Sweetheart*. Anu gently but forcefully admonished her twin. "We'll be needing our strength for the tasks before us—the worse for you an' ye make me waste one bit o' what I have left trying to comfort ye. Ye must away with ye an' not trouble yer heart over what cannot be helped." As if to lend force to her words, she wrenched her hand free.

Danu trembled violently. She wanted to cry out, to deny the truth, but she could not. Her sister's end drew nearer with each step. Danu sensed more than saw the wound carrying her twin closer to the Veil. A horrible rent tore down Anu's side, her heart's blood brimming and seeping from it. A muted sparkle of power kept the blood from flowing freely, but as her sister's strength waned, the stream gained force. Danu's grief held her silent. Anu was her strength...the completion of her heart.

"No! There no time for that. Now listen hard: ye must flee from here. Falias, Finias, an' Gorias are but scorched rubble, an' Murias...Murias has fallen into shadow, the gates forever closed to the *Daoine Maithé*." Anu cast a haunted glance the way they had come. Danu's gaze could not help but follow.

For the moment, she saw no sign of pursuit. The surface of the plain swayed beneath the stars with a deceptively peaceful air that clashed with Danu's memories of the carnage and destruction, of city streets painted crimson with blood, lit by the fiery glow of ancient homes turned to pyres. The ravaged remains of their people had been strewn about the cobbles in cruelly crumbled heaps, left to lie where they had fallen in their attempts to defend their kin and homes. The corpses were few, though no hope lay in this, for Anu's Sight had shown that the others had not fled to freedom; rather, they had been rounded up like livestock to meet their fate at the convenience of the enemy. Only the sisters had escaped, traveling between cities at the time of the attack.

No doubt, they would share the same doom if the *Namhaid* — the enemy — caught them.

Danu drew her attention back to her sister's words, eerily echoing her thoughts. "Even now the *Namhaid Conairt* follow us, as sure as hounds, an' soon there will be more on our trail. They must not find ye, they cannot be allowed to drag ye down like the rest o' us, or the *Daoine Maithé* will be dust forever."

Her good hand clutched painfully at Danu's shoulder for but an instant before her strength faltered.

"Ye do not understand, do ye?" Anu demanded. She paused a moment before continuing, her breath thready. "Sorrow has blinded ye. 'Tis only for now ye'll stand alone, an ye survive the hunt, 'tis yerself that'll see that the *Daoine Maithé* rise again." Anu's hand came to rest on Danu's smooth, flat belly. "I'll not be lost to ye forever, then. Now away with ye! I cannot last much longer an' I've one more task to see to."

Danu clasped her sister to her, barely suppressing the keen that welled up in her throat. Without even a thought, she sent a stream of power across the link that bound them. Before her sister could block her, she rooted her soul with Anu's, deeper even than the constant bond they had shared since the womb. Danu shared every ounce of herself in that instant before Anu ripped away with a burst of love and regret.

◈

"Ye wee fool, ye have not strength to squander." Anu struggled a moment. Her throat grew thick, and tears pricked her eyes. "Now away with ye, an' let me do as I may to see ye safely free."

Anu waited until Danu was well away before luring the hunters to herself. Only when she could neither see nor sense her sister's fleeing form did Anu release the barest trickle of her power, as good as a beacon beneath the ink-black sky. Already the wind carried the snarls and shouts of their pursuers. She must muddle the trail that would betray her beloved sister before the *Conairt* descended upon her.

Tearing a bloody scrap from her tunic, Anu fought to keep her hand steady as she probed the open wound in her side. Her teeth clenched and sweat glistened on her brow as she ruthlessly grasped a sliver of bone from the wreckage of her ribs and snapped it free. Not even the rigid control acquired over centuries of life could hold back the scream of agony the act tore from her. Triumphant howls mockingly echoed her wail, chilling her to her core as they drew closer.

Damn! She would have to work quickly. Gathering all she could spare of her dwindling energy, Anu pulled her travel blade from its sheath and sawed furiously at the thinnest of her braids. Then, with careful haste, she wrapped the bone in the scrap she had torn from her tunic and tied it fast with the severed plait. She held it in the now free-flowing stream of blood spilling from her side, all the while chanting fervently in the ancient tongue. Unhindered by her fevered mind, all manner of images began to form, fantastic creatures, both fair and foul, with jeweled wings and needle-like teeth, fey eyes and fickle manner, leviathans of the deep and wispy spirits; all that was darkness and light filled her thoughts, interwoven with her memories of joy and fear and grief. Her imagination formed legions of faerie folk never before seen upon the earth. Their sole purpose: to confuse and distract the *Namhaid Conairt* with tantalizing whiffs of borrowed power, giving Danu time to flee.

Anu kept nothing back for herself; death already held her close. She raised the crude fetish to her face and blew upon it, guiding her creations with all the magic at her disposal. A mist sparkling with power enveloped Anu as she sank to her knees, arms raised above her head in entreaty. The vapors took on her imagined shapes until one by one, she released her only children to the world, feeling a bit of her soul drain away with each one. In her mind, she whispered their names: púca, sprite, faerie, redcap, yeti, leprechaun, ki-lin, selkie, lamai, and so on until each of them knew themselves.

With what felt like her last breath, Anu crumbled to the ground. She could barely muster a sense of satisfaction as she lay upon the flattened grasses, vaguely aware of the approaching sounds of her pursuers.

And then she saw them. Their red eyes glowed in the near-black night, and their short white pelts shimmered like crushed velvet. Thick manes of fiery red hair whipped about their bare shoulders and breasts, while razor-like fangs gleamed almost daintily in their open mouths...open to allow their dragging breaths to taste the scent of the sisters on the air. Their musk rose heavy and cloying, leaving Anu longing for one last breath of crisp, clean air. How could they possibly filter out enough of their scent to track anything less potent than they?

She would never know.

They were upon her, and she could not even gather the motivation to cross the Veil by her own hand, rather than allow them the satisfaction of taking her. She just laid there, eyes raised to the stars, as they circled and baited. Vicious in their frustration, cheated by her lack of response, they sought to draw from her a more gratifying reaction; they lashed out with raking claws and taunted her with flicks of their rasping tongues as if she were a bit of candied fruit. They continued to howl their chilling cries. Moans and growls of battle-lust filled her ears and yet her only thought was to wonder where Danu would find herself when finally she stopped running.

And then she felt a sense of peace—a Vision danced before her, images of a strange, vast island of green, rolling hills and impressive granite cliffs surrounded by seas trimmed in white, lacy froth as they broke upon the rocky shore. Danu would thrive there among the ancient groves and moors, surrounded by her Clan of children.

Finally, her sister's face floated before her mind's eye. With her final breath, she muttered the words of a curse at that beloved one. The name Danu was on her still lips as they dragged her away to Murias.

"Imeacht gan teacht ort, A chuisle mo chroí!" May you leave without returning. The words whispered on the wind at her back, but Danu knew her sister's love had turned that common curse into an anchor to help her remain steadfast in the time to come. May she leave without returning, indeed; Danu had no doubt that it would be a blessing never to see this cursed shore again. She shared her sister's mortal agony, felt the hand of death upon her own shoulder, but she'd also brought away with her the surety of hope. It was time to take that elsewhere and resurrect their people, to be the vessel through which their souls would once again enter the earth.

Putting the darkness from her mind, she focused on what her beloved twin had called her: *A chuisle mo chroí!* O pulse of my heart! A phrase more typically shared between lovers, but in using it, Anu had given her a gift, for Danu could not dwell on the heartache without knowing her wounded heart beat for both of them. Anu's sacrifice had secured a future for them all. Danu would find a new home; there to bear her children...and the *Daoine Maithé*—the Good People—would once again lift their faces to the sun and moon and wind.

Chapter I

Cloaked windows turned a blank gaze toward the alley as a steady rain moistened the dust and grime on the cobbles outside, making them glisten with an oily sheen. In the murky storeroom of Pat Connelly's Pub, tucked away on a back street in Dublin, men silently prepared an arsenal to move against the most recent oppression.

Crates of AK-47 rifles sat where Connelly usually kept kegs of beer, and the massive and scarred oak table bore open boxes of bullets waiting to be loaded into their magazines. Next to the rifles sat white sacks of Swiss black powder and a keg of nails, screws, and broken glass destined to become the innards of pipe bombs. Half-pound blocks of C-4 filled another crate to the top.

Anticipation charged the atmosphere, fed by blind conviction. Ideas flew about the room until they drifted down in some semblance of a plan, a plan anchored in ruthless hearts that had grown indifferent toward those innocents who would pay dearly in the name of revolution. A malevolent force drifted through the rafters, its presence felt, if not recognized, in the heavy, humid air.

The Power waited patiently, feeling no need to provoke the self-righteous fervor and burning hatred wafting about the room. The negative emotions already fed upon themselves, thriving without any assistance. But alone they weren't enough. The Power needed a catalyst to direct things according to plan.

The gathered men railed and cursed about Brexit and English oppression. With the fervor and arrogance of splinter groups everywhere, they cursed the IRA, Sinn Fein, and half a dozen other factions, confident in their hubris that all society needed was their vaunted wisdom. Seeing themselves as the refined essence of the Cause and those who came before as lacking the purity of their ideals.

Eyes feverish with zeal, one man absently lit a cigarette and flicked the match across the room as he called for an attack louder than anyone else. As he continued his animated argument, the still-glowing match sailed in the direction of the weapons and explosives, just falling short. With a curse, the leader, John McDubh, reached over and smacked the man in the back of the head. As he moved, he momentarily bared the tattoo wrapped around his wrist and down the back of his hand — an intricate knotwork pattern of a viper poised to strike. A wisp of satisfaction flavored the air; the leader would be the perfect vessel.

With eyes like burnished coal and hair to match, McDubh leaned in and caught the fanatic's eye. The man paled.

"Watch where ye're tossing yer matches, Michael. Pick it up an' for chrissake, put that cigarette out. There's loose powder all over the place."

With calculation, the malevolent Power surged forward as Michael's gaze faltered. The pure essence of Evil seeped through the charged atmosphere, infiltrating Michael until his gaze grew contemptuous. He eased back in his chair to take the measure of the adversary before him, lingering on the gun in McDubh's pocket before allowing his gaze to travel back up to lock fiercely with the leader's eyes. Leaning back and propping one foot overtop of the other, he made it quite obvious he wasn't at anyone's beck and call before insolently speaking around his cigarette, keeping his hands free and deceptively at rest on his thighs. "Come now, McDubh, 'tis already gone cold, why would I pick it up for nothing?"

"If I choose to make an example o' ye, who are ye to say no?" The words sounded deceptively soft, yet they filled the room like a ticking bomb. "'Tis a dangerous lack o' forethought ye have. A careless match...a reckless, unsanctioned hit...'tis all the same." With a subtle tilt of his head, John McDubh signaled two cell members nearby. "I don't take it kindly when my orders are ignored...but maybe ye weren't ignoring them, then? Perhaps ye just didn't understand? I think I better make myself more clear."

Fear and fury flared to life in Michael's gaze, fed from within and without, as the two men who had closed in on either side of him hauled him to his feet. "I don't know what yer talking about! What the hell are ye doing?" Not a small man, he struggled against their grip with considerable strength but did not stand a chance.

"Do ye think I do not know 'twas ye behind that hit at the Brexit rally last week? An' right before the DUP conference, at that?" The room suddenly fell silent, broken only by the rumbling thunder outside. None of the others had known of this. They had cursed The Murphy himself for their failing luck...until now. The hovering malevolence encouraged their growing wrath. Pinned by so many glowering gazes, Michael redoubled his efforts to get free, but his captors held him wedged firmly between them. McDubh's black eyes glinted dangerously as his men restrained the troublemaker. "What do ye think o' yer timing now? Already ye've made it twice as hard for us to strike. Ye should be kissing my feet in thanks that all I ask ye to do is pick up a bit o' match."

With a surge bordering on glee, the dark force oozed down further into the room, malice dripping like condensation from the rafters, eager to enflame the rebellious glare in Michael's eyes.

Outside, the steady rain became a torrent, and the humidity in the air grew even thicker, but not as thick as the tension. The rumble of distant thunder went unnoticed by all.

"Kissing yer feet? I'd sooner spit on them than kiss them!" and he did so. "Ye're too slow to take a perfect chance when 'tis offered up to ye. 'Tis a man o' action I am, an' yer only sore I've made ye look the coward ye are. Ireland will never be free an it must depend on John McDubh. Ye cannot even take me on fair—ye need yer flunkies here to give ye a hand."

As Michael raged on, exhaling contempt with every spat word, McDubh merely stood his ground, hands fisted at his sides, shoulders relaxed, eyes hooded. They stood frozen in tableau eerily limned by green-tinged flashes of lightning slipping through the smallest gaps in the window coverings.

"Are ye sure that's how ye want to be taking this, then?" the leader's tone threatened all the more for its evenness. "Come now, Michael, use a bit o' sense. What do ye gain by fighting me? Tommy an' Owen will only give ye a bit o' hurt to remind ye o' yer place. A slow, painful death is what ye can look forward to if ye make me see to ye myself."

"So sure, are ye?" Michael snarled back, his lips still clamped on the cigarette that had led to the confrontation. Straining against the grip of the men holding him, he fell against the table as McDubh gestured for them to release their hold. He recovered quickly and lunged for his target.

Gracefully evading Michael's attack, McDubh snapped a punch at the man's face. He shifted easily around the room, a moving target, providing more opportunity for the bungler to wear himself out. Invigorated by the violence charging the air, the unnoticed Power funneled even more anger into the room, nurturing Michael's rage.

A nasty smile danced across his face, half sneer and half maniacal grin, and the cigarette bobbed precariously. "Who says there are no snakes in Ireland?"

"Ach, Mikey, 'tis a snake I'd rather be an' not a worm." The comeback dripped with scorn. An uneasy murmur traveled through the group of witnesses. Seeing the perfect opportunity, the Power reached nto Michael's heart, drawing out the primal ferocity of Man, suppressing every instinct but for domination.

Unable to stand against the overwhelming impulses flooding him, riding on a wave of adrenaline, Michael became the very reflection of the Viking berserker from whom his line had been spawned. Poised to lunge, eyes wild and muscles bunched, something more than just his stance had the observers backing as far from him as they could.

Unnoticed above their heads, the shadows deepened and writhed like a nest of vipers as Michael cast away his cigarette and, with a bellow, barreled into McDubh, driving his fist hard into the man's gut. Shock stole precious seconds. McDubh hesitated a moment too long. Torn between the need to protect himself and the horrible certainty of where the burning cinders would land, McDubh did not evade or defend; instead, he fell back onto the edge of the table beneath Michael's rain of blows. He lost sight of the cigarette as the table tilted, sending both of them to the ground. The boxes of bullets flew right along with the fists.

With an aim that could not have been better, the cigarette went tip over tail toward the stockpiled explosives as the rebel pummeled his leader. The rest of the cell stood powerless to intervene as their death landed in an open bag of Swiss black powder. The silence ended with a prophetic boom as a crash of thunder rattled the building.

Mingled with the cacophony of panicked screams, the repeated peals gathered force overhead as the green-tinged lightning continued to slash across the sky. Either foolhardy or brave, the moment they realized their reprieve, select members of the resistance scrambled forward, rushing to snatch away the flame. Others dove for the doors and windows, stumbling over the two men still fighting on the floor, until in horrific parody of the explosive thunder, the powder ignited and drew all but a fortunate few into a fiery nightmare.

It was as if the night were a black velvet sheet drawn over Dublin...a corner of that sheet burned. The very air was afire. The demonic roar of the blaze melded with both the echoes of continuing explosions and the screams of the unsuspecting to create a powerful mimicry of Hell.

Amid the chaos, the malevolent Power uncoiled completely, rearing up in triumph at the apex of decades of calculated manipulation. Feasting on the anguish and horror of those scurrying below, the dark hovering force, a demigod that had once been known—and feared—as Dubh, dove into the heart of the inferno to claim his fittingly named prize.

Down through the roiling smoke and consuming flames, slithering through the superheated air, the displaced godling hovered above the burning men. With a tendril of power, he reached out to caress the tortured nerves of his chosen tool. His victim shrieked in agony, drawing the fiery air even deeper into his lungs, only to spasm in worse torment, his body attempting to arch off the ground as much as the dead weight of his adversary would allow. Scorched inside and out, he longed for the mercy of death, only to have Dubh's insidious voice whisper directly in his mind.

"No, I think not. There shall be no comforting release; neither death nor oblivion will be allowed you unless I deem it so."

The tendrils of power again slid across the charred surface of what used to be recognizable as John McDubh, firing off every angry, enflamed nerve ending.

"Oh yessss...such sweet suffering...you will do well."

Weaving a spell ancient, powerful, and perfected by a millennium of practice, Dubh dipped beneath the surface of the man's thoughts, settling comfortably within the pain-drenched crevices of his mind. Drawing in the awesome energy of agony to achieve possession was a matter of but a thought. It took even less effort to cloak the body in a seeming, hiding its true and hideous condition.

No one witnessed John McDubh climb from beneath the remains of both Michael and the shattered oak table and stroll calmly out of the inferno, to all appearances completely unharmed.

The weak, dismal daylight diffused as it hit the shadows of Agnieszka Anne Michaels' sparse bedroom. Even dim, it raised a muted glow from her cloud of ivory hair and kindled flaring embers in her sleep-dazed, amber eyes.

The approaching dawn hadn't awakened her, but the sudden hopeless ache of unnamed loss had. Lying there, huddled in her sweat-soaked sheets, she felt bruised all over. She must have been dreaming, and whatever it had been about, she was just as grateful not to recall. The images could not have been pleasant to leave her waking in such a state.

She pulled herself up, perching listlessly on the edge of the bed as she wondered why she bothered. The sun-sparked glow in her eyes faded into apathy. What did she have to get up for today? What purpose did she serve, which couldn't just as readily be taken up by another? Not one person she knew would be lost, or even particularly distressed, without her. Anyone could handle the accounts at St. Michael's Orphanage, she had no close friends or family, and all of the nuns she had counted as such had passed away long ago. The only living things to miss her would be her plants and the local strays. Well... and the Kalderaš Clan, but with the randomness of their appearances, they had to know that someday she would not be here when they came to Wicklow Cottage. That old age or illness would eventually claim her in their absence. They would merely find another dooryard to grace upon occasion.

Resolutely, she pulled herself away from that train of thought before it wandered its usual path leading to her faithless love, whose betrayal and absence she could not help but mourn, even after forty-four years. Mists shrouded her memories, obscured them in her mind. All she could recall were flashes of a face, a whispered voice, or other brief, tormenting aspects. But even as nebulous as those glimpses were, she often lost herself in that sweet agony.

No. Agnieszka would not indulge that torment yet again; her mood was already foul enough as it was. She didn't know what had put her in this dismal frame of mind today, but she was going to snap out of it right now. She had no time for self-pity. No right to be ungrateful for being alive and well. Her life was not perfect—whose was?—but she was generally quite content with her quiet English cottage, occasional company, and peaceful solitude.

It took but a moment to rebraid her snowy locks in a thick, neat tail trailing down her back. She started to rise when a twinge in her abdomen threatened to fold her over, followed by a bitter, copper-penny aftertaste in the back of her throat that differed from her general morning mouth. Indigestion, perhaps? Her vague dreams had been unsettling enough to turn every stomach in the surrounding village of Cornhill, England sour. Another clenching of her gut made her wince. Unless she felt more herself after her morning cup of tea, she did not believe she would make it to St. Michael's today.

Wandering out to the kitchen, she did not even get as far as putting on the kettle when she doubled over in sharp, jagged agony. Catching hold of the edge of the table before she fell, Agnieszka could not reach far enough to pull the ladder-backed chair toward her. A wave of nausea followed another flood of pain. Fighting the compulsion to retch, she lowered herself carefully to the hardwood floor. She didn't know how long she lay there, huddled around her pain, but with unnatural detachment, she listened as mournful sobs filled the air. Her heartbeat seemed to match itself to the rhythm. Only once before had she felt such soul-wrenching despair...the image of forest-green eyes drifted fleetingly across the surface of her memory.

Gradually, as the desolate sobs faded, her world expanded beyond the pain until she could hear the steady ticking of her Regulator clock and the woodlark singing a morning song from its hiding place by her window. Her eyes returned to focus, locking in on her pale white wrist, mesmerized by the faint throbbing of the vein there...and the bright red trails of blood that led to deep, angry gouges in the meaty part of her palm where her clenched nails had dug in. With the metallic tang of a fresh wound overwhelming her sense of smell and the sight of the blood transfixing her gaze, she lost her battle with her stomach.

Loosing a quivering breath, she looked away, trying to ignore the oppressive odor of bile. It took her a moment to gather the strength to get up and deal with the mess.

Resting quietly with her head pillowed on her arm, she looked around her in something of a daze. She could not remember ever viewing her kitchen from this particular vantage point; tiny cobwebs formed under the bottom of the cabinets and motes of dust clumped beneath the icebox. She even spied a glint of metal that looked like it might be a lost piece of silverware. The mundane presence of dirt was like a safety line. Cleaning was a purpose, a goal, but first, it was time to climb up off the floor and make that cup of tea.

Maggie McCormick scanned the rooftop. The blood and evidence of the recent battle had been cleaned up by the *Sidhe* that came after, but they might as well have left it as it was. Purest evil had desecrated her sanctuary. After this night, she would never set eyes upon this place again, even should her god ask it of her.

It was enough that it would haunt her dreams.

It had happened so quickly. Lucien Blank and his men had invaded Yesterday's Dreams by traveling across the Greenwich Village rooftops. The *Sidhe* guardians, along with Patrick O'Keefe, had fought valiantly. Even so, two of the *Sidhe* had fallen, and it had seemed their side would lose. That is, until the very person they sought to protect—Kara O'Keefe, Maggie's sacred charge and blood of her blood—defeated the foe single-handedly. Just not soon enough...

Though the *Sidhe* and their allies had won the battle and Kara and Quicksilver were safe once again, her father Patrick lay in death's shadow. Unless they moved swiftly, he would follow both Cian and Demne into that final embrace.

Maggie's jaw clenched and her breath came shallow and quick as fresh grief stabbed through her chest at the thought of her lost mate.

There was no question of where they were bound, but plenty of doubt as to the reception they would receive once they reached *Tír na nÓg*. Yet there was no help for it, and she had better prepare herself. Many of the Good People would eagerly dissect her actions and call to question her judgment. Sweet Eri must stay, and Cassmail, Urias, and Donn, likewise. All four had tasks they could not forsake. Others could go or stay as they pleased, but Kara and her parents, Beag Scath, and half a dozen of the younger *Sidhe*—their only purpose in America to learn—they all must go to *Tír na nÓg*. It was not safe for any of them to remain. And one more she had not considered; Miach, he most definitely must come if Patrick were to survive the trip.

Where was the healer? Scanning the area around her, Maggie spied him, towering nearly half a head higher than any *Sidhe* there—and most likely anywhere else for that matter. His hair shimmered with iridescence, at once all colors and none in particular. Maggie felt a sudden rush of warmth and exasperation as he wended his way among those bearing the marks of battle. Even now, when he was pale, nearly faded with weariness, he sought to soothe the hurts and cares of others. She had to divert him before he spent himself on the multitude of minor wounds that could wait.

"Miach, are the O'Keefes set for the journey?"

Her gaze settled on the mortally injured man and his wife. Valiant Patrick, burdened with more than his share of both heartache and sheer Celtic stubbornness. He had stood beside them in battle to protect his daughter, and yet Maggie herself owed him her life. How poorly she would repay him, with more heartache and responsibility beyond his ken. Or worse, by offering a hope he may not feel free to accept, no matter how he may long to...or his family might strive to persuade him.

Maggie thought longingly on her solitary centuries here in New York as the pawnbroker at Yesterday's Dreams. Centuries where she had not had to consider such ramifications. She had not been alone, but neither had she been immersed in society. The company of her beloved sprite and self-appointed second shadow, Beag Scath, and a few carefully selected acquaintances had kept her in touch with the world, while still allowing her to maintain a fringe existence, more observer than a participant. Those times were now slipping away from her. Great Mother, how she missed them already.

As if summoned by her thoughts, the diminutive sprite, proportioned as an adult human but scarcely the height of an infant, climbed gracefully up to her shoulder. He rubbed his silky tousle of hair — a blending of every shade of red and brown imaginable — along her cheek in greeting. His burnt-umber eyes eloquently spoke their concern. Weaving an arm around her neck, he gave her a relaxed hug and gently rested his cheek against her forehead. She felt his sub-vocal hum as he instinctively sought to soothe her. Sprites were creatures of harmony and wonder; Maggie's turmoil disturbed his peaceful appreciation of the dance-like movements of the other, more industrious *Sidhe*. Scath drew her attention back to the here-and-now just in time for her to acknowledge Miach's affirmative response.

She managed to meet the healer's glittering lavender gaze, recognizing the reflection of her own horror in those depths. After seven decades without feeling death's touch, Miach had stood by and had to watch, powerless to stop two kin from crossing the Veil. But the day was theirs, Kara and Quicksilver were safe, and the attackers were dead or gone. The leaders, Lucien Blank and Tony DeLocosta — his name gleaned from his wallet by one of the *Sidhe* as they cleaned up the battle site — were all but mindless husks laid out on the rooftop. The *Sidhe* had attempted to banish these two to the formless void, as well, but something prevented them from sending the bodies to where they would never again do harm. This concerned Maggie, but if Patrick was to survive, there was no time to dwell on the uneasy feeling that she had left something important undone.

Anyway, Miach's spirit would heal, and she dared hope her own would as well, though she had trouble believing that at the moment. A glance toward the roof access and the pile stacked beside it confirmed that they had gathered all items of power from the shop and the rath below, the sword that was her ancient charge to protect — triple-wrapped by sheath, spell, and silk — along with the other items she protected by choice. Now to see to the people.

"An' have the...have our..." She swallowed hard to subdue the grief that reared up yet again. "Have they been gathered up, to be borne away to the land o' our kin?" The healer held out two bags of deepest ebony; Maggie caught herself just as her trembling hand rose unerringly to clutch the fullness of the grave bag on the right. She turned from Miach abruptly, snatching her hand back to her side. A deep centering breath restored her calm as her eyes tracked back across the rooftop, but her hand, of its own accord, continued to clench and unclench on the empty air.

It was time to leave. With the humans ready and the fallen seen to, Maggie needed to pull herself together and summon a cloud to take them all to the *Sidhe* Court.

But not quite yet, she realized, as a snowy white head wove through the bustle of preparations. At some point, her neighbor Molly Kelley had left the safety of her tavern and climbed the stairs to Maggie's rooftop. Right now, the woman made the rounds with a jug of cider in the crook of one arm, one of water in the other, and a plastic sleeve of cups across her back. The pockets of her apron bulged with items Maggie couldn't identify. A warm smile came to the *Sidhe*'s face: she never ceased to be amazed at the resilience of the Celts. Earlier that day, Molly had cowered in fear of Maggie herself, based solely on the fact that she was one of the Kindly Ones, the *Tuatha de Danaan*, and yet here the woman was, walking this devastated site after a mage battle, offering sustenance to Maggie and others like her with no more concern save whether she'd have enough cups.

Maggie chuckled a moment but sobered just as quickly. She needed to make arrangements for those left behind, those who would not be safe if the rogues they had defeated this night were not the whole threat. Mollie was of particular concern. Kneeling beside the pile of items, Maggie sifted through them looking for something she would be free to leave behind, an item that did not radiate with the soft glow that told her the person to whom it was linked still lived. There were baubles and instruments and a jumbled assortment of vessels, but most of them were to be sent off with Eri and Urias, who would return them to those for whom they had meaning and fate. So many dreams, so much destiny strewn before her, she prayed to the Mother Goddess the people tied to those destinies would have their opportunity to fulfill them.

Finally, near the bottom—of course—Maggie found what she needed, an item still charged with mystical energy, though it no longer emanated a pulsing glow, evidence that its original owner had no more use for it on this plane. Picking up the intricately carved wooden cross by its leather lacing, she called out to the tavern owner. "Molly...a moment, love, if ye don't mind?" The woman looked up, startled, and turned a questioning look upon Maggie. Molly gestured with the jugs; Maggie shook her head and beckoned the woman over. "I have something I would leave with ye, just in case."

Carefully making her way across the crowded rooftop, the woman stopped a few feet from Maggie. Molly's eyes narrowed. "Just in case o' what?"

"In case ye need help, or need to reach me. Short o' a phone, which we don't have where we're going, I can't hear ye from across the Pond, but I can give ye a way to reach others o' my kin here in New York. They will help ye, as they're able. An' if 'tis danger that has ye calling, they'll come to your aid as quick as if ye were me." Maggie stepped forward and lowered the cross over Molly's head. Her hands being full, the woman could not stop her, though she did flinch as the cross settled around her neck. Maggie respectfully did not acknowledge Molly's fear. Placing her hand over the object, Maggie embedded a magical message in the object — two actually, each triggered by urgency. The first, a call for help, to be answered immediately by whichever *Sidhe* was closest; the second, for less pressing needs, to be answered as time allowed. All one need do was hold the cross in hand and let the heart call out as it would. Maggie explained this quickly, making sure the mortal understood.

"Could I not just call them on the telephone?"

The question was a valid one. "Aye, ye could if the situation allowed, but mundane means can be unreliable. Should ye be caught unawares, goodness forbid, ye have another means to summon help...one that will always get through. O' course, reaching me will take a bit more doing, but they'll manage if 'tis needed."

Reassured that she would not need to worry so much about her neighbor, Maggie sent Molly back to her rounds. Now to make sure all was straight with those *Sidhe* left behind.

Quicksilver wailed and trilled, the notes spiraling up and around in an auditory whirlwind. She was the calm at the eye of the storm, unfeeling, distant, pushed so far by the evening's events that she stood untouched for this one moment. Just herself, the music she played, and the pulsating energy that charged the air. And yet, some part of her felt a deep, constant tug as another gathered up the strands of energy that she called and harnessed them to their intended purpose. The air on the rooftop grew misty, softening the remaining signs of battle. Something akin to a delicate breeze caressed her cheek; a gentle, accepting touch at odds with the barely controlled tempest surrounding her.

"Enough, Kara," The words sounded distant, foreign; they had nothing to do with her. The concept of 'Kara' had become disassociated by the musical equivalent to a lightning rod standing atop Yesterday's Dreams. A stinging slap drew her harshly back to herself, anchoring her once again to her humanity. Anger replaced languor as her eyes remembered the art of focusing.

Glaring into unfamiliar eyes steeped in such an ancient understanding that they could be nothing if not *Sidhe*, it was a good thing Kara's hands were occupied, one still locked around the neck of Quicksilver and the other clutching her bow.

"Enough, *leanbh*," — child — "else the power ye draw 'twill shred the very clouds we seek to call...an' ye with them." She didn't know his name, but, despite his spiked, metallic blue hair, this strange *Sidhe* vaguely reminded her of Grandda... and Papa.

As his words reached her buried awareness, Kara started to tremble. Then her knees buckled, and her vision dimmed. If not for the obsessive grip she had on Quicksilver, the violin would have been dashed upon the roof as she crumbled.

"Shhhhh...shhh...'tis well ye've done, lass, time to rest."

Kara found herself—Quicksilver and all—scooped up like a sleepy child being carried off to bed. She twitched in the elf's arms, and feebly protested his officiousness, but he continued without even tightening his grip. As he slowed to a stop, Kara muttered and moaned, so weary she ached. Had she ever in her life been as drained as this? She did not have time to ponder the appropriateness of the phrase "dead tired" before some other hand reached out and smoothed her hair away from her brow. Kara was too far gone even to wonder who it was, but as a familiar hum calmed her tremors and beckoned her to rest, she knew.

She was well on the way to sleep as the cloud carried them away.

New York City's less-than-wholesome air took on unprecedented thinness as Olcas, cloaked in Tony DeLocosta's body, rose from the deserted roof of Yesterday's Dreams. With a wave of his hand, he set the place ablaze behind him, just the first step in his ultimate revenge. Without looking back, he made his way from the Village to Alphabet City...once more traversing above the skyline. Stepping off yet another ledge, Olcas used the force of his will to draw the surrounding air together beneath his feet, melding it with his power to make it as firm as the pavement below. Behind him, he left a trail of dead pigeons and sparrows, suffocated in the vacuum created by his aerial walkway. A nasty smile twisted his stolen lips.

How glorious to be strong again. If not for the inherent physical weakness of the human form, Olcas's current capabilities would have approached what they had been before the destruction of his divine body. Exhilarated by the sudden rush of power gained with his new shell, he didn't care if he squandered it. No longer hindered by that psychic cripple, Lucien; Olcas could now unleash his full wrath upon this world. He found it intoxicating to once again draw upon a potential deep enough to conduct even a fraction of his god-self's formidable power.

In celebration of this newfound freedom, he flung his arms outward and indulged in a display of raw electrical power. Out of the cloudless sky, lightning danced above his head. With a sweep of his hand, he sent it dashing toward every antenna and transformer within sight. He laughed maliciously as whole blocks went dark.

As he settled on the roof of the building where Tony lived, an odd twinge across the surface of his skin dampened his enthusiasm. He was new to this body, and with all the ability it promised Olcas had to be careful not to overdo things too soon; he'd loathe to lose such potential. He thought of his time working through Lucien and sobered; he'd had such limited control he could not even possess the body without crippling himself further. Now *Tony*...Tony was another matter altogether. Olcas had more control over this tool than any other he had ever possessed. Thanks to the conditions under which he'd taken over, he didn't have to battle the original personality. It was so submerged by shock that it had taken a mere thought to shackle it in place, leaving Olcas the full benefit of Tony's memories without the hassle of the constant skirmish for supremacy or the need to eradicate the individual. Yes, Olcas would have to take care; if he burned out the tool now, he risked having to transfer to another vessel as unsuitable as the previous one.

Without another glance at the disrupted city, Olcas entered the building through the rooftop access, no longer interested in merely tormenting mankind when he could work toward its ultimate downfall.

Stopping before the door to the apartment Tony shared with — Olcas dipped into the boy's memory to find the answer — Gypsy Rose, he noticed a series of runes painted upon the door. They seemed vaguely familiar, but their significance eluded him. Impatiently, he pushed the unease aside; they were probably some pagan protection from thievery or break-in. Even in Olcas's day, the Rom had used thousands of such "spells" and rituals in every aspect of their lives. Putting the matter from his thoughts, he pulled Tony's keys out of his pocket and opened the door.

As he stepped across the threshold the world spun down into darkness.

Blinded by a brilliant burst of light, Tony shook his head to rid his ears of an echoing roar. What the heck was going on? Why did he feel like a Mack truck smashed into him?

Rubbing his hand across his face, he reached behind him to close the door. He was too rattled to move. Closing his eyes, he leaned against the cracked plaster wall and waited for his head to stop pounding. A persistent afterimage danced across his lids. It was as if a flash had gone off, or one of those disco strobe lights, burning onto his retina some of Gypsy Rose's queer writing. Tony took a deep breath and straightened, nearly falling back again in shock as he opened his eyes.

The furniture, the pictures, everything was gone! Not that there had been a lot, but even the dust had been cleaned away. The place smelled sterile. Moving in a daze from room to room, they were all the same, until he reached his door. It stood open and, as far as he could tell, everything remained as he had left it, with one exception: his grandmother's scrawl covered the entire door, written, by the smell of it, in oils and herbs. He couldn't read it, but he knew enough to recognize it as some serious mojo.

"Aw, man! Shit! Shit! What the hell is going on here?!"

Slipping into his room, carefully avoiding brushing against any part of the door, he looked around for some explanation. He found nothing, not even a letter on his dresser or a message on his answering machine. Fumbling in his pocket, he pulled out his cell phone, nothing there, either.

Making yet another search of the apartment, he noticed something he had missed earlier...every door and window bore a symbol he did recognize, the one barring evil from entering. Looking at the place with a new understanding, Tony got a sick feeling in his stomach. The apartment had been cleansed; Gypsy Rose would not be back.

He rushed back to his room. The ceiling panel where he hid anything that was important had been disturbed. He climbed onto the bed to investigate. Pushing aside the panel, he pulled down the meager bundle with both hands and sank to the mattress, scared shitless at what he might find. Flipping through the snapshots, a pattern became clear: not a single picture of his grandmother remained. She was the only family he had left that he knew of, and it was as if she never existed.

He cursed out loud, using every swear word he knew until his throat was hoarse. He even threw in a few he'd picked up from Gypsy Rose in the language of the Romani. He knew she did not approve of his business lately, but to abandon him? She was the only parent-figure in his life that he could remember. The only family at all. Regardless of how they had gotten along — or not — lately, he still loved her and to have her vanish like this tore his heart out. How could things have gotten this bad? Hell, she hadn't even left him with a picture! He finished looking through the pile, but he knew it was useless — he found nothing more than used-to-be friends looking up at him.

With a growl, he stood up and flung the photos across the room. As they fluttered to the floor, something caught his eye: a picture of himself as a very young boy, smiling in an open, happy way foreign to him now, his deep brown hair briefly kissed with red highlights brought out by the summer sun. In the background stood the heavily carved and brightly painted wagon they had lived in when they had traveled with the Rom. Gypsy Rose referred to that time in their lives as setting his roots. What an ironic phrase for a Rom to use. Her desertion hit him harder at that memory. For the love of him alone, she had settled down in the city, and now she had abandoned him.

Yanking his thoughts away from the memories and betrayal, Tony suddenly realized why the photo had caught his eye; while all the others had fluttered to the ground, this one had dropped as if anchored. Turning it over, he discovered an ancient-looking pendant taped to the back, a copper charm heavily engraved with spiraling runes. On the surface, it looked like any of the touristy, soul-seeker baubles Gypsy Rose had sold in her fortune-telling shop, but as he pulled it from the picture and held it up in his hand, it felt heavy with age. A tingle traveled up his arm and settled in the vicinity of his heart.

He didn't know what was going on, but this was a link. He no longer felt completely abandoned by his grandmother. Slipping the leather thong over his head, Tony pocketed the photograph, along with the money from his secret stash, then he turned to leave.

Taking one last look around to make sure he hadn't missed anything, Tony stepped through the front door only to find himself gripped by unrelenting dizziness that trailed off into oblivion.

Kara's heart thudded against her ribcage and her blood crackled in her veins like an electric charge. She felt giddy from trying to take everything in. How could the *Sidhe* sit there so calmly? Even with the horrors she had seen not two hours ago burned forever in her memory, Kara could not help but thrill in this experience. Experimentally, she minced her way across the cloud's surface, marveling at how much it felt like trying to walk on a trampoline or a bouncy house. She had the overwhelming urge to bounce on her butt. Only recalling the very long drop to the ground stopped her—that and the awareness that her timeless travel companions would witness such a childish act. But oh, how she wished to bounce!

"Ye could, ye know."

Startled, Kara jumped, almost unintentionally doing the very thing she restrained herself from moments before. Only the *Sidhe*'s steadying hand kept her on her feet. Cheeks burning, she could not respond. Miach's smile was soft, gentle, as he continued, "What a curse eternity would be without frivolous acts an' the joy they bring."

Kara smiled up at him in return. Though Miach radiated an intensity that far surpassed that of any of the other *Sidhe*, almost as if he had memories as far back as the dawn of *Sidhe* history pressing against his skin, she found she could not fear him. His tender nature quickly diffused any awe she felt. It was almost as if Grandda stood beside her once more. Though he was long dead, she could still picture him in her mind; his passion for nature and others had glowed similarly, if not as bright.

"Come, *leanbh*, let us see what there is to see, shall we?"

As if embarking on a stroll in the park, Kara took his offered arm and lost herself in the wonder of cloud-riding, trusting he would carefully skirt them around those seated on the pillowy surface. Running her free hand through the misty curtains of vapor surrounding them, she giggled at the soft, tingly feel as she drew her hand back covered in minuscule points of dew that glittered like diamond dust in the brilliant sunlight.

"How can we breathe so easily? Isn't the air supposed to be thinner up here? Why aren't we cold? How...." Kara trailed off. Realizing she sounded like a curious two-year-old, she glanced self-consciously at the others lounging nearby. Those not sleeping wore amused smiles and averted their eyes. Miach did not bother masking his laughter, but as she searched his expression, she saw no mockery. Freed of her embarrassment, Kara chuckled.

"'Tis good ye show an interest in what surrounds ye, *leanbh*, but give me time to answer." Miach smiled warmly, and Kara marveled at the beauty and serenity the *Sidhe* emanated. "Now...Let us see," he paused, and she caught a mischievous glint in his eye. "Oh yes, 'tis magic."

Kara couldn't help groaning, even as she grinned at him.

"Okay, close yer eyes an' picture a bag o' goldfish."

Suddenly, a water-filled plastic bag, tightly knotted, formed before her mind's eye. Twelve tiny little fish darted within its confines. She would have giggled if not for those around them.

She focused again on her bag of water, noting the tautness of the surface, how the water filled it only halfway, while the rest ballooned with air. An external sense of satisfaction and approval drifted across the surface of her thoughts, as comprehension blossomed within her.

She barely had time to bask in Miach's approval when suddenly the water in her cerebral goldfish bag rippled, bright colors playing across its surface. Kara flinched as sudden caresses glanced across her mind, darting and alien, both hungry and awe-filled. For a moment, panic flooded her as she tried to pull back from her mental landscape and the unexpected assault she encountered there, but terror locked her down as memories of Lucien and his intent to possess her surged up from where she'd submerged them. But fear lasted only for a moment before rage flared up in its place. She had vanquished Lucien, and his kind would never threaten her again—she would not allow it!

The mental intrusions abruptly pulled back and she sensed terror not her own in the wake. The sensation left her dizzy and disoriented.

"Easy...easy," Miach murmured. "They'll not harm ye."

"They? Who do you mean? Who was it?"

Kara allowed him to take her by the arm and draw her to the rear edge of the cloud. She looked out across the sky and could not fathom what he showed her. The view held nothing but wispy clouds such as she had previously trailed her hands through.

"Look...." he gestured toward the tiny, wafting puffs. Kara strained to see if they carried passengers of their own, but she saw nothing. "No...*lcok*...." and with a subtle telepathic touch, he guided her other Sight, the one she still did not understand, and then she saw. The dancing and diving bits of vapor *were* the creatures, kindly and curious, and when they had ventured forth to say 'hello,' she had blasted them with her anger and fear. Both her hands flew to mask the trembling of her jaw, stilling it before the tears could follow, leaving her eyes shiny and brimming.

"No, lass, no… They don't fear ye. Reach out to them an' feel it. 'Twas yer heartache an' pain that sent them to flight. Ye didn't harm them.

"If ye'll forgive me, I must check on yer Da; will ye be all right now?"

Kara nodded as he moved off to give her time to adjust to all that was new. As if that was likely to happen any time soon… She managed a small smile and wished that the turmoil was over and she could go back to being simply Kara O'Keefe…only she had never actually been simple as she had thought and, truthfully, neither had the world; not when clouds could think and feel, and magic was no longer bound harmlessly in the pages of a faerie tale. Kara took a deep, settling breath and waved him on.

All thought of the others fled her mind as she perched at the edge of the cloud mesmerized by the dips and dives of these magical creatures.

For the first time in a very long time, Maggie felt the complexities of the cloud-riding magic interwoven all around their little company. It sent tickling ripples down her nerves and filled her eyes with rainbows as the dazzle of sunlight on captured condensation created a jeweled haven in the air. She rediscovered the marvel of this mode of transport as Kara explored their aerial chariot on Miach's arm.

Maggie had not traveled thus since she first came to America. She allowed her mind to unfold from its tight little ball of concentration and took the time to relax and savor the moment of peace. Her spell was well set and no longer needed her complete attention. She scanned the group to see how each of them faired. Most of the *Sidhe* rested: those who had fought recouping their strength, and those who had not, conserved theirs. She smiled to see them perched on the cloud like so many brightly plumed birds, their sharp, molded features and ancient eyes softened by their beauty. Though the entire party wore similarly modern clothes, the humans were drab little wrens beside the *Sidhe*, or at least the older ones were. Kara radiated her own aura of timeless beauty, no doubt fed by the immortal blood flowing in her mortal veins; if her parents were wrens, she was the mourning dove.

Taking a deep, appreciative breath, Maggie turned her attention away from the people and savored the subtle perfume of the troposphere, rich and soothing after the tainted air of civilization. A solitary albatross settled on the cloud beside her, companionably warbling before taking wing into the endless sky. The tranquility was eternal this far above the world. Birds and the other inhabitants of this plane did not much care who shared their aerial space, as long as everyone coexisted in peace.

In the distance, she sensed more than saw a host of wispy elementals skating in the cloud's wake. Darting forward and swirling back, they were easily confused for bits of clouds themselves, caught in the intersecting currents of weather fronts. Knowing them for what they were, Maggie wouldn't have taken further notice at all if they hadn't shown such an avid interest in Kara. A glance revealed that the enchantment was mutual, though Maggie wasn't entirely certain if Kara realized what they were. While the girl's gaze constantly darted from one point to another, taking in every aspect of their magical journey, it always trailed back to the graceful wisps that followed behind them like the tail on a soaring kite.

A gentle smile kindled miniature faerie lights deep in Maggie's eyes, and the flow of magic coursing through her as she sustained the energy envelope encompassing their cloud made her soft strawberry-blonde curls dance about her head with the charge, though no breeze riffled through them. Careful not to startle Kara right over the edge, Maggie reached out with the briefest of touches. "Want to invite them over for a visit?"

Kara jumped and gave a nervous little gasp. It was obvious she'd lost herself in this wonderland. Maggie easily read the uncertain curiosity in the girl's eyes. At the same time, she couldn't help notice the shadow that also tinged her gaze. What had happened while Maggie wove her magic?

"Look at them with more than yer eye an' ye'll see—'tis the faerie folk, this time creatures o' the wind an' aerial dew."

Kara smiled back. "I know."

Maggie watched closely as the girl extended her untamed gift, wrestling it to her will with intense concentration. They would need to do something about that lack of sure control. The thought was fleeting as the atmospheric acrobatics began. The elementals were more than ecstatic, they swooped and swirled and pirouetted, clearly for the sole benefit of this unwitting girl. Maggie had never witnessed such a display, nor seen such an open approach from these somewhat timid kin-cousins. It was clear Kara enthralled them. Swarming close, they wreathed the girl's shoulders and twined gently around her in a way Maggie would have to call fawning.

What could be the cause of such behavior on the elementals' part? It was perplexing: typically, they were skittish and fickle, yet they acted as if Kara was divinity!

❧

The soft murmur of the evening news filled the screaming silence. Arn's grey eyes widened in horror, and some detached, far-away portion of his brain sensed Lynn's hand clutching at his arm.

"My God, Arn, it can't be!" His wife's voice trembled, but Arnold Barnert, Patrick's doctor and best friend, barely heard her, his attention riveted on the scenes flashing before him on the television screen. That was his best friend's house with the front door hanging from the hinges and shattered glass littering the ground. Arn had walked through that door just hours ago. That twisted wreckage was the couch he'd sat on as...

Desperately, he tried to latch on to the calm, matter-of-fact words of the announcer, anything to stop himself from slipping into the dark pit he felt gapping before his consciousness.

"The peaceful neighborhood of South Richmond Hill was rattled tonight by a bizarre and inexplicable occurrence. This wreckage behind me is all that remains of the home of Patrick O'Keefe, his wife Barbara, and their twenty-three-year-old daughter, Kara.

"Neighbors describe the O'Keefes as quiet and considerate, decent people that were well-liked by all... Or were they?"

The reporter looked so unmoved, her face carefully composed, her good side toward the camera as she paused dramatically for effect. It was almost as if the devastation she stood before did not represent the violent interruption of people's lives and that no one in her audience saw this story as a personal tragedy. But that wasn't so. There were people like himself whose chest constricted and eyes burned with every image that flashed by, people like Lynn, weeping uncontrollably. Friends, family, Kara's students, Barbara's co-workers...to all of them this was a moment of grief. For the reporter...it was a sixty-second spot, filler...not even likely to draw any ratings.

Arn forced himself to put aside his indignation at the shallowness of it all and focused once again on the reporter's words.

"...believe that sometime between eleven this morning, when the local mail carrier completed this portion of his route, and eight this evening, when the next-door neighbor discovered the scene, several parties entered this residence by extreme force through the back yard, somehow committing their violence utterly unnoticed by anyone in the homes nearby.

"It is not known if the O'Keefes were present at the time of the break-in. There is a car in the driveway, but neighbors confirm that the family's second car is unaccounted for. Though police have told this reporter that no signs of injury have been uncovered, they have not ruled out the possibility.

> *"Police have not yet named any suspects and are requesting that anyone with information that might reflect on either this case or the whereabouts of the O'Keefes, please contact the Tip Hotline at...."*

Arn clicked off the television as the news report segued into sports. Numb with disbelief, Arn pulled his wife toward him. They sat in the dark, wrapped tightly in each other's arms, unsure of whose sobs were whose.

CHAPTER 2

IT WAS AFTER SUNSET BY THE TIME AGNIESZKA WIPED UP THE MESS AND RETRIEVED the silver—that perhaps taking longer than all the rest. It had taken an hour just to pick herself up off the floor and crawl back into bed. And now, though her household was back in order, Agnieszka only felt more out of sorts. What happened that morning had truly unsettled her. Never having in any way been sick before, her imagination ran wild, fearing that a lifetime worth of illness even now prepared to beset her.

She suddenly felt very alone.

Isolation was nothing new to her. She was well aware of the subtle differences that stood between herself and others her entire life. Though not everyone had been cruel or uncaring, in her eighteen years at St. Michael's, without exception, not one *child* there had befriended her. They had either accused her of being fey or odd, or shunned her to avoid joining her as a target for the bullies. *They* called her witch-child and changeling and hid nettles in her bed and poured salt on her porridge when she wasn't looking. Behind her back, they made signs against evil, and more than once, she'd heard the more malicious of them "innocently" telling prospective parents how strange she was. Those harsh early years made it hard for her to trust in anyone's intentions. Instead, she spent her time with the Sisters or tending injured animals and birds she found during her solitary wanderings.

If only people were as honest and as accepting as the creatures of the forest. Some of those in town still treated her like a pariah to this day. They weren't petty, but to say they were distrustful would undoubtedly be accurate.

She went to a chest buried beneath the clutter in her seldom-used spare room. Like a child prodding at the gap left by a missing tooth, she excavated the pile until she could lift the lid. Resting on top was a small carton of photographs from her days at the orphanage. Twitching her rope of a braid out of the way, Agnieszka settled on the rag rug and withdrew her memories. With reluctant effort, they came out of their little box, one by one spread out on the floor. Before her lay the visual representation of her despair. It deepened as each photograph joined the ranks. So far, she spied no sincere smiles on anyone's faces and none at all on herself. There were two types of snapshots:

those the Sisters orchestrated, and those of Agnieszka by herself. It was a toss-up as to which was more dismal. She flipped and flipped without thought until a handful of photos in the faded shades of early color photographs caught her eye. Now she smiled.

This small grouping was from her life after the orphanage, just after she'd completed her A levels. The Sisters had put together a celebration dinner for those who were ready to move on. Agnieszka's silvery-white hair was twisted elegantly on top of her head with small tendrils framing her face. She had felt so lovely in the black sheath dress and low pumps. With platinum blondes and tall willowy figures all the rage, on that day, the others couldn't touch her. Even Matéo had been there, making the day perfect.

Matéo had been a kind giant of a man, one of the Romani. She supposed now that he must have actually been just normal-sized, her memories of him based solely on the fact that, as a child, she had to look so far up to see his face. He had seemed so very large and old then, as if one had taken Samson and combined him with Methuselah. But thinking back, it wasn't that he was wrinkled or grey. His actual nature was more indeterminable than that. No, it was his eyes and the intensity that emanated from him. He felt ancient.

What Agnieszka remembered most fondly, though, were the evenings he'd visit with them before prayers, taking whatever instrument was at hand and playing any song they asked. Funny that; she could not recall even one instance where he had faltered, no matter how obscure the tune requested. Not even when the little Pakistani girl called out a song from her homeland.

Matéo hadn't come very often, yet he had been one of her joys, if nothing else, but for the music and the smiles or bits of candy he'd always had for each of them. His presence in her life, his easy acceptance and unconditional love, was all that had made her feel special. Not to be ungrateful to the Sisters, but there was only so much they could do with so many little souls in their care.

Looking back, though life at the orphanage had not been kind, Agnieszka still thanked God that she'd had even that much love. So many others hadn't. They had come to the orphanage after being taken from parents who hit when they should have held. Or worse yet, parents who behaved as if they weren't even there until the bright potential of youth sputtered and all but went out beneath sullenness and despondency. Agnieszka might not have had a life free of torment, but at least she had not known abuse. She might not know her lineage, but at least she knew herself. It had been the Sisters who had given her that.

Everything she had, everything she was, she owed to the Sisters of St. Michael's; her name, her purpose, her life, her birthday...even that they had given her. She was grateful for it all. And yet here it was, packed away in one sense or another, for despite eighteen years in the Sisters' loving care and even more in their friendship, deep down Agnieszka still had trouble opening herself to others and did not care to leave about reminders of the time she allowed her longings to rule her. She had not known what it was to be loved because she was always looking past what she did have for something she wanted more. She had wasted so much time, so much potential for happiness. What a horrible way to treat the gift of life...the only gift her parents had ever given her. With but one exception, not counting the Sisters who ran St. Michael's and Matéo, she had never felt loved. And now she could admit the fault was hers. Agnieszka's face burned with shame as she remembered the exception, the one indiscretion of her youth, and the reason she never again allowed another near. The reason she now spent her "golden" years alone.

Having grown up at St. Michael's, she had a strong foundation of Catholic beliefs against which, unlike many of the other children, she had never felt compelled to rebel. That fact only made her fall from grace all the worse, intensifying her sense of guilt quite beyond any hope of redemption, not because she felt unforgivable, but because even now she could not bring herself to repent her actions...her carnal sin. The only person she had ever loved and trusted—if only briefly—with all her heart, had left her nearly before the mingled sweats of their passion had dried on her naked flesh. Was it any wonder there was not one person she had met since whom she trusted not to hurt her? But was that any reason to stop living?

She took herself firmly to task, vowing not to waste another moment in self-imposed exile from the human race. With shocking ease, she released her hold on the obsessive hope she had never even admitted to herself: that one day her love would come back for her. She had clung to that hope so fiercely and deep in her heart that no other could compete with the ideal image she had built of him. It was time for freedom.

As Agnieszka made peace with herself, she marveled at the shimmering tingle that swept over her from the surface of her skin right down into the core of her. She felt warm and content, almost the way she felt with a belly of the finest, richest, darkest hot cocoa she had ever had, only so much more. It was as if she had finally shed the skin of her former life, discovering she was a butterfly and not a tiny worm...ready to start anew. With wonder, she ran her hands across her face and body as if to discover it for the first time, following with her eyes. Her palms came to rest on her abdomen, the point that seemed to be the seat of the kinetic heat that infused her. She was almost shocked to note that she did not glow; such warmth had settled upon her that she'd nearly expected to be shining brighter than a star. Was this really how simple it was to be happy? Had she only known, she would have made the decision long ago.

Aí approached Goibhniu with dread in his heart, making his way through the heavy silence of those gathered. He had been sent on a task to gather news of ominous occurrences and visionary warnings. Instead, he stood here before the Court with his duty half discharged, driven by visions of the *Cosaint*, the security of his People, and another young woman he had never seen before. It was the *Cosaint* that concerned him the most.

Every *Sidhe* knew of her existence, a safeguard against the extinction of their race, but beyond that, none of them knew the details of her nature. Was she one of them? Was she of mixed blood? Could she even be something none of them could begin to imagine? The legends were not clear, with nearly as many versions as there were members of the *Tuatha de Danaan*, and even though the tales were vague, they were closely guarded and never told to anyone who was not *Sidhe*. Only one knew every detail regarding the *Cosaint*, and who would have the presumption to question Goibhniu?

"Ye return early, my envoy, surely ye have not discharged yer duty so soon." Goibhniu had no need to shout; his disapproving words hung above the crowd.

Kneeling before him, Aí bowed his head without remorse, his chestnut hair falling like a curtain to hide his face. The scrutiny of the Smithgod, to whom his kind owed their very immortality and continued existence, nearly overwhelmed Aí, but he knew he was meant to return with this knowledge. Even so, he did not know what this would mean for the *Sidhe* and that doubt…that fear…held his tongue.

"Then why have ye returned early, with yer charge not yet done?" The words were not harsh, nor unkind; they merely drew Aí out of his uncharacteristic reserve.

Rising, his bright blue eyes intense with the importance of the message he came to deliver, Aí moved forward with confidence, near enough to grip Goibhniu's arm with urgency. "'Tis visions o' the *Cosaint* I've had…never a face have I glimpsed, an' she always seems a different person, but I've not a doubt 'tis her; every time, beset by purest evil," he whispered intently, unsure of how those around him would react should they hear him. He did not receive visions often, as his gift lay in the understanding and healing of the heart. It had been a harsh lesson, learning to heed the intermittent revelations. These particular visions had continued uncharacteristically for weeks.

He hadn't known what to expect, but nothing he imagined came close to the sad, knowing smile tugging at Goibhniu's lips. Aí could not continue.

With all of his being, he knew that this was a seeing of the now, a fact that bode ill for the *Tuatha de Danaan*. The *Cosaint*'s very protection, and thus that of the *Sidhe* as a race, was ignorance of her nature. How could anyone have seen past the carefully wrought spells to her true being? Aí took a deep breath against the massive weight holding down his chest and prayed Goibhniu would take the burden of this vision from him. But it was no use; a deep conviction chilled him—he had been cursed with this vision because his fate interwove with that of the *Cosaint*.

"Come, the two o' us shall walk in the gardens an' ye can share with me all ye have learned." They might as well have walked up and down a darkened corridor for all that Aí was able to enjoy the scenery of the Smithgod's gardens.

"I've a new task for ye, Aí." Goibhniu began after a few minutes of wandering the serene paths. "The threat o' conflict hanging over the *Tuatha de Danaan* 'tis now a surety."

"But how? Who could rise against us?"

"In yer heart, ye know."

Aí felt as if his chest hollowed out only to fill with stone. Though indeed the coming conflict was part of his visions, he had desperately blanked the details from his mind.

"No! It cannot be! The fire claimed what little was left..." He turned panicked eyes on the Smithgod. Aí was young, or young for a *Sidhe*, a few hundred years, no more, but even he knew the tale of Carmán and her three sons. The horrors they had perpetrated against both Eire and the *Sidhe*, the lengths that had been required to put an end to their attacks.

It was said that when they were finally subdued, Carmán herself had been bound in iron chains from Goibhniu's own forge, unbreakable links that anchored her to the earth and suppressed her powers. In those very chains, she died of grief as son after son was put to death for their atrocities before her very eyes. Nothing had been left!

"'Tis my shame that those chains bound only Carmán an' her ability to destroy." Aí flinched as Goibhniu answered his frantic thoughts. "I thought nothing o' her having the capacity to preserve...to safeguard...there were no wards against that aspect o' her power. Some o' us wonder if she preserved the souls o' her sons, though not their bodies.

"An' whether 'tis them or some new threat, the signs are clear: now is the time we must prepare if the *Tuatha de Danaan* are to withstand them."

Aí felt the weight of Goibhniu's gaze. Something told Aí he meant "we" in a more direct sense, rather than a general one. Then the Smithgod's callused hand descended upon his shoulder, confirming his fear. With a deep, settling breath, Aí looked up to meet his eyes. Understanding and compassion filled them, but that did not make Goibhniu's words any softer.

"I'll be needing yer help with this, Aí. No other at Court has the anonymity ye have, an' no other would I trust with this responsibility. I must send ye out into the human world to gather those who can't protect themselves. None beyond our Lands are safe from this threat, but some are even more at risk for being faerie-touched. Humans, waterkin, and some number o' the *Sidhe* who've chosen to keep themselves apart...it falls to ye to draw them into safety, or at least warn them, before 'tis too late."

Aí swallowed hard before attempting to speak. "There is no other? Only me? I can't hope to stand against such..."

"Do not fear, ye aren't sent as a warrior, an' I won't send ye out ill-prepared," Goibhniu's words did not comfort him, faced as he was with such a daunting task. His eyes skated to the Smithgod and away again. Why precisely had he come back? Aí began to question if the idea had been his own. He swallowed hard as Goibhniu continued, "Other Halls shall send their own runners an' to be sure I'll provision ye well. The warning must go out. An' still, 'tis asking ye I am, not telling ye. If ye cannot bring yerself to face this unknown danger, another will be asked, an' another after that until someone goes. None will know I came to ye at all, an' not I nor any other will think less o' ye for knowing yer limits."

Goibhniu was wrong. Regardless of who knew, or understood, there would always be one who thought less of Aí if he turned away from this charge...Aí himself. He could not live with the shame of cowardice, even if it meant he would die in the duty.

"Well then," he drew his courage about him and stepped from beneath Goibhniu's hand, freeing himself to kneel before his god. "An' where would ye have me go?"

✹

The gloom of the darkened street lifted as the door of the pub swung open, releasing a burst of rousing music into the night. Laughter and drunken singing mingled with the pulsing beat, and yet there was a certain peaceful quality to the ruckus. The tall, poised man slipped out with inhuman grace and carefully closed the door behind him, more a calculated move to avoid attention, rather than out of consideration for those that must wake before the sun to earn their living.

Humming to himself, Ewan—once known as Dulachan of the *Tuatha de Danaan*—casually strolled down the sporadically lit street, his well-cut brown suede blazer and time-molded black denim jeans blended with the shadows, while his shoulder-length, bright copper hair shimmered like muted silk until he entered the pool of the streetlight, where it blazed like the setting sun.

He looked like he should be on the stage or the cinema screen, not strolling the streets of Aberdeen. But here he was, content to lurk in this peaceful haven, with all the comforts of society, yet free of the predatory competition he would find elsewhere. Or so he thought; as he rounded the corner of the street where he rented a room in a boarding house, he was confronted by the sight of a woman sprawled on the ground beneath the streetlight in front of his building. The blood streaking her pale, bare skin was nearly as deep a shade as the tumble of fiery curls draped across her face.

His heart raced, and he swallowed hard. Breaking into something more than a walk but less than a trot, he cast searching looks up and down the street. Had anyone seen what happened? Did the woman's attacker still stand nearby? Damn! It was too soon. So much careful planning and, if he didn't move quickly, it would all go to waste. The man's lips repressed a snarl as he again scanned the street, this time to determine if anyone watched from what they thought was the safety of their darkened windows. There was no one in sight, even to his heightened senses. He had time to deal with the mess. Fortunate for him...too bad for the woman.

As he drew closer, he noticed the long, ebony nails visible on her out-flung hand. They also looked to be filed to sharp points. A punker then, or a goth, probably up from London. She should have stayed there instead of coming up here and disrupting his plans. If she weren't dead, she'd soon wish she had been. He quickly stooped to get his arms beneath her and gather her up.

"Evening, Ewan, you're out a bit late tonight."

Ewan flinched and snatched his hands away from the body, a part of him noting her velvety skin seemed to twitch as he did so. With the grace of a stalking panther, he rose and turned. What a pity, MacDonald was not one of those he'd been eyeing, hardly worth the effort of reaping, though that would make little difference now. Keeping his face neutral and his voice friendly, Ewan stepped closer, angling his body to obstruct MacDonald's view. "Evening yerself, Jamie...Cameron was bending my ear at the pub, I couldn't get clear o' him."

Why did the man not react? He wasn't blind, and yet MacDonald acted as if there was no body right there on the ground. Still, Ewan could not risk it; better to secretly do away with two bodies, than one and all of his plans. He stepped even closer and called a bit of power to his hands.

"Did you drop something?" MacDonald asked and looked down toward his feet as if whatever it was would all of a sudden be right there.

Ewan could not help but look himself, though he knew there was nothing to find. Curious, though… he could have sworn the woman's hand had been just behind his foot. Damn! If she woke up, he would have much more trouble silencing the two of them.

He heard the whispering scrape of calloused skin on gravel and cursed more fervently. He would have to move quickly. His hard, slate-blue eyes hooded and his lips drawn up in the barest of smiles, Ewan gathered what mage energy he could as he advanced on his neighbor, whom he judged as the more significant threat.

As he was about to strike the man down, Ewan's eyes flew wide and the smile slid from his face. Instead of watching the pitiful human crumble before him as Ewan harvested what little energy the unGifted Scotsman's death released, the dark *Sidhe* found himself the victim. His back arched away from the burning agony that slashed from the nape of his neck down to his buttocks, as if a dagger ran length of his spine, tearing his clothes as if they were no more substantial than a butterfly's wing. A strangled cry caught in his throat, while the power he had gathered to strike down McDonald ebbed away...no, was *drawn* away.

In shock, Ewan watched as MacDonald's brow furrowed and the farmer's hands flew up to brace him. "Here now, what ails ye, Ewan? Tell me what's wrong, man!"

What a twist of fate, but he couldn't worry about MacDonald now; apparently, whatever struck down the woman had returned. Ewan tried to twist around when an iron grip locked his head in place. With dawning realization, he looked down at the hand flexing around his throat, noticing streaks of blood on alabaster skin and sharp, ebony nails that proved to be far more than for show. Ewan quaked inside. He had not known such personal fear since that long-ago day several centuries before when Manannan Mac Lir, no longer able to overlook Duluchan's dark...amusements, had cast him from the Land of Promise.

"Sweet Lord, what's wrong with you, lad? Are ye ill?"

He tried to focus on his neighbor, but a sickly sweet odor further muddled his thoughts, and invasive whispers drifted through his head, intermittent and indistinct, as blood and oxygen seeped through pinched pathways. When he noticed the pale movement of several more figures darting just beyond the circle of the streetlight, it occurred to him that MacDonald's reprieve would be short-lived. Ewan had his own concerns with this unknown foe demanding his attention.

In an effort at his own defense, Ewan gathered more mage energy, only to hear a pleased moan by his ear as it was again drawn away from his control.

His breath came only in panting gasps as shudders sent bursts of fire coursing across his back. The one thing he heard clearest of all was a snarling laugh as the pale arms wrapped tight around him, drawing him back into a final embrace.

Once upon a time, Kara had begged Grandda to describe *Tír na nÓg* to her. Begged and clung to his arm until he had looked down at her with weary eyes and sadly shook his head. She'd been five then and could not understand why this, of all things, was left out of the glorious tales he told her, though the name of the Land was in nearly every story. Already by then she could vividly picture her favorites among the demesnes of the *Tuatha de Danaan*; *Tír na mBan*, the Country of Women, and *Tír Tairnigiri*, the Land of Promise, came alive for her in the rich, colorful narrative Grandda excelled at, as did all the other Lands of the *Sidhe*. But never would he describe *Tír na nÓg* to her. When she'd persisted, tears actually welled up in his eyes, and, even as a child, she saw his internal struggle: In the end, he had disappointed her, rather than face that which he could not bear. He just hugged her and said, "'Tis too beautiful, too terrible for words, lass, 'twould tear my heart in two to try, an' ye still wouldn't understand the glory o' the Land o' Youth."

Looking back, it was the only thing he had ever denied her, and looking about her now, she saw why. When their cloud began its descent toward the mass of burgeoning greenery Maggie claimed was an island, Kara found herself breathlessly eager to finally see *Tír na nÓg*'s wonders, but from the air all she could see was a lovely postcard image of a great Hall nestled like gleaming ivory scrimshaw in the center of vibrant, velvety green, all of it peering through a not-quite-sheer mist, as if it would preserve its mystery a while longer.

Once upon the ground, it was like standing in the center of Eden. Trees soared to dizzying heights as if their roots were set in the very foundation of time, flowers bloomed so beautifully she wanted to weep just seeing them, and it was hard to say which delighted her more: The rich, yet subtle scent that perfumed the air, or the joyful sounds of the wildlife drifting like sweet music upon the currents. She spun about, trying to take all of it in. Her awed discovery eclipsed the horror of the past few days, and she continued to twirl excitedly until she nearly careened into her companions. Miach laughed and put out his hand to steady her, and Maggie merely smiled, too weary after her efforts to do anything else. The *Sidhe*, whom Kara did not know so well, just waited patiently for her to settle down so Maggie could lead them this final step of their journey.

Looking from their solemn eyes to the deep black grave bags two of the *Sidhe* cradled reverently in both hands, Kara gasped at her own unthinking callousness. Then her eyes went to Papa, himself carried by a third *Sidhe*; his shallow breath barely raised his shattered chest. Even unconscious, pain lined his expression. She winced and knew the true depth of her shame in keeping them all waiting. Kara fell still and stood with eyes lowered respectfully as Maggie and Miach moved past her, the other *Sidhe* following in procession. Though it had not been discussed, Kara sensed she and her family should not be in the forefront for this homecoming. She waited until the youthful *Sidhe* carrying Papa went past before taking Mathair's hand and falling in behind, feeling like they were both homely cygnets trailing behind a parade of full-grown swans.

Silently wending her way past the lush greenery, Kara could not see much of anything beyond the back of Papa's bearer. Her grip on Mathair's hand tightened gently as a confused and fearful moan, no louder than a whisper, escaped from her mother.

"Soon, Mathair, soon we'll be..." Kara trailed off as they broke through the brush, feeling the sudden urge to draw Mathair beneath the protection of her arm. Before them, towering above even the ancient trees, was the vast behemoth at the heart of *Tír na nÓg*...Goibhniu's *Mór Halla*. Unbidden, her eyes traveled slowly up its extreme height, taking in the seemingly endless expanse of filigreed marble that somehow managed to appear both delicate and mighty, and yet, like an enormous carved mountain, it flowed with the landscape, rather than breaking it up. The hand in hers began to tremble violently, drawing Kara away from her reflection. There would be time enough later to learn all Grandda had not been able to tell her of *Tír na nÓg*. Plenty of time once the future of her family...actually — if Maggie were to be believed — once the future of the *world* was resolved.

What a sobering thought, to have all of that rest at least in part on her shoulders, but she was not weak. She had stood against great evil when she vanquished Lucien, and she was the one remaining to tell of it. After all, as the wise knew, courage was the acceptance of one's fear and the ability to take action in spite of it.

Squaring her shoulders and taking a deep, settling breath, Kara led her mother after the solemn procession of *Sidhe*, up the graceful, sweeping steps that led into the epitome of faerie land, through towering doors that altogether reminded her uncomfortably of how she imagined St Peter's pearly gates. It was impossible to quell the tremor that ran through her at that thought, but she tucked her mother's hand around the curve of her arm and strolled through the entrance with a regal bearing that vied with that of the *Sidhe*. Only once inside did she have to remind herself to breathe.

What could Arn do? A trail would not suddenly appear, leading him to Patrick and his family. Tears burned unshed in his eyes, and his jaw clenched with frustration. He stood before the O'Keefes' home amidst a group of the morbidly curious and genuinely concerned. He might as well have been alone for all he noticed the others. His heavy brows drew down in a scowl as he tried to make sense of the scene before him. What had happened here? Were all of them carried away for some heinous purpose, or had their suffering already ended? More important...why? For a week, Arn had lived with the heartache of knowing his best friend would soon die, consumed by cancer Arn himself had been unable to eradicate. He had dealt with that, resolved the matter in his heart, and accepted it. This was different. Here he was robbed...may have been robbed...of the time they should have had left. And what of Kara and Barbara?

With each grim thought, the heat of his anger dried up the threatening tears. He didn't care what the news reporter implied; the O'Keefes hadn't any enemies. This was wrong, something evil had taken place here and, though he hadn't any clue of what it was or what he could do to right it, he swore to himself that he would not let it fade away until he knew.

As Arn turned from the devastation, he noticed a young man in the crowd. The punk's pale blue eyes bore the purest malice, sharing space with a voracious hunger entirely out of place in such a lean but obviously well-fed body. A bright blue silky swatch peaking from the kid's jacket caught Arn's attention.

With a physician's eye, he automatically noted other details he was used to gleaning from his patients, subtle clues to attitude and condition. The eyes were pinched, with faint shadows beneath, betraying some inner conflict and recent lack of sleep. The punk's stance spoke of insolence and indifference, but the fingers on his left hand faintly twitched as if he would reach out and snatch something away. Arn didn't know who this young man was, but he would bet his practice that the punk wasn't here out of idle curiosity.

"Okay, folks, I'm going to have to ask you to move along." The modulated bellow of a uniformed officer interrupted Arn's thoughts and drew him back to a reality from which he'd rather have distanced himself. "If you're not here on official business, you must vacate the vicinity."

Arn stole a final glance in the direction of the punk and the pole where he had been propped. The guy was already gone. What was his connection with Patrick? Or was it Kara who held his interest? The thought was not an easy one to bear.

From outside, *Tír na nÓg* appeared to have an understated, elegant beauty. Inside was anything but understated. After so long away in the human world, Maggie found the Court jarring. Like a jumble of opulent jewels in an equally impressive box, the *Sidhe* milled about in *Mór Halla*. In style, each dressed according to their own inclination, drawing on the fashions from every era, both mortal and *Sidhe*; but all equal in the sumptuousness of their attire. Neither the courtiers nor their garb would have been out of place on a Paris runway or at a Hollywood premiere, even those with more eclectic tastes. In stature, all were tall and willowy, surpassing in beauty and possessing an inner glow that made the blush of human youth seem sallow. The only notable blemish, at least in this Court, was an air of ennui characteristic of the celebrated or the wealthy. While the mortals so afflicted went to therapy, Maggie always figured the *Sidhe* went to *Tír na nÓg*, there to forget the rest of the world existed. Not all of the Court, of course, but a good number of those she saw before her clearly had done just that.

Such was the contrast of the new arrivals that the tumult of the chamber fell silent while the tattered troupe worked their slow and laborious way through the throng. Each of Maggie's people still bore some mark of battle—a dried bloodstain upon a torn shirt, fresh bandages twined hastily around weeping wounds, eyes haunted by the horror of combat, and pulses still beating a rapid tattoo at the base of throats tight with overwhelming grief. Three of their number were carried — two encased in ebony velvet grave bags, and Patrick, with the barest flutter of breath rising in his chest.

The glittering and graceful Court opened before them, closing ranks only when the wounded were well past, their curiosity and compassion restrained by fear. They could only gasp in horror. There was no warm reception here for Maggie, or those who followed her. To be truthful, she hadn't expected one. Her home had been in *Tír Tairnigiri*, when she'd still lived among her fellow *Sidhe*; most of what would be considered her friends and family — though that was a human concept and not the way of *Sidhe* interrelation — still resided there. In all of *Tír na nÓg*, she most likely knew only Goibhniu and but a handful of others. As few of the residents of the Land of Youth ever left, the same was most likely true for the *Sidhe* that followed her. Still, if she had been expecting respect and consideration, the Court was disinclined to oblige.

Their views were clear upon their faces: What had struck at the *Tuatha de Danaan*? How was it that Men once again walked the halls of *Tír na nÓg*? Who had allowed them to infringe on this tranquil retreat, bringing with them their violence and suffering? Surely the memories of mortals brought before the Smithgod were dim, mere wisps of thought worn as thin as spider silk by time. In every other *Sidhe* holding some aspect of mankind lengthened its meager line in the stillness of Underhill, sharing their children and their passion with the Children of Danu, but rarely were they brought so deep as this Court.

Knowing what was going through the self-consumed thoughts of many of these insular *Sidhe*, Maggie could not look into their faces and continue walking through their midst. At this moment, it was not even possible to think of herself as Cliodna, as one of them. She had stood in solitary guard and fought blackest evil that each of them might lose themselves in this illusion of a life; she had sacrificed her heart and her innocence to preserve their peace — all of her party had, *Sidhe* and human alike. The entire Court should have rushed to relieve them of their burdens and offer solace and care for their wounds, not draw back their precious garments and watch the warriors with guarded expressions.

Her jaw clenched in anger until only Patrick's dire need drove her on. But though she walked among them, she would not look upon these sorry representatives of her people. Instead, her eyes turned upward and found the courage to move forward, to ask a god for a most urgent and deserved boon, one rarely sought, let alone granted, in all the far-reaching history of her kind.

Above the heads of the courtiers, Maggie could see the endless, intricate, brightly colored carving of the Great Wall, filled with Celtic swirls and knots and images both as simple and as complex as each of their lives, all interlinked and magically engraved in the living stone. With determination, she focused on one far up near the vaulted ceiling, a graceful twining of a multitude of "strands" interlaced with runes of protection and strength. She already knew it's weaving as well as she knew herself. Its lines were rich and full of life, and in tracing those paths, she relived each change, triumph, and torment that led her to this single point in time. All of it became fresh again: The intense, agonizing losses, the dull, aching loneliness, and the invigorating joy she found in mankind's world—between the rise and fall of one breath she reclaimed its strength. It was astounding how many lifetimes she had lived, while those around her merely toyed with existence. And to think she had not appreciated it at the time.

Dazzled by the brilliant colors of this stone tapestry of *Sidhe* lifetimes, Maggie's gaze wandered, tracing other patterns, comparing them to her own. She found recognition in a particular curve here and there, marveling at the way all of them interlocked and repeated. It took her a moment to realize that she desperately sought one particular arrangement and, as they say, therein lay madness. Locking her gaze back on her own unending line, she continued walking. If she allowed her eye to wander, they would seek out what her heart could not bear to find. Then darkness would descend upon her for true.

Maggie came back to herself as two immense hands braced her shoulders. Lowering her eyes, she met Goibhniu's understanding gaze full on. She had run the gauntlet, and only numbness stopped her from falling upon him like a child fleeing to the comfort and protection of a father's arms.

"Rest easy, *leanbh*, ye are home." The low rumble of his voice reached all of the newly arrived warriors as if he spoke directly to each of them, *Sidhe* and human alike, filling the defenders with a peace that stood between them and their earlier horror. Maggie swayed as his hands released her. "Go care for yer wounded while a feast is prepared in yer honor. Our servants will bring provisions from a lesser Court that yer mortal comrades may join us."

"We must first be heard," Maggie answered, determined to come to her point while she had the attention of all. "We haven't faired well through our battle, an' one o' our number yet hovers at the edge o' the Veil. He cannot be permitted to pass through or *Sidhe* an' mortal kind alike are doomed."

With each word uttered, her chin jut out more and more rebelliously. She knew her eyes flamed with challenge as her hands fisted at her sides. As she finished, and the heavy silence of the Court radiated back at her, she remembered herself and quaked to her very heart. Here she stood before a god in his own Hall, and she'd all but thrown down a gauntlet at his feet! Dropping her eyes and forcing her hands from their aggressive pose, she waited for the uproar to begin.

"What is it that ye ask, Cliodna?" The soft-spoken words and the use of her true name nearly brought Maggie to her knees. She expected to be struck down, banished, whisked away by a wave of his hand; instead, she was granted audience. The Court was not so magnanimous. She flinched as they roared in protest, but no matter how loudly they yelled, they could not drown out Goibhniu. He continued as gently and as reassuringly as before, "Come now, ye dare to approach, do not falter now…speak."

Maggie motioned for the *Sidhe* carrying Patrick to come forward. "I swear to ye I wouldn't speak so were the matter not vital. As he lay dying, Demne charged me to bring this mortal to *Tír na nÓg*. I swore to my love as he took his last breath that Patrick O'Keefe would sup at yer table."

"An' what right have ye to make such an oath?" the belligerent words rose up loudly from somewhere among the Court. Others quickly joined the solitary protest. If there were sympathetic comments as well, they were lost in the uproar. "What right had he to ask it, as if the choice were yers?"

"What right? Need I yer leave to accept the final pledge o' Goibhniu's own messenger? Do ye tell me what is right an' fair, now?" Maggie whirled again to face the Court, her visage terrible in its fury. "I stand before ye with the blood o' an ancient caked upon my clothes, the blood o' my love beneath the very nails on my hands from trying to save him. I answered Demne's pledge as was right an' meet so to do an' have journeyed to *Tír na nÓg* to see it done, if it takes my own final breath to see it honored."

But it was no good; the hearts of the *Sidhe* before which she stood had gone cold and selfish. If she had needed to convince them, this effort would have been doomed. Whether it was the barely repressed rage she held toward them or the memories assaulting her that caused Maggie to shake, she could not say, but her voice trembled subtly at each mention of her lover's name. She could not allow herself to fall to pieces again, not if she were to honor Demne's final wishes. Breathing deeply, she tightened her resolve to claim for Patrick a place at Goibhniu's table…eating no lesser fair than the Smithgod's food, drinking his ale.

She challenged the Court with her glare, making sure each courtier knew she would stand against them all, she was that dedicated to her oath. In a few faces, she saw respect and understanding, but in too many others, she saw fear and indignation, the reflection of petty, self-centered hearts. Though they flinched away from her fervor, she still heard more murmurs of protest from the Court than of acceptance. They knew where she was headed and by the growing buzz most, if not all, were outraged at her presumption. Of course, the Court did not matter, she could ignore their clamor, she could stand before their disfavor, and she was more than willing to forever isolate herself from their circle to achieve this one deed. The hard part was standing before Goibhniu's penetrating gaze and still managing to get out the words she had to say, leaving no doubt of what she was after. "I ask for this man a seat at the *Fleadh Ghoibhnenn*." By the time the last syllable left her lips, it was uttered into silence, though only for a moment as the resulting pandemonium drowned out the echo of her words.

"Silence." Goibhniu need not raise his voice to command obedience, or to express disfavor for that matter. Maggie made a conscious effort not to cower before the Smithgod, though she was confident the admonition was not for her. No doubt, each *Sidhe* gathered in the Hall had the same impression. Objections that had been growing louder by the moment ceased immediately. "I allow ye the comfort an' security of *Tír na nÓg*. This does not grant ye a say in how I choose to reign here."

Maggie's face grew chilled as the god redirected his gaze solely upon her. She saw no anger there; faint comfort when she could read *nothing* in his expression.

"On what do ye base yer appeal, beyond the dying request o' one man, child o' Danu though he be?" Goibhniu's words seemed calculated; he did not chastise her for her impudence, but it felt as if he tested her resolve. She dare not waver for even a moment.

"Demne's gift had shown him that this man has a destiny, a critical part to play in safeguarding Eire, an' even the world, from an ancient Evil; I share his belief that this man is the Miller's Son, mentioned in our legends, the man fated to call forth *Gearoidh Iarla* from his slumber to battle in the defense o' Ireland an' her people.

"There's a great Evil moving forth, hungry an' ready to devour all; *Sidhe* an' human alike. 'Tis already begun...if ye'd seen what we've already faced ye'd recognize it even as we have. The minor evil we've vanquished was just a harbinger."

"A convenient claim, that," someone scoffed, emboldened by the anonymity of the crowd, "an' where's yer proof, then?" The others shifted subtly away from the one who'd yelled out. A hint of uneasiness took root in their otherwise smooth and untroubled faces. Looking upon the newly arrived warriors, seeing the shadow cast upon them and the all-too-obvious signs of battle that marred their perfection, the courtiers could not deny that something had risen up to strike at the *Tuatha de Danaan*. Fear crept into their eyes. Maggie sensed her kin weighing the potential. *Could it be that the one defeated was not alone?*

Meanwhile, the Smithgod turned his gaze unerringly on the speaker, letting the *Sidhe* feel the weight of his regard. No other comments were offered up by those watching.

"An'...?" Goibhniu again addressed Maggie, gently demanding she speak of what weighed almost equally on her heart. Maggie pulled her attention back to where it belonged.

"An' on the strength o' the life-debt I owe him...'tisn't this man's consuming illness that draws him so quickly to the Veil, but injuries gained protecting me when on the battlefield I was lost to the depths o' grief."

Even the full wrath of the god could not prevent the furor that followed Maggie's admission. Immediately, she knew what they were thinking: How dare this impetuous woman suggest gifting a mortal with the very immortality of the *Sidhe*, all to settle a personal debt of honor? Their kind did not owe mortals anything, not when it was mortal men who drove the *Tuatha de Danaan* from the land, forcing them to create new places for themselves Underhill. Not when mankind struck blows upon the *Sidhe* wherever they were discovered, fearful of what they did not understand. Not when...

"Enough!" The members of the Court cowered before this rare display of Goibhniu's anger. "Ye do not rule here. An' what's more, shame on ye that ye do not have half o' Cliodna's honor an' courage. 'Tis a good thing yer cold hearts have no say in how I decide, for I wouldn't have it thought *Tír na nÓg* is ruled by a petty an' heartless people." His words were heavy with reproach, and his expression with disappointment.

"Follow me," the Smithgod turned back and addressed Maggie and the weary group that had traveled so far with their heartache. Compassion and warmth replaced the steely displeasure that had been in his voice moments before, "We shall discuss this further in more...hospitable surroundings."

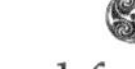

The instant the fighters stepped forward, the Court's muttering abruptly ceased. With curiosity as irresistible as that of Lot's wife, Kara glanced back over her shoulder and gasped out loud. *Mór Halla* was gone, replaced by the most enchanting of hidden grottos. Lacy wisps of greenery dangled from a lower ceiling, miniature waterfalls trickled down gradual tiers of water-smoothed rock, and thick cushions of moss softened the edge of still pools. In some corners, the open waters bubbled like music set to a merry dance; in others, thick walls of fern corralled rising steam above sheltered hot springs. Beyond the pools, through a fantastically carved arch, she saw gardens such as she had never imagined, flourishing along natural pathways. The landscape was magnificent, and so much more than Kara could take in at a glance. This was a private retreat of such awesome splendor, as one would expect from the demesne of a god.

Turning away from the inviting scenery, Kara stopped short at the more material opulence before her. Strewn everywhere were cushions of every description, long satin bolsters, full, plush pillows, even something that resembled a velvet beanbag chair. Drapes of gossamer silk in vibrant, rainbow hues softened the stone walls, and what appeared to be piles of sumptuous clothing waited for them on low, carved wooden tables. Well, it wasn't exactly how she pictured a god's domain would be, but then, on what did she have to base her opinion?

"This chamber is more for the comfort of others, rather than for my own," Goibhniu said softly, amusement woven into his words. Kara blushed as she realized he'd addressed her very thoughts.

At the sound of his voice, Kara's eyes came to bear on the man...*being* before them, Goibhniu, whom Maggie called the Smithgod. There was no denying that he looked the part, larger-than-life, with muscles etched and gleaming, harder than the stone walls surrounding them. His eyes, dark and smoky, their depths endless. Something inside them glowed like steel heated from his own forge. Short, blacker-than-oblivion curls framed it all.

This was how she had always pictured the god Vulcan from the ancient Roman mythology she'd studied in high school. Goibhniu radiated such power that she expected him to vibrate with the tension of it, and yet he sat there, calm and serene. He looked very out of place, lounging on silk and satin.

It was not difficult to see this man as a deity, though every ounce of Kara's parochial upbringing objected heavily to such a claim. She had been raised a good Catholic, secure in her faith that there was only one true God. This was not the God she'd been raised with, or at least not the one she was taught to believe was real. Of course, her conviction kept stumbling over the memories of Grandda sprawled on a beach blanket, sharing his stories with her, a rapt expression on his face, as with a glowing passion he taught them to her. She was not new to the legend of Goibhniu, and now that she was confronted with the living representation of those legends, she discovered that some part of her actually shared her grandsire's zeal. It felt uncomfortably like blasphemy.

Kara glanced at the others. Her mother looked frightened and confused while the *Sidhe* showed varying degrees of reverence. Maggie looked braced for battle, seeming unaware of her surroundings in the face of what was to come. And that brought Kara to the reason they were here; she refrained from looking at her father, unable to bear it with his future still uncertain and Death nearly visible beside him.

"Come, Children, let me first tend the wounded." It was clear that Goibhniu referred only to the injured *Sidhe*. Kara flushed with anger at the omission; though to be fair, the only human injured was her father, and matters had not yet been settled on that count. Each of those with minor injuries Miach had not had the energy left to heal stepped forward, all save Maggie. With a touch of Goibhniu's massive hand, a shimmering glow radiated from his fingertips, trailing across each wound in turn. It faded, revealing flesh and bone once more hale and whole.

"Cliodna, let me ease yer wounds."

"I cannot do it." Maggie stood firm between Kara and her mother, Patrick effortlessly cradled in her arms, passed to her as the others answered the Smithgod's summons. "My conscience won't let me."

Kara did not know whether to hug Maggie or drag her to him. She admired that Maggie would not step forward because of the debt she felt she owed Kara's father, but Kara was afraid of what that would mean for her friend. It could not be easy to stand up to a god... Was Goibhniu a vengeful deity, or a benevolent one? Kara's gut clenched with fear for both Maggie and her father.

The silence lasted long as Goibhniu contemplated Maggie and her mortal companions. With a gesture, he sent the newly healed *Sidhe* out into the garden. Even after they left, the Smithgod remained silent. Kara's nerves screamed for action, but he seemed in no hurry. Finally, Goibhniu sat forward. "Ye're loyalty is well placed, Cliodna, but have ye thought on what ye are asking?"

"I ask that this man be saved in the only way left to him," Maggie answered in a clear, calm voice, with no sign of the strain Kara knew she must have been feeling. "I ask that he be restored to follow his path preordained, that both his valor an' unselfish actions be rewarded."

"Quite commendable, *leanbh*," Goibhniu responded. "An' if I told ye there were many who walk this man's path, though only one will be needed at the end hour?"

Kara could not help wonder what they were talking about. What had they called her father in the Great Hall? The Miller's Son? What was this task he was supposed to accomplish? Maggie had said nothing about that in Molly's kitchen. Was that the only reason she was defying her god for Kara's father, because she wanted something from him? Kara was uneasy with the thought, though if it saved her father, she could not say it would make a difference what Maggie's motives were.

"I'd say 'twere o' no matter, for 'tis my oath that binds me, sworn on Demne's deathbed. What's more, I'd say I already know yer answer will be yes for 'tis been seen that Patrick will champion both humans an' *Sidhe* in the battle to come, though he'll not do it alone." Laced with conviction, Maggie's voice was far steadier than Kara felt her own would have been were it she standing up to Goibhniu, god or no. "An' even if ye deny all o' that, I'd say 'tis a life I owe the man, even if my own must be forfeit in making it so."

Kara gasped in horror as her friend's words sank in. At the same time, she selfishly prayed that her father would be healed...whatever it took. The feeling did not sit easy on her heart.

Maggie felt battered by the waves of emotion flooding the room and could not help but wonder: if it had been for Patrick's sake alone and not her promise to Demne on the man's behalf, would she have had the strength to stand before the Smithgod, rebellious and demanding? She would like to think it would make no difference, but deep in her core, she had a doubt.

Still, the point was moot. She had promised her love that she would champion Patrick O'Keefe. It mattered not what sacrifice Goibhniu required of her...she had nothing left that it would bother her to lose.

Putting these uneasy thoughts behind her, Maggie gently lay Patrick down on the cushions at Goibhniu's feet and remained on her knees before the god. She knelt not as a supplicant, but as a child would to share a bit of innocent wisdom with a loved one. "I can't say there aren't others as well suited to the task, Lord Goibhniu, but I can say this is the one Demne's Sight revealed as carrying out the prophesy, an' never have I known our god-given Gifts to prove untrue." She looked up into his face, her gaze unwavering, at peace with her conviction. "Do not make o' me an oathbreaker."

The absence of expression in the Smithgod's features did not shake her. She breathed deeply and relaxed against his knee, keenly aware of the sparkle of pride and love surfacing from the depths of Goibhniu's eyes. Maggie allowed her own eyes to flutter shut as she basked in the warmth radiating from the Smithgod, and she could not help but let loose a bit of a sigh as his massive hand came to rest lightly upon her head in a gentle caress. Through the communion, she could feel, if not his agreement, then his approval. The tension that had been building up even before Kara had entered Yesterday's Dreams drifted away as his comfort and compassion filled Maggie. His love ran soothingly through her, reducing her heartbreak from gaping wound to a more bearable aching memory.

Even as he healed her soul, Maggie knew he took the liberty of making her body whole as well, starting with the patches of scalp she'd torn out in her all-consuming grief. For a moment, she allowed herself to be lost in the warm healing glow, but only for a moment. With extreme effort, she pulled away from his touch, the worse of her battle wounds as yet unhealed. She now crouched with the mortal between her and her god, in more senses than one.

"What say ye, Goibhniu?" Maggie asked with quiet resolve, in good conscience unable to accept further healing while Patrick was closer to crossing the Veil than he was to the Smithgod's feet, even here in timeless *Tír na nÓg*. "Will ye grant to Patrick yer touch an' a bit o' yer ale, or will we leave here as we are an' search out another way?

Chapter 3

Murna o' Tir na mBan wandered the hidden recesses of the forest, those pocket clearings where the fallen trees brought sunlight to the stunted undergrowth, allowing it to erupt in patches of full, bright greenness; ferns and grasses and riotously colored wildflowers clustered in the circle of sunlight like the forest's interpretation of a fancy-dress ball. Her pouch already bulging with medicinals gathered earlier that day, she settled against the fallen forest giant responsible for this clearing. The noonday sun had baked its bark warm, a comfort in the coolness of the shady woods.

Reaching for a nearby clover blossom, she sucked the sweetness from the purple petals and relaxed, joined now and then by the creatures of the forest. Butterflies lit upon the trunk beside her, and hare and deer wandered companionably close. Lulled by the peaceful setting, the *Sidhe* closed her eyes and basked in the sunlight. It was hard to believe humanity lay just beyond the verge of the forest, blissfully unaware of the impact their cars and factories and other landmarks of "civilization" had on this natural haven, making it smaller and smaller with each passing year. No, she would not dwell on that, not on such a glorious day.

A thud against her thigh was her only warning. Her eyes flew open in time to see a frantic bunny butting and scrambling against her in its effort to flee. She scanned the shadows of the trees for an explanation. All appeared peaceful, though she did note a faintly cloying scent on the air that hadn't been there before. Frowning faintly, she looked back to the young hare, taking pity on it as its heart leapt beneath its pelt. She reached over and lifted it past the obstacle of her legs, watching with amusement as it bounded off into the dense undergrowth of the woods.

A pale blur caught her eye as she settled back. A sudden chorus of rumbling growls filled her ears. More pale blurs, accented by flashes of deep red, darted in the shadows beneath the surrounding trees. The wildlife sounds that had been abundant moments before fell silent. Rising to a crouch, Murna drew a short, curved blade. As a weapon, it wasn't much, designed, as it was, for harvesting herbs. It would have to suffice.

Murna backed against a tree large enough to shield her, positioned to make a stand. She watched the forest for attack but to no avail. A substantial weight dropped from above and forced her to the ground. The cloying musky scent intensified and a harsh whisper filled her ears. The words made no sense but the threat stood clear. Murna cried out across the ether, but her plea for help went unanswered. Something blocked her ability to touch another's thoughts. Fear and anger gripped her until her body shook. She tried to scramble away.

A clawed hand reached around her throat. Murna whimpered as it pulled her back to a kneeling position, forcing her to watch her doom slink out of the tree cover. Five women advanced on her, quite beautiful on the surface—beautiful until one looked into their faces and saw the bloodlust in their crimson eyes. And when they smiled...one completely forgot any thought of beauty in seeing teeth meant only for rending flesh.

Where had they come from? She had never heard of their like before. Her musings were short-lived as the hand gripping her withdrew, mimicking the gentleness of a fond caress right up until a slash of claws across her back propelled her forward, closer to the advancing pack.

A gasp, half pain and half rage, tore from her throat as she took a more forceful grip upon her insufficient blade and pulled herself upright. The smell of her own blood overwhelmed her. The feel of it streaming down her back sickened her. And yet it lent her strength and resolve as well, for those stalking her could likewise smell it and the sight of their nostrils flaring and their blood-red tongues darting out to lick their ruby lips was more than she could stand. She was an herbalist, not a fighter, but she would make them earn every last strike from now until they took her down. Loosing a few growls of her own, she shifted for a better advantage, trying to close with one or two alone before the others fell upon her.

She made an effort to turn, trying to keep all of them, including the one who'd leapt upon her, somewhat in view. The attempt was hopeless. They flowed back and forth across one another's paths, making the six appear to be a legion.

"Who are ye? Why do ye attack one o' the *Tuatha de Danaan*?" Her challenges were met with hisses and attacks so swift the perpetrator was back among her sisters before the *Sidhe* had even a chance to defend, let alone counterattack.

Letting loose another growl, she propelled herself beyond their reach, her supernatural agility serving her well despite her added wounds as she leapt for the nearest branch and took to the treetops. But it was to no avail. The pack followed their prey, even more eager for the chase than they had been for the baiting.

Too late, she sensed it made for them a much more satisfying kill.

"Oh, dear Lord, no!" his wife's fraught voice pulled him from the fog that had descended over him since his devastating visit to the O'Keefe's house. "Arn! Look!"

With an air of detachment, he noticed how close to hysterical she sounded. When he turned to look at her, automatically noting how bleak her normally bright blue eyes seemed and the tangled, unkempt appearance of her typically straight and neat brown hair, his heart clenched. She should not have to face such things. Caught up in his remorse, he struggled to refocus as she pointed frantically at the image on the TV. The local news channel had been on since that initial broadcast in the hopes that something more would surface. Arn wondered now if perhaps they should have left it off.

"There! Isn't that Barbara's car?" Lynn's voice grew hushed.

Arn's throat thickened until he could not answer. When he nervously licked at them, his lips were moist and salty. She wanted him to say no, but he couldn't. He had seen that car just yesterday when he'd confessed his and Patrick's falling-out to Barbara. There was no hope then. Barbara's car was parked in front of a blazing building and the voice-over spoke of arson.

Picking up the phone, he quickly dialed Lynn's sister, Sue. Lynn was too overwrought to leave alone, but he had to go find out more.

Heading for the downtown address mentioned in the news report, Arn was numb from all the turmoil over the past two days. First, his fight with Patrick, then the destruction of the O'Keefe's house, and now this. If Arn weren't so overloaded with emotions at the moment, the thought of how they had parted company would torment him. How trivial their argument had been. If he'd handled it differently then, would his friend be safe now? Arn swallowed against a dry heave at the thought.

He had to focus. If he played "what if" he could blow any remote chance of helping his best friend, or at least of tracking down whoever was responsible.

Driving through Brooklyn on his way to the Village, he saw billowing black smoke on the horizon, flaring every now and then with a sullen orange glow. *The blaze must be huge to cast such a light. You would think half of downtown was on fire.* Arn's jaw clenched at the thought. Already faint whiffs of acrid smoke drifted through the car's vents. As he crossed the bridge, traffic was already backing up, due to the incident. It would only get worse the closer he got.

Setting his jaw in determination, Arn plowed on. He had to find out something, starting with whatever had happened at that building and what it had to do with the O'Keefes. At the pace traffic was crawling, he would get there sometime tomorrow.

This was ridiculous. With every minute he was trapped in his car, the trail grew colder. He scanned ahead for a parking space he could swing into. The address was close enough that he'd get there quicker on foot. Pulling into the first available spot, he barely took the time to lock up before setting off at a marathon pace toward Canal Street. His eyes never left the mountainous cloud of smoke, which, with each step, grew colossally larger in his mind than it was in real life.

"I'm sorry, sir, but you will have to step away." The officer remained persistent if mechanical in her response when Arn tried to gain access to the scene. "No one but rescue personnel and emergency medical past this point."

Never having been one to shamelessly use his credentials to get his way, Arn nonetheless reached into his pocket and fumbled out his wallet, thrusting it toward her. "Here...here, Officer...Ryan, look, will you. I'm a doctor, please let me through."

The police officer looked him over with skepticism.

"Please! There could be people injured in there, people I can help save." *Possibly people I care for very much,* Arn finished to himself, trying to project every ounce of trustworthiness he could possibly muster. The earnest look on his face must have convinced her that whatever he was up to, it was with good intent. She returned his wallet with one hand while pushing him past her with the other, paying him no more mind as she began her spiel for the group of reporters trying to follow him past the blockade.

Finally on the right block, Arn focused on making his way down the street with single-minded determination. He vaguely noticed clusters of people off to the side, one or two being treated for smoke inhalation by emergency personnel, others just looking on in disbelieving shock. Their faces, where they weren't smudged black with soot, tinged orange by the reflected light of the fire, like the tortured damned from *The Inferno*'s City of Dis.

Looking from the onlookers to the unnatural blaze, he could not help but mutter Dante's oh-so-fitting lines, "'Eternal fire/That inward burns, shows them with ruddy flame/Illumed; as in this nether Hell thou seest.'" His Lit professor would have been astounded by the ready way the quote tripped from his tongue.

And yet he knew how the bystanders felt. When they had gone off to bed this night, these people had not thought to find themselves in Hell, but that must be what this was for them. They looked as though they shared amongst them that sick, floaty feeling, like they were watching events from beneath the surface of a pond—lack of air and all—followed by the panic and disbelief. The fear that all they had worked for would burn to ash. That feeling that even though they were safe, their very safety was an illusion. He couldn't afford to dwell on that. He was here to find and help his friends.

Forcing the bystanders from his thoughts, Arn pushed forward. Flashing his credentials at an EMT halfway to the fire, he borrowed a spare emergency kit from the man and tried to find someone with answers. He thought he had found what he was looking for in a cluster of police across the street from the burning building.

"I don't care what it takes! I want every person on this street questioned. I want to know where everyone was, what they were doing, and who and what they saw before, during, and after the period these guys say that fire started." Bright red in the face, his eyes piercing and intent, the detective jabbed a finger toward the nearest fireman. The patrolman stared straight ahead, swallowing convulsively, his eyes glimmering desperately as his superior continued. "I want every lead followed! I want you to find out who owns every car on this street, what they were doing here, and where the hell they are now! Am I understood? We have a five-alarm blaze on our hands that these guys can't put out. We don't know what was used to start it, and we can't even come up with a reason why! Now get moving—what the hell are you doing just standing there?" Turning away from the poor patrolman, the detective continued to roar orders to his men. "Somebody find me that old lady! I know she saw something and I want every last detail! I want someone from Arson over here now! The same goes for the Bomb Squad. And get these people downtown for questioning...all of them! I want this block cleared until the situation is under control! Move it! Move it! MOVE IT! What are you waiting for your pensions?!"

Arn trailed behind the patrolman, careful not to approach him until they were some distance away from the others.

"Excuse me," Arn waited for the young officer to focus on him before continuing. The officer raked his fingers through light brown hair coated with soot. He was clearly rattled. Arn couldn't help but notice how he continued to swallow as if trying to get rid of the acrid taste of the smoke no doubt coating his throat or the equally acidic taste rising from his stomach to meet it. "I couldn't help but hear all that back there." The officer swallowed again. Arn smiled reassuringly as he read the man's nametag. "Is he always that intense, Officer Patterson?"

"Detective Ruggiero? The place burning to the ground belongs to a friend, her whereabouts are unknown." Patterson's face was a study of hopelessness and he blinked as if dazed. The smudges of ash and smoke wreathing his face, combined with that look, gave him the look of a Dickens' waif.

Arn doubted if the kid had ever been at the scene of such destruction before. In fact, he'd bet anything Officer Patterson was fresh from the Academy. "I know how he feels."

"And your purpose here, sir?" Composure reasserted itself as the officer looked at him a bit closer.

Arn presented his credentials. "I'm a doctor, here to help out if I..."

The officer interrupted abruptly. "Sorry, sir, no unauthorized personnel on the crime scene." With a calculated look, he pulled out a note pad and began jotting down information off of Arn's identification. "Exactly what are you doing in the area, sir? Or do you make a habit of showing up at crime scenes?"

"No, but in this case, I made an exception," Arn answered evenly, his gaze unwavering and his chin set with determination.

"I saw the fire on the news," he turned and pointed in the direction of the blaze. "I happened to notice a friend's car right in front of the building. That friend is missing, his house mysteriously wrecked...I am here to figure out what *that* has to do with anything." In an eerie parallel to the detective's earlier motion, his finger jabbed forcefully toward the burning building, where several fire companies ineffectually battled the blaze. They couldn't even get close enough to hook the walls and bring them down to smother the fire; the heat was that intense. Most had given up on the one ablaze and were dousing the surrounding buildings in the hopes of preventing the flames from spreading.

"Your friend's name, Dr. Barnert?" Officer Patterson rubbed briefly at his forehead, swallowed, and returned his pencil point to the pad.

"O'Keefe, Patrick O'Keefe. The car is registered under Barbara O'Keefe, his wife." Arn felt as if a fragile understanding had been reached, though he could not help but allow the iron to creep into his voice. "Whereabouts likewise unknown."

"Which car is theirs?" Patterson fired off a half dozen more questions that Arn cooperatively answered, as best as he was able, until he wanted to grind his teeth with frustration. This was getting him nowhere. Finally, as the officer paused for breath, Arn interjected a question of his own. "May I see the car, please?"

Patterson shot him a sharp look, already shaking his head. "Sorry, Dr. Barnert, that would be a clear violation of police procedure."

"Please! You have to inspect the car anyway! I promise, I won't touch a thing, just let me look over your shoulder. How else would you know if anything was odd? You need me! I'm Patrick O'Keefe's best friend, for pity's sake!" Arn barely kept himself from gripping the officer's shoulders in desperation. Even so, something must have shown in his face because Patterson's expression softened ever so slightly.

"If the detective notices, I'll have you carted away in a heartbeat for interfering with a crime scene." The officer's tone was harsh but cushioned by the understanding in his eyes. Arn felt like crying with relief. Now he need only pray this was all worth it.

"O'Keefe...isn't that the family in Queens gone missing? House torn half-open like a dollhouse?"

It was Arn's turn to swallow his gullet, his face bleak as he thought of that apt description. He couldn't help but remember his little niece's legion of dolls...invariably scarred and maimed from her enthusiastic attention, plastic hair burned away by a curling iron, missing legs revealing plastic ball joints, faces permanently tattooed in indelible marker. The analogy made his gorge rise as he thought of Patrick and his family missing. Whose enthusiastic attention did they endure? Or worse, were they beyond enduring?

Confident in the power of *Sidhe* magic and not a little annoyed by the overbearing detective she'd encountered earlier, Molly hid in the alley between her tavern and the burning pawnshop. She marveled at the flames before her. They were no ordinary flames. With her Sight, Molly could see both black and blood-red tongues overshadowing the mundane flames. Evil green vapors shot through the billowing smoke, coming from the bright sparks that occasionally erupted in the heart of the fire. Could the sparks be the magic of the Kindly One being destroyed by the cursed inferno?

"...Holy Mary, Mother o' God, pray for us sinners now an' at our hour o' death, Amen. Hail Mary, full o' grace..." Molly muttered her Hail Marys and Our Fathers over and over, and for good measure prayed to Saints Catherine, Florian, Francis, and Lawrence that the very protections on her pub didn't call the fire upon her. As an afterthought, she threw out a plea to Goibhniu, the Smithgod of the *Sidhe*; after all, it was one of his own that brought her to this point. So far, the safeguards held. Staving off even the heat of the blaze. Under normal conditions, she would have been baked blacker than a burnt scone by now.

Turning away, Molly peeked out of the alley at the frantic effort of the city's firemen to subdue the fire. She knew they hadn't a hope to knock it down and yet felt respect and pride in them as they continued the hopeless battle. Too bad they would never believe her about why it was no use. That was why she hid here: Maggie's detective friend was anxious to find out what she knew. Only, as he would never believe half of what she had to tell him, she saw no reason to comply. Fortunately, they had stopped trying to enter the building, for the only thing that would induce her to step forward was the unnecessary screams of the injured.

As she looked out on this scene from a nightmare, a gentleman distinctly out of place caught her eye. He stood just a few feet from her hiding place. A fine-looking man of middle years, fit and well turned out in slacks and a shirt only slightly smudged with soot. But that was not what caught her attention. What moved her was the torment in his gaze, from his determined expression to his tensed shoulders to his clenched fists and, she suspected, toes. The man looked absolutely rife with anguish. Her heart went out to him.

As his lips began to move, she strained to catch his faint words on the molten breeze.

"Nothing...absolutely nothing! I can't believe it..." He brought his clenched fists to his temples, pressing them tight as if to halt a throbbing she couldn't quite see. "Patrick O'Keefe, where the hell are you! What could you possibly have gotten mixed up in?"

O'Keefe? She knew that name, but why? O'Keefe! The lassie's name was Kara O'Keefe. When Maggie had revealed herself to Molly, she had told her of great danger to the girl and that she and her family were fleeing that danger...fleeing to Yesterday's Dreams! Something told Molly that this man was not the danger she had been warned of.

"*Pst*! *Pst*!" Molly hissed to get his attention but to no effect. He was too deep in his grieving. Reaching around, she scooped some gravel from her tiny flowerbed. With a careful aim perfected long ago in Ireland against her brothers and the odd fox or two, Molly let loose with a cast that clipped the man's ear.

"Yeow!" Only as he turned a black glare in her direction did she realize the oddity of a white-haired granny pelting a grown man with rocks. Yet she knew that she must speak with him and was not willing to reveal herself to the authorities to do so.

"*Pst*!" Molly once again beckoned him. His face paled in horror, mortifying her, and she prayed he would not faint as she could never hope to catch him, even if she were willing to leave her hiding place. As he reached out a trembling hand, she realized how she must appear to him, ghostly in her fairness, white hair disheveled and pale robe torn. Why she must be the very image of the *Bean Sidhe* herself!

Searching the ground about her feet, she seized up her bright blue wrap and draped it around her shoulders before beckoning the man forward again, hoping desperately that the hominess of her well-worn shawl would ease his fears before someone else took notice of her. She didn't consider the effect her transformation from ghoul to granny would have on his composure. Molly could not help but let loose a strangled shriek as the gentleman lunged forward, his face infused with panic as his eyes danced from the flames to her and back again. A curse slipped her lips as he bellowed for all to hear.

"What is this? Would someone like to tell me what this man is doing in a secured area?" The bull-like bellow exploded across the chaotic scene, rivaling even the roar of the flames. The firefighters continued their concerted effort as if nothing existed but them and the blaze; the policemen, however, stopped dead.

"Well?! I'm not asking to hear my own voice, people. I want an answer. And while we're at it, how the hell did the woman I've been yelling for all of you to find, hide beneath your noses eight feet from an inferno?!" The detective stopped his tirade and glared at them expectantly, his nostrils flaring with each heavy breath drawn, his bloodshot eyes glaring from beneath thick furrowed brows. The atmosphere crackled, and the officers — plainclothes and uniformed alike — held themselves absolutely still, like rabbits hiding in plain sight. Arn felt sweat trickle down his own neck as the tableau remained frozen, save for the valiant efforts of those fighting the fire.

"Well, move, dammit! I want both of them downtown...NOW! I want to know everything right down to the last time they scratched their asses!" He pierced everyone with an intent glare as he stood there, huffing like a prize bull in the ring. "And don't think I won't find out who's responsible for them being where they were to begin with."

As Officer Patterson helped him into the back of a patrol car beside the glaring old woman, Arn squirmed in frustration. Nothing. He'd learned nothing! And he wasn't likely to where he was going now. He sighed heavily and settled back in the seat as they sped off, leaving behind the ominous backdrop of roaring flames and billowing black smoke.

"Ye be looking for the O'Keefe's, then?" The whisper was so low Arn had to wonder if he'd imagined it. Glancing sidelong at his companion proved differently, though. Her bright, intelligent eyes watched him intently, and he found himself returning her minute nod, both acknowledgment and answer.

"Aye...well, there are things ye must know, but we can't talk here."

Arn spent the rest of the ride wondering what to make of the cryptic comment.

Olcas lounged insolently against the bole of a nearby maple in clear view of the burning building, having traveled over the rooftops to easily defeat the cops' efforts to secure the area. He basked in the glow of the destruction he'd wrought. His eyes glinted with the reflected blaze, lending a hellish cast to his features; he did not even mind the soot coating his generally immaculate self. It was worth it to savor the cloud of terror and horror that had settled over the former haven; another bonus in this venture. The tranquility had been so thoroughly disrupted that he doubted it would ever restore itself, particularly without that detestable *Sidhe* to perpetuate it.

Certainly not above a bit of petty revenge, Olcas drew on the prevalent air of frustrated anger that continuously hung over parts of the city and with a drag on the cigarette dangling from his lips, released his little gift upon the stunned residents of this previously peaceful street. He allowed himself an evil little smirk at the thought of them, forced from their sanctuary and reduced to living like the rest of humanity must, victims of their environment...easy prey. They even looked like frightened mice, huddled in rough rescue services blankets, knuckles white and eyes haunted.

The smirk grew into a sinister smile as he turned his gaze back to the futile efforts of the firefighters. With a tendril of power, he added to their frustration by whipping the flames into a frenzy. An even more impressive column flared within the circle of energy he'd erected to guarantee the total consumption of Yesterday's Dreams. Though the expenditure served no purpose, it most definitely was satisfying, as was this little visit.

I may not have learned the whereabouts of the girl or her blasted Sidhe protectors, but perhaps the human can get me that much closer, Olcas thought, as he spied the arrival of the man he'd noticed at the O'Keefe's house. Since the man obviously knew and cared about the family, Olcas would let him find them, and once they were found, Olcas would ensure it was for the last time this side of their so-called day of judgment.

Olcas skimmed through the man's thoughts for anything useful. The only thing beneath the savory guilt were his worries over his distressed wife and the thought that the man — Arn, he called himself — could not return home without something to tell her that would ease her fears.

Frustrated, Olcas ground his teeth. He anchored a tether in the man's thoughts for future use and withdrew. Though no one seemed to notice him, he assumed the deceptive slouch Tony had perfected to distort his appearance and wandered off.

He did not make it far before a sudden uproar drew him back to the scene. The police were converging on an old woman, and the man Olcas intended to use as his own personal bloodhound. He hadn't noticed the woman earlier; perhaps she knew something.… With a small burst of energy Olcas brushed across the surface of the woman's mind. That brief contact revealed she was familiar with both the *Sidhe* witch and his tempting prize, Kara. He tried to sink deeper into her thoughts, but could not gain a hold before the police cruiser they'd been loaded in pulled away.

Olcas's eyes took on a murderous spark. He tagged the departing car with a bit of hastily gathered power. With more care, he drew enough mage energy to march unnoticed across the sky, following at an accelerated pace.

The holding room was full at the precinct, as were the interview rooms. Molly and the man were left to wait in an empty office. Old smoke and a faint mustiness mingled with the fresher odors of fear and fire coating both their clothes and hair. Molly sat primly in one of the chairs and watched as the stranger paced the room, his expression anxious. She searched his face for the concern she'd spied earlier. He'd appeared frantic, even desperate in front of her pub; she'd felt sorry for his uncertainty and the pinched look to his lovely silver eyes, as if something pained him. She wondered if what she sensed was genuine or put on to deceive her. Her Lady *Sidhe* had shown her how deceptive the enemy could be. Dared Molly trust him? Yet she hadn't lived eighty years upon this earth without gaining a certain amount of trust in her own instinct.

"They've gone to Ireland, the lot o' them." It wasn't much, but perhaps it would ease his heart a bit to know they were safe.

"Excuse me?"

"Yer friends, Patrick O'Keefe an' his family, they've gone with the *Sidhe* to Ireland."

The man's expression hardened with suspicion.

She cursed beneath her breath.

"Do ye wish to find yer friend or not?" she demanded with some exasperation.

"Would I be stuck here if I didn't?" he snapped back at her. "That doesn't mean I have to swallow this bull. Kara doesn't even have a passport; Barbara doesn't trust planes or boats. How have they supposedly undertaken this transatlantic voyage, then? Are they swimming it, or are the *Sidhe* taking them there in magical bubbles?"

Molly gritted her teeth. Why did she even care to convince him? She was pissed with him for exposing her, yet she had tried to ease his fear. Now he slammed compassion back in her face, and she didn't need it! "Fine! Believe as ye wish, ye small-minded oaf! I'll not waste my breath on..." Molly's biting words trailed off as a familiar face filled the Plexiglas panel in the office door. All of a sudden, her head seemed crowded as a burning, brutal force tried to sift through her thoughts. Her throat clenched, and a fearful pain shot through her chest. She fought to break his gaze, quaking as the ruthless raking through her mind continued. Something... someone...he was attempting to strip away everything she knew about anything. Nothing she had ever experienced in her life prepared her for this moment. She couldn't have been more terrified if she found herself before Satan himself. Molly felt the *Sidhe*'s protections resisting the trespasser's efforts, but something wasn't right...he didn't feel right!

This punk was supposedly as good as dead. And he certainly wasn't supposed to be capable of such things. She sensed as the plunderer— Tony...Maggie told her his name was Tony—broke through, skimming the surface of her thoughts. Molly added her own strength of will to the shields. She quickly buried all the critical things Maggie had told her under layers of trivial nonsense.

Her resistance cost her dearly. Gasping for breath that would not come, she slid to the floor. Her chest burned and exploded like a sun, all but obliterating her awareness.

"He's evil. Yes, pure evil..." she muttered brokenly as the one of whom she spoke echoed laughter in her head. "Maggie must be warned... must...Ire..." Agony clamped an iron grip on her and put an end to her feeble efforts, slurring her words and further twisting the tortured muscles of her heart. She was no challenge for the pain as it drew her down into oblivion.

Arn watched in horror as the woman crumbled before him. Regardless of what he thought of her mental faculties, as a doctor, he reacted instantaneously. Grabbing her firmly but carefully, he halted her uncontrolled slide toward the ground. With an efficiency that had become instinctive over his years of practice, he laid her out on the carpet and had her positioned for CPR without even a conscious thought.

"Quick! Someone get in here!" he bellowed as he checked for breathing, pulse, and obstruction before beginning the emergency procedure. "*Now!* She's had a heart attack!"

Not wasting any more effort, he focused on the woman before him, fighting to save her life. Having filled her lungs with a breath, he moved to the compressions, all the while trying to empty his mind of the lasting impression of her face filled with horror. He moved back to her head and began the cycle of breaths and compressions all over again, the lines of his face hard set, and his expression grim beneath his determination. The harsh, acrid stench of the fire teased his nose, clinging, as it was, to both of them, reminding him of his earlier thoughts of Dante's damned souls.

"No! Breathe, damn you! In and out...In and out again...it isn't as if you don't know how to do it by now," he growled at the unconscious woman through gritted teeth as he went back to the compressions, much too aware of her frail bones beneath his hands. "Dammit! Get the paramedics in here before this woman dies!"

Arn cast a glance behind him toward the glass-set door. Instead of the help he expected to see, the punk he'd first noticed at Patrick's house peered at them from the other side. Totally unsettled by the intense, avid look on the young man's swarthy face—a look of gleeful anticipation, if Arn was any judge—his hands stopped the life-saving actions they had been carrying on automatically. Only as the kid gave him a self-satisfied smirk and sauntered away did Arn come back to himself and frantically take up where he'd halted, desperate to regain the precious moments he'd lost. Rage filled him, and he redoubled his efforts. As he resorted to thumping her chest to jumpstart the rebellious heart a gentle but insistent hand pulled him away.

Standing off to the side where he'd been pushed, Arn focused intently on the paramedics who'd taken over the battle. Nothing else existed until the moment he saw the woman gasp, her body jerking as it reclaimed control of its autonomic functions. He swallowed hard past his clenched throat and forced a deep breath. He had discounted her as a loon less than fifteen minutes ago; now, he wasn't so sure, as crazy as it all seemed. Something about that punk and the way he'd watched made Arn reconsider what was possible in the world and what wasn't. What were the chances he would be both at the O'Keefes and here? Arn couldn't shake the chilling feeling that pure Evil shadowed him, an Evil quite pleased that this woman had been silenced. Well damned if Arn wouldn't listen a little more open-mindedly next time.

The rest of the world filtered in again, and the annoying buzz he'd pushed away while the old woman was still in danger now resolved itself into an impatient volley of questions.

"What happened here? Why didn't you get help sooner? What exactly is your relationship to Ms. Kelley?" barked the newly arrived Detective Ruggiero in rapid-fire.

Arn's thoughts clicked sharply as the last question registered; here was his opportunity to maintain access to this woman, whom he suddenly found vital in his search for the O'Keefes. "I'm her doctor," he barked back and brushed past the apoplectic officer to follow as the paramedics wheeled the woman out.

Chapter 4

father's future dependent on the outcome. The anticipation was so thick that she felt faint by the time Goibhniu spoke.

"Heed me well. Cliodna." His tone remained even and his expression revealed no clue to his demeanor. "'Tisn't as straightforward as ye would care to think. Have ye given thought to the feelings o' his family? Have ye spoken with them an' made it clear what ye propose?"

Maggie's response remained unwavering. "Aye, they know I call for the Feast, an' that 'twould make him immortal."

"An' is that all?"

Kara wondered at the mild rebuke carried by the god's soft-spoken words. "Haven't ye explained that he will be forever separated from them, even should he stay by their side until the end o' their days? He will not wither, sicken, or die o' age but he will be forced to watch them an' anyone else he cares about do so until his own heart either shrivels with the sorrow or hardens to the point where it won't matter to him to see another mortal cross the Veil for he won't have allowed them close enough to care.

"O' course," Goibhniu continued thoughtfully, "he would always have the option to distance himself from humanity forever, joining us Underhill where he would be safe from the heartache brought on by the ravages o' time, either now or at his family's deaths. Perhaps they would even join him, giving up their entire world to enter ours, all so they could be with him."

The blood drained from Kara's face with each word, and she could feel the frantic grip of her mother's hand on her arm. Was this what they came here for? Was this how they were to save him? She couldn't help but think of the immortal Court they had just left, their rejection tangible, even hostile. Was there any place among these faerie lands where the O'Keefe's would not be greeted so? Was there any welcome to be found amongst the *Sidhe*, or were Maggie and the other New York elves an anomaly, more accepting in their own isolation? Kara did not think she could bear to have her father saved only to find himself tortured by the choices of which Goibhniu spoke.

"Why? Why?!" Her mother's voice rose shrill and unstable as she spoke out for the first time since arriving in this surreal place. She looked nearly ready to launch herself at Maggie, her hands, flexing like claws eager to strike out, half-raised at her sides. "How could you dangle false hope before us? Telling us he can be healed, made immortal, without telling us what that would mean. Were you going to wait until he'd eaten at this 'Feast' and then let us know what kind of life we'd face?" Mathair's body rippled with shudders, and Kara knew her mother's deepest fear had been thrust upon her: being alone...not having Papa there to care for her, protect her. Even after almost twenty-five years of marriage, their passion and playfulness with each other had not faded, and Mathair had always needed taking care of. Papa was her strength. What Maggie proposed could shatter their family into dust. Kara pulled her thoughts back as she heard her mother's tirade continue.

"What of our God and Heaven? What of the blasphemy you expect us to accept in the name of your cause? What hope do we have for eternity if we will not share it? Why have you done this? Just so he can be this Miller's Son you didn't even bother to tell us about? Answer me!"

Kara grabbed her mother before she could attack the *Sidhe*, clutching her as if all of their lives depended on it; as well they might if she struck Maggie at the very feet of her god. Mathair trembled violently in her arms and the threat of madness in her eyes terrified Kara. Choking on a sob, she pulled her mother against her chest and desperately wiped the spittle from the corner of Mathair's mouth. She turned so that she was between her mother and the others.

"Mathair, no!" Kara pleaded. "Please...let them explain...there has to be more. And if not, I can't bear to lose you both. Mathair, don't give up." She caught her mother's gaze and refused to look away. It took everything she had to pull her from the brink of madness and despair. She did not notice Goibhniu rise and come to them until he towered above her. Before she could react, his immense hands reached around her and with the utmost care, removed Mathair from her grasp.

Kara was not sure of her own intentions, and she never would be for Maggie rushed forward and placed an anchoring hand on her shoulder. "No, Kara, he won't harm her." Kara jerked away and turned on Maggie, not caring about the silent plea for understanding she saw in those immortal eyes. She felt her own expression settle into rage.

Kara spared a glance for the one Maggie called a god as he returned to his pile of cushions and settled lightly upon them, still cradling her mother in his arms. She could not hear the words he whispered, but it was apparent from the caring look on his face, and the way he soothed her as a parent would soothe a frightened child that he intended no harm. Kara turned her attention back to Maggie.

"Explain," Kara demanded through clenched teeth, her own hands fisted. "*Now!*"

Maggie sighed as she moved out into the grotto, settling onto a secluded, moss-cushioned seat and beckoning Kara to join her. The story was not a long one, but she suspected the strain of the recent chaos began to wear on them both. She had already partially explained the Feast, so she merely filled in a few details before moving on to the legend of *Gearoidh Iarla*.

"Long ago, there was a man of the Fitzgeralds, greatly revered. Called Earl Gerald by all who knew of him, he was ever a champion for Ireland against the wrongs of the English government. Upon a time he brought to his home, the Rath of Mullaghmast, a wife of surpassing beauty. Now, the Earl was known for his skill with weapons and magic both, but it was his ability to transform his shape to whatever he wished that fascinated his bride."

"But I know the story of Earl Gerald…" Kara interrupted. "It's one of my favorites. Grandda told me that one often, how he disappeared forever because his silly wife screamed…"

Maggie stopped her with a reproachful look. "Ye'll kindly allow me to finish my tale, seeing as ye've demanded it be told.

"Through much pleading, she convinced him to transform for her, to which he agreed, though only after extracting from her a promise to not be afraid to any degree while he was transformed or he would be trapped until many generations o' man had gone to their grave." Kara sat quiet and attentive, and Maggie could see Conall's influence on the girl. At his knee, she had learned well to appreciate a good story, as well as to respect the teller. It warmed Maggie's heart to see Kara's anticipation overcome her anger.

"The bonnie lass was true to her promise…that is, until Gerald's own showing off put him in great peril. To please his bride, he had transformed into a goldfinch an' darted about for her delight. In flitting outside their chamber window, he was sighted by a fierce hawk, which stooped into a dive in pursuit. The Earl sought shelter in her bosom." Yet another pause as Kara shivered at the image of a fierce raptor diving in for the kill. Yes, Maggie watched the cold, harsh look fade from the girl's eyes, as she lost herself in the story.

"Being fair in love with him, she shrieked in horror that he might be caught, though there was no reason to fear," Maggie continued with the smooth voice and sure tempo of a bard, calling on every trick she had ever learned around the evening circle. "The hawk had dashed itself into a tabletop an' would hunt no more. Relief blossomed upon his lady's face until she turned to find her love was nowhere to be found an' never again would she see him."

"Nice story," Kara spoke out, her expression impatient. "But it tells me nothing of this Miller's Son you keep claiming my father is."

Turning upon her another measured look, Maggie took a sip of water from a goblet that had not been there before and went on. "'Tis said that in County Kildare once every seven years the Earl returns, even in his exile determined to watch over his homeland. On a steed with silver horseshoes, he rides around the Curragh o' Kildare. It is also said that when those shoes are but the thickness o' a cat's ear, *Gearoidh Iarla* will himself be restored to the land of men, along with a company o' his warriors, then to rise up in a battle against the English that will free Ireland forever. Upon the day he disappeared, the shoes were half an inch thick an' long ago that was."

"The English?! What do the English have to do with any of this? What..." drawing a sharp breath, Kara fell silent without a further reminder. Maggie could see that she struggled to restrain herself.

"Legend has it," Maggie continued. "That the Earl an' his men merely slumber, hidden away in a secret cave beneath the Rath at Mullaghmast an' on the day long prophesied the Miller's Son, born with six fingers to each hand, will raise his trumpet to the sky and with clear ringing notes sound the march that will free the warriors from their slumber, calling them to battle with the English, there to free Ireland for all time."

There was silence. A strained silence, as Maggie could tell Kara's need for understanding had not been met. With a nod, Maggie signaled she was, in fact, done.

"Knights?! Knights with horses and armor and swords?" Maggie watched as Kara shook her head and ran a tense and trembling hand across her eyes. "You have put us in this position over ending English oppression? What are you?! The *Sidhe* IRA?! And worse, you expect us to go through all of this heartache to raise ancient Celts armed with medieval weapons, to be used against modern-day soldiers with machine guns and explosives... How could you?"

"Kara, listen to me," Maggie spoke as calm and reasonable as she could manage.

"No, Maggie, you listen to me," Kara cut her off, resurrected fury sparking like lightning in her eyes. "Papa doesn't even have twelve fingers! And the only instrument I've ever seen him play is the violin."

"Can ye truly sit here, in the middle o' *Tír na nÓg*, an' question that there are things that just won't make sense? That doesn't mean they are false. Even I can't explain it, but 'tis the vision Demne saw." Maggie reached out and took Kara's hand, willing her to open her closed mind and see the sense in what Maggie was trying to say. "As for Earl Gerald's men, do ye think these are ordinary warriors? Do ye think after centuries o' slumber they wouldn't have perished were there not something more to them?

"For that matter, do ye think, after all ye've been through yerself, that the threat we're all called to face would be as simple as the English an' their oppression? The unrest in Ireland is but a symptom o' a greater Evil, one we've known o' but can't touch. An Evil more sinister than what ye spied in Lucien. One that has remained dormant for longer than I've been alive, but there's signs 'tis stirring.

"Kara, I'm asking ye to have a little faith," Maggie released the girl's hand and reached up to smooth the stubborn tension from Kara's forehead. "I swore an oath long ago, to ever protect the Clan O'Keefe from harm. If ye won't believe the legend I've told ye, I ask ye to at least trust in *me* just a bit longer."

Breath left Kara's lips in a shuddering exhale. For an instant, the tale charged something inside of her, gripped by the energy and promise in those ancient words, chilled by what they foretold. Kara then surfaced from the enchantment of Maggie's storytelling and shook off its grip. Did she have the faith to accept these claims? She did not know how much store to place in the legend, and frankly, it frightened her, the scope of what was expected. It was not for her or even her mother to choose if Papa would be responsible for calling men to war like some modern-day Celtic archangel. No, they had been foolish to think they could decide his future with no regard for his thoughts on the matter. They had been selfish and self-serving in their need to hold on to him but could not continue to be so, not if they truly loved him.

Kara was still furious with Maggie, but whether or not she believed it made no difference. With some understanding of what she needed to do, she rose from the seat. Leaving the grotto without a word to Maggie, Kara sought out the room of cushions, there to find the one the *Sidhe* called the Smithgod.

"Goiv..Lor...sir," Kara began awkwardly. She could not find a way to address him that sat easy with her. "Goibhniu" seemed too irreverent, "Lord" was downright blasphemous, and "sir" just seemed plain wrong, though it would serve.

Goibhniu caught her eye and held it a long, silent moment. "Despite what the legends and my people say," he told her in a sympathetic voice. "I do not claim or believe myself a god. 'Tis just they don't understand how else I can do what I do. A gift, like any other, but it doesn't mean I am all-knowing an' all-powerful."

She blinked...and blinked again, thrown off balance by his unexpected addressing her doubts. As what he said sank in, she gave him a smile. "Thank you."

"Now, *leanbh*, how can I serve ye?"

Nervous, Kara reached out and smoothed the tangle of honey blonde curls on her mother's forehead. Mathair looked to be asleep, which was probably best for her sanity. "Is she okay?"

"She will be," he answered as he gently lay Mathair down beside Papa. Goibhniu looked thoughtfully at Kara before continuing, "Some people only seem weak because they have yet to come up against that which will test the limits o' their strength. Yer mother has found the courage to face down an immortal, I don't think there is much in yer world that she will now find daunting."

Uneasy with the way Goibhniu's words again found their mark, Kara looked to divert the conversation.

"Maggie has explained the *Fleadh Ghoibhnenn* to me, and the legend of *Gearoidh Iarla*. I don't know how much I buy into her claims, or even how much that matters in the end, but one thing is clear to me: there is more going on here than us trying to keep Papa alive. It also helped me to understand what you were doing back there." Kara paused, ashamed by her own unthinking selfishness and distracted by something that was bothering her since Maggie finished her tale. Her stilted speech betrayed her discomfort. "The important thing is that we were all of us ready to make this decision in Papa's name, without a thought to what it might mean to him. Maybe what you said would happen could be true, or maybe not, but either way, it is not for us to decide what is acceptable when Papa will have forever to live with the choice we were prepared to make for him."

"Yer wise to understand that, Kara...what I have to offer is scarcely a gift if the one to receive it comes to view it as a curse." Goibhniu's gaze left her feeling revealed, as if no aspect of her nature was unknown to him. Looking up to meet his eyes, she was startled to see the evidence of a revelation there, completely out of place on his mien. In an instant, it was gone, leaving Kara to wonder at its significance.

With a troubled look at Goibhniu, she continued. "But it's more than that, more than our personal heartache and the mess it would make of all of our lives." She knew what she needed to say, but suddenly Kara had trouble finding the words. Not only would the decision of her father's mortality completely alter his world, but with it would come certain obligations of which he wasn't even aware. They had been so ready to grasp this final, unsuspected hope, and they had not even thought of the costs or obligations that came with it. Her thoughts more formed, Kara glanced back at Goibhniu and continued. "If he sits at this Feast, he lives forever, and in living remains your Miller's Son, the very gift of his life obligates him to fulfill this role regardless of what he might have chosen for himself. Have we the right to indebt him so?" She could see in Goibhniu's gaze that she had once again surprised him. He seemed to consider her carefully before he spoke.

"The only cure for yer father's cancer is immortality." He eyed her intently before continuing. "The only cure for immortality is unnatural death. Do ye think even he knows which he would choose?

"This is how we shall proceed," he decreed with quiet authority, clearly not wanting or expecting an answer to the question he'd put to her.

Maggie, left trailing her fingers in a moss-lined pool after Kara went off to approach Goibhniu, fell completely still in anticipation of his pronouncement. Kara had to wonder why it meant so much to her that Papa lived.

Goibhniu commanded her attention once more. "I shall heal Maggie's an' yer Papa's wounds an' then Maggie shall take the three o' ye off for some much-needed rest," his tone brooked no argument, "then later we'll all o' us talk o' cancer, the Feast, an' the future."

There were no words to describe her shock. Sitting there in Doctor Pemberton's office, Agnieszka felt the overwhelming urge both to giggle and to scream. It was impossible, utterly impossible. What was this doctor thinking?

"Ms. Michaels, are you all right?" If the doctor hadn't been so obviously concerned, she would have told him to have his head examined. Of course, she wasn't okay! But she controlled the urge to lash out at him, brutally suppressing it, like everything else.

"I shan't faint or be ill if that is what you mean," she replied crisply. Carefully releasing her grip on her handbag, Agnieszka pushed loose tendrils of hair away from her clammy forehead. "I dare say I could use a glass of water, though."

"Of course, I'll be right back."

As she waited for the doctor to return, she focused her entire attention inward. She hadn't been feeling herself lately, but how in the world did the doctor believe a sixty-year-old woman—one who had practiced celibacy for the past forty-four years, mind you—could possibly be pregnant?

"Here you go."

Taking the water from the doctor without her hand shaking called for all of her will and concentration. Some childish and resentful part of her longed to toss the contents of the glass in his face for turning her world yet further on end. However, she restrained herself. Only when she'd finished and set the glass down did she turn her attention once more to the man across the desk from her.

"I am afraid all of this is quite impossible, Dr. Pemberton," Agnieszka kept her tone as reasonable as she could, given the circumstances. "Even if I weren't too old, I haven't had...relations since I was a girl."

Looking perplexed, the doctor rose from his desk and went to the journals lining his wall. "Ah, yes. Here it is." Returning to his chair, he flipped to a page and held out the journal. "Read this. It isn't just the venue of the tabloids; there are documented cases of women giving birth well into..."

"Dr. Pemberton, you have not been my doctor long, perhaps we should go over a few details?" Agnieszka flushed hotly as she interrupted, "I am nearly over sixty, I am not married, and I do not even have a gentleman friend. What's more," Agnieszka was doubly red in the face, with anger and embarrassment both, as she struggled with the inadequacy she was about to reveal. "If you must know, I have never had my menses, not even once. Which pretty much confirms I am barren.

"And furthermore, if I am not mistaken, the women in question were artificially inseminated."

"Well," Dr. Pemberton looked taken aback by her aggressive tone, "perhaps chronologically you are in advanced years, but your state of health is well above average for your age group.

"Still," and here he looked discomfited, "you say that you have never had your menses and have not, and please excuse me, been with a man for quite some time?"

Mortified by the turn of the conversation, Agnieszka could not meet his eyes. "Correct."

"Tell me, have you had any occurrences of lost time in the past few months? Noticed any signs of trauma that could not be explained? Tenderness in your private areas, perhaps? Bruises that you do not recall the cause of?" She was more and more uncomfortable beneath his scrutiny. There was no doubting what he implied, and it outraged her. At this moment, his questioning felt more invasive than any physical rape could be. "Have you found any articles of clothing inexplicably damaged, or with blood on them that you could not account for?"

"Most assuredly not! I resent your implications, sir." Flustered by the whole situation, Agnieszka drew herself up to her most proper and pinned the doctor with an incensed glare. "Firstly, why in the world would you even consider a pregnancy test for someone of my age? Secondly, why would you imply that I am lying or suppressing memories of a violent act, rather than question whether the test results are even accurate?

"These things have been known to be wrong, as I am sure you know." Considering the situation, she was pleased with how steady her voice remained. Agnieszka could not believe she was once again being called a victim of rape, and this time with much less reason—she could not possibly believe the test.

Forty-four years ago, she had wandered into the forest near St. Michael's to avoid the taunts of the other girls from the orphanage and had not come out again under her own power. By all accounts, the Sisters searched and searched and eventually found her on a secluded path deep in the forest, curled in a fetal ball with her clothes in disarray. She lay there crying silent tears; they could not get her to speak.

Rape had been the logical conclusion, especially after several of the other girls had mentioned they thought they'd heard her scream. She had been so bereft that she had not bothered to try and hide the evidence of her activities.

She had no clear memories of the event, just fleeting impressions that had faded quickly, leaving her with only her conviction and an image of startling green eyes peering lovingly from beneath tousled black locks. One thing was certain; she knew she had willingly engaged in intercourse, naïvely welcoming it as irrefutable proof that she could be loved. She had told them so, but they misunderstood, taking her vehemence as a classic denial of her supposed trauma. They focused on convincing her it had not been so, telling her over and over that there was no fault of her own, that she had been a victim and nothing more, that burying it or trying to turn it into something it wasn't was unhealthy. She had never been able to convince them they were wrong. Or at least, not right in the way they thought they were; she was a victim of betrayal, not rape.

There had been pregnancy tests then as well, more than one, in fact, just to be sure. The tests had been much less accurate in those days, and she had had to endure visits to the doctor for months after. Each visit reopened her emotional wounds. She almost wished she had been pregnant, at least then she would have something more of him to hold onto than the shirt she had found mixed in with her own clothes. After each test, she retreated more and more within herself. The Sisters tried to console her, only worsening the agony of her abandonment.

Everyone at the orphanage had been forbidden to discuss the matter, but that did not stop the girls from whispering about her and casting knowing glances her way. She could not count the times she found nickels wrapped in scraps of paper secreted among her things, the scrawled taunt instructing her to keep it firmly between her knees next time, or how often she discovered chicken blood spread beneath her covers when she went to bed at night. Before she had been shunned because she was odd, different. Afterward, she was persecuted even more for being soiled and unclean.

"My apologies, Ms. Michaels," Dr. Pemberton's words drew her thoughts back to the present, "the initial test was a mistake. One of the lab assistants confused the samples. However, given the results, we re-tested just to be certain. True, the urine tests have occasionally been known to give false results, but that is why we took a blood sample. I wanted to be absolutely sure before I discussed the matter with you.

"Your distress and disbelief are most understandable, my dear, but please be assured that I would not have brought this matter to your attention if I were not completely confident in the results."

"Forgive me if I do not share your confidence," Agnieszka could not contain her sarcasm as she stood to leave, "While I revere her, I have never much identified with the Virgin Mother."

Looking understandably disgruntled, the doctor rose from his chair, moving to open the door for her. "You can, of course, obtain a second opinion. In fact, I would encourage you to do so."

"I seriously doubt that will be necessary, Doctor, good money after bad, and all that," she called over her shoulder on her way out the door, "Good day." Her patience stretched beyond bearing, she could not find it in herself to stand there and observe polite manners one moment more.

Hours must have passed before Agnieszka became aware of the pebbles pressed beneath her knees. It felt as if they were permanently embedded in the flesh. With her hands slowly sifting the rich loam of the flowerbed and her mind wandering both the far and recent past, she'd accomplished nothing more in her afternoon in the garden than a burnished glow to her cheeks and a well-turned patch of soil.

She'd come out to distract herself from the turmoil stirred up by the morning's doctor visit, but the more she tried to forget, the more the details came crisply clear. There had been many times in her life when she would have welcomed his diagnosis, but what cruelty to receive it now when it had to be a mistake. She had never had a family, beyond the Sisters at the orphanage, unless one counted the stray animals that came to her door. She'd fostered once or twice, but the agony of saying goodbye had been too much. Adoption had been the only recourse. Not a night had gone by, nor a day even, where she had not prayed for the chance to fulfill a child's longing for a parent, but as a young woman, she could not adopt, not being married. Couldn't have married really, even had anyone asked, haunted as she was by a vision with deep green eyes and silky black curls. Anyway, things were different now. Her single status needn't necessarily matter, but it had when she was young enough to consider the prospect of adoption. How odd it would have been to be the one searching, rather than the one desperate to be found.

Well, regardless of life-long prayers and lost opportunities, short of a miracle, the results had to be wrong. Of course, that left her no better off than before her appointment. She had no idea what was wrong with her, and she could not think of where else to turn to find out. She could try another doctor, but the thought of facing all those tests again was daunting.

Anyway, gardening had not given her the moment's escape she had sought, and twilight had setted in, lending a biting chill to the air; it was time to take her musing inside. Climbing slowly to her feet, Agnieszka felt perversely guilty at how easy it was. Anyone else her age would be half crippled after hours on their knees. She was a little stiff, and her toes tingled with the newly unobstructed blood flow, but she was otherwise none the worse for her hours lost in thought. Gathering up her unused trowel and the bulbs she had intended to plant, she took barely three steps to the back door before the surrounding shadows sauntered up and distributed themselves before her like so many graceful attendants.

"Well, hello, my furred children," she greeted the cats warmly, looking down to meet a mix of adoring and reproachful gazes. Her stomach mumbled its own reminder that it was hours past their normal mealtime. "Shall I go see what's in the cupboard for supper?

"Now, wait here, and I'll be right out." Climbing with care past the twitching tails, she laid her load on the bench outside the kitchen door and went to look for a suitable peace offering. Opening the door just wide enough for herself, nevertheless, she felt the unmistakable brush of silky softness as she closed it behind her.

This wasn't the first time one of her feline guests had slipped in with her, but she was quite firm that while she was more than willing to supplement their uncertain diet, they were to keep themselves, fur, fleas, and who knew what else, to the yard.

Peering into the dimness of the kitchen, Agnieszka reached for her sturdy, ever-present broom before flicking on the light. There was no telling from where she would have to flush out the miscreant.

Whatever she had been expecting, it wasn't the sight of a glorious, black-tabby tom sitting boldly on her counter. The cat was as large as a medium-sized dog and long in every aspect. Possessing more than the typical overdose of feline arrogance, this was no ordinary stray. The animal wore no collar about its neck and no fringed paunch betrayed a pampered, overindulgent life, but the full, glossy fur was clean and free of burs and mats, and his clear lapis gaze was unclouded by leeriness, as was second nature to the other strays waiting impatiently outside her door. This cat could not have been homeless for long if he even was at all. Either way, he did not belong in her kitchen.

She was no stranger to ousting uninvited guests. Brandishing her broom, she advanced, keeping herself between him and the rest of the house, ready to herd him through the pantry and out of the door.

Her guest had other plans. Though she was right upon him, the tom did not even flinch. Watching her with disturbing confidence, he lifted his front half up over the sweep of her broom and started a rumbling purr. For the longest moment, he held the upright pose, looking for all the world like a prairie dog surveying the land, without once losing his dignified air.

Astounded, Agnieszka stopped, the bristles of her broom lowering unnoticed toward the floor. This was like no other cat she had encountered. There was no hissing or swiping or mad dash about the room; he didn't howl or even cringe. He just sat there, a study in patience, waiting for her to realize the futility of her efforts.

Standing with a slow, majestic stretch, he casually leaned out across space to butt the silky down of his forehead along her arm. *Th-rrrrr, th-rrrr, th-rrrr.*

Backing away, incredulous, Agnieszka came up against one of the kitchen chairs. Not knowing what else to do, she sat and, without ever seeing him move, found herself with twenty-five pounds of cat in her lap. Carefully treading, making a visible effort to pull back his claws, the cat's brilliant blue eyes dared her to push him away.

She found she could not do it. Sitting there with her entire body vibrating with the rumble of his purr, for the first time that day, all memory of recent and past events fled her thoughts. There was no sense to it, but contentment descended upon her as he settled in, his head on her chest, and the rest of him overflowing her lap. Overwhelmed by feelings of unexpected love and trust, she felt the urge to purr all on her own.

"I shall call you Rex," she told him in bemusement, "for you have the bearing of a king."

She was so caught up in this new friend that had quite neatly taken his place in her home and heart, she barely heard the hungry protests outside her door, or even noticed when they slowly drifted away. The strays would be back tomorrow, but Rex was clearly here to stay.

The plan was well thought out and meshed with his own, even if half the people meant to execute it were in pieces down at the morgue. Still, more people could be gathered and prepared. By the time Dubh was finished with Ireland, mourning black would be the national color, and the *Tuatha de Danaan* would be less than a memory, not even to be found in children's storybooks. And if all that had to start in a seedy little pub in Dublin, well, there were less fitting places.

With an appraising look, he allowed his gaze to travel around the smoky, ill-lit bar. They were a scraggly lot; most of the men looked as battered and careworn as the benches and tables they gathered around, the nicks and gouges and grim looks were well-coordinated. A battered transistor, its sound tinny and flat, poured out '60's American tunes that did more to depress the atmosphere than brighten it.

Anyone looking in would not have considered it out of place that these working-class men drowned their lost dreams and empty futures in the bottoms of their pints, the music a harsh counterpoint of their own lives. Many of the men had more bluster than anything, shoulders slumped and eyes dull with resignation, and in any other circumstance he would thrill to see the Celts brought nearly as low as he and his brothers had been in ages past, but right now he depended on these men for the success of his plan. He might feed on their misery, but if he and his brothers were to have their vengeance, he would also have to nurture their failing convictions. The explosion, necessary as it had been for Dubh's own intentions, struck a crippling blow to this splinter group. He would have to see that they recovered quickly, with some small but significant triumph to fan those flames. And surely there was some way for it to benefit Dubh himself at the same time.

Of course, about ten or so of the room's occupants were actual treasures; they had the fire of pure hatred kindling their blood, and they looked on their world with eyes flat and cold for another reason; their souls were as akin to his own dark nature as to make it nearly worth preserving them once the final plan reached fruition. Perhaps...but for now, these would be his chosen few, his elite, his black vipers.

"Send out the word," he said abruptly to one of McDubh's lieutenants, cutting across the chaos the meeting had become. "We go on as planned; none were lost whose task cannot be taken up by another. I want everything back in order by tomorrow, an' contact McDermott's group down in Kilkenny to get those weapons replaced. Now.

"The rest o' ye listen up," Dubh paused, leaving a laden silence in the air, ensuring he'd the attention of all. "From this moment forward, all collateral activity is to come to a halt; no action is to be taken that I haven't sanctioned. Am I clear?"

The room went utterly silent, but none challenged him. A few doubtful looks were hidden by downward glances, but the rest of the eyes snapped to where he stood. The power was ambrosia. Scanning the crowd in calculated silence, he made a mental note of those whom he sensed were skeptical, and thus to be less trusted. And then some thought their true intent hidden, the moles; they were not to be trusted at all, but most certainly would be used. The information he would allow them to "leak" to the Brits—both fictitious and truthful—would go far to help him achieve his revenge. Between their unwitting assistance and the wealth of knowledge regarding the Movement that this tool possessed, Dubh's plans would advance much more quickly. Once he brought down Ireland, shredding it from outside and within, it would remain only to obliterate the *Sidhe* themselves. The trick was to do so without adding to Britain's strength, for there was another fruit he would gladly pluck. If he played things right, he would bring down more than Ireland in the end.

"Danny," Dubh called out across the room, his commanding voice holding everyone still and silent. "Ye'll be going down to the Clerk's office tomorrow morning to get a permit for a peaceful social gathering to be held in St. Stephen's Green in three days' time. Tell them 'tis some church thing ye have going on, or something.

"Timothy, ye'll be going in the afternoon an' ask for a permit o' yer own, only for Mountjoy Square, for the same day." Dubh made sure to catch the man's eye to reinforce his instructions. Timothy wasn't the most dependable of those gathered, but he had a sweet, boyish face that was the picture of innocence, just like Danny, and if they wanted the permits, these were the best two to send.

"The rest o' ye spread the word...the "church" o' Free Irishmen is having a couple o' revivals. I want it whispered in every pub by lunchtime an' on everyone's schedule by supper. Make sure they know to divide themselves between the two locations. 'Tis time to stir the blood o' our countrymen an' get them to stand beside us in their own defense."

He turned back to the lieutenant and beckoned him near as the others turned back to one another and buzzed excitedly over their pints about this revival. "Listen to me, Rory," he spoke softly so that it carried no further than to the man's ears. "Ye're to tag these soldiers an' meet me upstairs. I've another set o' orders I need carried out. Tell them to give it five minutes, an' then by ones an' twos leave out the front as if on their way home, then circle back an' come up by the back staircase. The others are to think they're just leaving for the night. Do ye understand me?"

As Rory gave a brusque nod, Dubh passed him the list to look over and then took it away from him, waiting until the man's back was turned before, with carefully focused thought and a stream of power, sending the scrap of paper up in smoke. His nostrils flared appreciatively, and a dark glee lit his eyes as he could feel the tool's crisped and crackled hand twitch beneath its seeming, as the heat of the short-lived flame drew near the tortured fingertips. Dubh did not know which was more enjoyable, sensing and savoring every moment of agony the real John McDubh suffered beneath this façade they shared, or allowing himself to wade through the fervor his blind fanatics exuded like a musk, knowing the true horror they would eventually realize when he revealed himself for what he was.

Well, in the end, both were fleeting fancies for one who measured time in eternities. But for now, terrorism and intrigue occupied his thoughts. Not only did they move him closer to his goal, but they also fed on hatred and suffering and anguish. Which reminded him, it was time to foster more of all three on the unwitting Celts.

The chosen few that joined Dubh in the flat over the pub were a sharp contrast to those left in the room below. Though as careworn, these few retained the strength and determination that had brought them to the Cause. Large men, tall and brawny, they could have been brothers, or cousins at the very least, with their uniform fair skin and brown hair and eyes, eyes that snapped with resolve and the need for vengeance. These were not broken and bitter men; no, they were dangerous, and their loyalty to McDubh was ensured. These were the men who would bring Ireland beneath his heel.

"I needn't tell ye to keep this to yerselves," Dubh stated, his gaze piercing each of their defenses until he knew what each of them harbored within, and they knew he had their measure. Those planted went cold inside; sure they were about to die. The others, the true rebels, swelled with satisfaction. Finally, their worth was realized, and they would accomplish something more than harassing the Brits and the traitors to Ireland. All of them were relieved when his eyes moved past them with nothing coming of it. "None are to be told what's discussed here tonight."

A chorus of "Aye," solemn and hushed, rose from the men. Satisfied, Dubh moved from where he stood in the middle of the room and spread a worn and creased map over the stained surface of the kitchen table. He motioned for the men to gather around. They quickly rose from the mix-matched sofas and chairs crammed into John McDubh's small flat and arranged themselves with minimal jostling around the table.

"What ye won't know is the DUP conference has been secretly changed, thanks to last week's little event in Belfast...what ye also won't know is that this is actually in our favor. They've moved the talks down here to Dublin, which is the reason I've set up those little rallies. Now, while the bloody RUC are trying to figure out what we have going on here an' here," Dubh pierced the map with two pin markers over St. Stephens Green and Mountjoy Square, "All o' ye are going to be making the real moves here...here...an' here."

Someone swallowed a gasp and, after the briefest of pauses, the room filled with an agitated hum. Dubh allowed it to continue while he made note of each man's reaction, but as the hum grew into a rumble, he planted his hands on the table and spoke in a normal, even tone. "Do ye want Ireland back or na? Or are ye too afraid to take a few chances to get it?"

He allowed a sneer to curl his lip and, unnoticed, he prodded their anger and pride from the outside. It was so simple to manipulate these volatile creatures. They blustered so much about their independent thought and freedom, but in truth, it couldn't have been easier to lead them around to his will.

His own anger simmered as he realized how Carmán and her children would have already dominated this land if the *Sidhe* had not stepped in to save these...sheep. What right had they to intervene? In a land where strength ruled, Dubh and his brothers had come forth to conquer righteously, as had many before and after. And yet they had not merely been rebuffed but destroyed out of hand, their mother cruelly made to watch. It was more than unjust. Even the humans themselves had a saying, "That each should act according to their nature." That was all they had done and had not deserved to be repaid with destruction. Well, the *Sidhe* and all of Ireland would account for the long-ago action taken against the *Tuatha de Carmán*, and the culmination of that retribution began now.

"Gather closer if ye've the courage to, if na, then take yerself away...far away if ye value yer lives, an' mind it can't be far enough if I come to hear ye've mentioned a word o' what ye've already heard." Dubh paused a moment, his eyes narrowing dangerously as he again searched the faces of the gathered men. He knew which of them would talk. He had, in fact, chosen them quite carefully with that in mind. "Very well then, David, Robert, an' Seamus, the three o' ye will collect a package at this address from our friends in Derry. Be sure ye take care with it; ye do not want to be around when it comes open. Once ye have it, lay low until the night before the conference." Dubh spread a set of blueprints across the table and stuck a pin at the juncture he knew to be a sub-ventilation system. "Unless ye hear from me, take it to the convention center an' be sure to plant it right here by midnight, when the shifts change. Any later an' yer on yer own for getting out, so get it right. The central ventilation system will have already been taken care o', an' by the time ye leave yer little surprise, the building searches will be done."

"An' for life o' ye, if anything happens to the package, be sure to shoot yerselves because there'll be hell to pay, an' I won't be the one collecting, if ye ken what I mean." Handing them a copy of the blueprints, he sent them on their way and turned to the next team. "Charlie, have ye replaced the goods that went up in the incident yet?"

"I've run into a bit o' a problem over the C4, but I should have it by tomorrow," the man to his left answered.

"See that ye do. This won't do a bit o' good if we can't hit the municipal buildings as well. My sources have told me those not attending the conference will be waiting there." Another set of blueprints was spread across the table. "I want three or so o' yer special little surprises at these points, but 'tis important they don't go off before the conference begins. Any problems with that?"

Charlie shook his head no, though a tic in his cheek betrayed his doubt. Dubh did not care if there was a problem or not, as long as everything was completed to his specification in the end. "Very good then, take two o' the others to help ye get it all done.

"The rest o' ye, arm yerselves well an' pick a spot within this perimeter," Dubh made sure to catch each man's eye, reaffirming their fear of him and gauging their dedication, whether to him or whomever they moled for. He allowed himself a satisfied smirk. "We strike in three days, men. We strike for Ireland an' the Cause; bring yer courage an' leave yer fear at home for we'll not have ye otherwise."

Maggie stopped in the doorway to look back at the girl she had so quickly come to care for. Asleep, Kara appeared peaceful. An illusion, perhaps, but either way short-lived. Maggie sighed, feeling intense guilt at her part in disrupting Kara's previously calm life.

"An' now, Cliodna, *we* shall talk."

She had to fight the impulse to flinch as the Smithgod addressed her, not realizing that he'd come up close behind. And why did she get such an uneasy feeling at his continued use of her true name? Turning, she nodded respectfully, marveling at how Goibhniu cradled the newly healed Patrick in one arm and Barbara in the other, the two looking like nothing so much as enormous babies, both enjoying a rest he no doubt 'encouraged.' The Smithgod moved effortlessly past her and laid the mortals down beside their already sleeping daughter.

Maggie longed for rest herself, but in all conscience, she knew this could not wait. She marshaled her remaining strength and followed him from the chamber where the O'Keefes slumbered. Given all they had been through, Maggie could not begrudge them their momentary peace. At least after centuries of living, she was familiar with conflict. They had been immersed without warning...without preparation.

Goibhniu led her through the sweeping landscape of *Tír na nÓg*. They were heading, she was sure, to the secluded waterfall known as The Flow of Danu's Tears, though most just called it The Flow.

Magnificent even by the standards of *Tír na nÓg*, the Flow towered above them to a height that dwarfed even the tallest New York skyscraper, much taller than any waterfall found in the mortal world. The cascading waters raised a peculiar voice as part of its course followed channels in the naturally honeycombed rock, and the rest danced down upon boulders that broke its surface from the initial descent, all the way to the bottomless pool at its base. Between its own mighty song and that of the birds that flocked here, it was as if a constant symphony was in progress. Over the millennia, Danu's Children had added their own elements in tribute to their Mother Goddess; crystal chimes and delicate bells shaped in every possible resonating substance dotted the expanse, adding to the ever-changing song, that Danu would never be without music.

More than a century had passed since Maggie had last been here with the Smithgod. At the base of this sacred fall, he'd charged her and three others with the duty that took them away from the land of the *Sidhe* and sent them to the far corners of the world. She had crossed the ocean—taking the invincible sword, reclaimed from the ruins of Gorias, and hiding it away until the time came when it would be called upon; now it fell to her alone to explain why she had seemingly abandoned that charge by returning home, unbidden, with the sword, a small host of *Sidhe*, and three mortals in her wake.

"'Twill be some time before we sit down to feast; are ye hungry?"

Not ready to find her voice, Maggie shook her head and turned her eyes from the food and drink that appeared, low table and all, beside them. Goibhniu helped himself to some mead and sent the rest away with a flick of his fingers. Maggie's hands nervously braided the long strands of sweet meadow grass in the tufts growing all around them, careful not to tug too harshly on the roots still sunk in the soil. There was no reason for her to be this nervous, but something ominous hung heavily in the air, unsettling her already rattled composure.

Enough...they were here to discuss the events of the past week and what they meant for the *Sidhe* race. Maggie looked up to meet the Smithgod's gaze. A part of her wanted to beg him to lift this burden from her, but for some reason, he chose not to sift through her thoughts to learn what had transpired. No, he would have her drag her heart across the jagged rocks of memory without even the passage of time to soften the edges. Gazing into Danu's waterfall—something struck Maggie as not quite right, but the thought was fleeting and lost among her own turmoil—she imagined that she knew something of the goddess's pain; being bereft of the soul that completed your own was not something one recovered from in an instant of time. Nothing Goibhniu could say or do would lift Maggie's heartache.

A sigh slipped from between her parted lips. She must not dwell on Demne. Falling back on her meditation breathing, she calmed herself, distancing the pain even as she called the details of the encounter into precise mental focus. As she told her tale, she noted several points where Goibhniu's gaze sharpened, obviously alert to every nuance of what she said. Kara and Quicksilver were of definite interest to him, though where he truly balanced on her words was when she spoke of Lucien and her sense of him being as much a tool as the boy Tony had been.

"I fear I wasn't able to close with the man, to get beyond his shields. All I have to bring ye are bare gut feelings, but I can tell ye this, Lucien was not even a Master. At times, he'd an abundance o' raw power, an' no skill to use it, but then something within him would lash out with the control o' an adept." Maggie did not bother to hide her bemusement.

"Ah...something *within* him, or something *outside* o' him? Did ye consider perhaps that puppet was a more fitting word for the man?"

It made sense, Maggie had to agree, for how else could a man unleash such power, yet show no fundamental understanding of the weapon he wielded? If she hadn't herself glimpsed the potential within him, she would have thought Lucien had accomplished all he did by simple will and faith alone, blindly performing the spells and incantations with no view of the outcome. Was it more likely that some other person worked through him? She pushed the chilling thought around in her mind, looking desperately for reasons it could not be so. Power was bad enough in the hands of those who knew what they were doing. She shuddered to consider the danger for all when a practitioner tried to perform acts they did not understand. But how much worse was it for such an individual to be guided by someone who did, in fact, know the danger and courted it? She was afraid Goibhniu had found the key.

"I think 'tis most likely yer answer, an' if 'tis, have ye an idea o' yer true enemy?" Ruthlessly, Goibhniu continued to pursue the topic Maggie would have been most willing to let pass by, mirroring her thoughts out loud. She didn't want to worry about who else lurked in anonymity, waiting to descend and further wreak havoc, not when she was safely in *Tír na nÓg*, but she had no choice. Their foe freely roamed the mortal world. Who knew what atrocities they committed as Maggie clung to her respite?

"Well, we know Tony was a tool, though he'd potential o' his own, an' we can assume the same for Lucien. In either case, the pair o' them won't trouble us again. Tony fell, power-blasted when Lucien sought to strike me; if he recovers, 'twill be slowly. Kara was kind enough to serve the wizard the same with more finality."

"Ah...Kara...There's the key. Quite a tempting lure, would ye not say?" The look Goibhniu gave her was patient and significant. "Ye throw in Quicksilver an' what ruthless rogue sensing that could resist her?

"I cannot tell ye for sure what ye were up against, Cliodna, only that I fear we haven't seen the last o' this particular menace. Ye say both this Tony an' Lucien won't surface again from the blasting they received, but what if they weren't the genuine threat?"

Maggie considered his question and had to admit the assessment was fair. They might have escaped the battle of Yesterday's Dreams, but they could not trust that the enemy was vanquished. It remained for them to discover who that was and what they were after, for all of this had the feel of being about more than just Kara and her potential, even with the charmed Quicksilver added in.

"I can't say I'm surprised by what ye have told me. Things are uncertain an' even Underhill the tranquility is unsettled." Goibhniu startled her further by sharing with her dire news of his own. "In the past ten years every Seer in the Lands, no matter the strength o' their gift, has had at least one dire vision," Goibhniu looked pained and he seemed to search for the proper words. "They all foresaw decreases in our number, but no deaths to explain them. Never in all remembered time has a *Sidhe* departed from this world in any way other than a mortal wound...an' never without the joy o' a birth to offset the heartache o' the burial. What's more, many o' the prophecies imply an ancient enemy as the cause. In some cases, those that threatened the *Sidhe* weren't known to the Seer; in others, they swore it was the *Tuatha de Carmán* returned, though there has been no proof o' this an' none can offer an explanation o' how. The visions have increased in frequency an' urgency both.

"The oldest Raths have been plagued with minor disturbances for quite some time, but the worst o' it has taken place in the last few months. It started as petty destruction against the Lands o' the De Danaan, an' none took it too serious." As she listened to the Smithgod explain, Maggie recoiled inside as

Goibhniu's expression transformed. Anger hardened the planes of his face, and aggression set his jaw, but most unsettling of all were the flames kindled in the depths of his eyes as if reflecting the fire of his forge. He was a vengeful god who spoke with her.

"Two weeks ago the situation became more than inconsequential; clear messages have been left upon the thresholds o' our sacred places, the faerie rings an' hidden glens where only our people enter." Here Maggie watched in complete stillness as Goibhniu's jaw clenched tightly, and he forced his words past bared teeth that rivaled a horse's in size and strength, though they were not over-large in his face. "The minor creatures o' faerie have come under most diabolically attack. Not one o' our holdings has gone without the remains o' at least one kin-cousin left for us to find, bodies torn an' souls fled."

Maggie gasped, and her hand flew of its own accord to the shoulder where Beag Scath most loved to perch; her fertile mind supplied the phantom grip of his hand around the earlobe by which he habitually steadied himself. Her heart rebelled against the image that rose unbidden in her mind: her little friend, crumbled and bloody, his empty eyes staring at her in final desperation. She could not hold back her angry sobs; though she vowed the imagined horror would never become a reality, her heart could not help but mourn even the possibility.

"'Tis no coincidence, this. Someone sends a message to the *Tuatha de Danaan*. What's more, just before ye arrived news came o' a further threat, seeming to confirm at least part o' the prophecies. A runner was sent with the message that in the village that stands in the very place where Carmán an' her children were brought down, the monument raised long ago to honor our Race was utterly destroyed in the dark o' night. Burned into the very granite was a message '*Ar Carmán...Scrios...Tógail...Díoltas...*'"

"For Carmán...Havoc...Destruction...Revenge... An' ye think 'tis her sons somehow returned?" Maggie could not help but be doubtful. "Calma, Dubh, an' Olcas...The Scourges o' Eire...Were they not utterly destroyed, bodies an' all? If 'twere them, why have they not struck well before now?"

"I can't say, but consider the visions, the trouble across the land, an' yer own encounter hard on its heels. I dare say there's a connection o' some kind." Goibhniu leaned forward to consider Maggie. She tensed even further beneath his scrutiny. "Do ye recall the *sowlth* o' Celtic myth?"

"'Tis what they call a supernatural being without shape or physical form," Maggie answered.

"An' what if we're wrong in thinking Carmán's children gone forever?"

"What? Ye think they yet remain as *sowlth*?" Maggie's heart quailed at the thought. While not beyond the scope of possibility, the concept terrified her. If this were to be believed, which brother had controlled Lucien? And what of the other two? The de Danaan very nearly had not brought Carmán and her children down; what if they were required to face them again? It did not bear consideration, not after all she had already dealt with. *There is no comfort in being taken into the confidence of a god,* Maggie thought wryly. *Seldom does it mean anything more than that you are the one expected to help put things right. Praise Danu, but I am weary.*

Waking with a start to a darkened chamber and the sound of peaceful, measured breathing, Kara instinctively knew sleep would not be quickly regained, no matter that weariness still weighed upon her. As she crept from where she lay, she was careful not to disturb her parents, who proved to be nestled together nearby. No one else was in the room.

What was she to do now? She would go mad if she tried to lie quietly until they awoke. Instead, Kara slipped off the robe she had been sleeping in and put on the tunic and loose pants that had been left for her. Silently, she crept from the chamber, hoping she would find someone she knew. At worst, here was an opportunity to discover the true beauty of *Tír na nÓg* without being self- conscious of her reaction before the *Sidhe*.

Wandering from chamber to interlocking chamber, the seemingly perfect and ageless beauty she observed everywhere dazzled her. Some of what she encountered bore signs of artistic manipulation, such as the carved lintels and the painted frescos—unlike anything she had ever seen by the Italian masters, but quite stunning, nonetheless. Yet other features of the palace had a distinctly untamed essence, such as the flowering vines that crept in and out of the open fretwork of the outer walls, burgeoning like some botanical colossus up to the very ceiling. Some of the blossoms were three times larger than her entire head. Then there were the singing waters; trickling through a secluded chamber she'd happened upon, they rivaled any of the interpretive compositions she had heard in recital or at the Conservatory. The wonders were endless. And for a while, everywhere she went, an enchanting group of faelings, what the *Sidhe* called kin-cousins, followed shyly at a distance.

Eventually, Kara discovered she was, unsurprisingly, lost. She had not understood the scope of this place and had been sure she would encounter a familiar face at some point in her wandering, but she was hungry, it had been hours now, and she had yet to come across anyone, familiar or not. Thus, when voices drifted down yet another unfamiliar corridor, Kara no longer cared how pitiful she appeared. Rushing toward the sound, she approached a handful of *Sidhe* that seemed to be both pleasant and of comparable age.

"Hello!"

Even to her ears, she sounded loud and disruptive; her cheeks flushed, but she smiled anyway, eager for someone to help her find her way. They just stared at her, and though they did not do anything so obvious as to sniff in distaste, Kara noticed a cool indifference transform their animated features as she'd approached.

"Yes?" one of them asked after a moment of strained silence, speaking slowly and clearly, with exaggeration, as if she were dim. None of their expressions were encouraging. They did not turn their backs on her or openly show their disdain, but she thought she sensed minute bursts, almost like static charging the air, only it moved between them and nowhere else; their eyes actually twinkled with each exchange—definitely a physical phenomenon, not a trick of the light. Though she heard nothing herself, Kara had no doubt they continued to speak among themselves. The way they looked at her, it wasn't hard to figure out what they were saying. Stunned by the unexpectedly cold reception, Kara slowly backed off.

The knowing looks most of them gave her seemed amused, almost pitying; one or two were openly contemptuous. Kara felt the heat rise to her face. Her smile faltered then slid completely from her lips. She moved away, forcefully holding back her anger, saying nothing. She would not give them the satisfaction of their superior attitude. Drawing herself up straight and tall, she looked them up and down, allowing a glimmer of her own distaste to show through before turning abruptly and gliding away. Whatever their problem, they were not worth any more of her attention.

But what was she to do now? Her parents were somewhere resting peacefully, utterly unaware of her plight. Kara had no way of reaching Maggie or the other *Sidhe* she knew. There was no one to come to her aid. Even Pixie and Beag Scath were off goodness knew where. Well, she didn't care if she wandered for days; nothing would bring her to approach another unfamiliar *Sidhe*. There was plenty here she didn't understand, but discrimination was an ugly face she would always recognize. So, she had found the serpent of this Eden.

Lost in her fuming, Kara dropped her dignified stroll as soon as she was out of sight and stormed about the corridors without paying much attention to where she was going...right up until she collided with an immovable object, firm and unyielding and clad in draped satin. Stumbling back, her hand flew up to the man's shoulder to steady herself. It was immediately caught in a crushing grip. Kara lost her hold of her anger. She had been about to apologize—after all, barreling into people was rude—but to use such a punishing hold before giving her a chance to ask forgiveness? Whoever had dubbed the *Sidhe* the Kindly Ones most certainly had not been familiar with these representatives...that, or they had been exercising extreme sarcasm.

"Excuse me..." She had to forcefully wrench her hand free, the bones clicking together, and her wrist left burning. Leveling a scathing glare at the man-handler, Kara nearly gasped at the unadulterated hatred in the stranger's inhuman eyes: a startling shade of off-white, like aged bone. Combined with hair like a drape of dark, ancient gold, Kara found the man quite disquieting. His coloring and his expression doomed him to look evil. Kara had a feeling that, in this, looks were not deceiving.

He leaned forward, and she instinctively drew back. Though physically stunning, even beautiful, as were his entire race, this *Sidhe* really did have a nasty, evil air about him.

"Please, excuse me," she fell back on formality in her discomfort. "Are you all right?"

A sneer curled his lip, and insolently his eyes traveled over her. "Is there a reason I wouldn't be?" He sniffed dismissively, and his expression settled into one of extreme distaste. "Really, if one must keep pets, they should be on a leash, or better yet kept penned away where they will not disturb others."

The startling lack of accent in his voice distracted her. She had grown so used to the Irish brogue so prevalent everywhere she turned. Truthfully, she felt he suffered from the lack of it. The soft musical lilt would have softened his harsh edges and lent true beauty to his voice, if not his words.

Then she realized what he had said. Her jaw clenched with outrage, and her eyes sparked. How dared he! Clearly, a long life did not ensure that one acquired manners. She would have loved to tell him so but could not find her voice for all of her anger. She managed a few short huffs as her fingers curled into claws, and nothing more.

Even growing up in New York, she had never been so pointedly disrespected. Not even Lucien and his thugs had been so ill-mannered; they had coveted her and underestimated her, but never had they offered her such an affront. Were the only decent *Sidhe* in *Tír na nÓg* the ones she'd come with? Perhaps she overreacted, but she had truly had enough! Except for her friends and Goibhniu, she was disgusted with the *Tuatha de Danaan*. With few exceptions, those she'd encountered certainly hadn't lived up to the reputation Grandda had built up for them over the years.

"Of course, pets that turn upon others should really be destroyed, for the good of all. I'll have to have a word with Cliodna about her obsession with waterkin; they are so erratic, so undisciplined." Only when his glance flicked to her hands did she realize what he meant by his not-so-subtle threat. With extreme effort, she forced her fists to relax. She would not allow him to bring her down to fit his view of her, though why she cared what he thought she could not say. All she knew was that when he called her "waterkin"—a phrase she was unfamiliar with—his tone reflected the same inflection and expression she recognized from the faces of every bigot she'd ever known, whether their chosen terms had been "nigger" or "dot-head," "chink" or "spick,"—only worse. She had yet to come face to face with a purist in her short life, until now.

Drawing her dignity about her, Kara stepped around the racist *Sidhe*, leaving him with a withering glance and no more. His dismissive laugh pierced her like a splinter beneath her nail, but she forced herself to move on as if she heard not a sound. Kara had, without a doubt, had enough. First, the Court with their self-denial and escapism, then the snobbery of the group she'd encountered in the hallway, and now *him*. If this was what she could expect from the elves of *Tír na nÓg*, then she wanted nothing more to do with them. As much as she would love to, she could not afford to fight back, not with her father's precarious situation. Besides, they were guests here; respectfully, she would not abuse Goibhniu's hospitality in such a way. Kara would just have to spend her time with her family, with those *Sidhe* she had fought beside, or alone. Now to find her own way back to familiar ground. After all, in the Land of Youth, she had forever to do so.

"The eyes! Eyes...filled with the fires o' Hell itself..." The old woman was less than coherent when she surfaced from her stupor. Still, she had recovered amazingly well, considering, with no sign of mental or physical impairment. At least, that was Arn's initial assessment; he would have to run some tests to be sure.

"Shhh...it's okay, he's gone." There was no doubt in Arn's mind whose eyes she meant — the eyes haunted him as well, taunting him the entire time he waited for her to regain consciousness.

"Ye don't understand...'tis him an' it shouldn't be." She gripped Arn's arm tight enough for him to be certain that her motor skills had not been impaired. "That one was after the lass, only Maggie told me he'd gone mush in the brain from the battle; he shouldn't even be alive but fallen to ash in the blaze. They'd left him an' his master in a drooling heap on the rooftop when they departed."

She took a deep, steadying breath and nervously licked her lips. "'Tis him an' yet 'tisn't," she continued slowly. "Lady *Sidhe*...Maggie, she let me read from her mind the feel o' the character, so as I'd know, should he come around to cause trouble. The face, 'twas right, but the feel o' him was off, as if 'twere jumbled with the feel o' his master...and the Evil..." She shuddered, and Arn took her hand, willing her to know that she was safe, and he was listening, though believing would be much harder. "'Tis as if something rides him, something more horrible than any o' us imagined." She gripped his hand back, and Arn winced at the iron strength of her determination. "Ye must go with me to Ireland, Maggie must be warned an' ye aren't safe with him knowing yer face an' yer interest."

Arn gasped and pulled back from her vehemence. He had to tug his hand from her grasp, and though his heart thudded in his chest with the zeal she inspired, his common sense revolted against the outrageous demands she made, nearly as outrageous as her claims. He did not want to believe she could see the things she claimed, and he certainly did not want to acknowledge even the possibility of a threat from a force of pure evil, but he fought his own heart, as well as her conviction. "Ireland?! You expect me to run off to Ireland and take you with me? You expect *me* to run away to warn the faerie folk against a punk from the streets of New York? You tell me I'm in danger…what about my wife? What am I supposed to do, bring her with me?! This is ridiculous." His hands flexed in agitation, drawing tight into fists and then splaying wide as if he would wrestle a sense of reality from the air.

"Ye have to hide her away, send her to someone ye can't be traced to, but ye must do it now." The woman—Molly, the name on her chart was Molly, and as crazy as this all seemed, he had better get used to using it—met his shaken gaze with one rock-steady. "He has the measure o' ye, an' ye can be sure he's spied yer weaknesses. There's a reason ye came to where we'd meet, an' a reason I spied ye. I can help ye find yer friend, but ye must trust me. We've all a part to play an' it matters not if we ken why."

Arn just turned away, wanting desperately to close his mind to what she said. It was too far-fetched. No. It was insane; there was no magic beyond the trickery seen on TV, and elves were stories for children. And still, her claims stayed prominently in his thoughts, along with that punk who kept turning up. Arn rubbed his bleary eyes. Rather than agitate her—or himself—any further, he turned to leave, stopping only long enough to speak with the nurse. "I'll be in the doctors' lounge. If you need me, call me, but only if it's an emergency."

Chapter 5

Aí watched the woman closely through shrouded eyes. He recognized something of his kind in that ageless face and slender grace. Her coloring would not be out of place among those of the Court, but still, though her eyes were of a fey shade, they lacked a particular awareness that marked his people. Could she be waterkin? Did *Sidhe* blood run through her veins, a pale shade of itself mingled with the thinner human flow? Regardless of the purity of her blood, she was the last one whom he'd been sent to bring to the Court. No matter; fae-touched or pure mortal, his immortal charm would convince her to accompany him.

"Awfully sure of yourself, aren't you?"

The calm, rhetorical nature of the question made it more of a statement. Baldly stated, it rippled the smooth surface of Aí's confidence. Was she merely making an observation, or had she the gift to glimpse his thoughts? It was possible...both races had a legacy of such talents. Watching her expression more closely, he decided it was merely the bluntness of the Bretons who'd raised her that motivated her comment. If she had any Gift, she made no conscious use of it.

"What could possibly make you think that I'm this long-lost relative of yours? We look nothing alike."

Aí wondered how he kept from either laughing at her almost petulant tone or backing away from the dangerous glow that flushed her translucent skin. Had she no idea of the haughty way in which she held herself at this moment? Perhaps a human would not recognize her reaction for what it was, but having grown up among his own kind, and with his particular Gift, he knew well the wounded anger hidden behind her disdainful expression. Her eyes flashed with the coldness so perfected by the *Sidhe* that it was now an instinctual behavior, rather than a learned one. The graceful arch of her brow dared him to respond.

Nothing alike?! By Danu's name, there were times she could have been the mirror of himself, in her posture, if not her features. Oh yes, he would never doubt her kin. In whatever degree her blood ran to immortal, this was a *Sidhe* poised to strike out in all her fury at one who attacked her at her point of weakness. And yet rather than being overwhelmed with fear, Aí struggled with his compassion. Now was not the time to offer to ease her heartache. He must focus.

"Do ye find it so hard to believe?" He smiled at her most winningly, willing her to thaw with the artful innocence of his electric blue eyes. This one woman was proving harder to entice than all the others combined. "Our features aren't so dissimilar an' I have shown ye the pictures o' my mother...yer niece. I do believe ye have the same smile."

As he stood there, waiting for her to respond, he felt the silky brush of a feline head butted against his hand. He'd wondered when his little friend might appear. Without looking, he allowed himself to carress the ears beneath his fingertips for but a moment, not wanting to draw the woman's attention to the interaction. He picked up a sense of contentment/love/protectiveness from the faeling and felt he had chosen well when placing his little guardian here. He would meet the fur-cloaked rogue later and see what he could glean from him.

"I rather doubt you could be correct, as you haven't ever seen me use one."

Aí stiffened. Her icy tone alarmed him no end; it held the stillness of a viper before a strike. He should not have mentioned her smile. How careless. He had not counted on her overcautious greeting as she answered the door or the skeptical way she had responded to the story he had given. All he knew was that he'd been instructed by Goibhniu to bring this woman to *Tír na nÓg*...without revealing their nature. Simple enough, or so he'd thought. Now it looked like he'd be lucky to return to those very halls himself unscathed. She was wrong, though: he had seen her smile, at the birds singing outside her window, at the strays that flocked to her door, at just about everything in nature, but rarely at any other person...never at a stranger.

This woman consistently withdrew when others were around, not rudely, but with reservation. He hadn't seen her once come out of herself in all his days of careful watching. Of course, there was little doubt in his mind that she would react badly should she discover any of this. He suspected the only reason she confronted him as she did now was for the same reason a cornered animal attacks. He'd reopen the poorly healed wounds in her heart and then stood between her and any form of escape.

Dammit! He'd had absolutely no problem getting the others to go into safety. She was the last one, and he was bungling it. He was so used to mesmerizing humans with the very nature of what he was that he had not given this situation the caution that it called for. Now, the damage might prove too significant to overcome. It was time to back away and allow the woman to think about what he had said...with a little help, of course. The Smithgod must have foreseen the hindrance Aí's over-confidence would prove to be, for he provided a verbal key to gradually unlock specific memories, leading her to the *Daoine Maithe* should he fail. Taking a deep breath, Aí did his best to salvage the situation. He would use that key and then wait and watch for his chance to approach her again under more favorable conditions.

"Please forgive me," he asked as he rose from the sofa, his contrition unfeigned. "I know 'tis a lot to take in at once an' I had no right to ask it o' ye. I believe what I say to be true, that ye are my kin, but I don't seek to force ye to accept my belief."

Making his way to the door, slowly, he turned to her once again, his hand resting lightly on the knob. "May I leave ye the picture? Perhaps if ye look at it when I haven't upset ye so, ye may see something o' yerself in my mother's face." Aí allowed himself to sound wistful.

Looking stunned and left somewhat off balance by his unforced departure, the woman nodded, her eyes filled with something that was not quite reluctance. Allowing some measure of hope and gratitude to show upon his own face, Aí placed the picture on the table by the door. "Thank ye, *geal leanbh*."

He was about to close the door behind him when some instinct caused him to freeze. Cautiously looking over his shoulder, his gaze locked on hers. With a supernatural speed, he was sure she did not realize she had, the woman called Agnieszka was beside him.

"What? What did you say?" The tone in her voice would have had a lesser creature quaking on his knees. Aí watched closely as her eyes glittered. Perhaps he imagined the flicker of new awareness within their amber depths, but he did not think so.

"Thank ye," Aí answered, carefully being nothing but respectful in his tone as he pretended not to understand.

"No! *Geal leanbh*—what does it mean?"

The phrase had hit a chord with her, and it was not altogether a pleasant one. For all his thoughtless arrogance, Aí was no fool; he chose his words carefully. "Forgive me, 'tis an endearment my mother often used with me, I didn't even realize I spoke it. It means 'cherished child.'"

"You could not be more wrong." Something in her expression told him she did not refer to the incongruity of a young man calling a woman her age "child."

The measured way in which she uttered the words and the thick cloud of bitterness that descended to darken the day were the only warning Aí had as she slammed the door in his face hard enough to rattle his teeth and sting his nose. With a weary sigh, he turned and walked away.

"I am Urias, what help do ye need?"

The young man appeared from thin air, but Molly wasn't afraid. He was vaguely familiar. She remembered seeing him earlier as she wandered the rooftop after the battle. Undoubtedly, he'd been summoned by the call from

Maggie's carved cross pendant, which the nurses had been unable to pry from Molly's hand.

Her visitor wore the full regalia of a punk rocker, and he wore it well if that weren't a contradiction. His long, spiked hair glittered a metallic blue she suspected was natural, right down to his roots, and his eyes were a bright gold shade Hollywood and the current generation desperately tried to mimic with contacts. His features were nearly too fine, giving him a pretty-boy appearance. She was sure he masked it with harshness or a glamory out in the world. Not that she cared what he looked like. What concerned her was what he was saying...or not saying, more to the point.

Urias looked pained as Molly explained the help she needed. He nearly winced as he spoke. "I agree, Maggie an' the kin must be warned, but what ye'd have me do I can't...I'm not able. 'Tisn't possible to just call a cloud an' send ye on yer way, someone must guide it an' continually hold it together beneath an' above ye. Even could I go with ye, I haven't the skill for it. My abilities lay elsewhere; a bit o healing an' some Sight, 'tis all." There was real anguish on the *Sidhe*'s face. This was no small thing she asked, but then neither was the urgency. Molly felt a twinge of remorse as she gathered her resolve and went in for the attack.

"He knows where they are, lad. He's pure evil with a power like I've never seen; the only thing stronger being his hatred o' yer kind." She reached out and clutched a firm handful of his artfully torn tee shirt. With surprising strength, she pulled his face to within an inch of her own. It wasn't easy. She was hooked up to so many wires that she felt like a tiny spider in an immense web. "'Tis the same one as was after the girl. Because o' him yer kin are dead...he sent the pawnshop up in flames that won't go out...he nearly tore from my mind all I knew or even thought I knew o' yer kind an' where he could find them. For God's sake! 'Tis because o' him I'm in this blasted bed an' it were nothing to him. Can ye imagine were he to get his hands on Kara an' Maggie?

"What exactly did we fight for, then?" Frustration drew the muscles of her chest tight. She tried to breathe shallowly to ease the pain. It didn't help much. "What purpose did it serve for yer kin to cross the Veil? An' for Maggie to lose the shop she held most dear? For that poor girl an' her family to flee their home...their country?" One by one, the cryptic equipment surrounding her bed chattered more quickly, sounding as furious as she felt, but Molly did not let her gaze waver. It remained steady right up until her web of machinery sounded a definite alarm, screaming a split second before the pain struck in ever-increasing waves.

A golden-haired nurse stormed the room like some modern-day Valkyrie, her mouth set sternly. "Who are you? What are you doing here? Out! Now!" A steady stream of medical personnel flowed in behind her.

From beyond the haze descending on her awareness, Molly saw a stricken look flood the punk's face, guilt and resolve clashing with the rebel image he portrayed. Her heart tried to stir in triumph and hope but only succeeded in clenching tighter. Molly's vision greyed out, her head falling upon the pillow, and her eyes fluttering back and forth, unable to focus. She felt no panic or fear, just remorse that for her frailty, the *Sidhe* would pay a dreadful price. And then the end drew near and she saw the light they all spoke of, only it moved toward her, not the other way around, until what she was sure was the hand of an angel reached out to ease her pain. Molly sighed and did not fight it. Why, when the tingling warmth that now flowed through her chest brought such relief?

"I'm sorry..." The whisper was the voice of heaven.

Molly tried to tell him it was okay. The pain remained a dull ache anchoring her where she lay, but she figured the angel was just the start of it; God himself must take care of the rest. She could not regret that.

And then harsh reality pulled her back. "Leave, sir, before I have you forcefully removed." Molly cried as the angel's touch left her chest, and most of the warmth with it. She wanted to protest, to fight...she just lay there in chilled, hollowing pain as mortal hands dragged her away from paradise.

Kara and Maggie strolled across the Irish countryside, Beag Scath capering shamelessly before them. Kara felt like scampering herself, excited to finally see the land her Grandda loved.

She had heard so many tales of Ireland she felt she already knew every inch of it, in her mind at least. The reality was so much more that Kara found it difficult to comprehend the contrast. Here she was, finally surrounded by the majesty of Eire, the land her Grandda had described as a mirror's reflection of Eden, and a part of her could not help but compare it to the perfection of *Tír na nÓg*. What she found it hard to comprehend was that the Land of Youth suffered in comparison. Kara felt she could lose herself in Eire's wealth of greenery, the rich, dark vibrancy beneath the boughs of its ancient groves, the velvety brilliance of the mantle that cloaked the worn, aged hills, even the steadfastness of the moss clinging to its craggy cliffs. It truly was like finding yourself walking in a world captured within the perfect facets of an emerald.

As she followed Maggie, Kara reveled in finally being able to lengthen her strides beyond an ambling pace. The New Yorker in her had chaffed at placidly walking along Goibhniu's ideal and sedate garden paths. More used to walking to get from point to point and the challenge in getting there quickly and safely, she had never developed an appreciation of strolling for its own sake. Now she could immerse herself in a more proper swiftness and walk easy in the knowledge that she had a goal.

"'Tisn't a race, love."

Kara laughed as she noticed a slight peevishness to the good-natured *Sidhe*. As much as she was glad to finally step out, she realized Maggie must be equally pleased to have returned to her homeland. Kara could hardly blame her for not wanting to be rushed through the joy of getting reacquainted. Agreeably, she slowed to a steady, if less hurried, gait. "Where are we now, Maggie?"

"Kildare. The cathedral we came out through is Saint Brigid's." The answer was brief, but Kara latched on to every detail she could learn of Ireland. She had never been here before outside of dreams, but she could not help but love it nearly as much as Grandda and Papa had.

"Kildare? Isn't that the place from your story? The one about Earl Gerald?"

"Aye, 'tis the same. Ye've a quick wit to remember that." Maggie looked pleased, which filled Kara with the warmth of satisfaction.

"And where are we off to first?" she persisted, though it was clear Maggie was in a quiet, pensive mood.

Maggie smiled anyway, and the light of anticipation kindled in her eyes. "We're off to Dublin."

"Dublin? We're walking to Dublin?!" It wasn't the chilled autumn air alone that caused Kara to shudder. She was a city-girl, more used to traversing vast expanses of concrete and dodging pedestrians, not hiking across the countryside.

Now Maggie laughed, and Kara blushed at the way she'd yelped in disbelief.

"Ye mean to say ye nor up to walking forty-five kilometers?" Kara's mouth dropped open; she could see no sign of jest in Maggie's face. "Don't fear, 'tis only twenty-eight o' yer American miles." Kara was too flabbergasted to point out that for the last century or so, they had been Maggie's miles as well. Casting her gaze over the lush, green expanse, broken only by brief white mounds of what were either boulders or sheep, Kara swallowed hard. Twenty-eight miles...She'd make it to Dublin just in time to be buried there. She cast a skeptical glance at her sneakers. Why couldn't they be Timberlands or something? Keds would never hold up to such a hike. Just the thought robbed Kara's steps of their verve, dropping her down to Maggie's more sedate pace. Didn't these people know what a bus was? Kara longed for the reasonable dependability of New York's Transit system.

"Can't you just, um, wink us there or something?" Kara asked half-heartedly.

"O' course na." Somehow that didn't ring quite true, but Kara wasn't about to call the *Sidhe* on it. Surely, Maggie had some reason for not 'winking' in. Kara did spy a glimmer of satisfaction in Maggie's eye as she continued, "But we will catch a bus down the road."

"Why are we going to Dublin?" Kara had a growing suspicion that the trip was simply a purposeless diversion. But then she saw the wave of seriousness that swept across the *Sidhe*'s expression.

"There's been a bit o' a carrying on that's left the Seers among the Kin uneasy." Maggie looked at her with such solemn regard that Kara nearly squirmed. "We're off to see if we can learn a bit more."

That explained Maggie's somber attitude. "Is that why you've brought Beag Scath along? To sniff out those with Power?" For a moment, Kara glowed at the impressed look on Maggie's face, though all the *Sidhe* answered was "Aye."

Well, that clinched it; this was no pleasure jaunt, though Kara found it hard to reconcile that fact at the moment as they were surrounded by rolling green hills, dotted with creamy fleeced sheep and thatched cottages, the epitome of pastoral peace.

Still, deep in her heart, Kara knew that Maggie and the Seers were right; the current serenity was but a thin veil. Swirling darkness lurked beneath its gauze, like a bride-to-be's corpse laid out in her wedding finery. What was worse...Kara had a chilling conviction that she knew this evil intimately, or something quite akin to it. Though the sun still shone over the countryside, the blue sky had gone pale and bleak.

Arn struggled up out of a troubled slumber, cartoon leprechauns, little red devils, and images of Molly as a banshee clinging to his thoughts. A hand rested on his shoulder, an anchoring line to the real world...until Arn opened his eyes, that is. Three feet away, a strange man with spiked blue hair and punkish clothes stood watching him intently — too far away to have just been touching him.

"What the hell?"

"Ye've the care o' a woman named Molly." It wasn't a question, and, in any case, Arn chose to ignore it in favor of more important matters.

Arn scrambled up from the battered leather couch, putting even more space between them, and quickly scanned the doctors' lounge. They were alone. "What are you doing here? This area is off-limits to the public."

The young man merely stood in place with his hands limp at his side, a patient expression on his face. He was the picture of non-aggression, but Arn did not let his guard down.

"How did you get in here? That door requires a passkey. Who let you in?" Arn was furious; between the events of yesterday and the concern over Molly Kelley, he had barely slept in over thirty-six hours. Glancing at the clock on the wall, he had an hour before his next scheduled check on her, and this was no emergency, as far as he could see.

"Molly needs yer help."

"Who are you, and what are you trying to pull?" Arn edged toward the paging system on the wall, hoping to reach it before the punk guessed his intention. "Unless this hospital has become very liberal in its dress code, you are not on staff. Not only should you not be here, but kindly leave the care of my patient to myself and the professional staff. You need to leave." Arn was close enough to hit the page button, with just a bit of a stretch, but as his hand came down on it, it was as if it wasn't even there. He tried again, glancing quickly toward the intruder. Neither button nor man moved, though the punk had an intent look on his face.

Arn shivered, as the finger trying to depress the pager grew very warm. He yanked his hand back and stared at it. Perplexed, he reached out to touch first the lampshade and then the couch and back to the button again. Each felt normal and reacted appropriately until he came to the button, which still stubbornly refused to depress. It wasn't broken—he'd used it just a few hours earlier. Was he still dreaming? This was certainly surreal enough.

Arn turned to face the punk squarely. "Who are you? And what are you doing here?"

"I'm Urias, kin to Maggie McCormick, an' I'm here because Molly called on me an' asked me to come."

"Impossible. Her room doesn't have a phone, and she isn't allowed visitors." The protests sounded lame, even to his ears. The guy wasn't supposed to be in the doctor's lounge either, but he'd managed it.

"Molly needs yer help," the punk persisted.

Arn gritted his teeth, "Ms. Kelley is getting the best care this facility and I can provide; now you need to leave." He reached for the door handle and quickly released it. His hand had not been burned, but the handle was warm enough to give the impression it would have been were the contact prolonged.

"Set yerself down an' listen to me, Dr. Barnert." The man spoke calmly and reasonably as he sat in a chair on the far side of the room and motioned Arn to the couch. Arn noted that the intruder, uncharacteristic of his appearance, sat with good posture and placed his hands in clear sight on the arms of the chair. "Please?"

Cautiously, Arn lowered himself to the edge of the couch closest to the door.

"Dr. Barnert, I'm sure Molly's tried to tell ye o' Maggie an' what she is. Well, I'm the same. I know ye're resisting the concept, but that doesn't make it untrue. We're *Sidhe*...elves...creatures o' magic, an' whether ye chose to believe or na, the facts remain, ye can't open that door, nor use that paging device." Urias paused as if waiting for Arn to speak. Watching the intruder through narrowed eyes, Arn didn't really have anything to say.

The young man sighed and rubbed his eyes in a very human gesture. "Whether ye believe or na, our very nature, an' that o' yer friends, puts both

Molly an' yerself in danger. Ye've seen the face o' evil, an' had no trouble believing that." There was determination in the eyes that watched him, and for the first time, Arn realized those eyes were brilliantly golden, without the tell-tale signs the guy wore colored contacts.

"Evil is a very human trait," Arn kept his voice firm through sheer will. "Magic isn't."

The unearthly gaze that locked with Arn's showed both wisdom and weariness that appeared ancient...ageless. The man shook his head solemnly; he looked as if he would dispute the statement, had he the time, energy, or inclination. Instead, he rested his head in his hand a moment and seemed to reconsider his approach. His breath shifted from a healthy, unconscious pace to deep, deliberate inhalations. His head lifted just enough that his eyes once more locked with Arn's, and his breathing transitioned yet again until he drew sharp, jagged pants. Still, his gaze remained steady, though he trembled as if from a great effort, every muscle tense and straining. The golden eyes seemed to glow as the rest of him paled.

Arn was overcome with a desire to look away. It took every bit of his determination not to, though the gaze across the room grew brighter...crisper, while everything else about the young man seemed to distort. Arn's vision blurred and his hands dug into the arm of the couch until his nails bit into the battered leather. His mind rebelled as the shadows across the room deepened in relation to the brilliance of those unnatural eyes. Suddenly, Arn regained focus, staring at what looked like a golden-eyed hawk hooded with metallic-blue feathers, where a moment before a punk rocker sat watching him intently. His mouth went dry as he tried to deny what he saw before him. Even as Arn struggled with the sight, the hawk shimmered and morphed back to a man, abet one that was a pale, spent shadow of what he had been just moments before.

Arn was not ready to confront what he'd just seen. He let his mind run right past it and settle on the pressing matter at hand: Molly Kelley and her blasted attempts to convince him to go along with her mad plan. Annoyance was familiar ground, comfortingly so; he let that well up in place of his confusion. "Did Molly send you down here to pester me? Why me? Why not send her with one of your elf buddies? Why does she need me?"

"She's had another attack, Dr. Barnert." The man now sounded exhausted, drained, and oddly guilty.

"Well then, she certainly has no business traipsing off to Ireland and trying to drag me along, does she? She belongs right where she is, and I will not be the one to take her away from the care she must have to survive." Arn's jaw jutted stubbornly. "If she insists on doing this, then fine, but I won't be a party to it. I owe this woman nothing further, and I certainly don't believe her wild tales. She's already disrupted my life enough in the last few hours. I'm not about to put up with it a moment longer." He had had enough; he was leaving this room...now, passing Molly Kelley's case off to someone else, and then going home to his Lynn and their nice, normal life of bills and dinner parties and people who didn't turn into birds.

Storming to the door, he reached out for the handle before he could hesitate, or the punk could intervene. He grabbed it with all his might and panicked when, for a moment, it would not budge. Arn growled and tried again, setting his feet and bringing all of his strength to bear. This time he felt a faint pop. There was no triumph in the success; behind him rose a pained groan, followed by a sigh. Immediately, the doorknob ceased to resist, and Dr. Arnold Barnert turned his back on Molly Kelley and the *Sidhe*.

Enthralled by the streets of Dublin, the mixture of ancient and modern, with a history that went clear beyond the time of the Vikings, Kara lost her earlier apprehension and eagerly attempted to commit everything to memory. There was so much to see she made herself dizzy, whipping around her head. The historic townhouses and the cobbled streets; the green squares and the bustling Moore Street Market; St. Patrick's Cathedral, where Jonathan Swift was buried; and Ashtown Castle in the middle of Phoenix Park. More than once, she stepped on Maggie's heels trying to take it all in.

"Fer goodness sake, love, have a little mercy on my feet," Kara back-peddled as the *Sidhe* finally turned on her, exasperation written across her face. "'Tis only the one pair I've got an' they don't heal so quick that I can bear for ye to keep trodding them."

Kara smiled and slipped her hand through Maggie's arm until they walked side by side. "I'm sorry, Maggie. I don't mean to be so giddy, but I've never been anywhere outside the United States, and to have it be the land that Grandda loved so very much...well, I just have to see it all!"

Maggie glanced sideways at her, and Kara could find no sourness in her eyes though her lips pulled a frown. "Ye'll be seeing more o' it than ye'll like when yer walking back, an ye step on my heels again."

Laughing at the idle threat, Kara kicked up her heels in a bit of a jig. Joy bubbled through her, and everything she saw was bright and clean and full of Celtic flare. She understood why it had remained so in Grandda's thoughts, even if he had focused more on ancient Eire than Herself, as he called the Motherland, in modern days. She could also begin to see why Papa was still bitter at being ripped from his Celtic roots. Kara certainly couldn't imagine leaving, though at some point she was sure she would have to; she couldn't live in faerie land forever—her short stay there had already shown her that—and to modern-day Ireland, she wasn't even officially here.

Another laugh nearly choked her as she realized that technically she, Kara O'Keefe, was an illegal alien. Maggie's puzzled look only caused her to laugh harder, and she had to stop to hold her side. While she didn't get nearly the looks she would have in New York, the locals were still bemused, passing wide around the odd American and her poor Irish friend.

"Well, an' have ye had enough attention, then? Or perhaps ye'll just have done with it an' loose some o' that power we've been struggling to get under control?" It seemed Maggie had had enough. Grudgingly, Kara had to agree. A little fun was one thing, but she was quite aware of the seriousness of the situation that had brought them to Dublin.

She forgot any answer as Beag Scath gave a growling hiss as he wove in obvious agitation around their feet. He arched his back so severely it would have looked more comical than fierce if they hadn't realized immediately what had motivated it. Neither Maggie nor Kara was inspired to laugh. To be truthful, both of them were too stunned. Until now, they had wandered the back streets of Dublin under the illusion of a casual stroll, enjoying the brightly painted storefronts and riotous tumble of the flowerboxes, but at the moment, Kara wanted nothing more than to bolt right back to the bus station. While they talked, the landscape had subtly changed. Run down. less polished. Depressed. Central to it all they found the burned-out husk of a pub and several other buildings. The damage was clearly weeks, maybe months old, but the stench lingered. Worse yet, malevolence hung over the neighborhood like a pall.

"Well, now. I think we've found what we were after," Maggie muttered.

"Shh...shh...Come here, Beag Scath, it's okay." Kara bent down and beckoned to the sprite. Catlike, he made a beeline for the safety of her arms. Turning an outwardly curious gaze on the sight before her, Kara extended her awareness as Maggie had shown her on the trip over from America.

She shuddered. Her mage sight showed a black cloud radiating from the wreckage, glittering with sparks of jagged, deep green, the color of a fading bruise. Instead of scattering as a mundane cloud would, it deepened in intensity as it spread out. Puffs of it broke off to settle over other areas of the city, where they hovered like angry storm clouds, oppressive and ominous. Here, at the epicenter, eddies swirled around them, as if stirred up by their presence.

Kara felt much the same weariness as she would trying to fight an ocean current close to shore. She had trouble focusing, but as she scratched the cat-cloaked sprite behind his ear, she redirected a bit of her will to try and soulspeak with Maggie, a trick she was learning with sporadic success. *Do you see it?*

Was it possible for telepathy to be slurred? If so, Kara feared that was how her attempt came out.

Maggie turned to her, clearly alarmed. Abruptly, she swept the surrounding miasma away with an out-flung hand before hurrying them out of the area.

Kara could not explain what had happened, but she sensed the difference, once freed from its influence. Reflexively, she rubbed her hands across her jeans as if to shed her skin of the slimy feeling left by whatever they'd encountered.

They were halfway back to the bus station before Maggie shared her thoughts. *Would that I could tell ye what that was, love, but I've never seen the likes before. We must return to Tír na nÓg an' warn Goibhniu. That thing… it would have drained ye dry in minutes.*

Maggie's distress — impossible to hide when soulspeaking — shook Kara more than anything she'd encountered that day. Clearly, they had found the locus of the danger the Seers warned about.

Now, what to do about it?

*Geal...Geal...*She knew that word. It teased at her memory, only it hadn't been followed by *Leanbh... Geal* something...What was it? What was more, how did she remember it? *Geal...Geal leannán!* At the memory her heart broke anew. They were not the same, but close enough, and as far as she was concerned, both grossly inaccurate; Agnieszka trembled as a few scraps of memory flittered to the surface.

She had never been told what *geal leannán* meant, but with what she just learned, she could imagine, and her eyes burned with tears she thought she was long past shedding. Long ago, in a moment of weakness and despair, she had so wanted to be loved that she gave her heart and her body to a young man who appeared out of the morning mist. He had called her *Geal leannán* in the throes of passion...and he had been gone before the sun burned off the dawn's hazy veil. At sixteen, she had wanted to believe him with all of her heart; it was the last time she'd believed anyone with talk of love on their lips.

She was ashamed at how close she'd come to believing another young man this very day. He was just as lovely to look at, and his voice had sent her every nerve tingling as the first had done long ago, though this time, it was in alarm.

Pressing herself even harder against her front door until she felt bruised down her entire length, Agnieszka pushed away those thoughts and bit down on her lower lip, as she hadn't done in years, replacing mental anguish with physical pain. When the memories were once again tightly closed away in their deep, hidden compartment in her heart, she stepped away from the door. She just needed something to occupy her mind; that was all.

On her way to her study to sort out her neglected accounts, her eye swept across the table by the door. She lingered there a moment too long, for the sight of the photograph left by her unfortunate visitor quite undid her careful composure all over again. Snatching it up with a snarl that would have left her utterly frightened if she'd realized it came from her own throat, Agnieszka nearly shredded the likeness on the spot. Perhaps it was the eyes...or that damned smile — she had to admit the young man was most likely correct about that—but she found she could not destroy the beautiful image. This scrap of paper seemed to hold life than she had ever seen in herself—except, perhaps, long ago on a misty May morning, some perverse voice whispered from the corner of her mind. She could well imagine this was how her daughter would have looked, had she had one.

She placed the photograph back on the table with exaggerated care and turned away, retiring to her study and the bookkeeping she ironically never seemed to have time for. Considering the care she took with the orphanage accounts, the Sisters would have been dismayed at the state of her own, not that there was much to keep track of. Agnieszka turned on the small stereo system that was her one extravagance and settled at the desk, forcing her mind to focus on the neat rows of numbers on the page before her.

Perhaps it was the turmoil of the day, or simply old age having its way with her, but as the music played softly in the background, the bold, black lines of her finances danced before her eyes. Before it could even register that she was drifting off and should settle herself more comfortably in her bed, Agnieszka's head pillowed on her ledger.

Agnieszka sang softly to herself as she made her way through the tall, verdant meadow grass. The Sisters had told them to keep to the fields, but the other girls were hateful, and she did not wish to stay with them. As Sister Michael Adele dozed off upon her hassock, surrounded by a gently swaying sea of pale green grass not yet baked golden brown by the sun, the others tormented each other and gossiped about the boys from the village. Agnieszka would just as soon distance herself from them before they turned their attention on her.

Trees formed a solid wall all around the edges of the field, ancient oaks and pine with a sprinkling of yew and hawthorn. The green boughs draped down in places, conspiring with the meadow grass to cloak the forest, adding to its air of secrecy...and sanctuary. As the others gossiped around her, she longed for the solitude of the forest, to be wrapped in the cool, protective shade of the clustered trees, with her eyes closed so she could better hear the whispered secrets that traveled through their branches. As casually as she could manage, Agnieszka wandered further from her companions, skirting the meadow, wending her way around the edge of the forest just far enough that she would not hear their shrill laughter.

They were supposed to be gathering flowers for the May Day celebration that day. It was an ancient tradition, and this was the first time any of them were considered old enough to be allowed a part in the preparation. All of the other girls were too interested in which of the boys would dance with them and who they'd like to steal kisses from later on. Only Agnieszka had any flowers in her basket. She had no illusion that she would be favored by anyone at the celebration.

As she slipped further away, her hopes were shattered. The girls caught sight of her despite her covert departure and now made her the target of the moment. "So, Aggie, who do you fancy circling the May Pole with?" Their tone sounded innocent enough, but Agnieszka knew better; they always sounded friendly before they turned hurtful. Moving off even faster, she fled their malicious giggles and shouts of "Oh! She fancies Ol' Man Brighton...'is 'air's as white as 'ers is!" and "She dare not show herself today...everyone'll think she is the May Pole!" and "Maybe it's a good thing she's named after the patron saint of the virgins, no one's ever likely to want to kiss her!"

Even as she fled further into the forest, Agnieszka prayed for the boles and the branches to block out her tormentors' hurtful words. The Sisters at the orphanage had always done their best to make her feel loved and wanted, first by them and then eventually by others, but "eventually" was not enough for a sixteen-year-old girl whose body and heart craved some caring connection...any connection, with others. Something inside her ached unbearably for at least one other person to agree that she was worthy of notice, deserving of love.

Overwrought by her isolation and tormented beyond bearing by the taunts that still followed her on the wind, Agnieszka bit down on her lip until the salty, metallic tang of blood overwhelmed her senses. Her anguished cries literally bitten back, she ran through the woods without a care for the path before her. At full speed, she tripped over some deadfall hidden in the undergrowth and sprawled full length on the forest floor.

Unable to outrun her heartache, Agnieszka wailed out her anguish as she lay despondent in the brush. The aches of her body were nothing compared to the agony she felt inside. She wanted to be angry, to curse them and lash out, but how could she, when even she felt unworthy? If no one but the Sisters could find something redeeming about her, and them with a predisposition inspired by their faith and charity, how could she think any different? Agnieszka had to believe that there were no qualities about her to inspire love, or even kindness.

"Aauughh!" Drawing herself into a tight ball, the white-haired orphan girl threw back her head and screamed in utter desolation. Totally devoid of thought and caught up in a whirlwind of deep, negative emotion, she funneled all of her pain—physical and emotional—into one continuous, shattering stream of sound until her voice broke with the sustained strain and she gasped for breath against the overwhelming tightening of her chest. She wanted to be loved. Dear God, she did.

"Shhhhh..."

Gripped tight by despair, Agnieszka did not notice the young man approach from the depths of the forest. She did not hear his attempts to offer comfort. Curling in upon herself, she lay listlessly as her tortured lungs fought to drag breath through her raw throat. As her awareness expanded from its center, she took stock of her pains. Part of her relished the sharp ache of her twisted ankle, the stinging scraps along her arms, legs, and cheek, and her throbbing head. Physical pain gave her something to focus on beyond her heartache and emptiness. Physical pain made her feel more real, rather than the shadow-self she feared herself to be.

"Come now, Shhhh..." A gentle hand brushing her hair back from her forehead snapped Agnieszka back into the here-and-now. Tearing away from the stranger's arms, she drew herself together in a heartbeat. She scrambled to her feet and back away from him, eyes wild and hands trembling as they fisted. Her gaze locked with his and she drew herself up straighter. She was torn between crawling back into his arms and slapping him silly for the condescending look that flitted over the surface of his deeper concern. Instead, she did neither; her eyes grew cool, and she stood before him with the composure of a queen, giving the lie to her rumpled appearance. If she had had any sense, she would have been frightened at how quickly she bottled up her heartache, but right then, she was too caught up in shielding herself from ridicule — or worse — from this strange young man.

"Are ye harmed, lass?" he asked in a calm tone, his hands falling limp at his sides as if to reassure her that he meant her no mischief. She wanted to believe him.

She tried not to be captivated by the soft burr of his Irish lilt or flinch at the way his gorgeous eyes flickered over her. Was he looking for signs of injury, or just looking his fill? Distrusting her voice, she shook her head and wrapped her arms around her chest, not sure if she was shielding her body or the gaping wounds on her heart. How would she get away from him? She could not back away clear to the field, and with her ankle twinging harshly when she simply shifted her weight, there was no chance she could turn and run.

"Are ye sure?" His eyes burned right into her, clearly noting each fresh wound, each half-healed scar, and catching every bit of her fear and anger, all of it hidden deep inside. She shook her head more fiercely, and that was her mistake; perhaps it was the fall, or more likely it was her recent emotional overload, but as she shook her head, the forest spun about her, and the mist closed in.

The worried look on the young man's face as he rushed to catch her was like an anchor. Hovering on the edge of darkness, for the first time, Agnieszka felt compassion from someone other than the Sisters at the orphanage. That feeling alone made her reel even more until unconsciousness drew her down. She took with her the vision of his beautiful, startling eyes.

She woke in a clearing she would have sworn did not exist before that day. For years she had escaped into these woods, using their dark wildness to keep the other girls away; she knew it better than she knew herself, and she had never come across such a dell before. Surrounded by rowan and birches, towering ferns edged the clearing, and thick moss carpeted the ground. In the center rose a massive pillar-like stone, rough-hewn and carved all over with swirls and at the base, a spring bubbled up from the ground through a pile of rocks worn smooth over countless ages. Mist veiled the forest beyond the dell, and yet, resting on the ground as she was, Agnieszka felt no chill.

As she took in her whereabouts, vague recollection of what had come before resurfaced. Scrambling upright, she ran her hands over herself to confirm that she was all right and her virtue intact. Then, as she glanced up and met the stranger's eyes, she *felt ashamed. Seated on the far side of the clearing, he watched her intently, concern still darkening his gaze.*

His intensity overwhelmed her. She forced herself to look away. That was when she realized she did not rest directly upon the ground. Beneath her lay a fine, soft coat, shielding her from the warmth-stealing earth. That more than anything touched Agnieszka's heart. To lie something of such value upon the forest floor, solely for her comfort, despite what the dirt and bracken must be doing to it...she was not used to such kindness. She was not worthy. This could not be real. It had to be like the falseness of the girls at the orphanage.

That was an uncomfortable thought, and she did not want to believe it. Agnieszka shoved it away and raised the edges of the coat around her. She kept her eyes locked on her feet, rather than chance that green gaze again. There were signs of her mad dash through the forest, but, for the most part, she had been cleaned up. What's more, her ankle didn't hurt, and if she hadn't felt it earlier, she would have sworn she hadn't scraped off what seemed like a third of her skin. Curiously, the only wound she still found evidence of was the bite on the inside of her lip.

Thoroughly chilled by the mystery, she put it out of her thoughts for now. If she examined it too closely, it might finally force her to the far edge of madness. Pulling the coat tighter around her, she swallowed hard and decided it was safe to try her voice.

"Th-thank you." She felt her cheeks burn as her roughened voice caught in her throat. "I'm sorry to have been trouble."

The stranger only smiled a brief smile, gently shaking his head as if to deny it could be so. Rising slowly, he moved toward the spring and cupped his hand beneath its flow. With a care and grace Agnieszka never imagined a person could use, he rose and came toward her slowly, his hand still full of the cool, crisp water.

If she had tried such a thing, there would have been a trail trickling away between her fingers.

"Drink slowly, 'twill help settle ye."

Something primal fluttered deep within Agnieszka's center, threatening her very balance as she lowered her mouth over the rim of the young man's fingers. She drained the reservoir of his cupped hands in slow, steady sips, sensing he would pull away if she drank too quickly. The crystal-clear water, crisp and delicious, soothed her abused throat, causing her damaged lip to tingle not uncomfortably. It was so good, she had to hold herself back from using her tongue to capture every last delightful drop.

Startled by her thoughts and the physical reactions they inspired, Agnieszka flushed deeply. She jerked back, her chin burning with a pleasant heat where it brushed against his fingers. The sensation seemed to travel clear to a point churning deep within her. Something was wrong here; she had never imagined sensations like this, and the images they called to her mind were enough to send her running to the confessional. Where did such thoughts come from? She wasn't ignorant or naïve, but nothing in her experience had ever inspired the like.

Looking up in confusion, she found his eyes upon her; they were like the deep green pools found in the most secret forest glades, hinting at hidden things. They held an intensity that frightened her and yet drew her just the same; she could lose herself within that gaze and never care that it would be forever. She sensed a willingness there, a desire, but he did not move. Not a word was said aloud, but there was an agreement reached between their eyes.

Trembling, Agnieszka reached out her hand to finger a tendril of his hair — it was black with a deep purple sheen, not blue — it was silky and thick and crackled with energy that sparked across her fingertips. She had never seen or felt anything like it. Pulling back, she drew a quavering breath. What was she doing?!

Still, her stranger did not speak but extended his own hand to caress the curtain of her glowingly white tresses. His eyes filled with delight as his fingers danced through the strands. Agnieszka could not seem to catch her breath; it raced through her, and despite her panic, it left behind a feeling of euphoria. She could not tell if it were because she wanted him to stop or conversely, that she was afraid he would.

She was losing control. She was being swept away. And though she would not acknowledge what this was, she did not think she cared to try and stop it. Closing her eyes tightly, she leaned into his hand, afraid to see what came next — or not — but aching for it.

For one long moment and then another, nothing happened. Slowly the hand drew away, and her heart nearly shattered. Building from that deep center within her, another devastating cry rose to the surface, tearing her apart along the way...only to be captured in the depths of her stranger's mouth, caressed away by the gentle, hungry thrust of his tongue.

Trembling near enough to shake her apart, Agnieszka's eyes flew open, their amber depths glowing like molten lava. At last, she would know what it was to be cherished.

Leaning back far enough to hold her gaze, Love looked into her eyes and kissed her deeply, cradling her in his arm much differently than he had just moments before.

His eyes burned with desire and devotion both. "I give myself to ye, for now an' ever. My place 'tis by your side."

Unable to speak, she clutched him to her breast and willed him to know her heart vowed likewise. He smiled at her knowingly and kissed away the joyous tears streaming down her cheeks. And once they were gone, the two came together as one.

Chapter 6

crumpled papers in her hand tighter and tighter, as if all of her pain and anger
and hatred could be redirected into that one act. The images were always the
same, wasn't that the way it went on the TV? 'The images are always the same,
only I can never remember them once I awake'...no...that part was no longer
true, at least for her. Ever since that strange young man had visited, she always
remembered each and every damned detail with a clarity she never had
before. Why? Did he have something to do with it? Or was it Dr. Pemberton's
ludicrous claim that brought renewed life to her nightmares?

Her youth had been tormented by the guilt of that one act and the loss that
followed that moment. She had thought she had gotten beyond it by leading a
life of penance. Once she had conquered the initial heartache, she had locked
away all memory of that day, vague though it was. But now, all of a sudden,
the memories were back more vivid than ever. She could not close her eyes
without her heart breaking all over again. Why now, when finally she had put
it behind her and chanced living once more?

The dreams should have been cherished. What could be better than
rediscovering and reliving the happiest...no, she must be honest...the only truly
happy moment of her life? Of course, the dream itself wasn't the problem, but
what happened after that moment continually broke her heart — waking up
alone in the forest, clutching her lover's shirt, and then never seeing him again.
Left with only vague memories, doubts, and growing guilt.

This time she could not swallow the sobs; they wracked her until her breath
rattled. Her heart threatened to burst with loneliness. Biting down on her
knuckles to muffle the cries, Agnieszka rocked back and forth in her chair
and waited for the grief to dull. For twenty minutes more, she focused on the
thunderstorm outside before she was finally able to breathe normally through
the crushing weight of her chest.

She had to do something. It had been going on for over a week; every time
she drifted off to sleep unassisted, she was forced to relive that moment. It was
to the point where she either worked herself into exhaustion to stem the dreams

or avoided sleeping altogether. Before much longer, something was going to give, and she was afraid that it just might be her.

Gathering her sweater closer around her, she went to the medicine chest and took out the prescription her doctor had given her to help her sleep. She disliked the medication, but at least there were never any dreams. No dreams that she could remember, anyway...

They lay together in the dell, totally entwined with each other. Agnieszka snuggled beneath the shelter of her love's arm as he fed her berries she had not seen him gather. She opened her mouth wide to accept the sweet gem, hoping he'd follow it with a kiss..

Running her hand across his smooth, hairless chest, she tried not to think of how long they'd been there. Some part of her knew the others — or at least Sister Michael Adele, anyway — would have begun to worry about her. She definitely did not want to go back; her breath caught in her throat at the thought. Here, in this dell, was the only place in the world where anyone truly cared for her.

Even as she thought it, Agnieszka was hit by a wave of guilt that she would think such a thing. What about the Sisters? And Mother Superior?

A small, selfish part of her heart whispered back that it was their job to care for her, not an emotional investment. Why not stay in this dell forever? She could happily live on berries and kisses...

"We could, ye know..."

Agnieszka nearly jumped. She hadn't been talking aloud, had she? Instead, she only clung closer to her love. "What?"

"I said we could stay here forever, in Tír na nÓg." The smile on his face shone brilliant as sunlight on clear ice as he brought down his lips to kiss her once again.

Breathless from his intensity, she smiled and lost herself in his endless eyes, not even questioning where his words placed them. "We could...I give myself to you, for now and ever."

Pulling her closer for yet another tender kiss, he murmured back, "An' I ye."

Content in each other's arms, they drifted off to sleep.

All that effort and the old hag had given up next to nothing. What was worse, she nearly killed herself resisting him, overtaxing her frail human heart with strain. How pitiful! And for what? Olcas already knew the *Sidhe* fled to their blasted Ireland, taking the girl with them. What he needed to know was where they intended to hide his prize once they got there! He'd lose precious time if he had to search for her. He didn't care how deeply they buried her within their world; he would not give up that tempting morsel. With the power Kara represented, he could bring the world to heel all on his own and forget his wretched brothers, who had not bothered even to seek him out in all this time.

Still, he had learned something important. They had no idea what they faced. When Olcas changed vessels he changed their essence as well. The shields the pawnbroker set were useless, giving Olcas barely a moment's pause, if anything. Satisfaction warmed him for a moment. That also meant the protections on Kara O'Keefe would likewise fail. Once he claimed the girl, he could claim ultimate revenge—and the power therein—all for himself. All he had to do was find her!

The old woman hadn't yielded much information, and her pain had hardly been worth harvesting. He had gleaned even less from his earlier plunder of the man's mind. Dr. Barnert knew nothing...yet. But, Olcas reminded himself, with the doctor's determination, it was only a matter of time before he might be useful.

All of this running around and playing with magic had begun to drain Olcas. He couldn't continue expending the very resources he was attempting to acquire. The old crone and the doctor sought the same prize, even if their reasons differed. Let them do his searching. But how to engineer it...fear had not quite broken the woman, though it may have increased her already considerable motivation. Yet too much more would damage her beyond usefulness. But surely the doctor could be manipulated. And suddenly Olcas knew, without a doubt, what lure would entice the man to do his bidding.

Entering the brownstone that had belonged to Lucien Blank, Olcas made his way to the rooftop. He knew the police would have taken his quarry to the hospital, but which one? In a city filled with millions of people, medical facilities were nearly as plentiful as churches. Olcas searched the skyline for the tag he had attached to the man earlier.

There! The reddish-black shimmer pulsed vividly to his senses, though he doubted anyone else in the city that would note it... Well, except maybe the *Sidhe*. Of course, they were more than a bit preoccupied, weren't they? Olcas chuckled evilly, anticipating the anguish he could cause by arranging things just right. Time to prepare for the doctor's homecoming.

Olcas headed for the rooftop.

Entering the greenhouse he had erected while controlling Lucien, Olcas closed the door and traced a temporary binding rune upon the glass surface. The rest of the structure was already warded, but as the door must remain accessible, he was required to repeat the process each time he entered and wipe it clear as he left. Such a bother, these mortal conventions, but the magic he worked now was learned, not a part of his inherent abilities, which did not depend upon such trappings. Still, the two elements—divine and mundane— represented potential nearly without bounds; he would deal with a little bother for that.

Once the particulars were observed, he turned toward the interior. Around the extreme perimeter of the enclosure, adding to the illusion of a recreational greenhouse, were various species of plants, both exotic and commonplace. All of them had one thing in common: their arcane usefulness. In the center lay an immense slab of polished, red-veined black marble nine feet square. Beyond that stood an opaque wall set with a second door, dividing the structure in two. The main section, comprising three-quarters of the length, or about fifteen feet, was open and eerily moonlit. The smaller portion remained cloaked in darkness. He made his way toward the back, careful not to disrupt any of the wards or runes already sketched in wax on the marble slab.

"Hello, my darlings," his voice was low and husky with unfettered anticipation. Time to replace some of that wasted energy, even if the bulk of it would go right back into the spell he cast tonight. A muffled whimper sounded from the far side of the door, but no other response. "Come now, I should think you'd be glad to see another face by now...even if it is mine."

Still no response, at least not verbally... But a heady essence of heightened terror seeped past the door. Too bad he did not have the leisure to prolong the torment. Opening the door to what would have been a potting shed in a typical greenhouse, he took a moment to savor the anguish of the mother and child trapped inside, before he reached in to pull out the terrified woman. Ruthlessly, he extracted the little girl from her mother's viselike grip and thrust the child back inside...frightened...alone...in the dark. Her piercing shrieks were delicious.

With quick economic effort and not a shred of mercy, he slew the pleading woman over the runes, activating the cantrip already prepared on the slab, carefully shielded from all eyes — mundane and magical. In only seconds a diabolical haze obscured the body.

For a brief moment, Olcas allowed the creature to savor the death energy used to summon it, before cutting off the flow. His actions quick from recent practice, Olcas sketched the proper rune upon the cloud in burning lines, feeding it energy to keep it strong. The rune writhed and twisted violently as the demon fought the binding. The energy flared bright pink and faded to a dull reddish black, but did not break or go out. Once the demon ceased to fight the rune settled into a steady deep red glow.

"Your name, creature, is mine," Olcas commanded the ethereal being. "No trace of it can be found in your consciousness, nor will it until I am satisfied you have completed my bidding."

The demon hissed and howled, straining against the mage bond that prevented it from attacking. Olcas laughed and ran his hand through its cloud form, taunting it with the essence of death and suffering that was fresh upon his skin, harvested from the sacrifice that had made this summoning possible.

The cloud whined and tried to cling. Olcas laughed again as the demon attempted to suck the death energy from his hand; he relished its frustration when the bond prevented it from harvesting from its master.

"Hungry, then?" Olcas's voice deepened in satisfaction. This one would be his, without reservation, with but one more binding. He lanced the formless demon with a bolt of energy. It flinched away and ceased its frantic and fruitless sucking. A second, smaller bolt—mustn't be wasteful—silenced its gnashing and moaning.

"You will do as I bid; you will heed my words and do as I set you to do."

Olcas turned and pulled forth the frightened girlchild from the storage room, her blonde hair tousled, and her cheeks smudged with dirt and tears. Mothers really shouldn't take their children through Central Park at night...what a tragedy when neither one came back. He chuckled mercilessly as the girl trembled and shook, her eyes wide and glazed, then he drew her to stand in front of him. Her whimpers were already sweet to taste but nothing compared to the ambrosia of her hopeless moans as she backpedaled frantically, trying to get away from the sight of her mother, crumbled on the floor, the blood trickling from her vacant eyes mimicking her daughter's tears. For about thirty seconds, there was nearly complete silence, broken only by a subtle sucking sound. As the girl fetched up against Olcas' legs, her stunned moans finally rose to high-pitched screams. For a moment, Olcas allowed himself to savor the sensual rush it incited before closing himself off from it. This was not for him. He brought his hands down to rest heavily on the girl's shoulders before it could occur to her to run.

"The mother called you; the child keep you. Feast, you fiery being, and bind yourself to me. All you claim shall be mine. If you hold to this, ever shall you feast on the souls of this world's children." Olcas waited, watching intently as the amorphous cloud grew deeper and darker, seething with voracious hunger. He thrilled as it drifted closer, right up against the temporary bonds that confined it. And then Olcas's face lit with a demonic glee of its own: death and magic called the infernal being here, but its hunger bound it to him with a strength it could neither resist nor rebel against, though he sensed it intended to. It would try, but once it drained this little tidbit, Olcas's plans would be ensured.

"Do you want the child?" With a little push toward the cloud—and her mother—the child rose out of her terrified stupor and fought to back away. The demon surged forward, finding an active lure more enticing.

"Yesss!" The breathless sigh drifted closer with the cloud.

Olcas echoed it in the hidden depths of his mind. This fiend seemed a grade above the others he had already called. Perhaps it could serve better than to merely harass the *Sidhe* in this land. After all, that paltry handful was nothing when he dreamed of crushing the entire race. No, let them continue in their mistaken sense of security. As for the demon—he would keep this one close.

With the demon bound, Olcas broke the warding on the door with a wave of his hand. Leaving his new creature inside the greenhouse, he approached the retaining wall and again looked out over the city, looking for the telltale smudge that marked the man's whereabouts, which were no longer at the hospital.

Damn! The summoning had nearly taken too long. Turning back to the open door, he motioned for his minion to come out. The child, her expression lax, crept from the shadowy structure. If Olcas had any of the softer emotions to stir in his soul, they would have been well churned by the sight of her wavering in the doorway.

Alas, to him, such a sight only inspired hunger, the suffering a snack to whet his appetite. He snapped his fingers and strolled to the roof's edge without looking back. His new creature followed obediently, if slowly. When she finally shuffled to his side and looked up at him, pale moonlight glistened on her tear-streaked face. Her dark blue eyes, empty and dim on the surface, became shadowy pits to swallow up the light. For there, in their hidden depths, seethed and smoldered the awareness of the bound demon, tucked ever so neatly in his pretty little prison. Olcas was not concerned that her chest barely rose or that her lack of fear and curiosity was distinctly unchildlike. Actually, he was glad of it. She would serve his purpose more than adequately, luring both *Sidhe* and mortals with her waiflike misery.

His satisfaction waned when she stepped up onto the retaining wall beside him; she was close enough for the faint odor of soiled panties to waft from beneath the shifting hemline of her white-and-pink cotton jumper. Olcas wrinkled his fastidious nose and looked at her with distaste. While she was the ideal vessel, her innocence masking the diabolical, and her all-too-obvious signs of trauma comprising the ideal lure, he had to restrain himself from throwing her into a tub and getting rid of her filthy organic stench. He had to remind himself, just one more stop and then off to Ireland, and the...odorous little girl was the key to making it all work. Besides, at least outside the smell would disperse. Taking her by the hand, he stepped off into the sky, following the sullen shimmer that tracked the doctor's progress to Queens.

🌀

Was he in Heaven? If he hadn't such long-standing doubts as to the state of his soul, he would have suspected so. As Patrick surfaced from the embrace of rejuvenating slumber, he stretched, working previously taxed muscles and flexing joints that, in recent memory, would have painfully protested such activity. Breathing deeper than he had been able to manage in months, he wondered if perhaps he was wrong. It was clear to him that if he wasn't in Heaven, then he must still be dreaming.

"Good morning, sailor." The tearful joy in his Bobbi's voice triggered the dawning realization that something momentous had taken place. "Welcome to Eden."

Belatedly, Patrick realized they were somewhere other than their bedroom, or anywhere else he recognized.

"Well! For goodness sakes, then...hide all the apples! I don't intend to leave any time soon, not if I get to pillow my head in the lap o' an angel while I'm here!" Gazing up at his wife, he smiled at her bright blue eyes and tousled golden-brown curls. She was the most beautiful thing he had never expected to see again.

Bobbi chuckled at him, her hand absently smoothing the tangle of deep red curls from his brow. "I don't think we'll be evicted anytime soon. There are too many of them waiting around to be impressed by your considerable charm."

Something in the way she said it, even in jest, tipped him off to her underlying tension, but he still wasn't ready for more than light banter. "Them? Ye mean angels?"

He could tell Bobbi was attempting to look amused...without much success. "Love, where are we?" His expression grew solemn as the playfulness drained away.

"I'm told it's Tír na nod, or some such thing." He watched as her smile wavered a second before she reinforced it.

"*Tír na nÓg*," he automatically corrected her, his voice faint. No one could grow up with his Da and not have the name of the *Sidhe* land emblazoned on his brain, though how they had ended up here must be quite a tale — one he would have to ferret out in short order, and from someone else, considering how his wife was reacting. "What's happened?"

Bobbi merely smiled fondly at him and mussed the curls she'd just put in order. "Conall would be proud of you."

He could tell she wasn't just speaking of his dutiful recall of the old Celtic lore. Something had changed in his timid little wife and, God willing, he was going to enjoy getting to know her all over again. All of a sudden, the details didn't matter to him. Understanding how they'd come to be in the heart of faerie land wouldn't change it, nor would it change how genuinely wonderful he felt for the first time in the last six years...at least it wouldn't if he had anything to say about it. He'd find out all the details in good time, but for now, he was going to look into his wife's eyes and rediscover the lovely lass he'd met over twenty-four years ago.

With more ease than he could ever remember, Patrick half rose from Bobbi's lap and, turning himself sufficiently to draw her into his arms, he kissed her soundly.

Patrick's soul sang. God, it was good to be alive again!

He'd thought at first this was all a dream. But was it actually madness? Ever since he woke up and discovered his world turned on end, he had to wonder. At first, he had embraced it as a blessing, a miracle. He had spent a few precious moments alone with Bobbi and life was good. That was before the others started wandering in; Kara, Maggie, and the *Sidhe* warriors Patrick had fought beside at Yesterday's Dreams, all came to share their joy in his recovery.

They meant well, wanting only to help him fill in the gaps of what he'd missed, but all they had done was send his head spinning. Patrick remembered the battle...the carnage...the intense pain. He could still see the length of pipe in the thug's hand, watching it as it descended, knowing that when it connected, it would be the death of him...knowing there was no way to block it. And if it hadn't been for Barbara and Kara and the danger he knew they would be left to face, he would have considered the release a blessing, but no, the anguish of leaving them unprotected remained fresh in his mind.

But why, then, was he so uneasy with how things had turned out? Having lived so long with pain, it was more than a dream to be completely free of it. He should be jubilant, grateful, in awe. And yet here he was, cradled amid paradise with his family gathered safely around, first dreading and then looking for the catch that would turn this dream into a nightmare.

He found it in the one called Goibhniu. The man—god?—entered last, filling the room with his mass and his intensity. The name and everything it implied—assuming Patrick remembered his father's stories accurately—shook him to his core, rattling his faith and making him tremble relentlessly, if only on the inside. The name suited the...being.

As if that wasn't enough, Goibhniu, in his deep, rumbling voice, made clear the depth of Patrick's healing and who was responsible.

Patrick refused to show how shaken he was.

"An' how long did ye say this would last?" he asked, a wisp of skepticism tingeing his voice.

"The healing, 'tis forever," Goibhniu answered, his voice so soothing Patrick found it difficult to hold on to his self-preserving doubt. For a moment, he even forgot the paradox between his Catholic faith and the existence of this powerful Celtic being. Miracles could do that. "That's not to say ye can't do yerself the same sort o' damage again, but 'tisn't as if the very same wound will come back once ye leave."

"What about the cancer?" The mixture of hope and desperation laced through Kara's voice tore at Patrick's heart. His baby girl shouldn't have to have such concerns; she should have been pursuing her own life, not sacrificing her dreams to ease his decline. For goodness sake, she hadn't even allowed herself to have a boyfriend because she felt it wouldn't be fair to either Patrick or the young man, given how any attention she paid to one of them would take away from the other. What kind of life was that?

"At the moment, ye're clear," Goibhniu answered.

Patrick knew a moment of joy. The years he now had to spend with his family, watching Kara fall in love and have children of her own. To hold his grandchildren and make them laugh. To move with his Bobbi into their golden years...

And then Goibhniu's next words sucker-punched him right in the gut. "For now it lies dormant, but eventually," the Smithgod continued, "once ye leave the Lands o' the *Sidhe* an' go back to the world where Time rules, yer cancer may well begin its progression again, though there's no telling how swiftly."

As Goibhniu turn to leave, Patrick nearly called him back. Almost asked him to take away this blessing. Only the joy in Bobbi's gaze kept him silent. He could not count the number of times he had prayed for just a few more years. Now that he had them, he wondered if it was fair to his family. True, they would have him back whole and hale for a while, but what if they had to go through the entire nightmare all over again?

After Goibhniu left, Kara exhaled a tremulous breath, barely noticing as her hands linked and unlinked in her lap. All of a sudden, she had been given, for all intents and purposes, her greatest wish...her father restored, and with that, freedom from the burden of responsibility. But what was the hidden cost?

"How long have we been here?" her father asked, his voice too neutral for her to read.

She went to sit beside him, taking his hand in hers. "Just a couple of days." Kara noticed that Mathair looked startled by her answer, but that was all it had been. Maybe to her mother, it had seemed an eternity, waiting, as she had, for Papa to awaken. "You were pretty out of it until just a couple of hours ago, even after you were..." Kara couldn't finish. By healing him, they had doomed him to either choose immortality or to accept the certainty that all of them would have to live through the hell of cancer all over again, without knowing when it would hit. And the worst thing was, he didn't even know he faced the choice. There was her cost!

Well, now was not the time to tell him. He already had enough to cope with at the moment. At least, that was what she told herself. In truth, she was afraid to tell him, but she buried that thought. A little more time would not make that much difference, not here in *Tír na nÓg*.

Forcing the worries to the furthest corner of her mind, she smiled for her parents, letting herself enjoy the restored bloom of health in her father's cheeks and the glimmer of hope in Mathair's eyes. Who knew, with the advances in cancer research, perhaps the healing would buy them enough time that the medical profession would be better armed the next time they had to fight it.

"Are you hungry?" For the first time in quite a while Kara did not have to fake cheerfulness in dealing with her parents. Reaching out with her free hand, she ran gentle fingers through Papa's silver-shot red curls. "I'm sure I could find what passes for a kitchen if I try hard enough."

Patrick didn't notice the problem until everyone had left, and Barbara was asleep, curled close against his side. Nothing had seemed off or odd in that first rush of waking, whole and alive, and in Bobbi's arms. Not when his brain had been steeped in the fog of long rest and healing.

During the first hours, speaking with Goibhniu and the others, caught up in the joy that swept his family, Patrick had barely glanced at himself, not even questioning the renewed feeling. Now, alone with his thoughts as sleep evaded him, niggling doubt crept in. For one thing, he was beginning to think this miraculous healing had the feel of cheating about it.

But that wasn't it, not really. The true horror rose out of the most innocent of motions. As he raised his hand to stroke Bobbi's golden curls, a nightmare unfolded before his eyes. Patrick stiffened, and his stomach churned.

No! Denial chattered in the confines of his head. Tension and an acidic burn flooded through him until even in her sleep, his wife protested with a petulant little moan. Cries of "demon child" and "changeling" echoed in his thoughts, memories of taunts and frightened looks, of signs against evil and iron crosses prominently worn: a childhood filled with suspicion and persecution, his family being forced to leave their home and even their country merely to give him a chance at a normal life. Years of heartache and buried longing all came flooding back as he held his hand up in the dim light of the chamber where they slept. Not again! Patrick clenched his hand into a fist. It took all of his self-control not to pound it against the flagstone floor until it was a bloody pulp. He tried that once when he was very young and had only succeeded in mangling his hand...no, in the end, it took a surgeon's scalpel to rid him of the curse that marked him.

A frustrated sob escaped as he extracted his other arm from where it cradled his wife and held both hands before his face, still hoping that it was a trick — whether of his mind or the dim light, it did not matter, as long as it was a trick. But no, black despair flooded his heart as he wiggled his fingers. For the first time in over thirty years, twelve corresponding shadows waved back at him from the chamber walls.

Agnieszka absently set down her watering can halfway through her rounds of the verdant jungle that was her country cottage. She had awoken again that morning with a profound sense of peace still intact, her self-acceptance still secure. The heartache that she'd wrapped herself around for as long as she could remember — only ever examining it long enough to add another small sorrow to the raw mass—that heartache was truly gone, faded to its proper proportions. Each night since her revelation, when she drifted off to sleep, she was certain what she thought of as "the glow" would fade by morning, taking the peace with it.

Despite her tormenting dreams, so far she had been wrong.

Coming to rest on the edge of the gently worn sofa that had served her well since the day she'd moved in, she looked about her in dazed wonder. Outside her window, Cornhill slumbered beneath its dense blanket of early morning fog. All around her, the air seemed to shimmer and dance and, though she scarcely understood it, her heart fairly sang with joy. With her entire body tingling gloriously as if caught up in the celebration of all Creation, she closed her eyes in peaceful relaxation. It was amazing what a difference self-acceptance made in a person's outlook on life. Not to mention companionship, she thought, glancing lovingly at Rex as he sauntered from the room, intent on his own agenda, even if they didn't speak the same language.

Drawing in a deep, filling breath, flooding her senses with the mingled scents of violets, greenery, and moist earth, she turned about slowly as if caught by the currents of possibility. She could hear her bashful lark singing from the cover of the bushes beneath her window. Her eyes flew open in astonishment at the sense of contentment that drifted down to settle around her like the folds of a cherished afghan. She had felt this way once before in her life, but she had always pushed those memories away, believing that whatever joy they held was irrevocably mingled with the deepest disgrace. Well, she had been wrong about much; she could not but consider that she was also wrong in this.

Agnieszka looked about her with eyes newly opened after a long time closed against the pain. As her gaze traveled from the rampant fronds of her favorite spider plant to the soft velvety petals of her new African violets, and on through the rest of her house garden, she regretted that they were among the only signs of life in the place that she called home. Nothing personal hung on her walls save a simple crucifix above her bedroom door. The tables were absent of photographs and knickknacks. She had acquired all the furniture through the thrift shop run by St. Michael's—not one piece of it had special meaning or memories attached. But there was no reason for her life to be so empty. Against the starkness of her surroundings, the greenery spoke to her of possibility, of hope.

With a feeling of imminent discovery, Agnieszka arose and wandered into the bathroom and the only mirror in the house. As if seeing herself for the first time in her sixty-plus years, she stared hungrily at her own reflection. An enigma—a pleasant, ageless face framed by thick, brilliant waves of glistening white hair, with haunted, ancient eyes peering out like large rounds of amber from beneath the fringe of her bangs. She had always been thus, to one degree or another. Since she was clearly not an albino, the nuns had whispered amongst themselves that whatever orphaned her must have been tragic beyond compare to leave a child with hair as white as a granny's.

The self-examination extended beyond her physical appearance. What was she accomplishing? Why was she here? One moment she told herself she was content in her safe routine, the constant cycle of plant-watering and accounting in the quiet, sheltered back room of St Michael's; the next she felt deep shame at the way she'd squandered the years she had been given. True, she volunteered at the parish during the holidays and throughout the year when the Sisters were hard-pressed to meet the needs of the community, but other than her activities at the church, she was mostly separate from all but her immediate neighbors, alone in a crowd of strangers. If it weren't for the new addition of Rex in her life, she'd drift from day to day in solitude, diverted only by feeding her strays and occasional and unexpected visits from her Romani friends.

Agnieszka searched the house until she found her furred companion sunning in the window seat. She settled beside him and basked in the warmth and the rhythm of his contented purr. It was time to make some radical changes in her life. She felt as if until recently she had validated the opinions the others had had of her, seeing her very existence as some great offense against the world. In doing so, she had squandered so much potential. Happiness was not something that happened to you: it came from deep inside, rooted in self-acceptance and hope. It was time she cultivated that hope with as much dedication as she gave her plants.

In the hush before dawn, Arn made his way home, walking, all the while cursing the cops and Molly and even Patrick O'Keefe for putting him in this position. Of course, the guilt that followed on the heels of the last left him wearier than before. He just wanted to be home, in his room, curled around Lynn's comfortable warmth. Instead, the chill of early-morning autumn fog curled around his own meager warmth, leaching it away. He shivered and drew his coat closer. The atmosphere was still and thin, and Arn found himself gasping from his exertions, only to discover that the air carried an ozone tang that bit at the back of his throat. Mingled with the stench of the fire that still clung to him, and combining with the stress of the evening, it made his stomach burn.

Was this his punishment for turning his back on Molly? For not being there for Patrick? Well, what more should he expect from this day...these days, rather? After he had turned Molly's case over to a resident, claiming an emergency surgery for another patient Arn had found himself stranded. With no cabs in sight and without the energy to try and find his car, he'd headed for the closest subway stop.

So now he trudged down the ghostly vacant Metropolitan Ave, approaching Forest Park. Even the most avid early-morning joggers and cyclists had sense enough to be at home in their beds—and yet, as he neared the semicircle of benches on the edge of the park, he could see two indistinct figures glowing bright white in the fog, crowned by twin blobs of deep, rich purple. That could only be Radu and Bertram Singh. The brothers' daily ritual included bringing their caged flock of tiny black songbirds out for some fresh morning air. Fresh in theory, anyway. Arn took shallow breaths through his mouth, trying to avoid as much of the odor as possible, only to find that the method spared his nose but coated his tongue. Utterly depressed, he gave up trying to minimize the smell and sighed. He would be home soon...a good shot of bourbon would rinse away the filmy taste, and a nice, scalding shower would take care of the rest.

"Good morning, my friends, and how are the little ones?" Arn greeted the Singhs as he drew closer, waving a hand toward the tiny birds the brothers cherished as they did the many children of their household.

"Good morning. They are doing very well, though most quiet this morning. We are thinking they are chilled today," Radu answered, his rich, chocolate brown eyes glittering with pleasure. His brother Bertram only smiled his reserved little smile, not quite meeting Arn's eyes, but looking a quarter-inch to the side. He seemed more jumpy than usual, particularly once Arn drew close enough to speak. Bertram was simple, his dull brown eyes generally a little vacant, any emotion showing forth only as a faint glimmer, as if he hadn't yet decided to feel it. That made his quite obvious agitation this morning all the more startling. His head bobbed in abrupt jerks, and his eyes were fearful as they flickered toward the sky, down the street the way Arn had come, and then circled back to touch fleetingly on all present, human and avian alike. As Arn stopped beside them a moment, out of politeness more than anything else, Bertram shifted more prominently from foot to foot, the odd motion carrying him inch by inch away from Arn. With sudden swiftness, he darted for the nearest cage and pulled it from its hook, taking a staggering step toward the walkway leading away from the park and, consequently, Arn. The only sound was the birds' frantic chirping as their cage swayed in wild arcs. They fluttered their wings in rapid strokes to keep from being tumbled about. Arn could sympathize.

Radu barked at his brother in the fluid melody of their native tongue, shooting out his hand to halt Bertram's panicked flight.

"I do not know what is wrong with him. He was fine when we left the house." There was concern tinged with embarrassment in Radu's open gaze. Arn felt more guilt for disrupting the brothers' peaceful morning. In fact, the guilt seemed to press down on him, oppressively robbing him of his breath.

When he tried to apologize, all he managed was a gasp. Looking up, he saw his own horror mirrored in Radu's eyes. They all gaped, as if opening their mouths wider would draw in air that did not seem to be there. It was like being smothered by ozone, only it was the middle of autumn, and, as Arn's vision dimmed and his chest burned, it seemed as if Death's cruel laughter filled his ears.

"Doctor Arn! Doctor Arn! Oh, my goodness! He is dead. I am certain of it!" Trembling hands grasped Arn's shoulders as the frantic words struggled to penetrate the haze surrounding him. He would answer quite willingly if only to silence the babbling, but he did not seem to have the energy to form the words. Struggling to force open his eyes, Arn found himself propped up against one of the park's decoratively strewn rocks. Radu knelt over him, hands wringing, and over by the cage still hanging upon its hook, Bertram sobbed as he peered with utter desolation into first the hanging cage and then into the one he still clutched in his arms, his entire body bobbed in sharp, short jerks. Arnold Barnert felt like sobbing with him, though he didn't know why.

"Praise be! You are alive!" Arn allowed Radu to help him up but when the man would have led him to a bench to sit and rest, he extracted his hand and staggered off toward Bertram.

"Doctor Arn! You must sit!"

It was not hard to ignore the man when the uncomfortable buzzing in his ears conveniently drowned him out. No, he would not sit down, not yet. First, he must look into those cages, for an impulse drove him to it. Bertram, lost in his grief, did not even notice as Arn approached. Such strong emotion! He had never seen the simpleton react this strongly to anything, good or bad. With dread, Arn peered into the cage cradled in Bertram's arms.

Arn gasped in shock. Strewn about the bottom of the cage, each and every songbird was dead, their tiny, bright yellow beaks gaping. A quick glance in the hanging cage confirmed the same.

What was going on?! What madness was taking place? The uproar about greenhouse effects and the ozone layer drifted across his jumbled thoughts, along with tabloid accusations of aliens stealing natural resources, and old grade-B movies where the sky was really an artificial dome preserving what was left of a shattered world.

Shaking his head to clear away the nonsense, Arn hurried away toward home, leaving the brothers to their stunned grief. He could not reassure them, especially when he found he needed reassurance himself...reassurance and comfort that could only be found in Lynn's solid and dependable arms.

The meadow stretched before them shimmering like a bolt of gold silk unfurled and rippling in the wind. Wildflowers dotted its expanse like rich, delicate embroidery, and sunlight danced across it like a loving hand. In a clear space beneath the drip-line of the forest, Miach settled companionably with Patrick and Barbara by the shady base of an ancient rowan, Quicksilver nestled carefully beside them. They chatted well out of the way as Maggie spread a crisp white cloth with assorted delicacies she and Kara had brought back from Dublin. The two of them had made sure everything laid out was a favorite of Patrick's, with a fine supply of Guinness taking the place of honor in the center of the spread.

Before they'd left for Dublin, Kara had confided in Maggie her concern. Patrick had been pensive and withdrawn when alone, more often sitting off in a corner somewhere, arms folded under and his thoughts far away. Caught in unguarded moments, he looked haunted and even defeated. Maggie knew his private torment, but it wasn't her place to share the revelation. Patrick would declare it in his own time. But emotional funk or not, it must be soon.

Perhaps this little picnic would help, perhaps not, but there was no doubt that they could all use the diversion. Giggles rose from the forest in two-part harmony, as Kara and Beag Scath lost themselves in a one-sided game of hide-and-seek. Fifteen minutes after they started, Kara raised the surrender flag as far as her hunting for the sprite was concerned. Just as well, she would never have found him if he hadn't chosen to be found, even were she a champion seeker. Not that switching roles had done her much good. Already the girl had jumped from hiding place to hiding place ten times. Maggie heard Kara's exasperated, yet good-natured groans each time the sprite immediately pounced upon her no matter where she hid.

Later she would have to confess to Kara that she hadn't stood a chance. Maggie herself had intimate knowledge of what it was like to flee before Beag Scath with her innate magic painting the most transparent trail behind her. That was how she had ended up with the sprite as a companion, to begin with...traipsing around the moors of Eire all alone before she'd learned to shield her nature or her abilities from the world at large.

Until the girl learned to refine her shielding technique, the sprite would be able to find her anywhere between here and the ends of the earth. It was his very nature to be drawn to her aura of power. Maggie thought it was too bad many of her own race looked at sprites and the other faelings as little more than pests to be run off. Hide-and-seek would be an excellent way to train the young ones in the art of shielding. It was something to think about, anyway. Perhaps she would pass the idea on to Goibhniu and see if his power was enough to overcome the prejudice of the People. But that was for later, not now.

"Kara! Scath!" Maggie called out into the twilight beneath the forest canopy. "Come along the both o' ye or I'll not be held responsible an there's nothing left for ye to eat." She didn't need to call out twice; even before she'd finished her idle threat, Kara came dancing out of the underbrush with Beag Scath scampering behind. Both were flushed and animated as they settled together on a corner of the cloth.

"Ah! Put it down, Scath. Ye'll be waiting for the rest o' us or ye'll get nothing at'all. Come along all o' ye, I've a fierce hunger myself." With a gentle swat Maggie batted a piece of fruit out of the sprite's hand and waited patiently for the others. He looked at her rebelliously, and Maggie knew he considered summoning his own fruit if she would not let him have hers. But all she had to do was frown with disappointment and he was the soul of contrition, crawling in her lap and hugging her fiercely. Beag Scath was not a bad or malicious sprite; he just needed to know something was important to her, even if he didn't understand why. Forgetting the fruit, he stayed in her lap, giggling merrily and playing peek-a-boo through her braids, though she couldn't tell with whom. The others were too busy getting settled to pay attention to him.

After a moment or two of allowing everyone to arrange themselves around the blanket, Maggie made a calculated move. Kneeling in her own chosen place at the edge of the spread, she reached out her hands to Kara on her one side and Miach on the other. Taking the unexpected cue, they, in turn, reached a hand out to their neighbors until all were joined. That is, all but Patrick. Stunned, he merely stared at the hands Kara and Barbara offered him and thrust his own even deeper in his pockets, leaving the circle broken.

"Patrick?" Puzzlement wreathed Barbara's face. "What's wrong?" On his other side, Kara started to reach out to her father, only to pull back at the look of panic that flooded his expression.

The silence hung thick beneath the boughs of the immortal forest as Patrick worked his mouth but could not manage to speak. For a moment, Maggie allowed herself to feel remorse for the position she had placed him in, but not for long. He had lost himself in melancholy long enough. Resting comfortably upon her knees she held her gaze on Patrick's face, as did all the rest of them. No more hiding, she thought. It was time for all to come out, and the revelations were up to him.

"Patrick, come on!" Barbara now reached for his arm only to have him flinch away. "What has come over you? Let's say the blessing so we can all eat, for goodness sake!" While she might have railed at him a bit more, one look at his face and the hopelessness in his eyes, and Barbara fell silent. Maggie held her breath and readied to leap to her feet should Patrick choose flight over confession. If all of this proved too much for him, she could not allow him to run off alone. She was responsible for the confrontation, after all. She had to be ready to put things right. With arrested breath, she watched as the muscles along his jaw twitched, and his eyes glistened. She didn't exhale until he drew both hands from his pockets and held them out before him. The first step had been taken.

Of all of them, she alone did not gasp at the sight of twelve fingers slowly clenching and unclenching upon Patrick's two hands. Painfully aware of the man's torment, Miach actually clenched his own fists in sympathy. Patrick's family only knew he was upset; the *Sidhe* understood the gravity of those extra fingers, though not precisely the heartache they'd caused the man in the human world. Betraying the burden of a true empath, Miach's lavender eyes deepened to violet as they shared the human's bleak despair.

Still, Patrick did not speak, at least not with words, but there was plea upon plea written upon his face. Maggie's heart—though nothing more—went out to him. It was not herself that he sought reassurance from.

"P-papa?" Kara reached a trembling hand out to grasp one of her father's. The girl's uncertain gaze darted from Patrick to Maggie, no doubt remembering the tale of Earl Gerald and the Miller's Son, not to mention her earlier denial of the relevance the legend held for the O'Keefes. "Papa, what is this?"

A broken whisper finally left Patrick's lips. "I couldn't tell ye...I couldn't tell either o' ye..." He then fell silent.

Maggie cleared her throat and took it upon herself to explain. She told them how she hadn't known herself until returning to *Tír na nÓg*, but Kara's grandparents, Conall and Moira O'Keefe, had not left Ireland for lack of work. They had left to have the sixth fingers surgically removed from their son's hands and to give him a chance at a new life. It was not difficult to imagine why he hadn't spoken of it before. Goibhniu had known; he had told Maggie all about it soon after healing Patrick, accounting for the persecution that the young family had faced long ago. From the beginning, when the extra fingers on his hands were noticed by the neighbors, it was whispered about that young Patrick was a changeling and a demon child. The kindest merely called him fey and watched him with awe. Because the O'Keefe's were respected, there was never more than talk.

Even so, with such constant suspicion and the apparent rift it engendered between the family and their neighbors, it was small wonder they hadn't fled sooner. But such was the love all three of them held for their home: none of them could bring themselves to leave. They bore the looks and the muttered words; they even bore the runes against evil repeatedly scratched upon their newly sanded door or worn upon collars and coats.

Not until Patrick was twelve and a rash of bad luck hit the village were the O'Keefes forced to give up the home they had clung to. One evening, after several fields were lost to lightning-struck fires, some of the older local boys had taken it upon themselves to beat the supposed mischief from Patrick. Before long, they were quite caught up in their own enthusiasm; only Conall's return from work had saved his son. Conall descended upon the group with full and righteous wrath when he saw the boards they had used to pummel Patrick take aim at his son's head. The next day found the O'Keefe's cottage vacant and Conall on his way across the ocean to America, having left his family with far-off relatives in the south of Ireland. That was when Maggie herself had first met Kara's Grandda, though he hadn't known at the time what she was.

When the tale was done, the soft sound of weeping carried over the otherwise still air. Maggie fell silent, feeling like an intruder spying upon the O'Keefes as Kara and Barbara cradled Patrick between them, each clutching one of the hands Goibhniu's healing magic had returned to its original state. Patrick himself bestowed grateful kisses upon the heads of his family, the look on his face one of relieved joy. Maggie knew he would never be comfortable with his restored hands, but at least Kara and her mother had made it quite clear the extra digits made no difference to them, one way or the other.

She waited until the tears had stopped before speaking again. "A prayer then, so we may eat?" With restored tranquility, they all arranged themselves for a quick grace to the O'Keefes' God before descending upon the bounty spread before them. Maggie partook as eagerly as any of them, more than willing to lose herself in the pleasure of the moment, at least for a while. There would be enough time later to speak of destiny and choices.

Chapter 7

appointment?

Perhaps, Agnieszka thought, *I just want a little time to daydream of the child I could have before another doctor diagnosed the real problem and put those dreams to rest.*

Imagine the uproar if the results were valid: amazement, disbelief, and the sensationalism of it all. From within and without, her world would spiral into complete chaos...goodness, what would she say to the Sisters? Instantly, her face burned with shame. Guilt overcame her as thoroughly as a thick London fog, though in truth, she committed no transgression.

This was utter silliness! Here she was, letting herself imagine her joy, were the results accurate, and instead, she all but did penance. She was still new to this positive thinking, and not quite used to it.

Taking herself in hand, she gathered up her cardigan from where it lay folded along the back of the armchair. It was time to get out and away from the solitude of her own company.

She wheeled her old Pashley from the shed, secured her market basket on the back rack, gave the saddle a quick wipe with a rag from the bin she kept out there, and set off down the road. Now would be a good time to collect the mail and get in a few supplies.

As she made her way down the lane, she felt the tension flow from her, defused by fresh air and the autumn beauty of the English countryside. Her dark mood died a quick death, the final blow dealt as the young lad from the neighboring farm came at her whooping like a red Indian. Either he was never anywhere but on his bike, or he was always watching on the off chance she would happen by, for no sooner had she passed their lane than he came barreling out on his shiny new mountain bike, zipping past her with his usual backward glance of challenge. Quickly dropping the dignity of her years, Agnieszka, indulging in the childhood she never enjoyed, gave chase to the little rapscallion, laughing merrily as this time he allowed her to pass him before they'd reached their target of the crossroads.

"Good morning, Master Charles," Agnieszka greeted him formally, but with a glimmer in her eye, as they stopped to gather their breath. "And how is your mother this day?"

"'Morning, Miss Agnes. You did cracking well today." Chuck replied, not a bit winded from their pell-mell pace. He looked more satisfied with himself than he ever did on the many times he won. They'd played this out many times before, she going slower than she might, out of deference to his youthful pride, he occasionally allowing her to pass out of respect to her greater age; the arrangement suited them.

He eyed her basket. "Off to market? Mum said if I was to see you, to let you know the hens are laying well; if you'd care for some fresh eggs, she could use some of your apples as she's baking today."

"Very well, then." Agnieszka smiled at him warmly before fixing him with a stern gaze. "If you'll be careful about the strays, you can let yourself in the back door to put up the eggs. You'll find a grocery sack in the cupboard below the sink for gathering apples on your way back." The exchange held the steady rhythm of routine.

"Thank you, Miss Agnes. Enjoy the rest of your ride!"

As he pedaled away, warmth flooded her. Who said she didn't have children? There were plenty like Charles, who looked to her fondly.

She was halfway to town before it occurred to her she'd neglected to warn him about Rex. Well, at worse, her new friend would find himself in the yard for an afternoon. She gave it no more thought.

Feeling fit and well, Agnieszka indulged in a bit more speed for the sheer joy of it, laughing merrily as she coasted down the sloping country road. As she zipped past a stand of trees, a startling sight broke through her enjoyment; through a parted section of the undergrowth, a reddish glimmer, like feral eyes watching her, and on the wind, a hissing growl seemed to tease her ears. She told herself it was nothing more than her overexcited imagination. A flight of fancy brought on by indulging herself with the child, nothing more. With a shiver and a stern shake of her head, she continued to town.

The sensation followed her to the village and back again. She kept telling herself she was being silly. Too much excitement... too many odd dreams... What did she expect, insanely barreling along the lane every time she went on errands? And she spoke more to Charles and his active imagination than she did with any adult, including herself! It was utter nonsense to think the countryside was watching her, wasn't it? Just the thing Charles would have come up with from one of his books.

Head throbbing and heart uneasy, Arn staggered the rest of the way home through the haze. How long had he been knocked out? The sky had grown noticeably lighter, and all around him, he heard the neighborhood stirring. Arn tuned out everything and focused just on getting home. It was his heart's desire to forget the world around him and lose himself to the thick, comforting weight of the down comforter on his bed, which he imagined was quite toasty at the moment with his wife nestled beneath it.

Or maybe not... As he approached his house, the porch light was off, leaving the doorway hidden in shadow. It couldn't be out; he just changed the bulb. Had Lynn forgotten to turn it on last night? It wasn't like her, especially with him still out. Was she awake then, having turned off the light with the break of dawn? He hoped she hadn't been up all night. Poor dear, things had been so chaotic last night that by the time he'd had a moment to call, it had been much too late—or early, depending on how you looked at it. She must have worried herself silly. Well, it wasn't as if he couldn't take her back under the covers so they could both forget the world for a while.

With the keys he dug from his pocket, Arn unlocked the front door. A frisson of dread made its way down his spine and back up again as he leaned against the door to open it. It did not budge. *What the hell*... Then Arn realized that he had not unlocked the door, but locked it. His mouth went dry, and his shoulders immediately tensed. He thrust key back into the lock and called out to his wife before he even had the way open.

"Lynn? Lynn, honey, can you hear me?" For good measure, he rang the bell before throwing the door open wide. Anxious, he left it gapping as he hurried from room to room in his still and silent house. "Damn it, Lynn, where are you?" he bellowed, fright crackled in his voice. He found the back of the house all lit up, but the front rooms and the upstairs in complete darkness. "Sue," he called out for Lynn's sister, "Are you here? Someone answer me!"

His wife and her sister were nowhere to be found.

In the kitchen, he discovered a single teacup shattered on the floor, the pool of amber liquid still warm. There were no signs of struggle or intrusion in the house; the only damage was to the china, and yet Arn had a sinking certainty what had happened. His nerves jangled violently as the phone rang, a harsh knell piercing the silence.

"Hello?"

"Oh! Good, you're home," Sue's voice came across the line, relief warming her words. "I was afraid Lynn was still alone. Sorry for taking off, but she insisted she was fine. One of Kimmie's friends got hurt horsing around at the park and they couldn't reach anyone but me."

The comfortable familiarity of his sister-in-law's chatter washed over Arn, but it did little to put him at ease. He became aware of the expectant silence on the other end of the line. He didn't know what his sister-in-law had said, other than that it had nothing to do with his wife or her whereabouts.

"Sorry, Sue," Arn muttered, "It's been a hell of a night. I just wanted to say thanks again for coming over on such short notice. Good night."

Hanging up the phone before she could go on, Arn just stood there a moment in stunned disbelief; he'd found no warmth or comfort at home, only a cold and empty house. Anger and fear lent him a sudden clarity of insight. Within seconds he called his usual car service and hung up before the dispatcher finished saying his ever-dependable "Five minutes."

It was a matter of moments to collect Lynn's mad money from the cubby in her writing desk and his own modest allowance from his sock drawer. On impulse, he grabbed their passports and credit cards, as well. His final stop was his office closet with its matching set of lockboxes, tucked away in the back, hidden behind his Polaroid One-Step, the dartboard from his college days, and the golf clubs that were too nice to keep in the shed. Moving the camera and the dartboard to an upper shelf and the clubs out into the room, he pulled out the one and only way he'd ever betrayed his wife. One box contained his father's Ruger Mark II .22 caliber pistol, unloaded, and the other contained a box of bullets and three loaded magazines. He had not been prepared for his homecoming, but he would not make the same mistake in hunting for her.

Though as a boy Arn spent many a weekend at the shooting range with his father, or out in a secluded field, rifle butt to his shoulder, taking potshots at old cans on his uncle's New Jersey farm, never in the world would he have purchased a gun of his own, let alone keep one in his home. The passion for firearms had skipped his generation. Arn went along because he loved his father and uncles, not the guns. There were only two reasons it was here: the pistol was Pop's pride and joy, which he'd left to Arn as a part of his modest estate, and Lynn didn't know the weapon even existed. She was deathly afraid of any kind of sidearm, particularly in the home. There were so many horror stories in the news that he couldn't blame her. Still, though he seldom went out to the ranges anymore, he had a license for the weapon and observed the strictest safety protocols for both its use and storage. And sadly, they had never been blessed with children, so he didn't have to worry about them finding it. Keeping it from Lynn had caused him endless guilt, but it had meant so much to his father that he couldn't bear to get rid of it. Now he was glad.

A car honked outside. Arn dashed down the stairs, tucking the gun deep into one oversized pocket of his trench coat as he went. He was nearly out the open door before he noticed anything amiss. Stopping abruptly, he stared at his old Polaroid, now propped on the key table by the front door. His blood turned to ice. The table had been empty when he'd come barreling in.

How? He had checked every room in the house and found them empty. The camera itself had been in the closet when he'd left the office. It was not possible. But there it was, without a doubt the very camera he'd just shelved in his closet not two minutes ago. And there was the smile that haunted him, materializing like some evil Cheshire on the snapshot even as he watched. His darling Lynn, trapped against the familiar hood's side gripped tight by his arm, stayed faded much longer, but then, her palpable fear left her paler than the ancient bone china tea set he'd inherited from his great grandmother. Like that china, his precious Lynn looked as if she would shatter at a glance.

Two more quick blasts of a horn out front dragged Arn back to the world around him. Making sure everything he'd gathered was secure in the pockets of his trench coat and gripping the Polaroid in his hand, Arn closed the door and sprinted to the Town Car waiting at the curb. He didn't take the extra time to lock the house behind him. It no longer held anything of meaning to him.

There was no sense of time in the *Sidhe* Court. It didn't mean it did not pass there, only that there was nothing to distinguish its progression. Kara wouldn't mind so much if there were an opportunity to accomplish something, but she sat there growing more and more bored as the *Sidhe* decided what should be done. The focal point of her entire life had always been achieving goals and making progress; from learning the violin, to helping overcome her family's financial woes, Kara had always had the comfort of a sense of purpose. For her, at least, *Tír na nÓg* sadly lacked one. It was like a resort...a perpetual holiday...limbo even; it was not a thriving community that she could see, but an escape: Life perpetually on hold.

Of course, looking across the Hall where Papa and Mathair stood speaking quietly with Maggie, Kara could not help but think that this was precisely what they needed. Her parents were at peace for the first time in years. Even Maggie looked relaxed. Was this limbo really so bad that Kara felt driven to be free of it? Why was she in a hurry to go back to a world where death, disease, and violence were a matter of course?

And no sooner had she thought that, than she remembered their reception here, not to mention her encounters since. Of course, all that aside, she had since met a few *Sidhe* of the Court who were not jaded or separatists. Not many, but at least a few. And that was only here; there were many Lesser Courts, as Maggie had explained. Perhaps not all of them were of the same inclination.

"Music, child." Goibhniu rumbled gently, interrupting her looping thoughts. "Play us some music to remind us all is not conflict and competition."

Kara reclaimed Quicksilver and did the Smithgod's bidding.

Something unsettling and unreadable surfaced in the sea of immortal eyes trailed on her as she began to play. Flustered, she turned from them, trained her eyes on Goibhniu, and lost herself in the music.

Surrounded by the unbelievable backdrop of *Tír na nÓg*, Patrick looked around him, still somewhat dazed. Not one for formal audiences, he was only here to stay close to his family. Of course, now Kara was playing, and Maggie had drawn Bobbi away for something, so Patrick stood alone in the crowd. Left to himself for the moment, he let his mind wander, more interested in this supposed faerie land than he was in the faeries. The inhabitants of this place looked little different than celebrities he'd seen on TV, attending shindigs in outrageous outfits. But the architecture...he had always had a weakness for architecture.

Far above his head, broad expanses of carved marble capped off the Hall. The impossibly delicate fretwork appeared more like a lace veil draped across the open space, translucent and glowing as beams of sunlight wove their way through designs. The whole thing reminded him of watching his Mamó tat doilies when he was younger.

How had they created such a vaulting ceiling? There were no signs of a support structure. And the craftsmanship itself...at the height of at least five stories, it would have been near impossible for a sculptor to perform the work in place. Patrick's mind boggled at the mechanics necessary, first to create the structure and then hoist it up. He would dearly love to know how they had managed it. No construction method he knew of to date would have made it possible. More to the point, how effective could it be? Did it not rain here in faerie land? Or grow chilled?

And that was just the ceiling. The fretwork continued down the length of the walls, except for the central one behind the massive throne. That one was carved in a bas-relief that was even more of a mystery to him. The pattern of knotwork appeared intricate and flowing. Though he could not point to a specific occurrence, the design seemed to change subtly even as he watched. The wall did not appear painted, and yet color shifted on the wall as if a prism refracted the light, or the tumbling colors of a kaleidoscope. He did notice two points the light did not seem to touch; the knotwork consistent with the surrounding patterns, but grayish, matte black, as if soot had accumulated on the stone.

"'Tis life energy. Each pattern is linked to one o' the *Sidhe*."

Patrick jumped. He had been so immersed in thought that he had not noticed the *Sidhe* approach. He was familiar, one of those Patrick had fought beside at Yesterday's Dreams, but what was his name? Miach!

Miach smiled gently at him, and Patrick had the uneasy feeling that any thoughts he had, no matter how closely guarded, were as good as spoken aloud around this *Sidhe*.

He shifted to face Miach but said nothing. All this magic and mental hocus pocus did not rest easy with him. The concept itself did not disturb him so much as the personal impact it had on his life. Not put off by Patrick's lack of response, the *Sidhe* began again. "The color represents our life energy; each pattern reflects the state o' the man or woman 'tis linked to."

Patrick looked back to the wall as understanding dawned. Sobering as his gaze drifted to the soot-black segments. "An' those?" he indicated with a brief nod.

Heavy silence met his question. Patrick turned and his heart clenched. Miach's startling lavender eyes had deepened to violet, stark with grief. Though he had not cried for over thirty years, until recently, Patrick felt the threat of tears gather in his own eyes. If he could withdraw his question he would, but it was too late.

"Cian...," Miach spoke the name almost too low to hear as he pointed to the blemish in the lower corner of the wall, to the right of the throne. "An' Demne." He shifted his finger to point at the other, the one closer to the center.

Patrick's heart cried out, though he'd already known, subconsciously. Dealing with the trauma of his own near-death, he had managed to bury the memory of Maggie crouched over Demne's lifeless body. Now the image flooded back, and he again heard her wails. Though they had known each other so briefly, Patrick's heart felt bereft of the kinship he and Demne had already begun to form.

"No *Sidhe* is ever lost...each soul returns to us, as never-ending as the knotwork ye see before ye." Miach's soothing voice broke through the fog that engulfed Patrick's thoughts. As he spoke, the *Sidhe* reached up and laid a hand on top of his.

Patrick had not realized until then that he had gripped Miach's arm. Gripped it with a hand that two days ago had been a deformed mass of splintered bone and pulped flesh. Patrick turned an awed gaze on the *Sidhe* as his anguish and pain ebbed away. Miach just continued talking in a low, serene tone. "The patterns spiral, those near the center o' the spiral are the oldest o' our kind; those on the outer rim, the youngest. As those two segments continue to fade, they'll diminish in size an' two new ones will begin to form on the tail o' the spiral. By the time the old patterns disappear entirely, the new will have fully formed an' our sorrow will be replaced with joy as *Sidhe* children once again fill our Halls with their laughter."

Patrick looked closer at the massive wall with new insight. His gaze went from pattern to pattern, coming back again to the blackened ones. Something confused him. "Didn't they die at the same time?"

"Close enough to make no difference," Miach answered.

"Then why is Cian's pattern more blurred than Demne's?"

Miach looked sharply at the wall. Patrick watched understanding dawn across the *Sidhe*'s face, along with something else quickly veiled. "Demne hasn't started his journey back, an' Cian has."

"So ye mean Demne will be back, he just has to be born again?"

Miach looked at him, compassion clear in his gaze.

"'Tisn't how it works," the *Sidhe* explained. "The soul returns, not the person; richer for the lessons already learned, but unburdened by the memories...the heartaches o' another life."

Kara lost herself in the intensity of the music, glorious and flowing, an enticing lure drawing her away from the crowded Court and deep into the magic of unearthly song. Only the song had ended, and she had no recollection of lowering her bow.

As she flexed her stinging fingers, Kara surfaced, once again aware of her surroundings.

Only she and Goibhniu remained in *Mór Halla.*

"Ye aren't happy here, are ye?" Goibhniu's gentle question turned her earlier words back on her, challenging her to deny her heart.

Kara blushed and dropped her gaze to her abused hands. It wasn't that she was unhappy, but so many things no longer made sense. "I'd say off-balance…"

Goibhniu made a soothing sound, but said nothing.

While Kara had played — for hours on end, as she now realized — she managed to distance herself from the strain. It had almost been as if the music had cradled her, soothing her soul, even as it comforted her overtaxed shoulders and arms, cooling the burn of fingertips unused to such prolonged playing. But now, the tension crept back.

As though her thoughts were laid open to him, Goibhniu's massive hands settled over her own. Warm comfort flowed across the contact, a tingle from her fingertips to the base of her spine, the muscles relaxing before she had the chance to realize how bad they ached. A relieved sigh escaped Kara's lips. She had a new respect for Maggie's battle on Papa's behalf. How had the *Sidhe* been strong enough to resist accepting the Smithgod's restorative touch?

Goibhniu chuckled as his hands slipped away from hers. "Ye'll never know the whole o' it, leanbh, an' Maggie will ever wish she didn't either, but honorable was her intent an' I shan't hold it against her."

Not wanting to dwell on immortal matters, Kara dared a bit of boldness she wouldn't have if others had been present. "Please...would you tell me of Danu? Grandda never told me more than her name and that she is the mother of your people. I'd dearly love to hear her tale."

The Smithgod smiled and settled back on his throne. He gestured for her to make herself comfortable on the cushions at his feet. Kara curled like a kitten upon her chosen mound of pillows, unsurprised when several smaller bodies joined her as the faelings that seemed to follow her everywhere made themselves at home. Some of them assumed the form of cats or other common domestic pets; others held to their own fantastic shapes. They were a comfort, emanating love and peaceful thoughts. She felt as if she were at Grandda's side again, with Pixie curled in her lap. The remembrance was bittersweet.

Goibhniu's deep, rumbling voice filled the empty Hall, pulsing and throbbing and flowing like honey. "'Tis a *Sidhe* legend, not a Celtic one, yer Grandda may not have known it. It begins so…In the time before time, just before the rebirth of our race, when the way to *Tír na nÓg* was not yet opened to our people, Danu, destined to become the First Mother, fled the *Namhaid*, a deadly enemy. She didn't flee alone, for with her was her twin, Anu. The two were as one in all things an' their love for one another was great, but Death stalked them, setting them asunder.

"Determined that at least one o' them survive, Anu, the Savior, sent Danu off an' cloaked her trail. Drawing from the magic o' the wild an' o' herself she shaped the faelings an' released them into the world, losing a bit o' herself with each that left her. She didn't care, as long as it assured that they would more than mask any lingering signs o' Danu's flight. That done, her final act was as lure an' sacrifice to the *Namhaid*—the Enemy—giving her sister time to flee, leaving Danu to ever mourn her sister's passing."

Whatever else he was, Goibhniu was a masterful storyteller. As he spoke, even the faelings hung silently on his words…right up to the point where he mentioned their pivotal role in it all; then they went wild, flinging themselves into a riot of excitement. Kara wanted more. She hadn't realized how starved she was for the legends she had learned at Grandda's knee, to hear the cadence of a well-told tale, and to watch the images come to life in her mind.

She turned imploring eyes upon him, very much as she had with Grandda, as a child. "What happened then?"

Kara smiled gleefully as Goibhniu gave her a measured look and settled more comfortably on his throne. All around her, the faelings continued to cheep and chitter, but her attention did not waver as the Smithgod began again where he'd left off.

"The last o' her kind, Danu ran from the Homeland in the North with the four great cities o' Falias, Finias, Gorias, an' Murias, smoldering ruins behind her. She remained the sole hope o' the *Daoine Maithé*—the Good People—an' couldn't look back.

"In her survival, she saw only unending heartache…all those she had loved having crossed the Veil. Nothing more than her oath to her beloved sister Anu an' the quickening she sensed in her own womb drove her on. She had to survive if the *Daoine Maithé* were to lift their eyes once more to the sun an' wind an' moon. Her only hope lay in a sanctuary where the *Namhaid* couldn't pursue her…her only hope lay in the safe haven o' the sea.

"Drawing on her grief to channel the raw, now-untapped currents o' the elven magics, an' transmuting the feral earth magics surrounding her, she gathered all o' it in an' made it her own, forced it to her will.

"With all the energy trapped, throbbing beneath her skin, Danu marched gracefully to the water's edge. The sand crept over her feet an' the wind tugged at her tattered travel robes, running itself through her unruly braids an' curls, but only as the Father Sun closed his eye on another day did she enter the cold embrace o' the waves. As they welcomed her, drawing her down to their hidden depths, she unleashed the tremendous energy that threatened to split her skin. Dancing through currents both aquatic an' magical, she wrapped her thoughts about her like a shielding cloak. When her lungs threatened to burst, an' her mouth opened wide to gulp at air that wasn't there, only then did the sea take her into its bosom. The transformation began as masses o' floating hair fell away to be replaced by close, glittering scales all up and down her body. It continued until Danu wore the form o' a mighty salmon, wise an' swift an' hidden by the sea.

"In that aspect she bore her many children in their true form until the race o' the *Daoine Maithé* climbed from the sea, once more to walk the earth."

Silence hung taut in the air as the tale ended. Kara barely drew breath, and all the creatures curled up with her watched Goibhniu with radiant eyes. It was difficult for Kara to break herself out of the well-woven wonder, but she could not keep silent. Even now she needed to know more.

"And whatever happened to Danu?" Kara's low whisper rose deafeningly loud in the silence.

She watched closely as Goibhniu shifted in his seat, turning just enough to view the wall behind him, resplendent with its spiraling knotwork and ever-shifting colors. Maggie had explained the wall to her soon after they had arrived. Kara herself found it a bit disturbing; the massive pattern, with its minute transformations, made her feel unfocused and small.

That was when something occurred to her, and the words were out of her mouth before she could curb them. "...but salmon die after they spawn..." Her voice trailed off as she took in the indeterminable expression on Goibhniu's face. The complexity of his emotions made it seem as if many people sat before her at once, all in the same massive form. Kara looked away, taking a moment to brace herself. When she looked back, his expression had settled into melancholy devotion.

Finally, so soft as to make Kara doubt he'd spoken out loud, Goibhniu answered. "Aye, they do at that, but she was no mundane salmon. Danu lives, ever among us. Do ye see the massive pattern in the center o' the spiral? 'Tis hers an' it hasn't ceased to grow since the dawn o' *Sidhe* time."

Kara could not bring herself to look at the wall again; if she did, awe would overcome her.

"Have...have I seen her?" she asked, unable to resist the impulse to glance around *Mór Halla* as if the Mother Goddess would suddenly appear.

"Och! No, lass, ye'd have ken it if ye had." The look on his face grew sad. "Can ye imagine what 'twould be like to bear an entire race at once? To shelter them in yer womb, an' them all magical? 'Twould be terrible indeed to have bound within ye the entire sum o' the power o' the *Sidhe* Race, just waiting to be born again. Ye couldn't hope to ever be the same after, when suddenly 'tis all gone. Danu's very essence was forever transformed by the experience.

"If that 'twere all, perhaps things would be different, but Danu suffered another blow when she birthed her Children. Though every *Sidhe* soul returns, an' always has since the first spiral o' Time, for some reason, her beloved Anu's didn't. To this day, we have no answer for why." It was difficult to see the haunted look in Goibhniu's eye. "To this day, Danu is something other than what she was an' none have seen her for nigh unto three thousand years, though from time to time she speaks to her Children. I myself feel her presence often." Goibhniu's eyes slid back to the Great Wall. "Someday, she will walk among us once more. She has promised it."

His words were gentle, but Kara trembled just the same as Goibhniu rose in silence and took himself away, leaving her alone to wonder at the deep sense of affirmation she felt inside. An affirmation thoroughly entwined with dread.

Olcas stood at the center of an emotional maelstrom: dark and chaotic and destructive. It began the moment he rent the void to cross from New York to the ancient and magic-laced soil of Ireland. The sensation was nearly orgasmic. Either his memory of this land had faded, or Eire had become more of a prize today than it had been when Carmán and her children last walked the earth wearing their own faces.

He was so dazzled by the tantalizing cascade of magic across his borrowed nerves that the pathway he'd opened nearly closed behind him, leaving his...*companions* lost in the ether. Olcas reestablished his focus. While the woman had already served her primary purpose, her usefulness was not yet exhausted, and as for his other little pet...he was even less willing to let her go. That would be wasteful, not to mention dangerous. He turned and spread the tattered folds of reality wide, drawing the woman and child through to huddle together beside him. Both bore signs of recent tears, and both had dull, glassy eyes, though, behind the child's gaze, something roiled and writhed as if testing the ethereal bonds that imprisoned it. Rather than feeding Olcas' rage, the creature's efforts pleased him; the moment it lacked the desire and drive to escape, it would be of no further use to him.

"Come along, my dears." His voice dripped mock solicitousness as Olcas took each of them by the hand and led them deep into his chosen lair. An ancient network of forgotten tunnels left long ago by rebels of another era, cozy niches carved deep into the Wicklow Mountains, it was all that remained to attest to one of the many conquests of Ireland and the lengths to which her mulish people went to resist. He loved the irony of lurking in one of their own defensive warrens as he set into motion events that would consume them utterly, crush their spirits, and siphon away their souls until no hope of an uprising remained. Eire and her people would be his at last.

It had been centuries since he had been here, and in all that time, his precautions had remained intact. Not one thing was disturbed...not even the thick layers of dust.

Well, something would have to be done about that. Closing his eyes and taking a centering breath, the godling banished every speck of dust, revealing a decadent opulence not matched since the glory days of the Holy Roman Empire. Silk hangings and velvet cushions, inlaid wood and jewel-encrusted goblets, all awaiting Olcas's pleasure.

Once everything was restored, he locked the mortal woman away in an empty chamber. He could not be concerned with her at the moment; her main purpose had been to lure her husband across the ocean, where Olcas could take advantage of his driving obsession with the O'Keefes to nose out both Kara and the *Sidhe*. He would let the good doctor spring any traps.

Before another step was taken, it was time to cleanse the child's body of its organic stench. Her beset condition had served its purpose admirably, gaining him ready access to the doctor's house and opportunity to abscond with his wife, but he would stand the odor not one moment longer.

"Stand before me, creature, and do not move." Thinking, not for the first time, that humans were filthy, earthy creatures, Olcas fixed in his thoughts precisely what must go, the urine and the feces, the tear tracks and mats in her curls, everything that spoke of dirt, decay, and weakness would be whisked away, leaving a child like any other, only clean...on the surface, anyway. Drawing on a particle of the power at his disposal, Olcas made it so.

"Now, this is what is to be done," Olcas spoke mostly for the joy of speaking, so long had he been deprived of the ability to do so. It certainly wasn't because the demon needed vocalization to be guided. "I will scan the island for the girl; in the meantime, you will earn your keep by seeking out those of the *Sidhe* blood." Here he imprinted on the creature the signs it would look for: stunning beauty that glowed from within and immeasurable power rooted in antiquity, "and plague them. Do not attempt to claim them, as you could not hope to survive the attempt, and then they would be warned. The time for that will come soon enough. See, however, that they are very much disturbed. I want them nervous and distracted, ripe for the picking, once my plan is in place.

"Now away with you, and be sure to return quickly when I summon you, if you value your existence." Olcas fixed the malicious demon with a piercing glance. "You do realize that unless I grant it, you cannot feed, don't you?"

He laughed at the frustration in those inhuman eyes, scoffing at the murderous rage that transformed the vacuous expression on the child's face, a reflection of the spirit encased within. It was too perfect...too delicious... The impotent fury of the demon burned behind that façade. No, the rebellious creature had not spied the precaution Olcas had woven into the binding spell, so that even should the demon prove strong enough to defy him, it would be incapable of feeding through the prison of the body that contained it. Should it run away, it would soon fade to nothing in its shell. Olcas smiled, savoring his own brilliance, before contemptuously banishing the creature with a wave of his hand, compelling it to do his bidding.

Still chuckling with sinister glee, he turned his thoughts to his true prey. Pulling a simple blue scarf from his pocket—pilfered from the girl's bedroom even as the police put up their ineffectual yellow tape around the building— he draped it across his lap and ran his fingers along it. Soaking in the feel of not just the article itself, but the person to whom it was connected, Olcas allowed his awareness to expand, undulating across the ether along a path that could not be obliterated. The scarf belonged to Kara, his delightful little prize. Just by the feel of it, he could tell she handled it often, invested as it was with a great deal of personal energy. It was a potent key to finding her again, should she surface in the mortal world.

And if she did not, well, that was where the doctor would come in handy. If Dr. Barnert didn't draw the attention of the *Sidhe* himself, Olcas would use his insidious ways to ensure they became interested in the man. And when they'd brought him into their domain to reassure him his friends were safe and well, it would be child's play for Olcas to follow the bond linking them, right into the heart of precious Kara's hiding place. Once the good doctor was within their realm, nothing would be able to stop Olcas from following!

His patience paid off. After only a few hours, it appeared he wouldn't need to wait for the doctor after all. As fading wisps of incense wreathed Olcas's head and the final remnants of deep, rich, sinful chocolate yet titillated his tongue, he suddenly brushed against the girl's awareness, a bright and tempting light flaring in the darkness. And so close. Walking the streets of Dublin, in fact. She might as well already be in his grasp, she was that close. He followed the link from the scarf to the girl.

Olcas cursed. She was not alone. He eased back and merely watched. Every instinct egged him to seize her immediately, but he would not make the same mistakes again. It was important to ensure she did not slip away from him again. With a subtle thread of power, he reached out and tagged her. Whenever she surfaced in the mortal realm, he would know, and he could home in on her with but a thought. Let her become comfortable and relaxed, ease her into a sense of false security that would increase each time he allowed her to roam unmolested. When she was lulled, then he would strike.

For now he must plan. Once he secured Kara, he needed a place to take her. Not here. He would not risk his personal lair. Reaching out with his thoughts, he quickly found the perfect place: an abandoned warehouse surrounded by other abandoned buildings. Perfect...only rats and the homeless would hear her screams. He was sure neither would take note of them.

"Ye resist, Cliodna."

Maggie cringed, something she'd been doing with uncomfortable frequency lately. Goibhniu had yet to call her by her kin-name without next charging her with some duty she owed her people. What could they possibly ask of her now? Her rebellion was not quelled by the disapproving look on his face. "Ye'll have to tell me what ye're after, I'm afraid I'm not up to figuring it out for myself."

"Tired ye might be, but ye'll remember to be respectful just the same." His tone was mild but firm. Maggie could not help but lower her eyes in shame. "Now put up yer bitterness an' follow me."

"I beg yer forgiveness," she murmured. "I don't know what's wrong with me."

Goibhniu beckoned her to follow as he left the chamber. "Come along, let's see if we can't find the answer together."

She swallowed hard and did as he bid. Her time in America had not served her well. Never before her stay there would she have committed such a breach.

She'd barely descended into self-recrimination before Goibhniu reached out and drew her alongside him, to shelter safe beneath his arm.

"Look up, *leanbh*, look an' tell me what ye see."

Soothed by his gentle voice, she lifted her eyes and only the Smithgod's grip held her there, forced to stare up at the blackened pattern toward the center of the Great Wall. If it were anyone else, this would be the worst betrayal. A dark pit loomed before her, waiting for one more thing to tumble her in.

"Look, at it...haven't ye considered why the lines are as crisp as ever? In yer heart ye deny his death, ye keep him locked to this life, though 'tis already fled an' o' no use to him."

Maggie blanched at Goibhniu's words and shook her head violently. She jerked away from his arm, and he let her. Forgetting about respect, she turned on him, her heart screaming in denial, though she could manage no words past her shallow, gasping breaths. It was as if a trap closed around her, and finally, she spoke. "No!"

"Yes, *leanbh*...yes." Goibhniu countered, and a part of Maggie marveled at how such soft-spoken words could make her feel both chastised and forgiven in one breath.

"But I've mourned him; I held his lifeless body, carrying its dust an' the tale clear to the halls o' *Tír na nÓg*." She gritted her teeth. "My heart still bleeds!"

She allowed him to draw her away, following him through an archway leading to the gardens. Nothing could bring her to sit on the bench beside him, though. He appeared to overlook her small defiance, as she instead paced the clearing.

"Don't ye see what ye do to him? How ye betray him?" Goibhniu admonished her.

Maggie wrenched her gaze away from the ground to look up at him. He would speak of betrayal? Which one? There were so many. Her heart, her faith, her trust, her future...all had been betrayed by Fate.

Goibhniu delivered a hard pinch to the tender flesh beneath her arm, making her jump and gasp. Without a thought of whom she turned on, Maggie whirled the rest of the way around, her teeth clenched, and her red-gold curls whipping behind her as her forehead gathered in a scowl. The Smithgod suddenly stood close beside her.

"In case ye'd not enough to pity yerself for," he commented simply, before continuing with his rebuke. "Ye mourn yer own loss, not Demne's passing; until ye let yer heart grieve him for true, ye make yer love a prison to him...a prison becomes hell before too long."

Outraged, she stalked a distance away, measuring her stride back and forth across the small clearing, protesting with each length. "No, no, I have grieved! I have accepted...accepted his..." She stopped pacing and swayed where she stood. Goibhniu's gaze locked with hers, and she could no longer deny the truth: Demne, as she knew him, was lost to her and the world; he had not just gone away to return someday. Only his soul would return. One of the People would be blessed to bear it, but *her* Demne was gone forever.

Maggie did not have the strength left to say it out loud, but inside the truth was clear. Putting aside her self-pity for the first time since she woke above his broken body, Maggie allowed herself the purifying comfort of tears. They streamed unchecked down her face, and tremors went through her in steady waves.

Maggie's grief broke. It was as if she were being torn apart and remolded. Everything that had died when Demne was taken from her: joy, hope, love...all the deadfall burned away, making room for new growth; perhaps not today, but soon. Her future no longer stood so bleak as it had been when she'd faced it alone. Sobs shook her, and tears cascaded down her cheeks. They rose as liquid crystal from her very depths, making her eyes sparkle like dew on new-minted leaves. They flowed over her until everything was bathed in their soothing, glittery shower.

As the anguish drained from her heart in the way of healthy mourning, she was left with its bittersweet memory to carry for the rest of her days—a much easier burden than having its full weigh as a lodestone around her heart. Her head fell back, and the aggression continued to flow away. Until now, she hadn't even realized she'd begun to raise fists to the Smithgod. Allowing her eyes to drift closed, she took a deep, cleansing breath, finding in her heart the truth of what Goibhniu said. Anger and injustice had consumed her completely, outrage that so little time had been allowed to them: Demne and herself. She felt cheated, she felt abused...She. Nothing in her reaction had been aimed toward Demne; in her heart, she did not acknowledge his death, only her loss, as if somewhere out in the world he lived...apart from her. The grief was always there, a hard little kernel buried beneath her indignation, and it was beyond time she set it free.

Lightness settled over her and only vaguely did she notice as Goibhniu finally gathered her to him and settled upon the secluded bench with her cradled in his lap. She had no more awareness of her surroundings; nothing existed for her beyond his encompassing arms. The stony hardness in her chest was gone, and her breath came more freely. Lost in the cloud of this more healthy mourning, Maggie found herself in a soft, brilliant haze, pulsing and caressing as a spring breeze. A dazzling spark settled on her heart, flooding her with warmth and love until she felt encompassed by something much larger than herself. A brief surge of recognition faded into acceptance and contentment. Then she felt it... a blaze kindled deep within her womb, drowning out every other sensation with the complexity of burgeoning joy. Sparkling green eyes gone wide and her face glowing, Maggie looked up at Goibhniu with a bemused smile tugging at her lips before a gentle weariness drew her down into a healing sleep.

Chapter 8

The *Sidhe* who carried the body into *Mór Halla* was so old it showed in his faded, periwinkle-blue eyes if not upon his youthful face...or perhaps it was merely the horror of his burden.

"She was gathering them for me...she didn't even need them for herself...they were for the villagers..." the ancient one's words trailed off to a quiver as he stopped in the midst of the Court, looking around at those nearest him as if he hoped they could tell him what he should do next. Or perhaps that they would have an answer to how such a thing could come to be. And most of them...again, they all but pulled their fancy, embroidered court robes aside, away from the taint that stood amongst them. How frequent a guest Death had become to *Tír na nÓg*—and it terrified them.

Maggie could no longer fault them the dismay upon their faces. Those who had taken themselves to the refuge of the Land of Youth had long forgotten their own potential for mortality. When she herself had arrived, bringing the first reminders, she had not seen their fear for what it was. Now, from the distance of her own disassociation in *this* matter, she could see that their haughty, dismissive looks were a defense against Death itself, behind the contempt lurked terror. Yes, they played at War—death and all—but that was more to feed their conviction that true death could not touch them. Here in *Tír na nÓg*, those who were slain in battle rose the next day to play at Death again, reinforcing their self-deception. In their fear of it, they had withdrawn from the very arms of life, only to exist in this dream-realm—static and safe.

That safety had been shattered.

Moving through the crowd, she brushed her thoughts across that paralyzing fear, drawing it away as she was able, adding it to her own, to which she was already immune. Freed from their terror, some few of those she passed fell in behind her, compassion finding its way back into their hearts and faces.

Drawing close to the center of the disturbance, Maggie was surprised to recognize the man holding the corpse as Abarta, her tormentor of long ago. She had not known he now resided in *Tír na nÓg*. He was so different from what she remembered from centuries ago; there was no mischief in him today, and seeing the anguish in his expression, she couldn't hold those times against him.

The thought occupied her for but a second as her eyes were drawn to the incongruous remains. Something was wrong...very wrong. The body had not returned to dust. Yet the wounds no longer bled.

"I don't understand," she looked in puzzlement at Abarta and those gathered around him. "Does she live, then?" The man only stared at her dumbly, his arms clutched tightly around the girl. His head shook slowly back and forth, but there was no understanding in eyes locked up in grieving. Reaching her hand out to confirm for herself, Maggie drew back with a shudder. The girl's skin burned, as if with a fever, yet there was no pulse that Maggie could find, and the chest did not rise and fall with breath.

Her nostrils pinched in protest when, in examining the body, she inhaled traces of an overwhelming musk that clung to the wounds. Maggie was sure she knew every species that called Ireland home, yet this pong was alien to her, alien and foreboding. The injuries seemed to be caused by an animal, though that in itself made no sense. No animal she knew of would harm a *Sidhe*; they lived in harmonious coexistence with all creatures of nature...all of them save man. A human had not done this.

Maggie turned to the head of the Hall, her eyes searching out Goibhniu's. "She doesn't live, an' yet she also doesn't fade. How can this be?" While she addressed the Smithgod, she could hear movement behind her, as others lifted the body from Abarta's grip. There was the soft sound of shuffling as they led him away.

"How can this be?" she repeated in earnest.

She motioned behind her. Unable to bring herself to assume the burden of the body, she beckoned to the Court attendant now carrying it to follow her and made her way toward the throne in an uneasy parody of her original approach just days ago. The Court once again fell away in front of the procession, leaving a wide swath of a path to the very feet of Goibhniu.

Already unsettled, what Maggie saw next made her want to turn and flee. She couldn't help noticing the ever-changing knotwork pattern on the wall before her; one small, simple pattern on the outermost turn flared an angry, violent deep red. Even as she watched, two more in the coil followed suit. Her gasp drew the Court's attention. As they saw what she did, everyone erupted into assorted cries of anger, anguish, and fear. All eyes turned to Goibhniu, begging for answers—for deliverance.

The Smithgod descended his throne and came forward, gently taking the lifeless body into his arms. One massive hand rose to close her vacant eyes, to trace the angry slashes across her face, and finally to tuck her limp head against his shoulder as if he carried a sleepy toddler to bed.

Maggie struggled to keep her gaze from locking on the deep gouges running down the now-visible back of the victim. Any death would be upsetting, and one as violent as this even more so, but Maggie found she was more than upset. It was as if this were a personal loss, though she didn't even know this particular *Sidhe*. The cut of the woman's clothes was characteristic of *Tír na mBan*, not *Tír na nÓg* or *Tír Tairnigiri*, where Maggie had divided her time before being sent off to America. Though all *Sidhe* were connected in a racial family, some connections were bound to be more deeply felt. This was not one of them, for Maggie, and yet just the sight of the young one's blood smeared along Goibhniu's arm triggered despair that would be no deeper if this had been Maggie's own child.

"There are no easy answers to this vicious attack." Goibhniu's voice cut across Maggie's thoughts and carried effortlessly throughout *Mór Halla*. Its very vibrancy and strength soothed the panic running rampant through Maggie. Everyone looked to Goibhniu. "I will find ye the answers ye seek but first to ensure no more o' our number fall to harm. From now 'til the culprits are caught, Danu's Children must in their Halls remain."

His eyes took on the clouded, unfocused appearance of one soulspeaking with many at once. As he continued in a tone unlike his usual speech, the Smithgod's words reverberated forcefully, his voice raised in concert with those of the other rulers of the *Sidhe* Lands.

"Only those whom We bid shall go forth, armored against this unknown enemy — this *Namhaid* na Tuatha — with weapons from Goibhniu's very forge, blessed by Our Own hands." The divine decree sounded as one echoing voice, at once in every Hall and Rath hailed as home by the *Sidhe*.

The Court murmured in astonishment; never had they heard such a multi-voiced proclamation. The collective voices of the rulers of each *Sidhe* Land, combined with the need for such a declaration, utterly terrified them. Maggie watched their expressions closely. It was so obvious which were here to hide from the world. They betrayed themselves with their pallid faces and the way they shifted behind one another to avoid drawing Goibhniu's eye.

Very wise, Maggie reflected, but they'd nothing to fear, Goibhniu would never depend on them in their weak-heartedness. He'd never turn to *them* as his warriors.

As if the thought were an invitation to a dialogue, a remarkable presence resounded in her mind. *Cherished daughter...faithful Cliodna, ye'll have yer time o' rest, though I fear 'tisn't now.*

Maggie gasped; whatever training in defense she had, she was no warrior. *Training or na, ye are one o' the only Sidhe to see actual battle in centuries, yer fighters were victorious an' the Tuatha de Danaan have faith in ye,* Goibhniu answered her unvoiced thoughts.

But I'm a guardian, not a warrior! Because o' me two o' our people are dust, an' I very nearly joined them, lost to grief as I was in the midst o' battle! 'Twas only the mortals that won the fight an' prevented even more death! Maggie could not help but argue. She was absolutely certain that no good could come of this, and more would die because of her if he insisted.

Cliodna...ye had the strength to put aside yer grief, an' a mind wise an' open enough to even consider fighting beside a mortal. Ye have honor an' courage an' wisdom, an' yer forces vanquished the foe. What's more, ye have the respect o' all gathered in this Court. No easy task, given most o' them trust nothing o' the world.

The Smithgod's soulspoken words shocked her like a live wire. What did it matter if she were trained or not? Why was this even being asked of her? Already new life unfolded deep within her womb. There was no question that she would never put it at risk; it had come to her at too dear a cost to squander it.

None other holds my faith as ye do. An' ye're not being sent into battle, but as messengers to our Children. Be assured I'll not send ye out ill-prepared.

Maggie could not sway his confidence in her, she could tell that now. With a sigh, she met Goibhniu's eyes, and, seeing the love and unwavering faith within them, she found renewed resolve. He was right. It astounded her, but he was right. She did not stand alone, and with this further threat her people needed her...her god called upon her. Strengthening her stance and squaring her shoulders, Maggie—no...Cliodna, daughter of the *Tuatha de Danaan*, took up the mantle of the fierce Celtic spirit that was the *Sidhe*'s legacy to the people of Eire.

Coming out of the inward focus of soulspeech, she first met Goibhniu's eye and bowed her head solemnly in acceptance, then she received her next shock. She looked around her to see who else had been selected for this uneasy honor only to discover not only was she one of Goibhniu's chosen warriors, but she stood at the forefront, as their leader. Ranged behind her stood a force reminiscent of the ancient Celts' *Fianna*. Numbered among her band were twenty-four of the Court and every one of her own fighters from across the ocean, all unified by the Smithgod's quiet confidence. They were not the only band organized this day, but they were Goibhniu's own chosen. Though her blood ran first cold, then hot in reaction to this daunting responsibility, Cliodna could do nothing but accept this position of command over the new *Sidhe Fianna*. She was assailed by doubts, but could not let the slightest hint of them into her expression, not before this Court or any other; to do so would be a disservice to her new force. Forearm clasped above her heart, she went to one knee with her eyes lowered deferentially; her new forces followed her example.

"We go forth upon yer command," Cliodna declared with more confidence than she felt.

Silence, save for a muttering from the Court.

Cliodna raised her eyes to look up at Goibhniu, her gaze full of questions. She blanched at the anger and concern battling in his expression. "Kara O'Keefe is missing from the Halls o' *Tír na nÓg*."

Without checking the denomination of the bills, Arn threw several at the driver and leapt from the taxi. As he barreled through the main lobby, no sounds of outrage pursued him from the curb. It must have been enough...in fact, most likely quite a lot more than enough, he thought as the car revved away.

Inside was another matter. The hospital staff converged like gnats, protesting as he flew through the doors separating Reception from the inner workings of the hospital. The Ruger immediately set off the metal detectors, but he plowed on anyway, dodging interns with crash carts, patients trailing IVs, and nurses whose pace was nearly as frantic as his own. He waved his ID at the security guards and duty nurses attempting to intercept him. Arn wove expertly through the obstacle course and reached the elevator bank before anyone could reach him. He had no choice. No matter how delusional he thought Molly was, there was still something going on here, and she was the only puzzle piece connected to both himself and the thug he'd first noticed lounging in front of Patrick's house.

Arn pushed through the elevator doors before they'd completely opened and made his way to Molly's room, anxiety sending fresh floods of adrenaline coursing through his veins. When this was all over, he would crash hard, but at least for now, the surge was a godsend. That and the thought of what he would do to the thug when he got a hold of him were all that kept Arn going; he hadn't been this sleep- and sustenance-deprived since his residency. Just as he turned down the corridor to Molly's room, a barrage of klaxons and the rapid-fire beat of the response team drowned out the muted, peaceful sounds of the hospital ward. Arn broke into a flat-out run, dread clutching at his heart. It was not uncommon for a heart attack victim to experience collateral episodes, somewhat like the aftershock of an earthquake. In fact, he vaguely remembered the punk from the doctor's lounge claiming Molly had already had one. In her reduced state, a relatively mild secondary or tertiary attack could be more devastating than the big one that had put her here. He prayed fervently as his last few strides carried him to her open door, only to find the room not just empty, but sanitized.

"Excuse me." He struggled to get the words out through his panting. "Can you...can you tell me what happened to the woman assigned to this room?"

The nurse he'd intercepted gave him an intent glance before pulling her arm out of his grasp. Before she could protest, he held up his id badge. He wasn't here often, but he did have attending privileges at this facility.

"What happened to her, Nurse Cranston?" he repeated as patiently as he could, reading her name off her badge.

"Sorry, Doctor Barnert." He could read the annoyance in her expression before she carefully masked it. "I'm afraid I've just come on shift and haven't checked the board yet. If you come with me, I can find out for you."

He followed her to the nurses' duty station and supplied her with the room number and patient name. As he waited for her to pull up the data, he watched the hospital staff continue to flood the other room, the one from which the alarms still sounded, in a determined effort to save the life of that patient. Arn prayed the entire time that for some reason, Molly had been released, that this crack team had not had to go through such efforts for her, perhaps with less success than they seemed to be having now.

"I'm sorry, Doctor, but it looks like Ms. Kelley died about an hour ago, massive heart failure."

The blood drained from his face and only his grip on the countertop kept him standing.

"Are you all right, Doctor Barnert?"

"Thank you, I'll be fine," he managed past the resulting numbness. "I'm her doctor...was her doctor. Has the family been notified?"

She scrolled down on the computer screen. "There is no family listed. There is a note of a nephew visiting just before her final episode. It says he had already left before she had the attack, and the nurse on duty at the time had no way to contact him. It also says that she left a message with your service."

"Nephew? Is there a name listed?" He watched as she scanned the record, desperate enough to hope, but knowing inside there was none.

Who had come visiting? Could it have been the punk rocker from the doctor's lounge? Urias, if he remembered correctly. Or perhaps it had been the thug that kept showing up. And, just maybe, it was her nephew, and Arn was seeing nonexistent shadows everywhere now that the nightmare had touched his life to such an intimate degree. Now what was he to do?

He missed whatever Nurse Cranston just said to him. Pressing a hand over his throbbing temple, he tried to cut off the tension headache that threatened to hit. "Excuse me, could you please repeat that?"

"You're her physician; what should we do with her personal effects?"

"Personal effects? Give them to me; I'll see that they get to the family." Arn didn't remember Molly having much with her, but maybe something would give him a clue to finding Lynn. He could not let go of that hope...if he did, despair would shut him down completely.

The brown bag the nurse handed him was discouragingly light. It was an effort not to snatch it and run for the nearest private space where he could root through it without having to answer any awkward questions. Please, Lord, let there be a clue. He headed for the doctor's lounge only to break away as a couple of residents reached it before him.

Spying a sign for the restrooms down the hall, Arn slipped into the men's room. The stalls were empty, and the only other occupant left as he entered. Arn quickly locked the door behind him before dumping the contents of the bag all over the counter. His heart sank even lower. He fingered the blue shawl that tumbled out with a few other articles of clothing, remembered the sight of her bundled in its warmth, peering from the smoke-shrouded alley. So alive, so feisty. And now she was gone. He shoved the items away with a groan. The clothing slid to the floor with an unsuspected clatter and out tumbled a wooden cross pendant strung on a leather thong.

Tears burned his eyes, and his knuckles went white as he clutched the necklace. He wanted to throw it. He wanted to punch something. He wanted to hurt those responsible. He wanted to find Lynn...needed to find her most desperately before something happened to her. Perhaps he should have called the police, but for some reason, the thought never occurred to him. If he called them now, everything would point to him. Arn was frightened...for both himself and his wife.

"Well, unless ye've Molly hidden in a stall, ye'll need to explain yerself."

Arn dropped the cross down on the counter and whirled, his fists raised and his heart pounding. His gaze darted from the locked door to the man standing behind him. Make that the *familiar* man standing behind him, Arn corrected himself as he took in Urias's spiked metallic-blue hair and golden gaze.

"And maybe you'll explain that little trick you have of getting past locked doors..."

"Ye'll still not believe me, so why waste my breath? What ye're doing with Molly's bauble there?" The punk reached past him to scoop up the necklace, stepping back so fast that Arn did not have time to react. "So are ye answering, or am I leaving?"

"What do I care if you leave or stay? I don't even know what you're doing here, and I don't owe you any answers." Arn's anger got the better of him before he could remind himself that he was only at the hospital at all because he desperately needed help. He took several deep breaths before going on. "Wait...I'm sorry. The truth is...Molly's dead. She's dead, and my wife is missing."

Urias watched him with a shrewd gaze. It made Arn uncomfortable, those unblinking golden eyes pinning him where he stood, reminding him oh so much of the hawk from earlier. "So 'tis help yer asking for now, is it?"

He had never felt so mouse-like in his life, his first impulse was to crouch and cower. Instead, Arn closed his eyes and attempted to swallow his dread. Only hours ago, he had essentially told this man to go take a flying leap; was it any surprise he was less than magnanimous now? There was nothing he could say in response.

"Molly, she needed help as well, ye ken?" The tone was conversational, no accusation, no belligerence, no recrimination, just a statement. "How did she die? Another heart attack?"

Was that guilt just below the surface of the young punk's grief? The nurse's words suddenly came back to him. Could this be the nephew who had been here visiting? Arn looked up, a calculating look lighting his eyes. Guilt was something they had in common, could that be used to sway him? "You mean, you don't know? But you were here, weren't you? You showed up and told the nurse you were her nephew, and then you went to her and got her worked up over this insane belief in elves and magic and evil bad guys. It was too much for her already taxed heart, and she died before anything could be done. Before you got whatever it is you wanted out of her!"

Not allowing Urias to deny any of it, Arn whipped the Polaroid from his pocket and thrust it in the punk's face. "Who is he? One of your posse...your crew...your gang? Who is he, and what is this game you're both playing at? One woman is dead and another missing. My *wife* is missing. The only thing Molly and I had in common was that the two of you kept turning up around us today... What the hell is going on here? Was he sent to convince me to help...by any means?"

Urias slowly reached out and took the snapshot from Arn's trembling hand.

"Where did ye get this?" Intensity transformed Urias's face as the laid-back, dismissive punk fell away, leaving a regal, commanding young man in his place. Arn simply watched him, waiting for his move, his flight, his attack. It never came. "I tell ye I don't ken what yer talking about. I haven't seen Molly since before I came to see ye. She had another attack then, but all was as fine as it could be when I left. This picture, though, is another matter... I need to know how ye came by it... What do ye ken o' him...?"

"Know about him? I never even saw him before the other day! You want to know what I know about him?" Arn asked through clenched teeth, "I know the bloody bastard has my wife!"

There was a thud as someone attempted to push open the men's room door, followed by frustrated complaints outside. Gradually the sounds faded as whoever was there went off to find another restroom. Arn tensed and shot a glance at the door before riveting his eyes back on the punk. So it was still locked. Then how...He gave the punk an appraising look; he noticed Urias do the same to him. Their gazes met and held as they took each other's measure.

"Ye wanted to know what I was doing here...well, the truth is, ye called me. Ye held that bauble in yer hand an' yer heart cried out for help triggering a spell placed there by Maggie McCormick, an' I answered."

Arn searched the young man's face for any hint of deception and found only openness and determination. It made no sense. Every instinct Arn had pushed him to trust this unlikely fellow. No matter the impression his appearance gave, every movement and gesture, every expression, everything about Urias at this moment screamed integrity. As farfetched as all this seemed, what else was Arn going to believe? Already he had seen half a dozen things he couldn't explain. Either he was going mad, or reality wasn't what he thought it was.

"I do happen to know the face in that picture, but 'tisn't because he's a friend or any kind o' acquaintance—unless ye'd be counting enemies. The other day this man was a part o' a magical attack on the pawnshop, Yesterday's Dreams. He an' his master were after a lass named Kara O'Keefe; I'm thinking ye know her." Urias again held up the photograph. "This is an evil man, an' Molly was certain he's still after the girl. 'Twould seem by this picture *he's* determined ye'll be involved, an' according to this, I think we know where he'd have ye go."

With each word out of the punk's mouth, Arn wanted to scream in denial. His eye darted to the picture, to the point where Urias indicated with his finger. There was a word written there along the bottom, a word he had overlooked before: Eire. He had to think hard for several moments before he realized why it was familiar...and what it meant. According to Patrick's father, Conall O'Keefe—may he rest in peace—it was the original name of Ireland. Rage and suspicion welled up within him anew. Any trust that had begun to form shriveled into ash. Interesting that everyone suddenly wanted him in Ireland. "Seems to me you and Molly were the ones determined to get me involved, and interestingly enough, that was the very place you wanted me to go. How do you expect me to believe you had nothing to do with this?"

"There's nothing I could say would convince ye, an yer determined to think otherwise." Those golden eyes closed, and Urias's youthful face seemed weary. "I know all o' this is unbelievable an' I can't blame ye for getting riled about it, but however we can help ye we will, if ye'll accept our aid. What do ye say we get out o' here an' figure out how to get yer wife back?"

It was madness, but Arn wavered. He could not do this on his own, didn't even know where to start. Every instinct told him this man told the truth, and Arn had always relied on his instincts. With a sigh, he gave a single nod of assent and turned to scoop Molly's belongings back into the bag.

"Okay, I'll follow you for...now..." Arn trailed off. Suddenly, all the blood drained from his face, and his body swayed as he turned back to Urias, only to behold a shimmering rent in the air with the punk half disappeared through it, his hand reaching out for Arn's own. All he could think was, 'Oh God! What next?'

It would be a very long time before Arn stopped shaking, he was absolutely certain of that. He couldn't describe what walking between the worlds was like, the experience had been too chaotic...too fleeting. To describe how he felt now would totally unseat reason; suffice it to say that it was like everything about him had been jostled until all the infinitesimal connected bits seemed subtly misaligned.

Not wanting to dwell on how they had gotten here, Arn took in his surroundings. It was like walking into a Shaolin temple or a Buddhist monastery. The only word he could think of to describe it was serene. They had come through into a generous loft dressed in natural, muted tones, with solid slabs of creamy stone running from floor to vaulted ceiling. In one corner, a hushed waterfall cascaded into a basin the size and general shape of a hot tub. From there, the water traveled along stone-lined troughs to a raised pond, edged with reeds and full of fish, in the center of the immense space. At strategic spots around the chamber, oases of greenery softened the austere setting; dwarf trees clustered along the wall in pots, and reeds and ferns punctuated the rill as it wended its way toward the center of the room. From above came the soothing sound of wood chimes clacking gently, a peaceful harmony to the burble of the water. Looking up, Arn discovered a bower draped completely in billowing white fabric, nothing more than a generous platform with silk walls. Embarrassed at the intimacy of it, he drew his gaze back down to the public area below, marveling at the way the low couches and mounds of gently colored pillows served as comfortable seats without disrupting the meditative flow of the space. That was when he realized there was no sign of anything resembling a kitchen...or other necessities. A gentle cough from across the room reminded him this was someone's home, and that someone stood by while Arn gawked. A heated flush flooded his face, worsening as he turned to Urias and could not help thinking that the room more than anything else convinced him the young man was something other than he seemed...well, that and the way they got here.

"If ye like, ye can help yerself to a seat; the others will be here shortly." Urias's lilting voice carried through the space as softly as the chimes did, and was just as soothing...so soothing that it took a moment for what Urias had said to sink in. Others? What others? The tension from the hospital reared up full-force. Arn barely trusted this one, and he was expected to wait quietly while more showed up? Gauging the distance to the door he considered bolting.

"I'll open the door if ye truly wish to leave, but it won't bring ye any closer to finding yer wife."

Arn ground his teeth. "Oh, and traipsing off to another country will? I'm not here so you can whip me away on your little errand. Hell, I didn't even set out to call you, I only have your word that I even did."

"Trust isn't a simple thing to grant, but ye have to do it sometime."

Arn struggled with himself. Fear, anger, uncertainty...a maelstrom of emotion ripped him to shreds on the inside. He actually wanted to trust, but doubt kept rearing up, continually throwing him off balance each time he was confident he'd found his center. He discovered he could not bear to hold Urias's open and infinitely patient gaze. His eyes locked on the abundant and soothing serenity that surrounded him. He had to admit he felt safe in this haven, beset only by his own doubts. What was he to do?

The task before him seemed utterly impossible, and his choices nonexistent, he was being led around like a starving dog after a bone. His heart cried out, *My God, Lynn, please be okay, please!*

Completely overwhelmed, he slowly sank down to rest on the nearest seating arrangement. His gaze, desperate and tortured, sidled back to the enigmatic young man responsible for bringing him here. Arn was afraid he'd never quite understand what had taken place this evening, and to try and accept it unquestioningly was to embrace madness, but regardless, he needed Urias's help.

"I don't care how you do it...please, I need your help." As the silence played out, Arn was mortified. This...man had come to him and not only had Arn not helped him, he'd violently refused. Now Arn was the supplicant and dread rapidly smothered what little hope he'd managed to cling to. And still, Urias just stood there with his glittering eyes revealing nothing whatsoever of the thoughts that swirled beyond them. In fact, it was as if Urias were staring through him. Never before had Arn felt so 'not there.'

He couldn't stand it. With a strangled groan, Arn looked away, gazing reluctantly toward the door. With as much dignity as he could muster, he rose and moved toward it. Only moments ago, he had had a driving desire to leave. Now that he no longer did, he must. He was totally lost, no idea where he was or where he should go next. His overwhelming fear was that he would fail his sweet Lynn the one time she most needed him to be there. Tears did not just threaten—they cascaded down his cheeks. Thankfully his back was to Urias.

"Did ye think ye heard me say we wouldn't help ye then?" The words were softly spoken, a gentle rebuke that pierced Arn to his heart even as it revived his waning hope. In that instant, he saw with absolute clarity how undeserving he was of Urias's charity. Of course, that wasn't to say that he wouldn't cling like a bulldog to the unvoiced promise of assistance.

"Sit yerself back down, the others are...on their way."

Arn wondered at the pause as he settled back on the low comfort of the couch. Perhaps someone else would have missed the hesitation, would have likewise missed an infinitesimal tightening of the *Sidhe*'s jaw, but years of practice in gauging the emotional state of his patients served Arn well. Something was wrong here, beyond his own personal nightmare. Arn closed his eyes and prayed for all he was worth.

Once again, Kara walked the streets of Dublin, past the brightly painted storefronts and majestic cathedrals. Maggie had taken her about mortal Ireland several times after their first foray, but Kara could never get enough, particularly of Dublin. She wandered down streets lined with elegant townhouses, thrilling in the smell of hops on the air, though the Guinness brewery was half the city away, and laughed at the children running by with happy, yipping dogs trailing at their heels. She was more drawn to this lively, vibrant chapter of her family history than she was to the other, rich in wonder as it was. Perhaps because Underhill, thanks to years of story time with Grandda, already felt so familiar to her, whereas it had been a rare event for Papa to open up about life in mortal Ireland, which hadn't interested Grandda at all. Kara had rarely asked, not when each time she did, Papa's face went cold and hard with what she recognized now as pain. Now knowing why her grandparents had chosen a life in America for their son, Kara understood what haunted him. Even returning to his homeland hadn't eased Papa's pain; she could still see the thinly veiled heartache of separation in his eyes, even here on Irish soil, and would not press him.

And so, Kara explored the cobbled streets of Dublin on her own. Some spanned more than a millennium of history, some were brand new. They all tied the past and present of the Celts together into a vibrant now. Today was a guilty pleasure. She hadn't specifically been forbidden to explore, most likely because they assumed there wasn't need to. And to be fair, Kara likely wouldn't have ventured out on her own, but something happened today, and the resulting turmoil had her so on edge until she fled *Tír na nÓg* out of self-preservation. So Kara had pinned on the brooch Maggie had given her when they first met, taking comfort in its protective spell, and set off to explore as if she were nothing more than a tourist.

For a while she wandered Dublin's vast Phoenix Park, enjoying the ornamental gardens, the zoo, and the grounds surrounding the Viceroy's Lodge and absolutely marveled at the graceful, towering beauty of the Phoenix Monument, but eventually she left the more open areas to explore the nature trails. Perhaps not the wisest choice. It was late in the afternoon, and not many people were about, especially in the middle of autumn. She grew uneasy, almost certain she caught glimpses of a face she recognized, a face that continued to haunt her dreams — Tony's. Kara picked up her pace, trying to trace her path back out of the park — or at least find her way out the other side.

She flinched as the distinct harshness of a Brooklyn accent call out. "Hey, Lady..."

She would swear it sounded like Tony, a man who, in New York, had repeatedly attempted to abduct her at the order of Lucien, the man who coveted her mage power. While his master had died, was it possible Tony had recovered?

Hurried steps approached from around a bend in the path. What if he was not alone? Her panic increasing, Kara cut away from her current course, abandoning the path. Taking off through the underbrush, she dodged branches and bramble, heading directly toward what she was pretty sure was the way out of the park. In her hurry, she stumbled on a rock hidden in the deadfall and fetched up against an oak. She yelped as the bark scraped the skin from both her palm and her cheek; her heart pounded, and she was sure she'd most certainly given her position away. Behind her, the brush rustled.

Frantically she tried to remember the little magic Maggie had taught her in far-off New York. Her efforts had turned out well enough back in the City, but there had been no further opportunity for training. Her confidence waned. Still, she prayed there was something she could use to defend herself.

Reminding herself to breathe deeply and evenly, she suppressed her unreasonable fear. What had gotten into her? Nothing she encountered could be worse than Lucien, could it? And after what she had done to him, there was no chance of him surfacing again. Tony himself had been left across the Ocean, lying in a drooling heap beside his shattered master; even if he had recovered, there was absolutely no way he could know where she was.

Still, someone or something was following her, and she had not survived the past week in one piece to fall victim to a chance encounter. Pushing the tangled brown wave of hair from her eyes, Kara scanned the brush around her for a branch or a rock small enough for her to pick up but substantial enough to be wielded as a weapon. There was nothing and nowhere for her to flee in time.

At a loss for what to do, Kara eyed the low-slung branches of the oak she'd stumbled against. With a little jump, she grabbed the lowest one and strained to haul herself up. This bit of cover, combined with the "I'm not here" spell Maggie had taught her in New York, would allow her to spy out whatever followed her, without leaving herself open in case it was trouble. Settling in the fork of the tree, she began to hum, her thoughts weaving the air about her, wrapping it across her form so that it appeared uninterrupted. Now she had only to wait.

Moments later, Kara felt the fool; she had scrambled frantically to perch herself up in the tree, forcing her thoughts into the proper pattern for the still unfamiliar magic, and for what—to gain her vantage point just in time to watch a squirrel leap from the rustling bush. Abruptly halting her hum, she felt the gathered energy flow away to its original channels.

With a groan, she laid her forehead against the cool roughness of the bark. Well, the least she could do while she was up here was to try and get an idea of where she was in the park. She caught her breath a moment before scaling higher. It had been quite some time since her tree-climbing days. Somehow, she didn't remember it being this difficult.

After climbing as high as the branches would support, she carefully turned herself about until she saw all around her. Yes! There in the distance, a tall, gleaming column with a white bird perched on top in a nest of marble flames—the Phoenix Monument would guide her to safety. It was in the center of the park with walkways surrounding it, open and easy to navigate. Safe.

Careful to note a landmark below, Kara shimmied herself back down to the ground, and determinedly set off toward her white marble "beacon fire." She would not get lost again.

⟐

Ice-blue eyes, distinctly out of place in an angular Romani face, watched her with cold calculation from the shadow of an overgrown holly.

⟐

Would Aí ever be able to approach the Smithgod's throne without a sense of remorse to bring him low? If so, this was not that time. He had tried. He had tried so very hard, but nothing worked. Never before had he failed to sway a mortal with his charm, not even waterkin. Until now.

He could not help but remember the very first time he'd come before Goibhniu in shame. It was etched upon his memory, as fresh as the day it happened; he had been full of rage and drawn down into ultimate despair. The blood of innocents stained his hands, and his soul was forever shadowed by what he had done over seventy years ago in the mortal realm, unjustly calling down balefire on the McGillicuddy's homestead to avenge his beloved Sadb. Too late, he had learned his vengeance should have fallen upon another. From where he stood now, cloaked by the shadows of the recess, he could not keep his eyes from traveling over the Court, seeking out the one of whom he thought, the true villain from that long-ago time. Finding him brought Aí no satisfaction. The renowned Bran lounged indolently against a pillar along the far wall, clearly staring right at him, waiting to be noticed.

With a curse, Aí tore his gaze away as if burned, his breath coming in ragged huffs. That time of shame was past and he could not dwell upon it. If he did, the bitter and dark *Sidhe* across *Mór Halla* would triumph and Aí would only end up diminished.

He was so focused on his inner struggle that he did not notice the Court stream out, leaving him all alone with his imposing god. Only the extreme control he wielded against his inner demons prevented him from gasping as Goibhniu seemed to address his very thoughts, or perhaps not, Aí thought, as he recalled where he stood.

"Ye can leave the shadows now, *leanbh*." Goibhniu beckoned him. Aí crept closer. Each step was a challenge, and in the end, he could only manage to bring himself to the leading edge of the dais's first tier before going to his knees. "Back again? An' alone, is it?"

Aí hung his head. "I've tried everything an' she won't budge. Na even the word ye said would sway her worked. The best I've managed is to set a sprite to watch o' the woman."

"Come now!" Goibhniu's expression was stern and unyielding. "Ye've seen what we stand against, what's been done to the faerie kin well before now. What good do ye think one o' the kin-cousins will be when she's beset by what's been leaving the creatures an' countryside in tatters?"

Aí brought both hands up to cradle his head. "I didn't know what else to do. An' I wasn't intending he'd protect her, so much as he'd warn her an' myself o' any threaten."

"Who are ye to say what the sprite will an' won't do? They make up their own minds in such things. I only pray he doesn't come to harm for agreeing to do yer bidding." Goibhniu seemed to consider his next words carefully before speaking. "Come, I would show ye something."

Aí followed the Smithgod, every instinct screaming as in the twilight they headed down several linked paths, drawing ever closer to one of the most sacred monuments of their people, the Temple of the Fallen. As they approached, Aí's dread continued to mount, leaving his brow beaded with sweat and his jaw clenched. Where were all the other faerie kin? This path always teemed with the creatures, faeries making the air sparkle with their dust, fauns lacing the forest with haunting melodies on their reed pipes, pixies dancing beneath the brush. Nowhere else in *Tír na nÓg* was as heavily soaked with magic as the area surrounding this tribute to the only member of their race to never return from Death's lands.

The stillness of the air and the absence of the faerie kin unsettled him. As they continued on, Aí's gaze instead darted back and forth along the path, hoping to glimpse some sign that the faeries merely hid and had not fled. Did they hide from him and his ill-considered actions? Or was it the threat to the kin that had caused them to make themselves scarce? Hiding would be bad enough, but for them to have left was a dire omen. The beauty of this sanctuary was muted, a vital element missing.

He was so focused on trying to spy some sign of hope in the surrounding forest, Aí had to stop abruptly or slam into Goibhniu, who now stood solemnly before him, as still as the beautiful marble statue that rose before them. The fierce expression on the Smithgod's face was terrifying, the uncommon tears in his eyes even more so. Aí followed Goibhniu's gaze to the foot of the monument carved in the image of beloved Anu, savior of the *Daoine Maithé*, sister to the Mother Goddess. What greeted his eyes nearly brought him to his knees. On the slab of creamy marble, which never before had been bare of tribute bouquets and sweet-smelling incense and candles, lay a shrouded figure, cloaked in ebony velvet, a fabric generally reserved for grave bags, and nothing else. A single midnight-blue pillar candle burned at the head and foot of the body. Laid upon the breast was a black orchid, perfect, fresh, and fragrant, though the stem had been severed.

"Goibhniu, what do ye show me?" Aí could not speak above a strained whisper, his heart pounding in his chest and the blood draining from his face. The presence of the body shook him to his core. This place was sacred to the *Tuatha de Danaan*. He knew none of the Kin had fallen, for the bonds of blood and magic linking his kind spoke of all such things. Besides, this was not the corpse of one of the *Sidhe*; their end was cleaner than this and free of the decay faced by mortal men. But if the corpse before him was not *Sidhe*, who was it? It was hard to imagine that even one of the Kin would be brought here, but for a mortal to rest upon the monument...it felt like sacrilege. Turning begging eyes toward the Smithgod, Aí was nonetheless acutely aware of the body laid out in state before them. Who could be so revered to rest upon the altar of the Fallen?

"No mortal, Aí...one o' our own." Goibhniu's voice was low and flat, the emotion too deep to show through. "Ye see lain before ye, Murna, o' the De Danaan, late o' *Tír na mBan*. She's the first o' which we know but hasn't been the last. We haven't recovered even the bodies o' the others. All the souls o' the stricken are yet lost to us."

Aí staggered forward and fell to his knees beside the still figure. The Smithgod's words were not real to him...they had no meaning. Nothing could strike such a blow against the *Sidhe*. It was not possible. His hand trembled as he reached out, barely bringing himself to touch the velvet covering, let alone draw it from the body. But he had to see; this would not be real to him until he looked upon her lifeless face. Until he saw her, his mind would continue to protest, to deny even the words of the Smithgod. His fingers flexed, crushing the cloth and no more. He could not do it. Letting his hand fall away, he turned his pleading eyes up to Goibhniu and felt his head shake in unconscious denial.

Goibhniu stepped forward and laid a hand upon his shoulder, offering strength and comfort to Aí's troubled heart. Aí just dropped his head, leaning into the Smithgod's grip. He could not do it. He was too frightened. No matter how much he needed to see to believe, his very soul rebelled against the concept, did not want it substantiated. Only one of the kin had ever been lost to them—this was her shrine. Even millennia later, the *Tuatha de Danaan* had not recovered from the loss, every day they felt the ache of separation and dreamed of Anu's return to them. What would it do to his people were more to be lost? Terror filled him until he gripped Goibhniu's hand with crushing intensity. It would destroy them...that is what it would do.

"Aye, ye have the right o' it." Goibhniu's other hand reached out and drew aside the shroud, baring the fallen to Aí's gaze. There was no peace in Murna's face, only terror and great pain. For a moment, he thought she flinched, but given her obvious state, it must have been a trick of the light. Gouges, black with dried blood, marred her once-immortal beauty, and though her eyes were open, the light had gone out of them.

Aí feared he would be sick, rare for the *Sidhe*, though completely under-standable. And as if the horror wasn't enough, the Smithgod opened the robes she had been laid out in, baring all of her to Aí. The *Sidhe* swallowed hard, refusing to disgrace himself. He exerted iron control and did not turn away. Unable to restrain himself, Aí extended his Gift, needing desperately to know if this was death before him or some other unexplained state. Instantly, he regretted the impulse and snatched his senses away. What confronted them was like nothing he had ever experienced before: not the clean void of death, but some other sickly, tortured state. He could feel no sense of the *Sidhe* he sought, but rather something alien, twisted, writhing... He wanted nothing to do with it.

"Why are her eyes na closed?" Aí asked. Once he separated himself from the horror he was actually fascinated by what he saw; here was one of the *Sidhe*, immortal and magical, and yet dead and decaying even as they watched on.

"Every time they are closed, they open again, even when grave coins are placed over them," Goibhniu answered with a similar detachment. They both fell silent.

Aí took in every detail, from the sickly sweet scent that rose from the folds of the robe to the discoloration that seemed to be spreading beneath the abdomen—a deep, unhealthy green color whose mottled appearance made it seem as if the flesh moved—to the ancient runes slashed across her breastbone, belly, and pelvic area. "Scrios...Togail...Dioltas..." he read them out loud. Confused and disturbed, he turned a questioning eye toward Goibhniu. "Havoc, destruction, an' revenge?"

The Smithgod returned his gaze without wavering.

As Aí had discovered, that phrase had grown too familiar, gouged or burned in trees and rocks and the hides of slaughtered wildlife around all the major Raths, *Sidhe*, and sacred places, and no few of the minor ones as well. There was no doubting the message.

"The battle cry for Carmán's cursed sons." Goibhniu drew the grave cloth back over the slain. "Do ye now see why ye must bring in this last? If the *Sidhe* aren't safe, then neither are any touched by them."

In her unsettled state, Kara became turned around as she left Phoenix Park for the city proper. No matter which way she went, she could not find the hidden gateway that would return her to the safety of *Tír na nÓg*. She certainly wished now that she'd been able to lure Beag Scath into joining her on this illicit jaunt...but the sprite had had too much sense!

She spent quite some time wandering the city before she finally found herself on Amiens Street in front of the Bus Eireann bus station. It wasn't what she had been looking for, but it would do. When she and Maggie had come to Dublin the very first time, this was the bus line they had caught and the station where they disembarked. If Kara could find the right route, she could take it to Kildare and make her way back to *Tír na nÓg* from the gateway there...she hoped. Fingering her brooch nervously, she entered the station.

Inside was a stifling crush of travelers haphazardly hauling baggage and children in their wake. The noise was a comforting contrast to both the park and the *Sidhe* Court, where everything was hushed and muted.

Kara purchased her ticket and picked up a bottle of water from a newsstand before making her way to the seating area to wait, watching the people hurry past, so colorful and varied, and vibrantly alive. Just observing them made her feel more animated.

A harried matron, trailing a flock of redheaded children of varying ages behind her, brought a smile to Kara's face. It faded quickly as she noticed that the one who appeared to be the youngest trailed behind, her expression a veritable storm cloud threatening to let loose, her riot of tight, fiery curls bouncing to the tempo of war drums only the girl could hear. Cradled tenderly in her arms was a rag doll, looking more raggish than Kara supposed it was meant to.

Two children ahead of the little Mórrígán, a slightly older boy with close-cropped red hair kept casting glances back at the little one. His face was set in a taunting leer, but Kara fancied she saw a cloud of fearful doubt in his eyes. The exchange made Kara wonder exactly how adept the girl child was at exacting retribution. Did children really learn vengeance as young as that?

The thought was disheartening. And yet, before the gaggle was out of sight, she witnessed as the boy thrust his tongue at his sister, crossing his eyes in a manner Kara would have sworn was impossible. Rather than intensify the child's anger, the little girl burst into delightful giggles, the abundance of freckles on her face dancing with the fit. Peace and hope were restored as the children found their own balance. Kara felt she had learned something important this day...more important even than staying put where she belonged.

Losing sight of the family that had so engaged her, Kara turned her attention back to the crowd. Her gaze encountered something that thoroughly chilled her — sitting in the shadows across the terminal was a horrifying image of carnage: a man so severely burned you could not distinguish a scrap of clothing upon his blackened body, the carbonized tissue still smoldering, and his face locked in a rictal grimace of agony. It was as if someone had torched him in that very seat, without a single traveler noticing, except nothing save himself was burned. Even now, those passing by totally disregarded him. Couldn't they smell the stench of burnt flesh? Had the world become so insular that these people could just saunter past such a sight?

Kara didn't remember standing, but she was halfway across the seating area before she realized it. Her hands clutched the water bottle as she half began to run. It was impossible to know if the man lived, and it never occurred to her to instead look for a porter or security guard. She hurried forward until she was within a few feet of the victim... Kara stopped dead as his blood-red eyes flew open, piercing her very soul with their venom. There was hatred in those eyes. They narrowed as the man leaned forward, pulled a strip of charred skin from his arm, and sniffed it as if it were a fragrant bouquet. The arm it had come from showed the red of tormented muscle in sharp contrast to the carbonized skin surrounding it.

Her eyes widened in horror, and her stomach heaved as the ghoulish figure proceeded with exaggerated relish to chew the strip as if it were jerky. Panting for breath, she began to rock as if trying to shake herself loose from the morbid fascination that kept her eyes locked on the man and her feet anchored in place. Only as he made to rise did she turn and flee blindly. Nothing... nothing she had seen in the past week could have prepared her for this. As she reached the safety of a service corridor at the far end of the station, Kara could not resist looking back, something she wished she had never done. There, in the chair where she had thought she'd seen a live charred body, sat an ebony-haired man with a scruff of beard darkly shading his jaw. Completely normal, not a burnt inch on his body. The man's head was tilted back, his eyes closed restfully. She noticed his hands clasped and resting in his lap, one wrist encircled by an intricate tattoo of some kind. With a trembling gasp, she rubbed her hand brusquely across her eyes.

So utterly distracted, Kara did not notice the arm that snaked around from behind her until the hand had already clamped down over her mouth. As she was pulled back into the vacant corridor, the man across the station opened one blood-red eye and mockingly winked.

Chapter 9

The uproar of rattling wagon wheels and chattering children was like bird song in the morning, though the moon still hovered in the sky. The Rom had come to visit.

Agnieszka hadn't had as much company in a year as she had this week. Struggling up out of her drugged stupor, she dredged deep for the smallest bit of energy to greet her sudden guests. At this hour, her Romani friends would not expect her at the door, but it was better than lying back and courting more dreams. They came more frequently, either terrifying visions of being stalked by some unavoidable predator or heart-wrenching images of herself first round with child and then standing before an empty cradle. Each time she woke up sweat-soaked and frantic, unable to convince herself the dreams had no truth. No, now was as good a time to rise as any.

Vigorously rubbing at her face to shed the last remnants of sleep, she drew her robe about her and went to the kitchen. She didn't have nearly enough kettles to provide everyone with tea; good thing Carl, young Charles' father, had just delivered several kegs of cider. It wasn't the type of thing she had the inclination to try her own hand at, and while she puttered around her garden quite well, she didn't really know the first thing about orchards, so her arrangement with her neighbor suited her admirably; he and his sons harvested the apples from her land in exchange for producing cider enough for both households. His wife sold off any extra on market days and the earnings were split. The arrangement pleased Agnieszka, particularly as Carl made the best cider in the county, better than anything she would have managed if ever she'd tried.

Glancing out the kitchen window, she counted a mere trio of brightly painted wagons limned by the moonlight in the clearing past the cottage garden. Generally, there were at least five or six. One keg should do this time. Taking her largest pot from the cupboard and kindling the flame beneath it on the stove, she then hefted one of the barrels to her shoulder and started pouring the contents into the pot.

"Here now, little mother, you shouldn't be lifting that big old thing. Why aren't you in your bed?"

Agnieszka wasn't startled by either the sudden voice or the rough, weathered hands that carefully lifted the weight of the cask from her shoulder. This one was always first in her kitchen, eager to see what she might have put up and not too shy to help himself if she weren't around to offer. This rascal was the reason anything with a purpose was locked in the cellar—not that a paltry lock could stop him, but he did respect that it was there for a reason and would leave it be. Matter of fact, if she thought on it, the Romani man was very much like Rex; both felt they had free run of her house, when the others must stay outside; both made it quite clear that any rules they followed were because they chose to; and both cat and man would be sorely missed should they ever wander without returning. It was not easy for her to admit this, even to herself. Very few had been allowed close enough that she would be bothered by their absence—people or animals.

"Sleep? With all the lovely magpies singing outside my window? Good morning, Jacko." She only needed to tilt her cheek slightly for the peck he always gave her and made no comment on the many contradictions in him calling her both "little" and "mother," not the least uncomfortable of which being her doctor's...her *former* doctor's recent and inaccurate diagnosis.

"Surely, this isn't all for you? It is too much. I think you are lucky we happened by in time to help you drink it." Jacko's head tilted slightly, his black curls tumbling over his forehead, and his thick, dark brows arched gracefully again in what she was sure he thought was his innocent look. Batting him out of her way, she reached into the cupboard for her special blend of mulling spice. "You're all of you about awfully late this season, where are you wintering over?"

"We were to head down to Dover until the granddame traveling with us insisted we must make our way to Dublin."

"You'll have fun convincing the ferry to take you on. Why are you going as far north as that? My poor sparrows...What will you do when you find yourselves over your axels in snow?" Jacko just laughed at her exaggeration and called out the open door for a couple of strong lads to come carry the pot to the outside fire pit.

"Here now, aren't you forgetting something?" Agnieszka called crisply to the Rom, holding out the still-empty mug she had taken down for herself. Now that she was awake, there was no way she was letting that lovely cider go by without at least a little to warm her belly.

"Not at all," The glint in Jacko's eye was danger of another sort as he glanced at her bare feet, peeking from beneath the simple ruffle that edged the bottom of her long, pale-blue cotton nightdress, which hung just below the hem of her robe. With a mischievous gaze that hinted at the smoldering embers banked beneath, he closed the gap between them in one fluid step and gathered her up in his arms before she could begin to protest. For a moment, she could do no more than cling to his shoulders with her bare feet dangling high above the ground. As he cradled her, the backs of her knees burned through cotton that seemed much thinner pressed between them.

Then the indignity registered fully with her sensibilities, and she stiffened, pounding his shoulder with her balled fist, only to cling again as, shaking with laughter, he nearly dropped her halfway to the clearing...right over the tiny compost pit she'd dug on the outer edge of the garden. Only, having seen him in the past toss multiple lasses about in dance with a sure grip despite his laughter, Agnieszka was more certain than not that this was more mischief.

Holding herself ramrod stiff, she focused all of her attention on the slow burn that climbed her cheeks, making sure Jacko could see the displeasure igniting her amber glare. He only laughed harder as he set her down on a log before the communal fire, right beside an unfamiliar woman whose face was as deeply wrinkled as her own was smooth, though each of them had hair more brightly white than the sun on virgin snow. Making a great show of it, Jacko knelt before the two of them and mimicked pressing his lips to the ground before each of their feet, his mischief glittering in his gaze. With a fluid curse in her native tongue, the old woman kicked out at the seemingly irreverent Rom, though the affectionate twinkle gleaming from the dark little gems that were her eyes gave lie to her anger. When he simply laughed and turned away to collect two mugs of cider to offer to both of them, Agnieszka was puzzled; never before had she been pulled into their midst. In the past, the visits of the Rom had consisted of her making some hospitable gesture and then leaving them to the peace and privacy of their traveling camp. One or two beside Jacko would venture to visit her at the cottage, but mostly they had left her to her solitude.

Sitting there by the fire, her skin felt too tight and her robe and gown too small and thin to protect her—from what she expected to need protection, she could not say, even to herself. Looking around the circle with quick, sidelong glances, she did not recognize any of her guests, save Jacko, his sister Sveta, and her three children, with whom Jacko shared a wagon. Everyone else was a stranger, and Agnieszka could not stop herself from wondering what they really thought behind the façade of their bright smiles and rousing laughter. Always before she had been quite comfortable with all of her Romani guests, familiar or not, but this dawn she was filled with some unnamed dread.

Her stomach clenched with nerves and doubt; the warmth of the fire could not dispel the clamminess that crept along her entire body. The previously enticing sweet, spicy smell of the cider mingled with both the applewood scent of the fire and something else, something cloying that wafted on the autumn breeze, to add to Agnieszka's growing nausea. What was wrong with her? She'd never been ill in her life until the other morning, and now she was afraid it would happen again, this time before all of them. Locking her eyes on her bare toes, she realized there was no escape, not without either allowing Jacko to scoop her up again or braving the expanse of her yard in bare feet, in the dark of predawn. By sheer will alone, she brought her fractious stomach under control, but could not seem to manage the same with her irrational anxiety. Confronted with two options, equally dangerous in nature, her breath came in short, panting gasps and her fingers dug into the log with a punishing grip.

"Calm yourself, granddame, you've no need to fear," Agnieszka jumped as Jacko gently disengaged her death grip and held both hands captive in each of his own. Both his actions and his words snapped her out of her trance. Granddame? The cheek! She wasn't that much his senior. Without success, she strained to yank her hands from his grip. No longer lost in the depths of phobic fear, her head whipped up, and she lanced him with a penetrating glare only to find that though he locked her hands tight in his grasp, it was to the ancient woman beside her that he spoke. Flushed and confused, Agnieszka found herself limp and exhausted by the emotionally charged atmosphere that had superseded the peace of her private meadow.

"You're safe here, Rose, and well on your way to where you're driven to go." Jacko's soothing voice and the cool comfort of his hands calmed Agnieszka's own fears, even if she could not tell what effect they had on the woman to whom he actually spoke. As if she had said so out loud, he gave her fingers a light squeeze, and she suddenly found herself looking into the endless depth of his dark sable eyes. She looked away, flustered, and felt lances of pain run up her arms as her hands attempted to flutter. Jacko immediately loosed his hold. Gasping, she looked down. Her hands lay like bloody trophies across his callused palms, her nails torn and raised with remnants of bark and wicked lengths of splinter still wedged beneath.

She whipped her hands behind her back and looked in horror at the newly torn surface of the log on which she sat. What had she done? Feeling as if everyone watched her, she longed for her lost solitude; instead, she sat stiffly and proud, willing herself away, though she only succeeded in her mind.

An anguished moan rose, too deep to have come from her throat. Gradually soft, soothing murmurs replaced it, filtering through her distance, speaking to her heart. "No, little mother, do not hide. You've nothing to fear from the Rom." He smoothed her hair back over her ear and tried to lift her chin. "I'm sorry, love, I only meant to make you feel welcome, to thank you for your years of hospitality, with precious little you would accept in return. Oh, your poor hands!"

Agnieszka felt him draw them forward and could not bring herself to resist. The cooling caress of his powerful hands over her abused fingertips almost seemed to ease their burning. She heard him call out to someone in his fluid Romani tongue and couldn't help but wonder what he said, knowing that whatever it was, it wouldn't have been nearly so musical in English. Her heartbeat began to slow its frantic pace as Jacko kept up a steady murmur, most of which she couldn't understand, though that scarcely mattered.

"Okay, little mother, I'm going to ice down your hands so Granddame Rose can tend to them. You must keep them in the cold, okay?"

Still somewhat dazed, she merely nodded, though she couldn't help but gasp at the frigid chill, which made her all of a sudden conscious of how heated his touch had grown. Putting the thought from her mind, she sat there with her fingers immersed, losing herself in the growing numbness.

"Enough! You, girl, fetch my satchel." Agnieszka jumped at the brusqueness of the heavily accented voice, a mingling of Jacko's soft lilt and something else, something familiar, yet foreign…New York…the old woman sounded as if she'd spent some time in New York. "Hurry up!" This time Agnieszka nearly stood, though she hadn't the faintest idea of where to find the asked-for satchel. A gnarled hand that bore the remnants of crisp green scent from crushing herbs settled on her shoulder, pinning her in place. "And where are you going? You just sit there and wait for the child to fetch it." The woman's tone was as harsh as her voice, and Agnieszka got the feeling it wasn't all the grouchiness of age; something disturbed this woman, something to do with Wicklow Cottage.

There was a thud, and a rumbling chirp rose from beside Agniezka on the tattered log. The chill of a moist nose pressed against her cheek distracted her from her thoughts. The old woman gasped, but her grip on Agnieszka's shoulder also relaxed considerably.

"Well then, that's a right little guardian you have there." Granddame Rose sounded nearly respectful. Agnieszka was not in the least surprised when Rex answered the Rom with a solemn, almost condescending *yeow* as he watched closely everything she did to his mistress.

"Aye, I know it's no joke," Rose answered as solemnly. "I can feel them; they grow bold despite you…even despite all of us."

Was the woman daft? She spoke to Rex as if he were human, and the way they both looked at the darkness that still lingered beneath the boughs of Agnieszka's orchard was quite unsettling.

"Here comes your satchel, Granddame." Jacko broke the tension with his mundane reminder, and Agnieszka allowed her eyes to wander as the woman finished tending to her tattered hands, slathering them with an ointment that smelled of freshly bruised herbs, wrapping the worst fingertips in a few passes of gauze. All the while, the woman muttered and cast suspicious looks about Agnieszka's land.

What did the Rom see when she looked out on this acreage? Agnieszka herself had been uneasy of late, though she had thought it only a lack of rest caused by her plague of recent dreams. But no, she had to admit to herself how edgy she'd grown recently just walking the grounds or riding her bike to the village. It was as if she were always watched. A fleeting impression of glowering red eyes flashed in her thoughts and was gone before she could remember where she'd seen them. And now, with the woman putting ideas in her head, Agnieszka looked for the flicker of furtive movement she suspected was there all along, just teasingly on the edge of her sight. Was she going mad? Was this senility?

"You have quite a grip there." Agnieszka gave a shuddering breath as Jacko's words penetrated her thoughts. She looked down and found he'd been holding her hand and that the others had retired to their wagons. She also noticed his fingertips had turned a plumy purple.

"Oh! My goodness! I am so terribly sorry; I don't know what's wrong with me." She tried to release his hand, but he would allow her to do no more than loosen her grip, tightening his own when she tried to pull away.

"Little mother…Agnieszka, what frightens you?" There was genuine concern in his eyes, and something else, something that would have been one of her first answers to his question if only she could put a name to it.

"Don't be silly, I've just not been myself lately, I've been a little unwell."

Jacko's face paled, and his jaw tightened until it twitched. He shook his head. "No, you are never sick; you are healthier than I am. It is something else…you worry too much, you keep too much to yourself…"

Agnieszka had to laugh at the irony of one of the Rom accusing anyone of keeping too much to themselves. She patted his hand as she would young Charles and was relieved that some of his concern drained away. The look in his eyes instead grew more intent, and he went completely still until she had to look away and in doing so, noticed her battered hand again rested on his. Self-consciously, she drew it back to her lap and glanced over at her cottage. Why had she left her bed? She almost believed herself when she thought that even nightmares would be easier to face than how her waking life tumbled out of her control.

"Come, I'll take you back in." Before she could protest that she had two perfectly good feet to carry her, he scooped her up again. The jolt was instantaneous and shocking as if something passed between them. Agnieszka was torn between the fear she would be dropped and the fear something was wrong with Jacko. He might be fifteen or twenty years her junior—give or take—and healthy as someone as much *his* junior besides, but that did not rule out a heart attack or stroke if he were susceptible. Steadying herself in his arms, she twisted around for a better view of his face. His cheeks were flushed, and his eyes bright, but not glassy. He also seemed to have a little difficulty breathing. She struggled to drop her legs to the ground, needing, of a sudden, to stand clear and on her own feet, but Jacko only clutched her closer, his eyes for a moment fearful.

"What is wrong with you? Put me down, you…young pup, now."

Jacko ignored her, instead walking briskly toward the house, all the while casting predatory glares into the surrounding fog that had crept in with the dawn. Cursing beneath his breath at the way the landscape of hedges and saplings and burgeoning autumn gardens prevented him from shooting straight across the distance to the back door. He wended his way around the obstacles in a state of haste that only agitated Agnieszka's already jangled nerves.

"I said, put... me... down!" She punctuated the last three words with a slap of his shoulder, each one a little more forceful as he continued to disregard her. "I most certainly know the way to the cottage across my own field and gardens. Put me down or you are never welcome in my kitchen again!" Her growl was laced with honest threat; he was beginning to frighten her, and she would have no one around her she did not trust implicitly. Struggling with more determination only caused her pain as his arms locked down like steel bands.

Agnieszka's heart nearly broke. How many times had they sat at her kitchen table, talking until all hours? Why did he betray her now? What was there to gain from it that she didn't already give freely in friendship? Food, shelter, even money had passed between herself and his Clan, the very wagon he drove for his sister only traveled the roads by virtue of the axel that she had helped pay to repair—in exchange for some handiwork, of course. Searching his face for some clue, she quickly looked away from the focused expression transforming him from the delightful rogue she had allowed herself to care for.

As she cast her eyes down that she noticed Rex moving before them, growling and spitting not at Jacko, but out into the foggy haze. Rex, of whom she did not entertain even one doubt, acted more the advance guard for her abductor when she would have expected him to attack the man in her defense. With sudden realization, she stopped her struggling and would almost swear the Rom sighed gratefully through his clenched teeth. Whatever relief he felt did not, however, translate into his hostile expression. Even more frightened by this unknown danger, Agnieszka pressed closer to her friend's chest, feeling suddenly very small...small and cared for as she'd never been before. Softening for the briefest of moments, Jacko pressed his cheek against her lowered head. Pushing through her kitchen door, he made sure Rex was clear before he kicked it closed behind him and leaned hard against it. She could only suppose this was to make sure the lock had taken.

This was insane. Never before had she been toted around like a rag doll, particularly in her own house; in fact, she nearly laughed out loud as she realized that twice in one day she'd been carried over the threshold and she wasn't even a bride! The amusement did not last long as she found herself carted through the house and laid down upon her bed. Cared-for rogue or not, she did not think much of his marching into her bedroom as if he belonged there. She started to sit up in protest only to be pushed gently back. Jacko drew the eiderdown up over her then Jacko moved to peer out her window. He seemed to search the twilight intently before securing the shutters and locking the window down. He then drew a copper penny from his pocket and placed it on the sill. The entire situation was so absurd and unsettling that Agnieszka was too startled to protest when he perched on the edge of her bed and pulled more change from his pocket.

"Hold tight to this and don't leave this room until I come back," he said as he pressed another penny in her hand. "I'll not be long."

Not one to be ordered about in her own home, Agnieszka crept from beneath the comforter as soon as he'd walked out of her room, leaving the door open wide behind him. How curious that he would make such a show of locking the windows and then not close this. Positioning herself just inside the entrance, she watched him go from room to room, repeating the ritual he'd begun in her room: secure the shutters, lock the window, and place the penny. Always the door was left open. His actions mesmerized her until she forgot to duck back when he turned around at the last room. Agnieszka flinched as he stalked forward, no longer knowing what to expect from her old friend. He surprised her yet again as he gripped her shoulders roughly and pulled her into a desperate hug.

"I don't like you here alone, not now...not ever, to be truthful, but definitely not now."

The ghost of a sensation drifted across her memory as she stood there wrapped in Jacko's arms. Well, perhaps ghost was not the right term...phantom, poltergeist, wraith...those were better words for the feelings that were over four decades old. Stepping back out of his embrace, she patted his cheek with calculated care, again mimicking a gesture she would have used with young Charles, an old auntie responding to a young lad in a much more appropriate way. "You're sweet to worry, but there's no need. Hardly anyone ever comes this way, and if anything happens, I just call Carlton and his lot."

"This is supposed to reassure me?" He reached out and claimed the hand still holding the penny he'd pressed on her earlier. The grip he exerted was almost painful as he clenched her hand around it once more, but his eyes were earnest. "You must come with us to Dublin."

"Dublin? Must?" Agnieszka gave an incredulous look, shocked and outraged by his presumption. "You are deciding for me that I must go to Dublin? In one of your wagons? I think not!"

"Please. You need more protection than your little friend..."

"I never have before, and precious little has changed since the last you were here, nothing more than that little friend, in fact." Agnieszka drew her hand away and made a show of tucking the penny in the pocket of her robe.

That done, with both hands freed she pushed him toward the kitchen and out the back door. "Good night, Jacko. See you in the morn...afternoon."

Perhaps it was the excitement-induced exhaustion. Perhaps it was the "protective" pennies. Whatever the cause, Agnieszka did not wake that afternoon. No, she slept peacefully through to evening. Pulling herself from the warmth of the covers and slipping immediately into her robe, she then rummaged around in the bottom of the wardrobe for the slippers she never normally troubled with. Given Jacko's recent and erratic behavior she figured perhaps she would put up with the unfamiliar sensation in favor of not getting caught out again with nothing to protect her feet. It was silly, but just the mere thought of him made her flush warmly; however inappropriate, the attention was flattering, and she could not help but look forward to seeing him. Her hand went to the pocket of her robe. Perhaps she would have the penny pierced for a chain. The thought really made her blush, but it was innocent enough, wasn't it?

Anyway, she needn't have bothered with the slippers; wandering out to the kitchen for a bit of tea, she found only the kettle and a teacup waiting for just a bit of heat. Generally, when they were visiting, one or two of the Rom were perched here enjoying the rare comforts of a kitchen that did not sway, such as chairs you could move and running water, at least for those who traveled in traditional wagons, without the conveniences found in the more modern caravans. Someone had been here, for the cider pot was clean and up-ended over the drain, but they had already gone. Not even Rex was about. Moving to the back door, she peeked through the glazed glass, expecting to see the glow of the Rom' fire. Instead, there was only an empty clearing.

Her restored peace was hollow and empty, an ache in her breast she would not have anticipated. Less than a day had passed since she had wished for her solitude back, but to receive it in such an abrupt manner. They had not even waited to say farewell. And what about Jacko? So much for not wanting her here alone! He hadn't even left a note. Sighing deeply and shrugging off her thoughts, she told herself it did not matter; these were Rom to come and go at will, fickle and carefree.

The image of Granddame Rose's face drifted past Agnieszka's thoughts in dispute. There had been cares there, in fact, that was most likely why they'd gone. Something had driven the woman, plagued her. It was clear she'd prodded them to proceed with haste, or so Agnieszka tried to tell herself, but her gaze went dim and distant, and a familiar ache radiated through her chest as she closed off her heart.

Absently replacing the teacup in the cupboard, she went to the medicine chest for her faithful prescription before petulantly raising her window sash, throwing wide the shutters, and tucking herself back into bed, all thoughts of Rom and pennies walled away.

Caught in the grips of medicated sleep, Agnieszka thrashed and moaned, tears streaming down her cheek to soak her pillow. An intense thunderstorm rattled the windows and lightning cast odd shadows across her walls, aided by the wildly thrashing tree branches just outside. Agnieszka continued to shake and, without waking, unconsciously slipped her hand beneath her pillow, pulling forth something white and silky. She drew it close to her huddled chest. Though her tears still flowed, her sleep grew less troubled, and she drifted deeper into one of those dreams she never remembered.

Maybe it was the sudden chill that woke her or the sound of broken sobs muffled against her chest. Whichever it was, Agnieszka opened her eyes and felt terror take her as she saw only vague, misty shapes and the ghosts of color. She wanted to call out to her love...to call his name and comfort him for there was no doubt that the sobs were his, but she did not yet know his name, and her body was frozen in the grips of her own panic.

What could be the matter? Trying to reach for him, to return the solace he had given her, she was alarmed when her arms would not respond. Lying there in the mossy depression they had formed, she was aware of her surroundings, but she couldn't help noticing that it all seemed far, far away. Though her love's hands must have held her in a death grip, it was as if he barely touched her, and his sobs, no longer muffled against her, had not grown any louder.

What was going on? Her very being strained to resurface from a vantage point somewhere deep inside her. Instead, her body betrayed her, remaining limp and unresponsive as if her life had fled, and her love mourned her.

Could that be so? Had she finally found happiness and not been strong enough to survive the encounter? Had something happened to her as they slept? Rebelling against the thought, she fought the paralysis until the sounds around her came clearer to her ears.

"Don't torture yerself so." The deep, rumbling voice was gentle and filled with regret. It sent Agnieszka further into a panic. Who was this strange man, and what was he doing here? What was wrong with her that she could not move to cover herself? And why was her vision clouded over with a silvery mist? She listened intently as the voice continued to murmur, trying to make some sense of this nightmare. "Ye have to leave her, leanbh, *'tis the only way."*

"Why, Goibhniu? Why?!" The anguish in her love's voice warmed her, giving her the strength to focus her will and fight for movement. Her heart cried out to him, 'I am here, I am well! Do not leave me, my love. We are to live here forever...on berries and kisses!'

Trying to reach for him, to comfort him, she felt the smallest thrill of victory as her finger slowly and lightly brushed the smoothness of his stomach, not even caring that the sensation felt so distant it was as soft as if a butterfly's wing flapped against her hand. She could hear him groan and imagined he clutched her tighter. She prayed for the strength to hold him back. Maybe it was her imagination, but she thought she felt more of his gentle kisses showered over her face.

"Cian, Stop!" The strange voice grew stern as if calling a recalcitrant child to task. "Ye couldn't know she is the Cosaint, but she is the hope o' yer people an' ye cannot have her for yer own. She must remain hidden away, unaware o' what she is, lest her nature be betrayed to our enemies."

His name was Cian! She clung to the knowledge desperately. But what was a Cosaint?

"Hide someone else!" Her lover's voice grew fierce, even muted as it was by whatever cocooned her. "I love her, I can't leave."

"Ye must, my child. There is no babe to take her place." The voice was thick with regret, but unswerving.

"But my heart is hers — I'll die without her." The turmoil in his voice rang through her. She gripped it like an anchor, trying to pull herself closer to complete awareness.

"Will ye, then?" The words were quite neutral, but to Agnieszka the stranger seemed skeptical. They were met with a stillness that made her frantic.

The silence grew so solid that she feared she had failed, slipping further into oblivion in her efforts to climb out. But then she heard him, speaking no louder than a whisper, so low she felt more than heard what he said.

"Could ye…could ye…" her love seemed to struggle with the words as if in uttering them, he risked losing the hope they represented. "Could ye make me the same as her, then?"

What did he mean by the same as her? But the answer did not matter because in her heart she knew he asked so that he could remain with her. She prayed with all her being that the answer would be yes.

"Oh, leanbh…" The compassion of the words pierced straight through Agnieszka's soul, and her hope flowed out through the wound. "Would that I could grant yer heart's desire, but the magic that veils her won't work but on a soul that has never been recorded on the Great Wall. Ye ken yer own pattern is there in the spiral."

"Then my pattern won't be there for long, as I cannot live knowing she's forever lost to me." The fierceness of her lover's words left Agnieszka aching, frantic to call out and deny what he implied. She'd rather herself dead and him living on without her than to think of him taking his own life.

"Aye, lad, with that I must agree," The man answered remorsefully, "for neither o' ye can be allowed to remember…the Cosaint must be protected."

"Och! Goibhniu, No!" her love wailed. "Ye' can' t mean it! Please, do not do it!"

No! No! Agnieszka echoed his thoughts. She could not bear the idea that they would not even be allowed the sanctuary of their memories. How could they be taken from them? Desperately she wrapped her heart around the gift of love she had received that day, willing the memory to root deep enough that some fragment would remain, no matter what. Triumphant, she could feel the tiniest kernel of memory take root, hidden deep within her heart. It wasn't much, but she would take it.

Trying to clutch him to her, in her despair she only felt him slipping away as the mists claimed her, leaving her only the echo of his agonized roar, the fading images of blissful moments in a moss-covered grotto, and a feeling of abandonment with which she was already so familiar.

Chapter 10

THE AIR SMELLED OF MILDEW AND EARTH AND ROTTING BITS OF PLANT MATTER when Kara came to. She was strapped face up over something thick and solid, her arms dangling down and cuffed to something else that rang like metal on metal when she jangled her wrists, her legs rope-bound separately at the ankles with her feet flat on the floor. The way she was tied forced her thighs uncomfortably wide. The muscles across her stomach and chest ached with the strain the position put on her, and her shoulders burned. By the feel of the rough slats under her back, she was on top of a steel-banded packing crate.

Surprisingly, she was still fully clothed, though her jacket and shoes were gone. There wasn't even a blindfold, though the omission scarcely mattered since wherever she'd been taken was as dark as the grave, and there were no sounds to pinpoint her whereabouts, only the steady drip-drip of leaky pipes. She was also startled to find she was not gagged.

She tested her restraints half-heartedly, more out of a sense of obligation than with any hope that they would miraculously give. If she didn't depend on her hands for her livelihood there was a chance she might work her way free on one side; she found she could partially slip her right thumb past the burning cold metal of the handcuffs before it would go no further, but what good would it do her? The way she was secured, she'd never reach the other hand or even her feet to undo them. It might allow her to strike out at whoever had taken her, but she would still be bound and at their mercy...not that they had any, clearly.

Her back threatened to cramp something horrible, arched as it was by her awkward position, but other than that and the discomforts caused by her bindings, she was as yet unharmed. She was afraid that would not mean much if she didn't get free. If they left her in this position too long, she would not be able to walk for the pain.

Kara could not tell if she still wore Maggie's brooch. If she did, the spell would alert the *Sidhe* something was wrong. Kara couldn't depend on that, though. Gathering her mental composure, she tried the far-calling spell Maggie had taught her, only to find that something imprisoned her mind as surely as her bonds trapped her body. The moment she tried the spell, something clamped down tight on her thoughts and scattered her concentration.

Lying restrained in the dark, hope fled. The longer Kara lay there, the more silent tears streamed from the corner of her eyes and down into her hair, leaving stinging tracks of salt-tightened skin in their wake. What was one more misery? Trivial, given her many others. Suddenly she felt very, very cold. Shivers traveled down the length of her, leaving her teeth chattering despite the warm air of her prison and sending needles of pain through limbs already beginning to fall asleep. Even living in New York she had never felt threatened or unsafe. Now her sense of security had collapsed around her.

A blaze of light overhead interrupted her thoughts. She flinched away, squinting as a figure advanced from the shadows, looking like an angel in all its glory. Kara could not distinguish the features from where she lay, but she prayed she had been found by one of the *Sidhe*.

Kara's heart plummeted as a familiar face walked out of the light. No! It wasn't possible! Why hadn't Maggie's protections worked? She had trusted them to keep her safe. Tony came closer, looking as if he'd never been left with a broken mind on a rooftop in America.

"Welcome back, Kara." His voice was cold, and though it was as she remembered it, there was something different too, something that felt both ancient and malevolent. "It's time for us to get to know each other better, though I might untie you later just for kicks. I didn't bother with a gag," and here he bent to whisper the last directly in her ear, "because I *want* to hear you scream."

Tremors ran down her spine, and her throat tightened. Even though she rebelled against giving him what he wanted, a moan forced its way past her lips. Straining against the cuffs around her wrists and the ropes around her ankles, she used every bit of her will to wish them gone.

Tony laughed a nasty laugh as he stepped back to get a better view of her desperate efforts. She glared at him and made no comment as her thoughts unconsciously filled with music. A familiar feeling came over her, and she remembered how she had vanquished Lucien. Making herself breathe deeply, she relaxed the restriction of her throat, allowing instinct to take over. She gathered in the energy as quickly as it flowed to her. It had worked against Lucien; she would see how Tony liked a deluge of unlimited power. After all, it was what he was after, wasn't it?

"Ah, ah, ah...I don't think so, my dear." Kara's head throbbed to the tempo of his laughter, and a piercing pain lanced through the area just behind her eyes as he flooded her with power her faster than she could tame it. "You'll notice I learned that trick the last time we met."

She screamed, physically and mentally going limp. Tony only laughed harder. Though it frustrated her to lose her grip on the only kind of power she had right now, Kara willed the energy to flow from her, down her limbs and harmlessly into the ground before it burned her out as it had Tony's former master, Lucien.

That is when what Tony said hit her. The last time? Though she had only learned his name after, she had seen for herself at the battle of Yesterday's Dreams that Tony had been reduced to a near-mindless state by the time she had climbed to the rooftop to take out Lucien. Miach had said he would likely recover, but not for quite some time. How could Tony have learned anything? For that matter, how could he even be here only days later, hale and whole?

Wide-eyed, she watched as he slanted even closer, his lean, powerful muscles rippling like a panther's as he dipped low enough to sniff at her appreciatively as if she were an apple pie fresh from the oven. It sickened her. She could smell the stench of her own fear, and there was no doubt in her mind that that was the aroma he savored now.

Tony's eyes closed blissfully only to snap open mere inches from her own. Kara blinked, then thought she must be hallucinating. Over the past week, she had come eye to eye with both Tony and Lucien, and though there was no doubt it was Tony suspended above her, his eyes were ice-blue, like Lucien's.

Tony's eyes were deep brown.

She tried to suppress her terror, but it grew beyond anything that she could contain. Lucien was gone! She knew Lucien was gone because his empty, blank face still haunted her. As she shook her head in denial, Tony's hand snapped forward and closed painfully around her hair. With a sharp jerk, he locked her head in place. Parodying a lover's caress, he rubbed his cheek against her own, nuzzling her neck and raining kisses upon her unwilling person before biting down full force upon her earlobe. He groaned suggestively as he released his hold, breaking the skin but not rending the flesh.

His mouth remained right against her abused ear and with a voice as hard as steel and as insidious as a serpent's hiss, he whispered, "My wishes...my way...and if you are fortunate, you will come to appreciate my attentions... eventually. For mark this, I shall never let you go, not even into death, my little treasure. Your power and pain will feed me for millennia."

Kara couldn't help notice that every trace of Brooklyn accent was missing from Tony's speech. She lost that thought, as Tony's hands began roaming freely over her, alternating between gentle and hurtful without warning. Kara cringed and prayed for this to be a dream...for deliverance...for oblivion. She could not pull away, she could not move or fight. Beyond the point of caring if she gave him exactly what he sought, Kara whimpered uncontrollably as tears flowed unchecked down her face. She did not have the strength to be strong in the face of such hopelessness. Evading Tony's look of perverse pleasure, she noticed a leather thong around his neck, laced through a bur-nished copper disk. The adornment was so out of place, for a moment, it held her attention to the exclusion of all else. But not for long...as Tony stepped back, she held her breath, still staring single-mindedly at the charm, trying not to think of what came next.

Her awareness took on a surreal detachment as if she were looking at the situation from a distance, or through a curtain of water. The mingled sounds of her suffering and his pleasure grew muted. Kara lay there numb and unresponsive as her spirit withdrew into itself, attempting to find sanctuary in oblivion. She even watched calmly as Tony drew a knife from somewhere off to the side, beyond her field of vision. It was a long, thin, wicked-looking knife gleaming along its edge of cold steel.

She screamed as the point bit just below the collar of her top and straight into the thin flesh covering her breastbone before the knife ripped down the length of her cotton shirt and through her delicate bra. The look on Tony's face was obscene as, with his other hand, he gripped the remaining cloth and completed the upward cut that left her bloodied chest bare. She hissed with the pain and instinctively crushed herself against the crate as if will alone would force her past it and away from the madman.

"No! Please, no!" Kara begged to no avail. No longer caring about her future in music so long as she had a future that did not involve more torture, she worked her thumb into a gap in the slats of her crate and left it there.

As she waited, she slowly gathered back some of the magic that had drained away from her earlier. She might not be able to direct it toward what she wanted to do, but perhaps it would lend some strength to her efforts. Meanwhile, in desperation, she tried yet again to make the far-calling spell work, but it was as if there was a wall in the way...a thick, soundproof wall.

Her concentration shattered as Tony put aside the knife somewhere close to the right of her and reached out to fondle her bare breast, bruising it as he bent his head to lick away the trail of blood that followed the curve of her rib. Kara stared in horrified confusion as he lifted his eyes to hers and smiled, his teeth both brilliantly white and predatory. He reminded her of a wolf...no, worse...a feral dog.

Her mind rebelled against what she saw coming, blinding her eyes and fighting to bring her away into the darkness, but no, this was her only chance, she could not let it slip away or he would only have the opportunity to wreak worse atrocities upon her. Though her eyes remained unseeing, she kept her wits about her long enough to twist her hand forcefully against her bonds, snapping the thumb wedged between the slats at its very base. The agony swept over her just as Tony bit down hard upon her flesh, rearing back abruptly to tear it free.

"Auuugh!" The scream erupted from Kara's throat, and her back arched even further than it already was in protest. As Tony bent over her once more to press his bloody lips to hers, Kara's freed hand flew up and wrapped itself around the copper charm dangling around his neck. Fiercely intent, she barely noticed the flood of warmth that engulfed her hand as she did so, as if a circuit had been completed and energy flowed freely between her and the charm. Gratefully adding it to her own waning strength, she twisted the thong tighter. Stars danced before her own as her broken thumb protested the action. She ignored it and held on with tenacious determination.

Rather than collapse unconscious as she'd hoped he would, Tony struggled for a moment to pull the pendant from her grasp and then went completely stiff, chest heaving with his attempts to breathe. He paled. As the blood drained from his face, along with the anger and malevolence in his gaze, his blue eyes deepen into brown.

Suddenly Tony looked down at her in befuddled horror as he took in the scene before him. He choked and spat out her flesh.

"What da hell..." Tony's Brooklyn accent was back thicker than ever. He looked worse than stunned, and his movements were jerky and uncoordinated, as if he had overdosed on muscle relaxants, or had taken a severe blow to the head. If not for her grip on the pendant, he would have back-pedalled, looking desperate to put distance between them.

What was this?! The man who had abused her so viciously just moments before transformed completely as if he were a different person with the same face. He was still the enemy, but the Tony she'd encountered in New York had not been nearly as brutal and cruel as the one she'd encountered here in Ireland. And somehow the Ireland one was now gone... It was a trick! Weary beyond bearing, Kara shook with outraged sobs that sent shafts of intense pain shooting through her mutilated chest. She did not know where she found the strength, but with new resolve, she gave a more forceful twist, tightening the thong around his throat. Despite the pain, she continued to fight even as this other Tony reached for her hand, attempting to pry away her fingers before unconsciousness could take him.

"Untie me!" she growled hoarsely. "Untie me, or I get free, you will have to run from me your entire life!"

He just stared at her, faint tremors running through him as he struggled harder to release her grip. It was as if he didn't even understand her words. Well, if he wanted her to try it the hard way, fine. She redoubled her efforts to tighten the thong, the veins on her hand rising with the effort. There wasn't much time, her strength was giving out, but if she could get him to pass out first before her own pain took her, she might be able to reach the knife. The blade was long enough that it could be able to saw through the binding on her right leg if she did it while Tony was still out, and then... Her gorge threatened to rise at the thought—whether at the thought of what had been done with the knife, or the thought of what she would do with it, she could not say.

It felt like staring through a door at freedom and having someone hold you back just enough that you could feel the cool, liberating breeze on your face, but were denied that one final step that would allow you to claim it. Terrified in every aspect of her being, she twisted the thong with all her might and cried out to the very universe.

It was not enough.

As her numbing fingers lost their hold, she swore that somehow, even if not today, she would gain her freedom — and Tony's lifeless body would cushion her feet along the way.

The pendant pulled away from her failing grasp, and a veil once again dropped over Tony's features. No longer did he tremble or sway; no longer was there doubt in his gaze. In an instant, the bewilderment was gone, and the sadistic leer restored, the cruelty intensified. Her mind cowered, hiding from what took place, from the hatred and evil telegraphed so openly in those once again ice-blue eyes, from the violent intent written across that hardened face. Again she experienced a fractured vision of two separate Tonys: one cold and sadistic and evil with a capital E, and the other, well...not quite that bad. It made no sense to her. There was no difference. Either way, she was still captive.

But that didn't mean she gave up. Kara flung her hand as far to her right as she could, desperately reaching for the knife he'd set down. And yet again, cruel Fate baited her; as her questing fingers came down directly on the handle, she found no amount of determination would close her damaged hand around the hilt.

In a matter of seconds, Tony kicked the empty crate on which the blade rested out of her reach. The knife clattered across the floor with the force of his blow. If she weren't so sure that he intended to prolong her suffering indefinitely, she would fear for her life right now. Ironically it occurred to her that she actually had cause to be thankful for his brutality. The more he delighted in hurting her, the more time she gained to think of something. No matter the pain she experienced, as long as she lived, there was the chance of rescue. She could not allow herself to forget that.

And still, despair settled over her, and her eyes squeezed shut. It wasn't that she didn't care what would happen to her now, but she didn't think she had the courage to watch it coming. Better to drift away on that dark cloud she had abandoned in her effort to get free, better to lose herself in oblivion than to wait open-eyed for the horror destined for her.

"Don't ever think you can hide from me. Since you're impatient enough to do the damage yourself, I wouldn't think of letting you be deprived now."

The only warning she had was his voice by her damaged hand. She screamed again as a vise-like grip grabbed that hand and twisted the arm back down to where it had been previously secured. Despite his threat, she nearly passed out anyway as he ensured the handcuff had no give at all. He made it so tight, in fact, the metal cut into her flesh.

God, she ached. Every nerve was on fire from strain or from pain until it all blended into one eternal torment. What more could he really do to her? Instantly she regretted the thought as cold metal brushed her ankle and her ears filled with the sound of humming rising and falling to the rasping clip of a pair of scissors making their way steadily through thick denim. The brush of air on naked flesh already chilled her right leg.

Though she did not recall stopping in the first place, Kara once again began to sob, her tortured throat adding to the misery that consumed her. Bad enough, he would soon have his way, but as he snipped up one in-seam and down the other, he had no vested interest in keeping the sharp points from periodically piercing or clipping her flesh. Each time they did, he cooed at her and offered comfort. What cold comfort that was. Finally, she felt the fabric fall away, leaving her completely bare before his lecherous eyes.

Nothing happened.

Minutes passed in complete silence with only a warm current of air caressing her mutilated body, and still, nothing happened. Dazed, she struggled to lift her head and opened her eyes, hoping to find it all a dream. Instead, she saw him poised above her, only the pendant remained around his neck, and she knew it was not mercy that stayed him but a desire to make her suffer to the fullest, forcing her to witness her own violation. Even knowing that was what he was waiting for, she could not close her eyes against him; she was transfixed and mesmerized by the sight as if he were a mantled and swaying cobra preparing to strike.

Clustered in what Patrick was told was Goibhniu's private audience chamber, the *Sidhe Fianna* made preparations to venture forth. He fumed as he watched them. Never in his life had he felt so whole, so healthy, and so ready to stand against any who would threaten his family, yet they thought to deny him, to leave him behind. Not bloody likely!

Noting Maggie McCormick off in a corner with the massive Goibhniu, he made his way over to confront them. "Who the hell are ye to tell me I can't help find my daughter?"

The room fell utterly silent as his challenge hung heavy in the air. All eyes save Maggie's were trained on the Smithgod; hers met Patrick's, filled with compassion and regret.

"Are ye so anxious to return to the state in which ye were brought to me, then?" Goibhniu asked.

Patrick was taken back by the Smithgod's mild, curious tone. Well, fine, if Goibhniu didn't care enough to be angry, Patrick could manage enough for both of them. He was angry at life, angry about uncertainty and danger and death. And Kara...he was angry with Kara for being the reason he was again faced with the potential for all three...angry with her for not having sense enough to stay safe...angry with her...angry for her!

"Oh, an' I suppose ye expect me to wait here for yer precious *Fianna* to bring her back to me...like that poor soul carried in today? I'll not do it!" His chin jutted forward, and his jaw set firm.

"I expect ye to have sense...sense enough to stay safe," Goibhniu answered him evenly, echoing the words of Patrick's private thoughts. Stepping forward as he said it, the Smithgod pointed toward a pile of cushions in another corner of the room. "Do ye not see the lass sitting there? Do ye not see the strain o' her face? She's looking for yer Kara. Her name is Brid. She's the most gifted Seer o' the *Tuatha de Danaan* an' there's sweat on her brow.

"Did ye know that the one ye call Maggie has a link with yer daughter an' even she cannot sense her?"

Patrick looked over in confusion. Maggie, why would she have a link with his daughter? And what did that have to do with his joining the search? He didn't care what they said...they couldn't keep him here. He would bring back his daughter.

Even as he thought it, two massive hands reached down to grip his shoulders, giving them a little shake, then letting go. By no means, a short man, Patrick looked up, supprised at the considerable distance before meeting Goibhniu's unrelenting gaze.

"Patrick, there is something out there with the power to block the *Sidhe*, something strong enough to not only stop us from knowing where Kara is, but powerful enough to block from our knowledge the dying o' one o' our own, nay...worse, many o' our own. None...*None* we are familiar with can do that, which means we don't know what else they are capable o' bringing against us.

"Now, both Kara an' yerself are dear to us, an' we won't stop until we bring her home, but we can't have the two o' ye at risk. If ye won't listen to reason, then at least consider yer wife...would ye risk her losing ye both?"

Patrick swayed off-balance, body and soul. Shaking his head and breathing deep, he could do nothing but force down his pride...and his fear...and acknowledge the sense he had earlier refused to see. He would stay behind, waiting for his precious Kara when she returned.

He had but a moment to resolve the matter in his heart when he looked toward Maggie and noticed all color drain from her face. With one hand, she clutched her chest, and with the other, she gripped the pillar beside her, struggling to remain standing. Patrick couldn't help but remember Goibhniu's words...Maggie and Kara shared a link... Before he could move to help her, a cry rose in the corner of the chamber.

"Ayyy!"

Patrick, as well as everyone else, spun around. "Ayyy!" the *Sidhe* woman keened again. "Only a moment, but I've found her." Patrick's heart nearly stopped at the anguish in her voice, and he almost cried out himself. His daughter...his lovely daughter; was she already lost to them, then? Darting a desperate look back at Maggie, he nearly wept to see her restored, though tension lingered about her eyes that spoke of pain. His attention whipped back to where Goibhniu stood beside the Seer. Patrick barely comprehended as she continued to speak.

"You must fly to her, *Fianna*, fly fast. I've lost the vision, but I have not lost the path to where she's held. Ayyy! Save her, save her!" The Seer's face drained of color and she collapsed upon her cushions. Immediately, Goibhniu moved to her side, gathering his faithful servant into his arm.

"Patrick, I'll be needing yer help, if ye'd be so kind." The Smithgod motioned to the pitcher across the room, and Patrick rushed to fetch it. As he brought it over, he heard Goibhniu address the others. "Go an' deliver our child back to the safety o' Home." The Smithgod reached up to slip off the torc around his throat and beckoned Maggie over. "Wear this well, Daughter o' Danu. It will protect ye an' the precious child. No matter where ye be an' ye wish it, it'll bring ye all safely to this very room straight away."

In no way would Patrick have believed that the neck ornament would ever fit around Maggie's throat — more likely she could use it as a belt of sorts — and yet as it settled upon the graceful sweep of her collarbone it lay ideally, as if it were made for her.

With a brush of Goibhniu's hand across each of their foreheads, one by one, the *Sidhe Fianna* faded away, off to wherever Kara had been found. Patrick remained by Goibhniu's side, haunted by their expressions, fierce and intent to the very last. He no longer feared they would bring back his daughter...he only feared the condition she would be in when they delivered her.

Once again, she prayed for deliverance, staring into the distance in the failing hope of seeing Maggie's face, anger and all, as long as she took Kara away from here. She wanted it so badly her mind supplied the image and her ears the sound. Her smile was more of a grimace, and more tears filled her eyes at the enthusiasm of her imagination, for it had not only had it called forth Maggie as her personal avenging angel. A host of others materialized from the air to charge beside her. The same fire that forged their swords glowed menacingly in their eyes. To her terror-twisted mind, it was a pleasant sight.

Great was Kara's surprise when imaginary Maggie's enraged yell once again set off the pounding in her head. Down came the blazing sword, and only when Tony wheeled around did Kara realize her rescuers were really there.

As she witnessed her own salvation, she strained against her bond eager to see the bastard struck down. And yet, as she watched, the fiery blade halted in midair, denying her the satisfaction of witnessing as it cleaved his sadistic head.

"NO!" she raged, roaring and spitting like a lioness deprived of her prey. In her fury, she nearly didn't notice the pull as her energy drained away. Filled with a deadly suspicion, she focused her thoughts down and inward as Maggie had taught her. Sure enough, a link had been forged this day. Tony used her own power to halt the *Sidhe*'s attack. Venom rose within her like an acid core. It was too much for her. Wrath flooded her, deadening her pain. With her newly sharpened awareness, Kara abruptly severed the connection, damming the flow. "No!" she whispered this time, low and deadly.

Tony staggered and barely evaded the redirect of the suddenly released blade. Eyes narrowed, and expression pinched with pain, he threw a murderous glare in Kara's direction as his magical parry faded. Though for a second, Kara's breath seized in her chest, she bared her teeth in a snarl. Their gazes locked until he was forced to whip his attention back to the intruders, but not before he cast into her mind a deadly threat: *By the Great Mother, Carmán, you will live to regret resisting me. I curse you, Kara O'Keefe; I am every man you will ever see. Every man who touches you will touch you like I have. Every time a man speaks, you will hear my voice. Every man is me.* Each malicious word he spat into her mind felt like a shard of glass shredding her heart and soul. And then he was gone... But she wailed because, in truth, he would never be gone again. Even as he drew back from her, a small taste of the potency of his curse surfaced. She merely thought of Papa, wishing desperately that he were here to take her away from all of this, and even in her memory, Tony looked out from what should have been Papa's face. Kara's wail became a scream.

Aloud, a staccato intonation left Tony's lips, and his hands wove chopping patterns in the air. Before Maggie could pull back for a second strike, a portion of the surrounding shadow pulsed. It was as if reality itself stretched past the point it could bear, leaving a gaping hole whose jagged edges fluttered along Kara's senses, torturing her nerves, blinding her gaze, breaking her heart. So close and yet he would escape. Kara could not bear it.

"No! NoNoNo!" Until every *Sidhe* halted and trailed their battle-enraged eyes upon her, Kara hadn't realized she'd screamed again. "No..." The last was but a final, desperate whisper as Kara crumbled in on herself, dissolving in an unstoppable flow of tears as her rage evaporated, and her failing strength gave way, leaving her wracked by wave after wave of intense pain as each mutilation sent up its own cry. Her despair was all-encompassing. The last thing she saw was Tony blowing her a kiss as he disappeared through the rippling shadow; the last thing she heard was his peal of mocking laughter as in her mind he promised he'd be back...to continue their little game.

Terror followed her into the darkness of her private hell. She wrapped it around her like a steel cocoon, a hard protective shell...impenetrable.

It was time for something soothing, something to ease her soul. Agnieszka had already tried to lose herself in cooking. It had not occupied her hands or thoughts for near long enough. Neither had her bookkeeping. Though the figures dominated her thoughts to the exclusion of all else, they had done nothing to pacify the jangle of her nerves or the viselike sensation circling her head from nape to temple and back again. No, it was time to head out to the garden. Closing her ledger, she went and changed into her tatty, grass-stained gardening slacks.

"Come along, Rex," she called to her steadfast companion. The cat had remained by her side since the Rom had left. He followed closer than her shadow wherever she went, so much that when she had gone back to the village after a forgotten errand, he protested quite loudly at being left behind. When she returned, he was waiting for her where her private lane met up with the road to town, pacing back and forth. Ever since then, reproach interlaced with concern radiated from his posture. She could tell he still hadn't quite forgiven her. Without lifting his head, he responded with a disgruntled rumble.

"Well, suit yourself," she called over her shoulder as she turned away, "but I'm going out to tend my garden, I've some bulbs that still need setting."

Agnieszka had not even reached the kitchen door before the cat was at her side, displaying obvious annoyance at being forced from his grudge by his stronger urge to watch over her. Used to cats being moody, she chose to ignore him.

Just outside the door she picked up her gardening gear and the long-neglected bulbs. If she didn't get them in the ground now, they wouldn't have a chance to set before the soil froze solid. With a certain amount of annoyance, she had to practically dance to avoid the cat's long, thick tail, as she made her way to the patch of garden she'd prepared. Generally, Rex's standard flew high and with unwavering confidence. Today it was so low as to nearly rest between his legs, twitching back and forth with quite a degree of agitation.

"Away with you, already!" Agnieszka snapped at her companion. "I've brought myself out here to relax, not churn things up even more. Now settle down or go away."

Rex grumbled deep in his throat but stretched out on the black, wrought-iron chair nearby. However, his tail did not stop twitching, and not once did he lie his head down. Agnieszka ignored his uncharacteristic behavior. If he wanted to jump at every rustle and flicker in the underbrush, so be it, but she was going to leave all thought of the world behind for a while and get some gardening done. Marching with a purpose to her chosen spot, she turned and scanned her flowerbed, her forehead wrinkled subtly with puzzlement. This was the patch, she was sure of it. Not three days ago she had cleared the dead brush right there in preparation for a bed of iris, hadn't she?

Turning slowly, she scanned each of her beds. Was this senility? Had she prepped another spot and merely gotten confused? Or worse, had she not done as she remembered at all? She saw no gaps in the garden, no reasonably fresh-turned earth. She could not explain it...she remembered so vividly. Not only had she cleared it—and yes, it was this very spot!—but on the same day Rex had entered her life, she had sifted the soil to a fare-thee-well, so lost had she been in her thoughts. Yet now, every patch was filled. In fact, the space she had paid so much attention to actually burgeoned, now that she looked at it. There was no explanation for it, but the lavender and heather that had filled the space previously were back again and in full bloom. Healthier than such plants had the right to be at the onset of winter.

At a loss, Agnieszka ran her fingers along the vibrant stalks and blossoms before letting her hands fall to her side. It was as if the world had turned upside down on her yet again. Things that oughtn't to have been possible suddenly were. She found she was not as interested in gardening at the moment as she had thought. The bulbs would keep for another day. Making her way back to the cottage, she barely took note as Rex overtook her, no more than to acknowledge she was not alone in her uneasiness.

Hours later, Agnieszka was still shaken by the episode in the garden. She had settled down at her desk, trying to put all of it from her mind, but her progress was minimal at best. What was worse, her tension had clearly begun to affect her companion. Clawing persistently at the front door, Rex turned demanding eyes upon her. When she did not move quickly enough, he encouraged her further with a tense, half-vocal yowl.

"Well, now," she addressed him in her clipped British speech, her mouth pursed. "Is that the way you think it is?" She was only half-serious. He stalked anxiously between her and the door and back again.

Rising with a sigh, Agnieszka joined him in the foyer. This did not have the feel of a randy jaunt or frivolous roaming. It seemed more as if the cat had a dire purpose.

"As you wish, your majesty. Please, allow me to get that for you." Her halfhearted teasing fell flat. With an anxious look out the window, Agnieszka cracked the door just enough to let him through before closing it again and throwing the bolt fast. Just that barest waft of outside air was heavy. It crackled across her nerves, and the trace of sickly sweet organic scent that it carried assaulted her nose. It was as if the very night was a beast, lurking, watching her. For the first time in all her many years living in this house, she felt both isolated and exposed.

Uneasy, without even Rex to comfort her, Agnieszka gathered up her mother-of-pearl rosary and recited the litany, vocalizing a bare breath above silence, her fingers flying over the beads. Making her way through the house in constant prayer, she checked the windows in near-perfect mimicry of Jacko's previous efforts: where there were shutters, she closed and secured them; where there weren't, she drew the curtains. She most assuredly locked every window, and even made sure the pennies were still in place on the sills. For good measure, she added more over the door lintels. And, needless to say, she left a trail of bright lights in her wake as she moved from room to room. There would be no dark corners tonight, and, as much as she longed for her furred companion, the door would not open again until morning.

Compulsively, she checked and double-checked each room, barely aware of the continued rounds she made. Outside those windows without shutters, ghostly movements haunted her through gaps in the curtains. Like the aftereffects of a flash, she thought she caught a pale glimpse here and there, pacing her as she pulled curtains and peered through blinds. With a shiver, she drew a shawl from the back of her chair and wrapped its soft, comforting folds around her shoulders. Never once did her fingers halt their own rapid circuit across the beads.

Knowing full well that there would be no sleep this night, Agnieszka made her way to the kitchen to put the kettle on for tea. A flick of this last light switch and the house was—for perhaps all of the second time since she'd moved in— completely lit from baseboards to rafters. Now all she needed was something to mask the eerie howls of the increasing wind; without a pause in her recitation, she switched on her transistor by the sink, just in front of the kitchen window, the only one in the house with nothing to draw closed.

Needing the comfort of her faith, Agnieszka subconsciously accomplished her tasks, from filling the kettle to setting the table and pouring the tea, entirely one-handed, accompanied by a continuous and pious murmur. The comforting aroma of tea filled the kitchen, dispelling the odd mustiness that had crept in when she'd opened the door. Settling into her chair, she relaxed sufficiently that she gave it not a thought as she laid aside both the words and the beads of her rosary to take up her teacup.

A crash of what seemed like thunder shook the house. The lights flickered, and from the depths of her nightmares rose another pale blur, as something large hurtled against her kitchen window. The fragile bone china teacup tumbled from her nerveless fingers and plummeted to the floor, showering the kitchen with Earl Grey and china shards. In a matter of seconds, the first white blur was replaced by countless others, over and over, with flashes of red like flickering flame. The window and the very wall itself rattled with the force of the collision, though thankfully neither gave. She could not make out if it were human or beast or even, as she prayed, bits of flotsam tossed about by the wind, but she shook with each blow.

And then she noticed, by the glow of the moon in the clear night sky, no wind blew, not even a breeze to rustle the leaves of the apple trees she could see through her kitchen window. The howls continued, accompanied now by hisses and growls, and if she strained quite hard, she swore she could hear words, faint and unfamiliar one moment, clear as day in tone and meaning the next. "Breeder...feeder...fool...food."

Eyes wide and her pulse beating a rapid tattoo in her throat, Agnieszka stood and pushed away from the table in one panicked motion. She barely noticed as the chair clattered to the floor behind her; she was too transfixed by the brief, horrifying glimpse of what she thought was a face in the window, a vicious, feral face. A woman had gripped the sash as if she would tear it and the frame away...a woman with blood streaked across her lips and bare breasts and hatred in her eyes. A woman with a tiny shred of fur caught in a burr on the claw-like nail gripping the wood of the window. A woman that was there one moment and then gone like a hallucination.

Unnoticed in the background, the howls and hisses and growls continued. But Agnieszka only heard the disembodied chant: "Breeder! Feeder! Fool! Food..." The last trailed off as a contemptuous whisper, which was perhaps more unsettling than the yelling of the rest.

Trembling, shaking, barely able to keep her feet, she fought for breath. Why...why had she let Rex out? Why was she under attack? What had she done? The hisses faded, and she was afraid. One by one, white faces adorned with varied streaks of red filled the window. The hunger and hatred warring in their gazes mercilessly seized her heart and paralyzed her feet. Panting furiously, eyes wide, and her hands clenched in useless fists at her side, Agnieszka was trapped in a staring match with Death.

"Breeder...feeder...fool...food..." The hateful whispers continued as the sound of rending wood filled her frantic ears. The cloying scent returned a hundred-fold, making her stomach heave, though the rest of her was doomed to remain immobile.

Confident in the outcome of their conquest, the many faces of Death all smiled, revealing dainty, blood-dipped fangs. One of them licked at her incisors, intent as she savored the tang of blood, anticipating more. The horror was too much. A misty haze descended over Agnieszka's vision, and her knees lost all semblance of support. As she crumbled to the floor, she made a frenzied grab for her rosary and, with all her straining heart, cried out to her Lord for deliverance.

Olcas's body shivered and shook with tremors, his blood boiled. He had been so busy sipping at the sweet, terror-tinged power that peaked with each passing act that he had not bothered to gather it in greater draughts, instead preferring the anticipation of the powerful jolt he would experience when he ultimately harvested it all at once. Blast those interfering *Sidhe*. How had they found his hideaway past his layers of wards? He'd barely had time to reestablish the loosest of links with Kara through his parting curse before he'd been forced to flee. It linked them enough that he could savor the curse's effects, but not enough that he could follow it like a trail.

Damned if he wouldn't have to wait for the blasted doctor to surface now. Olcas seethed inside at the upheaval of his plans. Having his prize torn from his grasp did little to improve his demeanor. A shiver of anger-laced pleasure rippled through him as he walked, but his fury was too fresh for him to feel any satisfaction that his curse had already come into play. The energy burst he received from Kara's first experience was nothing compared to what he would have harvested from their little games. Olcas ground his teeth and continued on.

He stalked past a shabby little hospice, with its cheerful window boxes and peeling paint, and lashed out viciously. Whipping the power currents into a frenzy, he smiled as first one fading spark fluttered before a gust of savory pain, only to be followed by half a dozen others. The power he gathered was a pittance compared to what had been snatched from his very grasp in the warehouse, and there was no satisfaction in ending lives nearly spent. More an act of mercy, really, but still, it was better than nothing, and the panic of the attendants added a zing to the experience.

Olcas continued on, drawing away the wisps of joy and exuberance for life that made existence in such a depressed environ bearable, leaving the residents mired in hopelessness and despair. Pleased with the suffering once again trailing his wake, Olcas cast his senses forth in search of a more substantial, if still inadequate substitute for the delectable Kara. The distracting impulses of Tony's mortal frame had to be dealt with before the mounting pressure further scattered his thoughts. In a back alley, he found his victim, and not too soon as his assumed body spasmed with need.

This one was as sweet with potential as he was sour with stench. Olcas's lip curled instinctively, and his first impulse was to draw back, but as distasteful as the vagrant was, there was at least a glimmer of power in him. A bare shadow, once again, of that which Olcas had lost thanks to the *Sidhe*. He had to remind himself the vessel was not important as long as the need was satisfied.

It was time to yank his new victim from the grasp of blissful oblivion and introduce him to the pleasure of intense pain—well...pleasurable for Olcas at least, even if he was not free to linger as he had with Kara. Still, just the thought of what he had lost gave his actions added brutality as he vented his rage on the unwitting fellow, viciousness somewhat making up for what he lost without the leisure of technique.

The smells of fear and death were heavy on the stagnant air of the back alleyway. In the gloaming, all was cloaked in an indistinct haze, but standing out against the black-upon-black of the shadows, a pale furtive movement caught Dubh's eye. "Well met, brother. I thought I finally felt you surface." his voice was low, but carried quite clearly to one who did not need ears to hear him. "Having a bit of a snack, are we? Or is it dinner and dancing?"

"Oh yes, I just love eating between interrupted meals," Olcas' clipped growl amused Dubh, though the implications did not.

"Having problems with your food, little brother?" One would have thought they had last seen one another yesterday, rather than several millennia ago, before dear Mother had cast their souls out into the world — hiding them from their enemy and allowing them the time to regain their eminence, to prepare for the battle to come before returning to crush cursed Eire beneath their heels.

"That's a fetching look you have there — take you long to pick that outfit?"

He was intrigued when Olcas chose to ignore his question but went along with the redirect anyway. "Signature black, you know," Dubh quipped, keeping up the seemingly meaningless banter. Though this tool's true appearance was hidden from the view of most mortals, John McDubh's charred flesh was visible to Dubh's brother and fellow demigod, Olcas. "So, what happened to the lovely little thing I saw you pick up at the bus station? She also saw this body for what it is, by the way."

Dubh really did not like the implications of his brother's reaction to his question. Instead of answering, Olcas snatched violently at the local power currents and unleashed a massive levinbolt at the indigent corpse shrouded by the gloom. The body arched and incinerated in a matter of seconds, so exorbitant was the amount of energy used. The look of dark, murderous rage on his brother's face more than communicated the severity of the situation. "I know quite well what she is capable of, but some...friends dropped in to see if she was free."

The way Olcas' teeth gnashed together, Dubh fully understood his meaning. "So, the Danaans crashed your private little party, did they?

"I'd wondered why you'd resorted to junk food." His indifferent gaze slowly followed the dissipating plumes of smoke wafting upward, recalling the condition of the victim that had lain there. Only a thwarted feast or desperation would oblige the fastidious Olcas to resort to the filthy, destitute pariahs of society. While the end results gave Dubh some satisfaction, he was curious as to what forced his baby brother to such vulgar takings. Had Olcas fallen so low since that fateful day?

Dubh had been casting into the ether since acquiring his current tool, yet, not a whisper of thought from Olcas or Calma...until now. At least one of them was here on Dubh's doorstep. And at the perfect moment to help exact a bit of vengeance. The timing was as excellent as ever. "Well, it seems as if you've pretty much cleaned your plate. Shall we?"

Olcas did not stop seething as he followed Dubh from the dark alley. In fact, Dubh would never have to ask him the details of what had happened; they were clear in his mind now, having listened for the last half hour to his brother's mental griping. Dubh could readily understand the frustration caused by all of this, but enough was enough!

"Are you quite done?" Dubh spun until he and Olcas were face to face, stopped in the middle of one of Dublin's cobbled alleys. "It is rather distracting having to listen to your mental rantings when I am trying to devise a revenge both sweet and fitting, one that will ultimately regain you your treasure, and all three of us our ancient prize."

"The three of us...and what of Calma? I have not been able to sense him, let alone converse..." Dubh hid his contempt by glancing away. The whelp had never shown nearly the potential of his older brothers. Pitiful really, but it was no surprise Olcas was unable to sense Calma or Dubh: Olcas's opinion of himself was far and away more grandiose than warranted. Fortunately, fate provided Dubh a diversion before Olcas noticed the disdain he barely suppressed.

As his vision briefly lost its crisp focus, Dubh abruptly interrupted Olcas. "Come! They have cornered another." He could tell the look of voracious glee on his face was similar to Olcas's, even after millennia of separation, for corresponding anticipation replaced the petulance on his baby brother's borrowed face. Together, they swiftly slipped through the void of space Dubh handily ripped in the air before them.

Intense, piercing shrieks echoed through the mage-lit warehouse, bouncing off the bare walls and feeding back in a constant loop. Each time a male member of the *Sidhe Fianna* came within Kara's visual range or was careless enough to speak where she could hear, the screams began again and did not end until the frantic girl ran out of both the breath and the strength to sustain them. Even then, she maintained an eerie, broken moan. Through it all, the flow of tears never ceased.

Maggie sighed wearily and blinked back her own tears. She could not afford to indulge in them now, though every instinct demanded she wail for the suffering of her friend...her kin. The battle had taken mere minutes, from the first charge to Tony's escape. How he had come to follow them to the land of Eire she would dearly love to know, and all of a sudden possessing such strong magical skill. The fighting had been brief, but they had yet to calm Kara enough to move her. Forget about touching her, Maggie had to admit they'd barely been able to cover the girl…and keep her covered. The restrictive weight of a blanket alone set her off.

Nothing at all could be done for her wounds. She would suffer no one—not even the women—to touch her. Being a man, Miach had no hope at all of coming near, and he was the only healer among them. In fact, all they had managed to do was run off Tony and sever Kara's bonds. Neither one had been a minor feat, but how much had they really accomplished? And what to do now?

Maggie did not want to send away the bulk of her warriors when the very real possibility remained that Tony might attempt to pop back in and spirit the girl away, but it looked as if she had no choice; their very gender sent the newly rescued Kara into hysterics and Maggie was afraid that in the girl's mind, she had yet to be freed. All of the *Fianna* bore injuries from their initial attempts to lift the tortured girl; their last efforts had gained Maggie a raw burn down the length of her forearm where Kara's panicked instincts had lashed out with a bolt of pure power. Until that moment, Maggie had not realized the depth of the girl's potential. If she were not taken to safety soon, none of them would survive what terror unleashed. Kara was spiraling down into madness and, should that happen, she feared the girl would claim them all. Moreover, Kara needed care. If sending back the men of the *Fianna* was the only way Maggie could provide it, then thus it would be. She summoned the warriors.

"Gather 'round," Maggie ordered her forces to her side, a half-dozen meters away from where Kara still lay. With a nod, Maggie motioned two of the *Bean Fianna* to hold their position in guarding the girl. At their salute, she turned her attention back to the rest.

"The *Fear Fianna* must return to *Tír na nÓg* ahead o' the rest o' us." She met each gaze around the cluster, waiting for them to nod in turn before looking to the next warrior. Though every eye held compassion, she couldn't help notice they were also laced with relief. The repeated bouts of screaming were tearing out their hearts. "We'll move quickly as I do na care to leave behind a reduced force with the monster responsible moving about freely, an' with magic at his disposal.

"*Fear Fianna* to me; *Bean Fianna*, see that Kara comes to no further harm." Maggie gripped Goibhniu's torc and wished the way to *Tír na nÓg* open to her.

A rainbow-hued, shimmer in the air was all the warning Patrick had that the warriors were returning. Seated as he was in the corner beside the recovering Seer, it was an effort to twist around for a better view. He would have leapt to his feet, save for her hand clutching his own. They had been sitting thus since the *Sidhe Fianna* left half an hour ago; the woman would not release her frantic grip.

Slowly Maggie folded herself through the portal, one hand wrapped tightly around the torc. Upon sight of him, she stopped dead and merely stood there, all but in the way, as the men of the *Sidhe Fianna* flowed around her to clear room for the next warrior to come through the gate.

Desperate for hope, he had convinced himself over the last thirty minutes that all was well. In thirty seconds, the growing anguish on Maggie's face shattered that hope. He could not speak.

"We've found her," Maggie confirmed, her tone grave. "But I won't bring her through 'til ye've left the chamber."

"What?" He finally managed to vocalize.

"I won't bring her through 'til ye've gone."

"Ridiculous! I'm her father; I have to be here for her." In his fear, Patrick would not allow himself to ask why she was so adamant. "She needs me..."

He watched as Maggie stiffened, and her chest heaved with the deep breath she drew. "Ye can't help her now."

A moan escaped him, and he trembled. "Precious *Jea*-sus! Ye can't tell me she's dead." His grief-stricken eyes continued to plead for him as his voice broke. "Dear God, tell me no!"

"No...no..." Maggie's eyes were filled with both pity and pain as she reached out her free hand to him. "She isn't dead, but trust me, ye can't help her now, an' she won't want ye near, if even she realizes ye are."

"No..." It was all he could whisper past the grief as the warriors closed ranks around him in solidarity. Many of them were the *Sidhe* he'd fought beside just days ago, and he clung to the comfort they offered as he was led from the room, not even looking as Maggie disappeared back through the ripple.

Chapter II

Dubh watched closely the deadly dance performed before them. He thrilled at the economy of motion. Turning to his envy-ridden brother, he could not resist pointing out the finer points of his new minions. "Notice the minimal expenditure of energy. See how much power they reap for me. They are the perfect predators, and yet they heel to my call."

He made sure arrogance and satisfaction laced his every word. Though he made a point of not bringing up Olcas's most recent bungle in those regards, it was quite clear from the tightly clenched jaw and the venom in his little brother's gaze that the point was suitably thrust home. It was as important to establish dominance with Olcas as it had been with the *Bás*, whom the de Danaan had upon a time known as the *Namhaid*.

Little had Dubh known when he'd ventured north to follow his ancient vendetta that he would encounter yet another that was older than time itself, or that the object of both was one and the same.

He had been displaced for over a millennium before he was free to follow through on his plotted revenge. Once again, he offered up thanks to the memory of his beloved mother, Carmán, who, with the ultimate sacrifice of her very being, preserved her sons...preserved him, despite their heinous murder at the hand of the de Danaan. Though there were limits to what they could do in their unbound state, the most important of those limits had always been that they could not leave the land where their scorched bones lay forgotten, unless they linked themselves to another creature, one able to carry a bit of ancient bone away to serve as an anchor for Carmán's children wherever they chose to go. At least, that was how it had always been. But Dubh had not been content; he had thrust against his bonds over a millennium, gaining more and more ground until that very day when, with a shower of sparks, the mage bond that tied him to Eire's soil disintegrated.

When he had been bound by physical constraints, even as a god, he would never have been able to follow this pursuit, never would have spied the ages-old trail, let alone follow it. Now, soaring above the frigid oceans of the north, Dubh was determined to find something to vanquish his ancient enemies.

All around him, the winds howled and bellowed as conflicting currents tore across each other's paths. Dubh gloried in the violence that shredded the very clouds, even as it threw them together. The crashing peals of thunder and the crackling buzz that charged the air were sweet nectar. He reveled in the awesome power as he harnessed the unleashed fury and brought it and himself to ground. He was close...so close. The trail was ancient but, thanks to the Sidhe, he was not limited by physical senses, in his noncorporeal state it was as if he were a magnet feeling the pull of the planet's power, only unlike a simple magnet he could choose what drew him, and time was no hindrance; one minute or ten millennia, it was all the same.

What he had chosen to follow was the Sidhe, but not just any in particular; the ancient trail he pursued was that of Danu herself. It led him to the ancient homeland of those who had become the Tuatha de Danaan, the land they had fled age upon age upon ages ago.

Circling from above, he could see why Danu had chosen Ireland; it was much like the land below him. Though this clime was dryer and lacked the boggy moors of the Celtic lands, the majestic cliffs, riddled with so many caverns that they must whistle with every wind, dropped straight down into the crashing sea. Inland, the boulder-laced downs gave way to gently rolling meadows, interspersed with stretches of forest that so rivaled the smallest of Ireland's mountains for height, that they might have been sown from acorns at the dawn of time. Yet Dubh did not find what he sought.

If he'd still had teeth, he would have gnashed them by now. There were ancient signs of civilization, what he could only assume were the remains of the four ancient cities from which Dubh's enemy had fled, but there was no sign of life of any kind. Was there famine or some natural catastrophe? No...from what he knew of the Sidhe, nature would never turn against them, so there must be something he was missing. He gave a soundless roar and whipped the surrounding clouds into a frenzy that lashed the land below.

That was when he saw them, six pale, gaunt figures streaming from the cover of the mountainous forest. They were to all appearances women, huntresses by their steady, measured movements. He did not recognize the race...or was it species? Noting their alert gazes and whipcord bodies, poised to strike, Dubh observed them closely but did not approach. He saw no weapons among them, other than the teeth and claws they were born with. One look at their lethal movements made him consider that they did not need more. Could this be the source he searched for? Graceful and deadly, they were all that was beautiful to his wicked heart. They must be the ancient foe.

If he'd still had eyes, they would have narrowed, and his lips would have been graced with the slightest of mirthless smiles. Triumph expanded his awareness as a deep, satisfied breath would have puffed out the chest he'd once possessed. Here was the weapon he would wield against the Sidhe, the very demons from their past, the enemy that had driven them from their lands.

They looked like nothing but a promise at the moment, cheeks sunken and eyes feverish, starving madness markedly present in their expressions. With his sight unbound by physical restraints, he could see they searched with a likewise nonphysical sense, searched with a desperation often seen in the doomed, who clutch at any hope with the fear it will be their last. He watched as they milled about in confusion, and murderous howls floated past him on the air. If he'd been much closer those seeking tendrils would have drained him away to nothing, for he recognized in them his own power-hungry quest. These creatures did not feed on flesh, though perhaps they did rend it as a savory spice to their supping.

And suddenly, they stopped their aimless stalking back and forth in the meadow below. All six dropped to crouch in what could only be subservience, silent, with their heads and eyes cast down.

Interesting... Dubh glanced away from the women and scanned the landscape. There...a man, naked and powerful in the way these women were, left the cover of the forest, moving with the flowing grace of a serpent. A commanding stride brought him even with the huddled huntresses, where he planted himself, eyes locked defiantly on the very point in the sky where Dubh hovered.

Perhaps you will come down and we will talk. *The mental voice was arrogant and brooked no question, any intent hidden behind hooded eyes. There was no doubt he was used to being obeyed. He would have to learn to deal with disappointment.*

Perhaps I will stay safely where I am, and we can talk from here.

The battle of wills ensued, but no mere earthly being could hope to withstand a god, even a fallen one such as Dubh. The creature tried, of course, but Dubh hovered in his chosen space as solidly as a boulder anchored in bedrock. No amount of coercion would move him. But it did give him ideas. Annoyed by this bid for dominance, he unwound a bit of his own will and set it against the newcomer; each time the man pushed at Dubh with his will, Dubh pushed steadily back.

To all appearances, those below looked primitive-minded, but that was deceptive. Rather quickly, the man perceived what was happening and withdrew the pressure, sending him to his knees. Dubh's laughter floated down on the wind, leaving no doubt that the little alpha male amused him. The man snarled viciously and turned to lash at the huntresses, herding them back beneath the protective canopy of the primal forest.

Oh, come now, don't be like that, *Dubh sent a sly tendril of thought after their retreating backs,* *I only thought you might like to know where you could find the Sidhe.*

Abruptly the natives stopped where they stood, the women once again dropping into subservient poses as the man whirled back around, his gaze unerringly setting on the point where Dubh had advanced closer. He sensed the man's confusion at his words — perhaps they had known them as something else — but had no doubt of the flaring, bitter hatred surfaced at the mental images that Dubh sent with those words.

Yes! Now to convince them a cooperative effort would be eminently beneficial. *Shall we talk?*

Listening to the last of the Ard Namhaid — the Sidhe name, he had been told, for the male of this species, the females being the Namhaid Conairt — tell the ancient tale of the Daoine Maithé, whom Dubh knew as the Sidhe, he began to seethe. It was clear the Sidhe had a long tradition of destroying those who sought to detract from their power. They even robbed this species of their name, though he could see why. These predatory creatures, he had learned, had an interesting name for themselves...Bás, or to translate: Death. Not a name the Sidhe would have been comfortable using in polite conversation, though Dubh found it absolutely delightful himself. He would see they lived up to it.

But by his inattention, he was disrespectful to his host...actually, and more importantly, he was missing valuable insight into both races. Dubh brought his focus back to the story being told aloud in the hissing, snarling speech the Bás used among themselves. From where he hovered in a haze just above their heads, Dubh had no trouble gleaning the true meaning of their language from their thoughts.

"A great drought overtook the land and famine followed, driving us from our domain to the East. We roamed the earth to find a new home, there to whelp our young and preserve the memories of the Pride. Survival is all. The weak exist to provide for the strong. None are as strong as the Bás." The Ard Namhaid took a measured pause — long enough for the Conairt to raise their voices in chorus, "The weak exist to provide for the strong. None are as strong as the Bás."

He observed them as the Ard continued, more fascinated by the race's interplay than he was by the tale. Contrary to most pack mentalities, there was no jockeying for position among the women; they were all equal and operated in concert. And, without exception, they all showed complete deference to the Ard, not moving even once as he spoke, their expressions absolutely rapt.

"We came to this land, and it was good; it nourished us, and we made it our home. But also here we found the Daoine Maithé, both plentiful and powerful, and they would not have us share their land or draw upon their power. They stood against us, but their strength was not like ours. They could not withstand our might, and the Conairt brought them to their knees." Dubh found it interesting that the Bás had incorporated the Sidhe names into their culture, somewhat like badges of honor. "Those who would challenge us, we slew. Those who were weak, we took to serve to our young."

The mental image that followed that last was alien and disturbing even to Dubh, but he had nothing to fear. Even if he had a body that would serve their needs, he was not weak; whatever the Bás chose to do with their vanquished meant nothing to him.

"But one, one eluded us," the Ard hissed, his shoulders taut and his fists clenched, until, with his abbreviated version of the Conairt's claws, he nearly did himself damage. This went beyond hatred. What Dubh saw now was wounded pride, festering and oozing since the day the blow had been struck, whatever it had been. "The Danu fled before us, escaping to another land, there to spawn her race again. The Daoine Maithé's method being quicker, she sent her children back to slay all the hosts save one before our young had been whelped and that because they could not find the last.

"We are the kits that survived that time, hidden away deep in the caverns...we are all that is left."

It was as if Dubh were at a banquet. The anger and bitterness rising from the Namhaid — Ard and Conairt alike — were sumptuous delicacies. Having aged longer than the history of mankind, it had achieved a smooth, intense bouquet that was, to Dubh, richer than honey wine. Looking at the hatred burning in their blood-red eyes, and the way their wicked claws flexed upon the ground as if gouging flesh, he knew it would be no effort to bring them to his side.

There are more than seven Bás now. Forty-nine to be exact, Dubh thought with satisfaction as he withdrew from the depths of memory, and another seventy soon to be whelped. But, as he had promised them long ago when he'd delivered the first of the new hosts, he would see that the *Bás* — the *Namhaid* — flourished with each *Sidhe* they struck down.

Speaking of which, this one was more able than the rest. A warrior, full-bore. Quite a refreshing change from the mewing sheep his pets had cornered previously. The show should be quite pleasurable, sweetening the eventual feast.

Dubh watched on in eager anticipation as the delightfully ferocious creatures he'd forged an alliance with stalked their most recent quarry. What inspiration it had been, to follow the ancient trail back to the very creatures that had sent the interfering *Sidhe* nearly into oblivion. And to have found the key to making them allies was pure genius. There would be no "nearly" this time around. Dubh would not rest until not one *Sidhe* walked the earth.

The deadly dance was enchanting as the Pack circled and lashed out, and the *Sidhe* did likewise. With his white-blonde hair drawn back from his face in a multitude of warrior's braids, his leather hunting outfit as close-fitting as the pelts of the *Conairt*, and the cunning and vigilance in his midnight blue eyes a mirror of their own, any hunter would recognize this one as kindred; even Dubh felt a glimmer of respect, though he was loathe to admit it. It was written in the hard angles of his face and the piercing intensity of his gaze. Yes, the combatants were well matched, and perhaps, if the odds were not so lopsided, the *Sidhe* would have stood a chance. As it was, the Pack merely toyed with their prey, dagger-like claws marked him from thigh to knee, another swipe left furrows down his scalp. In a matter of moments, a scattering of other minor wounds added to the tally.

Diving away and rolling to his feet, the warrior bared his teeth in a feral grin and exacted retribution. Leaping clear of a pouncing attack from two of the *Conairt*, he drew a sword that glowed with the sheen of well-tempered steel and something more. With a downward-slashing sweep, he severed a clawed hand and reversed the sword to gut the other.

The remaining huntresses growled ferociously, abandoning the playfulness of their assault. All attention was now on the *Sidhe*, no regard was given to their stricken sisters, and no care would be tendered when all was done;

instead, retribution for their deaths would be exacted this day. Though one still drew breath, she was dead to the *Conairt*; along with any progeny she would have fostered to strengthen their numbers. Dubh knew to be the cause of such a loss carried quite a price; this prey would die most horribly, worse than his kin if such a thing were possible.

He allowed himself to savor their fury, the bloodlust in their eyes. It was all the more interesting to see their battle-rage progress as for the first time, for this group, their prey actually marked them, both with the slim elven blade in his right hand and the biting dagger he now drew in his left. Dubh saw the dawning realization as the *Sidhe* read his fate in their murderous red glares. And yet, as intoxicating as the encounter was, Dubh reluctantly acknowledged that it was not in their interest to draw this out. The *Bás* had only so many hunters left until the new spawn whelped; they could not squander them.

Dubh caught Olcas's eye, and they joined each other in a harsh, mesmerizing chant focused on the combatants before them. The battle stopped, *Conairt* and *Sidhe* alike halted in place to form an aggressive montage. Only their eyes were active — both sides turning their venom on Dubh and his brother. A mere gesture sent the reluctant huntresses back through the fissure to the void, bearing their fallen back to their Ard, leaving only the tattered *Sidhe* standing frozen before them.

Dubh took up their earlier banter. "Care for afters, Brother?"

It took the combined power of all the *Bean Fianna* to bring sleep down over Kara. They would not have done so if it were not for the screaming; if even their feminine touch descended on any part of her, the round of shrieks began again.

Maggie swallowed her own sobs as she moved in carefully to gather Kara into her arms. They were desperate to return the girl to *Tír na nÓg*. Already she fought to escape the oblivion they had drawn around her.

"Focus, my *Fianna*: we must have her safe before the spell lifts or we'll not manage it at all an she's free to fight us." Maggie sensed their effort to tighten the magical bonds over the girl. It was nothing short of cruel given what she had just been through, but it was the only way they'd been able to approach her and remain intact.

"Now! Keep her in the grips o' sleep," Maggie called to her warriors. "'Tis our final chance, for I fear neither she nor ourselves can stand another attempt."

Confident they would maintain the spell, Maggie held Kara close, focusing her thoughts on Goibhniu's torc, and willed open the way to *Tír na nÓg*.

There was nothing but silence as they crossed the void into Goibhniu's private chambers. Though the *Bean Fianna* still held the sleep over her, the girl's terror-driven strength and will to fight increased tenfold. For both her own and Kara's well being, Maggie lowered her to the cushions. Short of dropping her,

Maggie couldn't have set her down quicker, and yet already, Kara's whimpers turned into shrieks.

Horrified, desperation written boldly across her face, Maggie turned to her warriors and immediately dismissed both them and those who had been waiting to help. As they fled the room, Maggie sank to the floor and released her hold on the silent tears that threatened to drown her heart.

What was she to do? Of all of them, it had been her charge and her charge alone to keep this girl safe, and she had failed. In her pride, she had assumed there was no place safer than the Land of Youth—the very realm where the powerful *Sidhe* ruled and not even death and decay held sway...the land where the 'dead' of fierce battle arose with the dawn to fight another day...where at Goibhniu's own feast immortality was ingested with every bite—what place could be safer? Better to ask why Kara had left such a place alone, a possibility that no one had considered...or guarded against.

Breathing deep, she forced her way back from the edge with unexpected ease. She must find a way to soothe the child's anguish, and she had to find it soon before Kara slipped any further into the grips of the demons haunting her soul.

Speak to her, leanbh.* The touch of that awesome soul with hers was of no surprise. Maggie knew the peace she enjoyed was temporary...Goibhniu's way of helping from afar. *Go on, Cliodna, ye're her only hope. The only one strong enough to help her, maybe the only one she'll trust enough to let ye.*

Maggie took another deep breath and did not answer the Smithgod; she didn't have time: Kara needed her.

"Shh...shh...'tis safe ye are, love," Maggie crooned, just barely aloud. "None will harm ye with yer Maggie here."

For hours she kept up her murmuring from halfway across the chamber. The only sign that Kara even heard her was that the girl's moans followed the cadence of her voice. Still, Maggie continued: sometimes talking, sometimes singing lullabies, and sometimes reduced to humming as her voice gave way under strain. From time to time, Goibhniu would join her in her thoughts, but when she noticed that Kara sensed even this much male presence, Maggie shut him out, knowing full well she could not stay him, but hoping he'd see her reason and not intrude again.

Goibhniu did indeed leave them be from that point. Food and water materialized by Maggie's side, but she could not pause to partake of it. She could not recall the last time she had remained so still; her very muscles screamed at being held so tightly in check, but she could not risk setting Kara off again. They were making progress, though it was not reassuring. She had no way to tell if the girl was coming out of the shock or slipping deeper into it.

The surf roared and clapped ruthlessly against the hull, causing the deck to dip and dance beneath his feet. Overhead the wind howled, and thunderheads loomed like great grey boulders. So far, the rain only threatened. Jacko prayed that they reached the docks before Mother Nature made good on that threat.

If they had known the weather would turn so quickly, they never would have risked the caravan to the sea. The precious wagons—their homes, transport, and the badge of their racial identity—were making the crossing on the barge of an ancient Romani, whom age had forced to give up nomadic ways. Old Tomias contented himself with wandering the waterways instead and the challenge of crossing the Channel. He would continue until death itself took him away, and then he would begin his serious roving.

May that be a long time in coming, Jacko thought, as he paced from one end of the barge to the other. As uneasy as a caged wolf, he always ended up with his eyes unerringly locked upon England as if he might see clear across the other side, where Agnieszka was. With a snarl, he tore his gaze away and resumed his stalking.

"I do not like this! You had no right!" he growled at his sister, Sveta. "She is not safe there with none to help her. Something is not right, did you not feel it?"

"I did, which is why we did not linger in harm's way." She looked at him with understanding in her jade-green eyes, but the pressed line of her lips was disapproving and unyielding. "Would you have me drive the wagon alone, and me with three young children? Aye, I could manage if you chose to forget your blood. Family first before all others, Jacko." Sveta scooped up her youngest from the deck and walked away from him, her coal-black hair whipping about her shoulders and swaying hips. She looked back only once before entering the shelter of the small cabin. "Unless you'd care to explain to Marco and his brothers why some *gorgio* means more to you than they do…"

The words she spat at him were harsh, but Jacko saw the fear in her eyes. He then understood that what she said was meant to prick his pride, and nothing more. She didn't really think of Agnieszka as a *gorgio*, but something frightened Sveta enough that she was willing to bind him with guilt rather than free him to follow his heart. Looking from the slowly approaching Dublin port to the faint silhouette of England's receding shore, he wondered which frightened his beloved sister more: what they were to face, or what they had left behind.

Turning back toward their destination, he clutched the cold metal of the guardrail with a punishing grip, feeling its biting chill seep in to fill him up. He knew he would not leave the caravan, and he hated himself for it. No matter that he had no choice, especially since they had been halfway to Holyhead before his sister roused him to take a turn at the reins. He was furious and nearly turned back except for the whip of Granddame Rose's tongue. Wisely, he continued on with not a word spoken, keeping his curses to himself until they began the crossing. They had intended to catch the commercial ferry, only somehow old Tomias had been waiting for them, his crew poised to cast off the moment the wagons were aboard.

As Ireland drew closer and the coast of England faded away, Jacko took up his pacing again. More and more, he thought he should have kidnapped Agnieszka, bundling her away before anyone could say yeah or nay, especially her. It sat heaviest on his heart that he had been forced to abandon her without even a word. *I did not leave by choice, little mother*; he willed his thoughts across the channel and all of England.

They were all worried, and that worry drew them together. Everyone who knew Kara had gathered without prearrangement in Goibhniu's private chamber. Scattered in little groups, some sat on piles of pillows against the silk-draped walls; others stood in small clusters in the room or wandered just past the arch to sit on natural benches cushioned with moss. All of them remained uneasily silent, their eyes following Goibhniu, Maggie, and Patrick himself.

"I cannot heal her." Goibhniu's words echoed like thunder through the room. Patrick explored them in his head at least ten times before he could think to speak. Vaguely, he took note as everyone else in the room recoiled; whether it was from the unexpected finality of the Smithgod's words or the expression on Patrick's face, he would not hazard to guess.

"What do ye mean ye can't heal her?" his voice came out more confused than anything else. Wasn't Goibhniu's ability to heal the very reason they were here?

Goibhniu stared at him, his face calm and expressionless. "This 'tisn't as simple as taking away ye're battle wounds, Patrick. I find I cannot do it, no matter that I gladly would."

Patrick felt his rage build. "Ye'll be telling me why, then." His words were taut with fury as he cut off this *Sidhe* god, who played at benevolence when it suited him, and showed his indifference when it truly mattered. Patrick had lived his life, and if it ended this second, well then, he'd not count it wasted, but to sit back and watch Kara's end when it should just now truly be beginning—he couldn't live with that. "I said, ye'll be telling me why ye'd leave her to suffer! Her, who ye'd only just claimed is so very important to ye..."

Patrick could feel the hands of the nearest *Fianna* reach for him, pulling him back. Only then did he realize he'd actually started to go for the Smithgod. What he would have...could have done, he'd never know.

"An' are ye done, then?" Goibhniu's reply was mild, unfazed. Its very ease infuriated Patrick further. Did all that had happened to them mean nothing to this being of legend? Was Kara merely an idle interest to him? Patrick could feel his jaw clench and his lips peel back and close again over his grinding teeth with no words uttered. The pressure of those words set his temple throbbing as his hands clenched at his sides. What did they call the murder of a god?

"Lose yer anger, Patrick. 'Tis wrongly placed, an' while I can understand yer frustration that ye cannot vent it where ye'd dearly love to, ye'll not be spending it on me.

"Now, are ye ready to listen?"

Patrick nodded brusquely and felt the grip of his anger loosen, as if some outside force had contained it, turning it in on him when he would have otherwise have unleashed it against any number of—at least to him—well-deserving targets. Goibhniu slowly returned his nod, and Patrick went weak with awe as he realized the gesture was both an acknowledgment and an answer.

Patrick felt a renewed sense of calm descend on his soul.

"To answer yer question, then...I didn't say I wouldn't heal yer daughter, I told ye I couldn't do it. I've already tried." Goibhniu's pause and his indirectness were frustrating, but Patrick forced patience. "I can't explain it, but something blocks my attempts. 'Tis as if she's making every effort to keep the whole world out. I could force my way past, but to do so would likely shatter whatever composure the lass has left, or worse yet, her very mind."

Patrick cringed away from what Goibhniu said. What good was magic if it couldn't whisk away the heartache, the suffering? And yet as much as he wished to deny what he was hearing, he couldn't; his heart knew the god's words to be true. Patrick loved his daughter, but at the moment, she was the biggest obstacle to her own healing.

"I'm afraid in this there isn't a thing I can do. Until she opens the way to me o' her own will, I can't heal her. There is something at work here that I cannot slip past without risking harm to her." Goibhniu fell silent, and Patrick forced himself to accept the reality of the Smithgod's words. Kara was worth the world to him, and it tore at his heart that he could do nothing to take away her suffering. And worse, given the nature of that pain, he could not even help her bear it.

He was glad that Barbara was by Kara's side, and not here to witness this defeat. Patrick would break it to her gently and hope she was strong enough to stand by and watch the struggle to come.

Something was wrong...so very wrong. Aí stopped beside the road to Wicklow Cottage, uneasy with the silence. No birds sang, and the wildlife was ominously missing. They never responded thus to his own presence, nor to Agnieszka's, and even if there were other humans about, the creatures usually only hid. Today they were completely absent. Not even an insect made its methodical way across the underside of a leaf.

Aí settled deeper into a meditative trance, immersing himself in the very soul of the countryside, speaking to the spirits of the earth. His nose filtered through the fragrances of nature to settle on the foreign musk lacing the air. In every limb, he felt the aches of scored bark and savaged wildlife that had hidden either too slowly or not well enough.

Whatever waited ahead, he was most definitely outnumbered. Assault on foot was not an option. But from the air...perhaps that was his answer. He sent out tendrils of thought to more specifically search his surroundings. He would need power for what he was about to attempt, and stranger that he was to this area, the local magics would take too long to subdue. But in the middle of the English countryside he found what he was looking for: not far away was a cache, a stockpile of *Sidhe* power. Aí's very nature was the only key needed to unlock the safeguards. Taking the barest measure of *Sidhe* magic from the reserve, he called to him a wisp of cloud. Riding it, he would come in beyond the reach of whatever hunted here and deal with it, if necessary, or descend safely if all was well.

High above the treetops, hidden from all below by his misty cover, Aí continued on. As he drew near, alarm supplanted his earlier concern. The cottage gardens, previously immaculate, were upturned in shambles. Scattered across the yard were branches freshly torn from the surrounding trees. The woman's odds and ends of gardening equipment were broken and cast about. Above vacant dooryard, horror took hold of him: everywhere he looked, blood splattered the cobbles and walls of the country cottage. Patches of fur and stripped bones too small to be human littered the ground.

Aí retracted the magic in the cloud, holding it in anticipation of further need, and leapt to the ground from a height that would have shattered the frame of a human. He landed before the front door in a defensive crouch, ready for any attack. Ears straining to pick up the sounds of stealthy approach or further destruction, he didn't know whether to be relieved or disappointed when all he heard was a hoarse and pitiful caterwauling from around the back.

Aí recognized the yowling immediately. It was the sprite, still cloaked in his cat seeming. Continuing to move cautiously around the house, Aí maintained a balanced crouch, eyes and ears acutely focused on picking up any movement or sound. A quick reconnoiter of the area surrounding the cottage revealed that whoever was responsible for the present havoc was no longer here.

"Garda Faoi Rún," Aí called out, searching the wreckage as he made his way to the back of the cottage. "Where are ye, laddie?"

"Come along, Garda," impatience colored Aí's words. "Show yerself...I need to know what happened."

Still, the sprite did not surface. "Garda! Come now! We haven't time for this nonsense! Garda!"

Though he heard a rumbling, nearly sub-vocal growl, Aí could not pinpoint where it came from. He gave up scanning the yard. The sprite would not be found if he chose not to be, and for some reason, he so chose.

As Aí rounded the house and spied the damage to the back of it, he actually blanched. There was debris everywhere—the garden disrupted, trees torn from their roots, everything demolished, save the house itself, and even that showed signs that it wasn't for lack of effort. Moving warily forward, he examined the gouges in the back wall and the splintered remains of the window casement. He drew an unsteady breath when, in his examination, he discovered a series of five linear scratches across the very glass itself. He drew his spread fingers across the damage and a shudder shook him. While there were things other than diamonds capable of cutting glass, none of them left claw marks.

A look through the damaged window revealed an out-flung hand and a shadowy mass crumbled beneath the table. Draped across the open palm, a string of pearly beads glimmered softly in the gloom. Dear Goddess! Let her be alive!

"Garda! Show yerself, ye wee fool! I can't help her without ye!" As Aí called out he tried the handle on the back door. Finding it locked, he threw himself against it, both blessing and cursing the sturdy construction of the English cottage. His affinity was for nature, reading and healing the souls of both the land and of people—human and *Sidhe*—not in manipulating soulless objects. How was he to get in? "Garda!? Why won't ye help me?"

What had the woman called his little friend? Roy...Rhett...Rick.... no, close though...Rex! "Come now, Rex..." The *r* rolled gently off his tongue as he coaxed the sprite forward.

Before he finished his entreaty, a fur-clad bundle leaned heavily against his calf, pleading blue eyes locked with his as a strained, broken meow filled his ears. "Ach, my friend, there ye are. Can ye get us past the door, or must I break it down?" Aí certainly hoped not. It would offer them little protection if he blasted it to get in. But no, the weight of the sprite lifted off Aí's leg. Rex's massive head, with all of him behind it, butted the fresh-scarred hardwood of the door. Aí sensed the tingle of magic flowing from the battered countryside into his furred friend. A final, well-placed thud and the door creaked open, unbarred by the sprite's instinctive magic and his sheer will.

Full of dread, Aí followed the cat-cloaked sprite into the silent kitchen. He could not bring himself to reach out with his ability, though it would instantly tell him Agnieszka's condition. Once inside the door, he reached back and closed it behind him, throwing the lock for good measure. It would not do for the attackers to return and find the way unbarred.

There was movement beneath the table, but hidden as it was in the shadow, Aí could not tell if it were Agnieszka or Rex, who had immediately disappeared into the gloom. Aí switched on the light, only to discover there was no power. With a thought, he lit the bulb from a trickle of his own energy, flooding the kitchen with light. The sight that greeted him filled his heart with dread. Bright red blood streaked the floor beneath Agnieszka's head. Her face, robbed of its rosy fairness, appeared like a death mask, the skin stretched across the delicate bones of her fae-like features. Only the erratic flutter of a pulse at her throat gave him hope.

Moving forward, Aí watched the sprite rub against his mistress in a completely cat-like fashion. He could not help but notice that with each pass Rex made, both appeared more restored to their former, unharmed selves until only the matted blood in hair and fur betrayed that they'd been injured.

"Ms. Michaels...Agnieszka..." Cradling her head, Aí gently brushed the hair from her face, his own abilities further easing any lingering pain. "Come now, can ye hear me, lass?" Dazed amber eyes flickered open only to drift closed once more. He suspected the wound on her head had been acquired as she fell, not inflicted by whoever had attacked the cottage. A quick look around confirmed they had not gained entrance. And yet, though to all ends she was healed, the woman did not awaken. Glancing around at the Spartan décor, he decided that other than the cat there was little she would regret leaving behind. Over Rex's protests at being separated from his mistress, Aí gathered her into his arms.

As he lifted her, all suddenly came clear. It nearly brought him to his knees. Only the close contact betrayed her secret, that and the fact that all of his attention was intently focused on her. Aí had no more doubt as to why Goibhniu was so assertive about bringing this woman to safety. What he now carried in his arms was more precious than gold or any other element coveted by man or immortal—at least it was to the *Sidhe*. But why had the Smithgod not told him?

Taking a deep, steadying breath, Aí secured his hold on this dearest of treasures. As he repositioned her, the beads Agnieszka clutched—which he recognized as a rosary by the tiny crucifix dangling from the end—threatened to slip away from her. Instantly, her hand snapped shut, trapping the beads firmly within her grasp. Other than opening her eyes earlier, this was the first indication that the woman was alive and even vaguely aware. Aí thanked the Goddess there were signs of responsiveness to give further hope.

Moving out into the yard, Rex glued to his heels, Aí prayed he had enough energy remaining to open a temporary gateway to *Tír na nÓg*.

The Hall was subdued, the Court silent. All eyes sought someplace to dwell, someplace other than the Great Wall, where an increasing number of strands in the eternal knotwork glowed an angry, evil red. Seven had fallen to this faceless foe that rose up to smite them. Seven souls were lost to the *Tuatha de Danaan*, with no blessed wombs to bring joy from the pain of loss.

Maggie sensed that none of them wanted to stand by this glaring reminder of their new vulnerability, but neither did they care to leave the company of their kin. Though they crushed together on the extreme far side of the chamber, with obvious and understandable anxiety, they all continued to cast sidelong glances at the Wall.

A collective gasp rose from the Court. As one, they turned as a haunting wail drifted down the empty corridors of *Tír na nÓg*. The cry went on until Maggie felt it echo from the depths of her heart. A familiar agony, one she shared herself. The agony of wanting...needing to heal a beloved, and yet being powerless to do so. Her eyes were drawn to where Kara lay nearby, still hidden in the deepest recesses of her mind, though her healing body rested in its nest of pillows, wrapped in the lightest, least-binding silk robe to be found. The girl whimpered and thrashed, continually caught up in her private nightmare.

It was then that Maggie knew the voice; it was the violin, and she knew for whom it cried. She also knew that no hand drew the bow, for everyone presently in *Tír na nÓg* was in this room. Quicksilver herself voiced her mistress's pain and her own frustration at not being able to reach the girl. Maggie had glimpsed some small reflection of the instrument's true potential when Kara had brought it into Yesterday's Dreams for pawn; that minute glimmer was nothing compared to what it now revealed.

"Fetch the fiddle, Maggie, before it has the entire Court succumbs to its cry," Goibhniu commanded.

Wending her way past *Sidhe* already lost in the depths of grief, Maggie dodged grasping hands that tried to cling to her for comfort and others that struck out, defending themselves against the faceless menace. Closing her ears to the cries was harder.

Once across the Hall, she fairly ran down the corridor—a chorus of sobs trailing behind her. Unerringly, she headed straight for the chamber where Quicksilver lay all but forgotten. The fiddle felt her coming and its song muted to an agitated discord. Not bothering to come to a full stop, Maggie merely pivoted. She reached out, grabbed the instrument, and let the redirected momentum carry her back the way she'd come.

She was breathing heavily as she reentered the Hall, caught up in the pervasive air of desperation that clung to the violin. She stumbled and barely managed to place Quicksilver in the cradle of Kara's arms before collapsing beside her, wracked by heart-wrenching sobs. The Court joined her in voicing the violin's cries, caught up by Quicksilver's anguish. Gradually, just as their tears seemed exhausted, the dirge transitioned into a soothing, healing melody.

Emotionally and physically drained, Maggie struggled to lift her head, only to witness a most bewildering sight: the entire host of *Sidhe*, joined by the humans, were laid low with weeping. Goibhniu knelt in their midst—revelation mingled with recognition on his face, and both were tinged with awe. It created such a fierce look of joy that Maggie finally understood how such a contradiction as terrible beauty could come to be coined. As with all the *Sidhe*, there were tears in the Smithgod's eyes. His gaze was riveted just past Maggie's head. She shuddered, relieved such intensity did not focus on her. But that led her to question, what did hold his attention so?

With a monumental effort, Maggie rolled her head until she shared Goibhniu's line of view. Her eyes blurred and burned as she forced them to her intent. It was a moment before she realized the distortion was not from her sight. Inches from her out-flung hand, the world itself lost focus. A glittery shimmer, softly radiant and ever-shifting, filled Maggie's vision. There was no substance, no definition, but as Maggie closed her dazzled eyes the afterimage of a woman burned upon her lids...a woman cradling Kara just as Kara cradled Quicksilver. The ghostly image of a hand soothed away the girl's suffering. Maggie fell into a gentle slumber accompanied by a vision of terrible beauty akin to that she had seen in Goibhniu's features. As she drifted off, a soft, loving caress reached out to soothe away Maggie's heartache.

Darkness was good. Darkness hid the ugly truth...the festering wounds... the dirt. They couldn't find her in the dark. They couldn't touch her here. There were no voices.

Sinking gladly into the soft black folds of oblivion, Kara hugged her pain close as a reminder of why none should touch her, why no one could be allowed to come near. The darkness would hold everyone off, because if it did not, they would know. They would know and they would find her. But they wouldn't...because darkness was good.

The darkness was her friend, it wanted to protect her...it warned her when anyone drew too near, when *he* drew too near. Brilliant yellow sparks shot through her ebony mantle whenever the world infringed on her space, sparks that came at her call, and willingly lashed out at those who pressed against the barrier, those who would draw it away until she lay once more bare and exposed. No. He could not be allowed to find her; no one was allowed to reveal her hiding place. Her heart screamed in unfocused protest.

Kara drifted deeper, away from the piercing sound that screeched across her tattered nerves and the copper-penny scent of blood, mingled with the stench of fear. Her haven was a cold one, bitter and biting, but the numbness that crept through her at its touch was most welcome. It supplanted the intense burning that consumed her, spreading from more than a dozen points of her awareness. Soon she would be unseated, no body to concern her, to betray her. No need for senses that brought her only unpleasantness and pain. She could not wait to be free.

The shivers and a persistent tug in the vicinity of her heart were the only reminders of her physical bond with the world. Even that was too much. Burrowing deeper, she sought to escape. No part of her wished to confront the world, and every part wished to be free of it.

Again that persistent tug slowly inched her back. An annoying rebuff of her convictions, it was a continuous hindrance to her progress. If it were not for the tugging, she would have already lost herself in the depths of the darkness.

The realization only strengthened the pull that anchored her. In admitting to herself that any part of her held back, she gave power to the resistance. Well, she would not go back. Darkness was good.

"*A ghrá!* O, love! No!" It was but a whisper, faint and frail as it strained against the cocoon that wrapped Kara away from such things. "Ye can't leave me, not again!"

No, no one was allowed to come close to her. The darkness would hold her alone. She strained to lose herself in engulfing shadows. The path to safety was clear, but the intruder stood in her way. Veering off, Kara cringed in horror as something slithered past her to either side of the road she traveled. Dark and heavy masses loomed up in front of her as she diverged; sharp metallic glints were thrust upon her of a sudden; something moist and slimy flicked across her cheek until she cowered, unable to move forward and prevented from turning back. This darkness was not good.

"Come, *A chuisle mo chroí*!" the whisper urged. It was nearly drowned out by the chittering hisses that closed in now that she had abandoned the safety of the path. "I won't let them harm ye."

Kara yearned for peace and safety, and if the darkness were denied her, then she would move toward what was offered. She only prayed that were it a trick, it was at least a better choice than what now pursued. As eagerly as she had strained to climb deeper into the darkness, she now crawled toward the iridescent shimmer that threatened to disperse the black curtain enshrouding her.

"That's it, love, that's it! Reach for me now!" The murmur gained volume, no longer muffled by the cocoon. The darkness faded to a smoky grey all around, except in the direction from which the voice called to her; there it was more pearly, with gentle, soothing colors rippling across the diminishing expanse of Kara's oblivion.

Uncertainty gripped her once again. Without the slithering shadows, the dark was no longer frightening. Could the same be said for what lay beyond the greyness? Kara could not force herself to move forward. Right now, she was safe—what sense was there in leaving?

"No! No!"

Kara recoiled from the vehement protests of the disembodied voice, and the roots of doubt set a little more firmly. She would not move forward from this place. This was a deception, another ploy to further torment her mind. Safety was an illusion.

"Oh please...'tis sorry I am to have frightened ye. Don't run. An' if it suits ye, stay where ye are, just talk to me...please?"

Poised to flee, Kara held her stance, instead pulling the faded shadow toward her, wrapping herself once again in its protective veil, if only loosely. She would not answer, she would not speak, but neither was she quite ready for flight. Crouched and poised, her attention remained focused on the iridescent patch of grey that grew all the brighter as the surrounding shadow deepened once more. She would listen.

"Kara, ye're no longer in danger, not out there, but the deeper ye go into hiding, the greater ye risk losing yerself." The voice rose no higher than a gentle, soothing murmur as it continued to talk to her. It sounded so reasonable; she wanted to believe, but each time her grip on the cloaking darkness loosened, a different voice drifted through her thoughts, also whispering, also soothing, only that voice had been accompanied by pain.

"No, love, yer kin have freed ye, there'll be no new pain inflicted on ye, just the ache o' healing."

The voice sounded so reasonable, and Kara wanted to believe, but here was a choice, a decision, and the last time Kara had made one of those...No! No! The images crashed down on her, bombarding her from every side: charred bodies winking, a firm hand across her mouth, a blade glistening red with blood, frigid eyes that one moment were blue and the next nearly black... No! Her back arched violently, and her wrists burned anew, the sticky warmth of blood once again trickled between her breasts... No! Her feet were tingling stumps at the end of her legs, vague sensations that would not resolve themselves into the appendages she depended on to be there. The smoky grey of her surroundings deepened to charcoal as she struggled against the phantom bonds. No!

"Shhh...shhh..." Cool, soft hands stroked away the tightening pressure from Kara's brow; no pain followed. "Shhh...'tisn't real...shhh..." The feather-light caress, reminiscent of her mother's comforting, continued down her arms to her burning wrists, to her agonizing shattered thumb and back again in the barest of touches. "That's right, love, ye aren't bound, there're no restraints, an' the healing will come in yer own time when yer ready for it. Ye've but to let us near. Ye've only to ask."

Dazed and deadened, still struggling out of the depths, Kara puzzled at the words. In her numbness, she was unable to find the sense in what was said to her.

"The nightmare's over, love, our Maggie's set ye free. She's waiting for ye...they're all waiting for ye with tears shining on their cheeks. We need ye, love, do not take away the joy an' hope ye mean to us. I couldn't stand to lose ye again."

Kara felt the sobs building, as something in the voice reminded her of Quicksilver, the words floating through the expanse with the graceful flow reminiscent of the violin's notes. Her heart threatened to burst with despair, and fresh tears burned furrows down her cheeks as she finally found her voice. "Hope...there'll be no more Hope...no Hope and no Quicksilver, not anymore."

As the words ripped themselves hoarsely from her throat, the silvery mist brightened blindingly into white, before dispersing to reveal above her the vaulted ceiling of *Mór Halla*. Cradling her ruined hand to her chest, Kara wept as deep and gentle sleep replaced the darkness of oblivion.

✺

"What will you do with her after she has served your purpose?" Dubh showed only a remote interest in the answer to his question.

"I thought, perhaps, to make her a gift to your little pets..."

Dubh sniffed as if at something distasteful beneath his nose. "Perhaps as a plaything, but for anything else...totally unsuited."

As they stood watching the cowering human, Olcas tucked away the tidbit of knowledge he had just gleaned. His brother was stingy with information on the *Bás*. No matter, it would just take a little longer this way. Already Olcas had learned so much. Like now...he knew the Pack would bring down humans and use them as hosts for a litter of kits, so it was not the woman's species that rendered her unsuitable. It must have been because the doctor's wife lacked in another way—she was utterly mundane, not a glimmer of mage potential to be found. Made sense; if she had any, Olcas would not have offered her to his brother. No, all she was good for was as bait or as a sacrifice. He would keep her just long enough to draw out his true prey, and then there was no question of her fate, only in the manner in which it would play out.

"And the other?" A glimmer of Dubh's interest surfaced, though Olcas doubted his brother realized just how much he betrayed himself.

"I haven't decided yet," Olcas affected a slightly bored indifference and allowed his hand to run across the child's hair in a manner that would have severely alarmed any parent or decent-minded adult. Dubh's faint flash of condescending amusement, too quick to be caught except for Olcas's intimate familiarity with it, kindled satisfaction in him, not anger. Let his oh-so-superior brother believe the child was nothing but a sadistic plaything; that suited Olcas well and confirmed his suspicion that Dubh had never been in a position to learn how to summon and bind demonkind. He had absolutely no idea what this little pet was capable of. No doubt he sensed some sort of potential there, but mistakenly took it for some variation of mage energy. That assumption would prove to be Dubh's downfall. Glad to reinforce his brother's misconception, Olcas continued to absently caress and fondle the...child. He gained a thrill from the fact that were his safeguards not in place, the creature would have latched on and devoured him through just such a casual and careless contact. Even now he sensed the demon's frustration as it strained beneath the surface of its assumed innocence, its essence sucking harmlessly at his own primal force. No mortal was safe from the unshackled potency of this fiend; even he and his siblings would have been hard-pressed to emerge unscathed from a confrontation. And that was with proper precautions in place.

Olcas quickly shrouded his gaze and his thoughts, though, with the way his brother disregarded his presence, he needn't have bothered. A delightfully vicious plan sprouted in his thoughts, one he intended to carefully nurture. Dubh would soon wonder that he had ever been so dismissive of Olcas and his ability to plot a diabolical course, let alone carry one out.

Chapter 12

The feast was long overdue, and though it was not the Feast she requested for Patrick days ago, sparking so much controversy, it was at least a well-deserved celebration for them all. The *Sidhe* had been victorious in several recent encounters, Kara was safe again and on the road to healing, and though a threat still lurked beyond the bounds of their Land, there was hope that it would be vanquished. But that was for tomorrow. Tonight was for honor and merriment. That was the theory, anyway. In truth, Goibhniu had conspired with Maggie in this effort to draw them all together, especially those who would have been first to absent themselves had they known the true purpose of the evening: to force open the eyes of those willingly blind to the approaching danger.

Looking out at the gathering, Maggie marveled at how well they'd turned their backs on the world. Not all of the *Sidhe* had, but *Tír na nÓg* seemed to draw a good many of those that did. And there were so many of them. Long, low tables lined the walls and smaller round ones dotted the center of the chamber. Everywhere else, there were cushions, without even a clear area to walk between them. It did not seem possible, but there was room for everyone; no matter how many came through the arches to join the festivities, there was a space for them all among the sea of satin and velvet and sumptuous fare.

The beauty of the surroundings rivaled only that of the celebrants — *Sidhe* and human alike. There was something about the reaffirmation of life that lent them a certain glow. What Maggie was about to share would dim that glow, of that she had no doubt. She tensed exponentially as she waited for Goibhniu to call her forth. Was she ready for this? Had the festivities dissipated her temper enough? If one of the Court vexed her, could she respond without undoing all the recent good? Even as she wondered, Goibhniu's words committed her.

"Children o' the Mother Goddess, Danu," the Smithgod's commanding voice boomed through the chamber. "I would have ye listen to a tale o' bravery an' courage, not o' ages past, but o' yesterday. Our blessed daughter, Cliodna, known as Maggie in the mortal world, shall tell the tale o' her an' her companions."

Nodding, Maggie began. For the sake of the humans, she delved back slightly further than yesterday, as Goibhniu had said. She started first with the legend of the Children of Carmán, telling of the great evil out of Athens that had plagued Eire so very long ago. How the witch-goddess Carmán and her three sons, Calma, Dubh, and Olcas, preyed upon the mortal Celts to strike out at the *Tuatha de Danaan*, hoping to draw them into battle. The goddess and her sons had yet to meet a force that could stand against them and only saw the wealth of power they could consume in their conquest of the *Sidhe* and Eire itself. Power to them was like sweet nectar, sustaining them and enflaming their hunger. They engaged in the battle they sought and found themselves with no hope of standing against the Fair Folk. Attempting to flee, they instead were captured. Carmán was chained and left to watch as her sons were executed for their cruel atrocities. She died of grief, witnessing their destruction before her own judgment could be passed.

"All o' Eire rejoiced that their greatest demons were destroyed, but none suspected, even to this day, what Carmán's sacrifice had wrought." Maggie ruthlessly caught the eye of every *Sidhe* before her, those guilty of the same overconfidence that had brought down Carmán and her children. Members of this Court were confident that no one in the outside world could strike at them...well, they were wrong. "Have ye never wondered at the awesome power released that day with nary a sign to show for it, then? Such power doesn't just fade away.

"Carmán saved her children that day." Maggie's voice rose to fill the very heights of the chamber, louder and more forceful even than the strike of Goibhniu's hammer upon his anvil. It lashed out at the gathered crowd, those who looked down their noses at her and her "common" company. Ignoring the angry mutters of the dozen or so *Sidhe* who had actually been present at the vanquishing of Carmán and her sons, those who had helped subdue the ancient foe, Maggie continued.

"Ye don't believe me?" She braced herself, drawing strength from her conviction. Before she was done, this crowd would have no choice but to acknowledge that they were wrong. She had seen the very thing they denied, though she hadn't known it for what it was. None of them had known or appreciated the true depth of their victory until Kara had climbed out of her darkness and confirmed everything Maggie and Goibhniu had only speculated. When they realized the enormity of the encounter, Maggie set aside her sense of personal guilt for the suffering of her fellow fighters and instead felt burgeoning awe that they had not paid even more dearly for their victory. "Those o' us who fought the battle at Yesterday's Dreams stood together against an evil so great that most o' us nearly didn't walk away from the battle...an evil not unfamiliar to the *Tuatha de Danaan*. Carmán's sons live!"

"Impossible!" There was no telling who spoke, but the murmuring that followed confirmed that the speaker only voiced what was in most of their thoughts. "The bodies were burned, and the remnants given to the sea."

"The will o' their mother, the goddess Carmán, preserved their spirits, not their flesh," Maggie answered, her tone steady and sure.

"An ye doubt me, step forward...share my thoughts," she dared them, her voice low and full of challenge. Let them step forward; she would gladly share with them the hopelessness of that battle and the maddening grief of her loss. Maggie would be genuinely amazed should any of them prove strong enough to bear the burden that still weighed upon the hearts of her and her fellow fighters. But none came forward; they weren't given a chance.

"Better yet, try sharing mine, if you dare." The low voice carried ominously above the mutters of the Court, fiercely challenging all those who raised their voices to scoff at Maggie's revelations.

Her anger drained away, replaced with concern as Kara glided from where she hid, unnoticed in the shadows of an alcove. This was the first time she had ventured forth since she had recovered her senses. The girl was pale, a feverish flush just barely colored the curve of her cheek, and her eyes now appeared ancient and clouded with the weight of what they'd seen, their innocence fled. At the moment, her gaze was glassy as if she forced herself to look at her worst nightmare, without the luxury of blinking or looking away, trying merely to look through it.

As for the rest of her features, all softness was gone from them, and while the transformation did not give her a cold air, it definitely lent her a regality that rivaled that of the *Sidhe*, lending her features a fey cast. There was no doubt this mortal girl had changed: her indecision was gone, along with her sense of security, as Maggie could see by her subtle wariness, the edge of terror in her eyes, even here in the safe haven of *Tír na nÓg*. Kara may have been freed from the prison of her mind, but she had not yet rid herself of the demons. Worse yet, she refused to speak of it, rebuffing any help or healing, suffering no touch or contact. Still, that only proved all the more the strength she possessed, as she no longer allowed her fear to cripple her. It was worrying though, as if they had only her likeness back, with everything else that was *Kara* safely tucked away. Until now...

Maggie abandoned her observations as Kara again spoke. "Twice, I have seen great evil beyond anything you have ever reckoned. Twice it has looked out at me from different faces, but with the same eyes. I can't say if it is one of these sons of Carmán, but whether it is or not, the threat is great just the same. Dare any of you look into the face of the evil I have fought? The evil that has done this to me? The evil that has sworn, in its own words, by the Great Mother, Carmán, to gain revenge upon us all?" The girl spoke through clenched teeth, the intensity of her sweeping gaze silencing the room even before she tore the front of her simple shift, revealing the still-raw wound that ran down the center of her chest. Her dignity as she stood bared before them would have put a queen to shame. Her next words should have done no less to the members of the Court.

"Scrios...Tógail...Díoltas..." *Havoc...Destruction...Revenge...* Kara spat the Gaelic words in their faces, unwittingly speaking them as accurate as an ancient Celt would, accent and all. "Those warnings were not left for the Irish...they were left for the *Sidhe*. This will not pass you by while you hide here in your precious Hall and deny the menace at your door." Though it was barely perceptible, Maggie noticed as Kara trembled from the effort of stepping forward and speaking her heart. Maggie hurried to her side, steadying her before any of the Court could notice. She was not alone; as she put one arm around Kara's shoulder and reached her other around to draw the torn shift closed, every member of their original party came forward to stand united before the crowd. Astutely, none of them touched her.

"All o' us stand before ye today for but one reason," Maggie continued, her steely voice slicing through the prolonged and strained silence. "Because o' the strength an' courage o' this mortal girl, with the blood o' the *Sidhe* mingled strongly in her veins."

"We didn't know then that we faced one who stood against the *Tuatha de Danaan* long ago, whom we all thought dead with the rest o' his treacherous kin. As a *sowlth*, his strength still remains, though he must steal his form from others, using them as one would use a tool." Maggie drew herself up in the face of their disbelief.

"A tool, ye say," a contemptuous voice rose up from the crowd, "Like a puppet? Seems I'd like to know who'd be pulling yer strings. Who are ye speaking for, Cliodna? Sure enough, ye couldn't come up with such a fanciful tale all yer own."

"Goibhniu himself has confirmed this." Maggie clenched her jaw against speaking further, though a retort rose rather quickly to her tongue. It would serve neither her nor those who followed her to walk that path. Let the foolish Court mock her, attacking her with barbed words and derision masking their own fear. She would walk away with dignity before she jeopardized the seeds of thought she—and, even more, Kara—had succeeded in planting in the receptive minds scattered among them. Even now, she saw considering looks that turned toward her, the glow of comprehension as the concept took root—accepted, if not as fact, at least as a possibility.

With utmost decorum, Maggie turned and guided Kara from the Hall, the others following her, not in defeat but in disdain of the small minds that would strike out with petty taunts at any who disrupted their sheltered little world.

◈

Aí climbed through the shimmering air with his precious burden to find *Mór Halla* in disarray. As the temporary gate closed, Rex huddled at his feet, understandably wary of the turmoil that greeted them. Aí gripped Agnieszka's body carefully and lowered himself down on one knee so that the sprite could climb to his shoulder. He waited patiently as the creature transformed from the cat-seeming to his faeling form. Bright blue feline eyes remained unchanged, though now they looked out from a fey face, all angles and slopes and deep gold in color. The sprite's gaze was guarded and trusting all at once; the tresses framing the face maintained the aspect of cat-Rex's tawny, tabby coat shot through by bold, glossy black strips. With agility ever-characteristic of his kind, the sprite scampered up the offered knee and gently over the woman to settle himself upon Aí's shoulder. Once there, he stared defiantly out at the crowd.

Fortunately, all attention focused on the other end of the Hall. With haste, Aí ducked the three of them into the closest alcove. He did not think it wise to reveal his prize to the Court — not before he could discuss her significance with Goibhniu himself.

"Welcome back, poppet...or do I mean puppet?" The tone was deceptively polite. There was no trace of an accent, every word carefully enunciated, pretentious, as if the speaker shunned any connection to his heritage or to this land.

Aí wheeled about, muscles taut and blood gone icy cold at the unexpected voice in the sheltered corner. Was he cursed? *Mór Halla* had been bad enough, but to end up face to face with the single *Sidhe* he'd most rather have avoided, it was really too much.

"Bran," he answered. He tried for civility, but his mind and tongue conspired against him. "I can't say I'd hazard a guess at what ye mean. In fact, yer thinking has ever been so disjointed that I'm really not surprised ye can't be sure yerself."

Bran snarled and stalked forth, his cold, flat eyes burning with hatred and malice, his lip twisted into a sneer. If it were not for the immortal beauty of his heritage, Aí dared to think his foe would have been one of the most hideous creatures found upon the earth or even in its hidden places. Of course, he was biased.

Why doesn't he leave if he bloody well hates this place that much? Aí couldn't help but wonder. Unfortunately, when he met those aged-bone-colored eyes, burning with a familiar hunger, he was afraid he could guess the answer.

Once they had been the closest of friends, before Bran had sought to make it more. Aí did not share that inclination, even had his heart not belonged to the lovely lass, Sadb. The vengeful response to his polite disinterest forever altered all of their lives. Memories flooded unbidden through his mind before he could suppress them, and Aí forced himself to tamp down his immediate and burning hatred. He could not afford to let it influence him now, not with others present that could be hurt.

Bran's gaze swept across them, his eyes hooded with distaste, though it could not completely mask the longing that still smoldered there. "And you've brought company. Or is it a present? Oh, please...another waterkin?"

This was prejudice refined to its purest level. Aí saw nothing but loathing in the way Bran drew himself up, assuming a superior pose, distancing his person from the 'filth,' before speaking his poison once more. "One of its ilk dared to consider attacking me just the other day before I made it clear she still existed only on sufferance."

Aí felt a surge of wrath for the implied threat in his nemesis's words. Only extreme restraint and his awareness of the danger to Agnieszka kept Aí from snapping at the lure. For his efforts, Bran just pushed him harder. "And a vermin of a sprite? They are overrunning the place as it is these days. You really should be more discerning of the company you keep."

"Ah, in that I must agree with ye," Aí answered, his voice deceptively pleasant, while his darker side wanted to tear the other to shreds. He restrained himself to a verbal flaying. "'Twouldn't do to be seen with the like o' ye."

He was careful not to reveal in any way the error Bran made in referring to Agnieszka as waterkin. For some reason, whatever cloaked her in a mortal seeming still clung to her. Though Aí himself could see past it, he suspected that was due to the perception of his particular Gift. Just as well: safer for her to be mistaken for waterkin...at least until she learned what she was and what that meant. He knew for a fact she was just as ignorant of her own nature as this serpent was.

Every instinct told him to leave, but he dare not turn his back on Bran. Instead, with a thought, Aí sent Rex scurrying off to fetch Goibhniu. Now his only concerns were the woman in his arms and his own back. Did his foe dare to strike in the heart of *Tír na nÓg*? Always before he had reserved his attacks for the mortal world, where Goibhniu was less likely to notice his indiscretions. Still, this open confrontation itself was bold for Bran. What had changed to cause him to set aside his caution?

With each step toward the openness of the garden path just beyond the far arch of the alcove, Aí felt his nerves stretch taut. Bran's eyes never left him, though he made no move to strike out. Apparently, now was not the time. There was no doubt the reckoning would come, though. Aí heard the whisper of a promise in his head like a chilled draft robbing him of warmth. A quick glance back over his shoulder assured him Bran, and not his agitated imagination was the source of the promise.

"Then again, she does seem to be quite a treasure-trove of power. Nice to see she'd serve some purpose other than to spend oneself in." The parting comment sent rage shooting through Aí's already aggravated heart. Visions of his lovely Sadb flooded his memory: Sadb laughing...Sadb playing with the sprites...Sadb driven from *Tír na nÓg* by Bran's hateful lies, trapped in the mortal realm without even her true form to ease her way...Sadb with a human's crude arrow through her perfect throat...all because Aí had loved her more than he could ever have loved Bran. With each memory, a burning tide of fury washed over him. Not again! With swiftness only one of the *Tuatha de Danaan* could manage, he laid his burden gently upon the ground and whirled to confront the black-hearted *Sidhe*.

"Watch yerself, Bone Raven. She'll notbe used by any, an' especially notby ye." Aí's stance was rock-steady and his voice full of iron as he stood between Agnieszka and one who most definitely wished her harm. He had not gone through everything he had to ensure her safety, only to allow her to be victimized in the place meant to be her haven. His piercing eyes flared brilliant blue as he scanned the shadow, only to find the antagonist fled, his comment a parting barb.

Gathering Agnieszka back into his arms, Aí experienced a twinge of concern that she was still insensible. What had happened to her? Had he actually been too late? His memory conjured up images of Murna stretched out upon Anu's shrine. There did not seem to be a similarity in their states, but could he be certain? It wasn't as if any of them had encountered this before. What if this was the beginning?

Concern furrowed his brow, and indecision held him in place. As he stood there, his burden was lifted from his arms. No! His first thought was that Bran had returned and taken advantage of his distraction. That is until he felt a silky caress as the sprite's once-more feline head rubbed gently against his knee.

His gaze slid from the sprite at his feet to the towering figure beside him. Agnieszka looked so frail cradled in Goibhniu's colossal arms. Yet relief eluded him, his heart feeling only bereft. Aí had not realized how weary he had grown, his energy sapped by all that had transpired. Now that he had discharged his duty he could rest. Later would be soon enough to wonder what Bran was up to. And then he remembered what Agnieszka was...what she meant to his people, for there was no doubt in his mind that she was the *Cosaint*...and she was pregnant.

"Come now, *leanbh*, let us see what can be done for this most precious one." Goibhniu's voice rumbled from high above his head and echoed deep within his heart, all at the same time. "No doubt we'd be better off going somewhere a touch more private."

Numb and unsettled, Aí followed silently along a familiar path. It was no surprise to him when the unforgettable shrine came into sight, unfolding from the embrace of the forest. His chest grew tight, and dread shadowed his eyes as he looked from the shrouded figure on the slab to the enigma carried by the Smithgod. Did this herald doom or deliverance?

A whisper drifted on the tranquil air, echoing like a shout in the silence. "I'm ready, Maggie."

Maggie's heart stilled and the rest of her with it. Had she heard true? Forcing herself to breathe normally, she turned slowly to the girl beside her. The two of them sat alone in one of the many grottos around Goibhniu's palace. They had been trying to find their moment of peace after the most recent confrontation with the Court. "Aye, love, are ye now?"

It was a simple enough response. Completely understated, in fact, considering the monumental step this was in Kara's recovery. No matter how much she wanted to know why, or to crow with joy, Maggie kept silent. It was up to Kara to divulge as much, or as little, as she was comfortable with. That was the most important thing Maggie had learned since reuniting the girl with Quicksilver.

"I'm clinging to the pain." Kara's voice was distant, detached, almost as if it were not herself she referred to, but some third party. As she spoke, Maggie watched her good hand travel a familiar circuit across her ear, down her chest, and finally along her ruined hand. "Just like the Court clings to its anger and contempt toward us because they feel it keeps them safe from the outside world, I have not let go of my pain because it shields me from the responsibility that waits for me."

And still, Maggie said nothing. She was not here to offer advice or agreement, let alone to refute any of what Kara said; there was no doubt in her mind of that. Her sole purpose was as witness and foil for Kara's own internal debate.

"Maggie, I've been selfish for too long." Fear and remorse darkened Kara's eyes to a deep shade of raw honey, but could not diminish the renewed sparkle of life that Maggie spied therein. "I've been told more than once by Goibhniu himself that he can make me as if new, that he can restore my wreck of a hand so I can play again if only I would let him. All I need do is draw aside whatever barrier I've raised around me and accept his healing. I've refused to believe that that is all it will take. To say the words, to ask... I've clung to the misconception that somehow it would all be less real and my suffering less justified without that constant reminder." Self-disgust crept into her expression. "I have cradled the pain and the wreckage until I only remember my sacrifice and not that my own disobedience was the reason it was required."

"No!" Nothing could hold back Maggie's protest. "Kara, ye can't believe ye deserved this! No matter what..."

"Hush, Maggie." Though her words were not harsh, Kara's gaze was unyielding. "I said nothing about deserving, just that I myself am responsible. I am the sole reason I was in that situation, and inside, I have kept myself there ever since. I will not begin to be free until I let go of this. I am ready to heal,

Maggie; if I don't, I will be no better than those we left behind in *Mór Halla*, those who turned their tongues against you when you warned them." Maggie nearly flinched away as the newly kindled flame in Kara's eye flared with intensity. She kept herself very still as the girl shot to her feet, and her good arm whipped out to point back in the direction of the Court. "Those *Sidhe* cling as blindly to their denial as I have to this physical pain, and for the same reason. That doesn't make me as bad as them...it makes me worse! I know what is out there...I know what we face. By hiding here behind my wounds, I allow him to continue to victimize us all. There is not a moment that I don't see his face over me or feel his touch, but I have to admit it doesn't have to be that way, or at least not forever. But by refusing to take the first step that will set me free of this, I remain crippled in more ways than one. I can't continue this way, not if I am to reclaim my life."

Maggie sensed there was something more Kara did not reveal, but she didn't push. Instead, she took a deep breath and nodded sharply before rising to hold out her arms to Kara. It tore at her heart to see the girl tremble, knowing instinctively that it was with equal parts vehemence and fear. There were any number of *Sidhe* in Maggie's acquaintance who did not dare to admit such a fault, let alone take steps to overcome it. Maggie smiled softly and allowed her pride to sift into her gaze. "Shall we, then?"

❋

Settled among the roots of the most ancient tree in *Tír na nÓg* with Agnieszka cradled in a grass-filled depression between them, Aí cast a considering look at Goibhniu. For some reason, the Smithgod had withheld a significant fact about his charge. Anger and doubt regarding that battled in Aí's heart. Would it have complicated his task, to have known the woman's true nature, or made it easier? He could not deny that the stakes would have risen much higher.

"There was no telling ye, notwithout putting both them an' yerself in grave danger." Goibhniu's words aptly intruded on Aí's inner struggle. "Ye're thinking she's the only one, but in truth, half o' those ye brought back to the fey lands were *Cosaint*s—full-blooded an' unknown to the *Tuatha de Danaan*. Did ye never wonder why so many different tales existed, hinting at different aspects o' the hope o' our kind? Were there only one, 'twould be a faint hope indeed.

"Alas, it seems the time o' the *Cosaint* is past. More than ten o' the *Sidhe* have been lost to us, though only that many are reflected on the Great Wall; at least three o' the hidden ones have likewise fallen in this way, targeted for their unknown magical nature. The spell that protected them an' hid them has failed. Without that, we can't leave them vulnerable in the world o' men. The *Daoine Maithé* must find new hope, a new way to safeguard the future." Goibhniu's voice remained calm, and his body relaxed, but there was no hiding the sorrow in his eyes. The Smithgod suffered the loss of Danu's Children. Feeling Goibhniu's pain, Aí was unable to keep the tears from streaming down his cheeks.

"So ye see, I couldn't tell ye until the last one was safely home," Goibhniu explained. Aí understood, but still, it did not rest easy with him. It had been doubly shocking to find that not only was it a full *Sidhe* he bore away, but a pregnant one. No wonder she had withstood him. But how had she gotten with child? And why had the seeming not lifted? He did not get a chance to voice these questions, for there was a stirring at his feet.

"I...I know you." The words were faint...breathy, and the accent decidedly British. "I know you!"

It was Agnieszka, and the fury that replaced her initial confusion was frightening in its intensity. Instinctively, Aí leaned away from the newly awaken *Sidhe*. He needn't have bothered.

"Why?! Why did you do it? Why did you take him away?" As if a tether had been released, she flung herself forward, pounding upon Goibhniu's chest with furious fists. The Smithgod merely sat there, not moving to strike her, making no effort to halt her assault. Aí was dumbfounded by both of them. "Where is he? I've waited so terribly long...*where is he?!*"

These last words were desperate, filled with longing and half-hearted hope. Her eyes remained glassy and unfocused as if she were dream-walking.

"Yer heart holds the answer to it all, *leanbh*, an' ye know that, do ye na?" Goibhniu answered in soothing tones. There was no excuse in his tone, no false hope, no patronizing. As he spoke to her, his massive finger brushed across her forehead, and then her heart, and back up to caress her lips, as if wiping away a veil or protective film. "Look to yer heart's deepest paths, child. *Cuimhnigh*... remember."

Her eyes grew wide and her chest heaved as if she gasped for breath. For a moment, she went utterly still, arching with the tension until the moment she crumbled.

"Oh, my God! No! My God! This isn't real. What have you done to me?" Aí watched as Agnieszka wilted. Her fists continued to pound Goibhniu's chest, but only halfheartedly, as if her mind had retreated from that which she'd no desire to see, without telling them they could stop. "He's not dead, he's *not* dead..."

The woman drew shallow, labored breaths and looked ready to flee, her eyes wild with remembrance. Aí watched as a lifetime of knowledge flooded through her mind, leaving her heart pounding with unexpected self-discovery. It was torture to stand aside and not try and offer her comfort. It was not his place at this time, though. He was relieved when Goibhniu drew his hand down across her eyes, bringing the sleep upon her before she could crumble beneath the onslaught.

"Well, I'd say ye got more answers than ye bargained for," Goibhniu commented wryly. Aí sensed he was about to say more, but Goibhniu just turned and looked off into the forest. His gaze grew distant and even more somber as he turned back to address Aí. "I know, it doesn't make much sense. Yet, I've one more task for ye before I can explain..."

Aí winced. Many questions pounded against his skull. But he understood now was not the time for them. Someone approached, and the Smithgod clearly wanted both him and Agnieszka gone before whoever drew near entered the clearing. "What would ye have me do?"

He rose to his feet and watched patiently as Goibhniu gathered Agnieszka up. "Come closer." As Aí did so, Goibhniu laid her in his arms. "Return her to the Hall an' see she's settled. Don't give her over to another *Sidhe*. 'Tis Barbara O'Keefe I wish you to take her to. She'll notwake until I lift the sleep. Tell Barbara she has need o' a mother's care. Once ye've seen to that, return here."

Kara moved silently through the elemental forest. Some indefinable sense led her, as in a game of hot and cold. She could tell, vaguely, that Maggie trailed behind. And Goibhniu lay somewhere ahead. She tried not to cringe at the thought, but the curse still had her tight in its grip. At times, only Quicksilver's ever-present voice running through her head made it possible to endure the ongoing nightmare.

As she moved forward, the forest unfolded before her. It seemed somehow incomplete, vacant, bereft. The boles were massive and glorious; the canopy, an impenetrable crown of jewel-green leaves, but all was silent. Even the gentle wind had gone elsewhere, leaving the trees without a voice to wail their palpable sorrow. That was when it struck Kara what was wrong. No matter where she had gone in the Land of Youth, faelings flocked to her. A myriad of kin-cousins had trailed her every movement. There were no faelings here, where they should be most evident. Mother Nature's children had fled.

There was no time to dwell on the anomaly. Before her, the forest opened its arms to reveal a breathtaking shrine. But that was not what caught Kara's eye. In the very heart of the forest, a dreadful poison spread seemingly unnoticed. She didn't know how she recognized it for what it was. Its effects were evident, though. All around the clearing, harmful growth encroached on the greenery, sapping the trees of their strength and poisoning the soil. Leaves fell where they had never fallen before and insidious moss found a foothold on smooth, graceful branches that knew nothing of parasitic growth until now.

The source of it all lay in reverent state upon the shrine.

Shrugging off Maggie's hand, Kara rushed past Goibhniu to sink to her knees before the creamy marble slab. She stared up at the glorious statue whose features were both awesome and disturbingly familiar. Her eyes then dropped to the base of the slab. Compelled, her hands reached out to brush away the deadfall, revealing the inscription carved into the marble:

To the Valiant Soul of Anu, Cherished Sister and Savior,
Torn forever from the Heart of the Daoine Maithé
Stolen from us, by the Namhaid,
Denied the purity of the Eternal Flame.
All honor and love to your memory.

Kara's heart clenched as she read the haunting tribute. Tears streamed down her cheeks. The words touched her deeply, though she could not fathom why. Regardless of the reason behind her reaction, the engraving was a vital clue to the horror she hadn't even realized they faced. It revealed to her both poison and cure, though she could not explain how she recognized this. Before either of those present could stop her, she whipped away the cloth of black velvet, her efforts made clumsy by her ruined hand. She barely noticed, just as she barely noticed the exotic orchid that slid to the ground or even the way Maggie leaped forward to knock away the candles that would have set flame to the impromptu grave cloth. Nothing penetrated her awareness once the malignancy was revealed.

What lay on the sacred shrine defiled the memory honored here in the worst way. It could not continue. Guided by the soft, insistent strands of the violin music running through her thoughts, Kara reached out her awareness beyond the forest, calling back the nymphs and faeries, the pixies and brownies, summoning the sprites and undines and every other kin-cousin imaginable. She called them to her side. Frightened and unwilling, nevertheless they came. Kara sent them a silent plea; erect a barrier between her and all nearby, leaving only the body within the confines. The shield they raised was glorious and primal, glittering and vibrant and solid as the foundation of *Tír na nÓg*. None would pass through it. From her side, or the other.

Hands spread wide, as in supplication, Kara ran knowing fingers through the magical currents, the very threads that wove the fabric of the Land of Youth. For but a moment, she allowed herself to glory in the crackling caress of all that power. It embraced her, protected her, and recognized her as she did not recognize herself, filling a need she had not even known existed. There was no describing the heady sensation of acceptance. She was finally home.

She split the energy, directing two thirds back to the pathways they had followed for endless ages, momentarily diminished for now, but not broken. The remaining third she wove tightly until no seam was evident. Casting it in place of the black velvet, by sheer will she drew the edges closed, binding them together until they sealed in the corpse and the poison it contained.

Trembling with the unfamiliar effort, astounded by the confidence of her own actions when she hadn't a clue how she knew what to do, Kara stopped a moment, allowing the peace and certainty to settle back around her. She could not resist the compulsion to cast a glance beyond the faeling shield. Maggie and Goibhniu stood there, intent and unmoving, trying to see through the shimmer of the shield. It was humbling. No matter what wonders she wove before the shrine, nothing compared to the magnitude of the barrier her friends...her children had erected.

Children? Had she really thought of them as children? True, ageless as they were, they were innocents, childlike in their perception, their actions, their needs, though not in their wisdom or experience. But her children? They followed her around as if they were precisely that, but still, such a mindset was a dangerous one she dared not foster in her heart.

Taking herself firmly in hand before the distraction disrupted her focus, Kara turned back toward the energy-bound corpse. Ancient words rose up from some racial memory hidden deep within her genetic code. At least, that was how it felt, as hokey as it sounded in her private thoughts. The haunting strains of the violin still ran through her mind like a comforting hand on her shoulder, reassurance that her instincts were accurate. Kara found herself standing, her hair whipping about her, though no wind blew within the barrier. Her arms no longer supplicated; they were raised commandingly as she directed the power she had woven. Her voice cut like obsidian through the charged air. In a language neither her native English nor the Gaelic she'd heard spoken by both *Sidhe* and Irishmen alike, she commanded the eternal flame to burn. She wasn't ready for the fiery power that shot through her, the final component needed to do her bidding.

It certainly had not been Olcas's intent to be drawn into his brother's machinations, but shrewdly he could see the wisdom of seeming to. At least, until his own were assured. Dubh's plan was masterful: plant enough false information to keep everyone guessing, enough redundancies that even if one or two were discovered it would do the targets no good, and have enough multiple diversions to disrupt the enemy's forces without splintering his own.

Seated unnoticed in the back of the locked-down pub, Olcas listened carefully as the members of the Cell reported on their progress. All the components for the attack had been secured, except for the guns. There had been a raid down in Kilkenny, and McDermott's group had either been taken or had fled—all thanks to the moles in the Cell who had leaked the information to their superiors. One would think that Dubh had been sloppy, allowing that to happen, but the truth was, Olcas knew his brother had planned on it...invited it, even. It did not serve Dubh's plans to have either group triumph over the other. No, what he sought was balance, a weakening of both that all might tumble equally beneath his heel. Olcas respected the cunning of that twist.

Dubh's ultimate goal had absolutely nothing to do with these people, anyway. Olcas could see they were just a diversion for his brother, a subtle way to get a head start on subjugating Eire while they pursued their vengeance over the *Sidhe*. Of course, the rebels did serve quite well as a powerhouse, in either case. The amount of energy garnered from their anger and violence alone was enough to keep both Dubh and Olcas quite sated...for now. It was nothing compared to what they would harvest at the hour of their triumph, but satisfying nonetheless.

It was as if the universe itself screamed. Seven distinct and interwoven shrieks shot across Maggie's nerves and away on the wind as the glittering dome that separated them from Kara collapsed. They were inhuman and violent, evil and unclean, and if she weren't so concerned about Kara, Maggie would have given pursuit and shattered them into nonexistence. As it was, she gave them barely a thought. Shrugging off the frisson they'd sent coursing through her, she scrambled past the frantic faelings to reach her charge.

"Easy, Maggie, easy." Goibhniu gently pulled her back. A silent command must have quelled the faelings, for they ceased their wailing and retreated to the edges of the clearing, allowing them access to Kara. Once the kin-cousins were safely out of her way, the massive hand lifted from her shoulder and Maggie fell upon the ground beside the girl, frantic with the need to confirm she was unharmed.

"Nothing, I find nothing wrong...Why does she not wake?" Maggie felt a keen rising. Blood will always out, they said, and right now, Maggie felt herself slipping into her hereditary role as Bean *Sidhe* to the Clan O'Keefe. Her heart was breaking.

"Maggie-love, will ye not take note o' what is all right?" The gentle rebuke was like an electric shock across her taut nerves. Dazed and shaken, she lifted her gaze to Goibhniu, who stood beside the marble slab at the foot of Anu's likeness. She blinked and then shook her head as if to clear a fog. What was she missing? It was then that she realized.

The body was gone. All save for a fine layer of glittering dust. Goibhniu swept this remnant into a summoned grave bag, to be delivered to the woman's kin in *Tír na mBan*. What was more, even with the glittery *Sidhe* dust gone from the slab, a faint glow lit the marble. Blessed Danu, what had Kara done?

Looking down at the girl, Maggie saw her with eyes unclouded by fear or grief. Kara's chest rose and fell slow but steady. Her arms were out-flung as if she hugged the earth, making it clear that both hands were whole in all respects. Gripping her by the shoulders, Maggie gently rolled the girl into her lap, brushing the wild mane of hair away from a face left newly serene by whatever had taken place beyond the now-fallen barrier. With dawning realization, the *Sidhe* lifted the edge of her young friend's shirt, forsaking privacy in the face of her driving need to confirm what she suspected. Maggie beheld two perfect breasts cradled in a simple cotton bra and an unblemished cleavage beneath.

Somehow, Kara was healed.

With confusion and wonder mingling in her gaze, Maggie looked to Goibhniu. "How?"

"That even I can't say, nor even why, only that it wasn't my doing. Other than that, does it really matter?" As Goibhniu spoke, he tilted his head at a curious angle, staring intently down at Kara. "Haven't ye noticed what else has changed?"

Maggie looked closer and gasped. How could she have overlooked it? The difference was stunning, disturbing even. What could have caused such a change? Amazed, Maggie ran her fingers through Kara's fiery red tresses, searching in vain for even a single chocolate-brown hair.

The chaos of JFK Airport was nothing compared to the insanity Arn's life had become. And yet, it had taken the cabbie four shots to get them to the correct terminal; twice, they ended up leaving the airport proper altogether. How he missed his own car. Even airport parking would not have been nearly as costly or stressful as the taxi turned out to be. He'd probably never see his car again, for that matter. Still parked somewhere down in the Village, it would most likely end up in a chop shop or impound yard long before he returned to claim it.

Finally disembarking at the curb, he heaved his lone carry-on to his shoulder and patted the sealed pocket containing his passport and e-ticket to confirm all was secure. Arn slowly shook his head in self-disgust and entered the terminal. He had resisted hard, yet here he was headed for Ireland. Urias, whose task was most easily assumed by those remaining, journeyed with him. None of the *Sidhe*—particularly the one in question—were pleased with that twist, but there was no way around it. They had tried for two days without success to reach the Irish mortals akin to the *Sidhe*. Everyone capable of contacting Maggie McCormick had vanished. Without that help, he had to bring his own guide to *Tír na nÓg*.

Arn ground his teeth hard at the thought of all the time they had wasted. His temper was shot. With a sigh, he forced the tension and anger away. In the end, none of it mattered, as long as he got Lynn back.

The only good thing about the wait was that he had convinced one of Urias's friends to magic the Ruger so it would not set off the scanner at the airport. Arn had to restrain himself from touching the concealed weapon. The *Sidhe* told him he wouldn't need it; that against what he would face, it would do him no good, but he insisted. Call it his security blanket...his insurance.

"Are ye ready then?"

Arn just growled at Urias and stalked off in the direction of the customs line. At least he was finally doing something constructive. God help the *Sidhe* if he found out that he was leaving his wife behind with no hope of rescue. Arn would relieve them each of their burden of immortality himself...with his bare hands. He had to get to Lynn.

Please let me be in time, Arn thought furiously. *By God, Jesus, Mary, and all the saints, and for good measure whatever the Sidhe held sacred, please let me be in time.*

❧

Aí delivered Agnieszka into Barbara's capable hands and headed back to the clearing. He was nearly there before he noticed the changes surrounding him. The forest was no longer silent. Everywhere he looked, he saw signs the faelings had returned and life once more filled the forest. Excitement and relief coursed through his veins. He quickened his pace until he nearly ran to the clearing—only to stop dead at the sight that greeted him.

His eyes traveled a quick circuit around the now-peaceful glen. The plants and trees were extraordinarily vibrant even for the heart of *Tír na nÓg*; they nearly pulsed with life. The change was quite dramatic. Then his gaze came to rest on the shrine itself. The body...it was gone! The stone bore nothing but the glow of gentle, insistent power. What had happened here?

He turned his gaze to the small group huddled before the shrine—Goibhniu and a *Sidhe* woman he didn't recognize gathered around someone on the ground. His gaze returned to the empty shrine.

Murna of Tir na mBan was nowhere to be seen. Was it she they stood over? Had she somehow risen from what they had thought was her final rest? He exerted his senses, bracing himself for the chilling miasma he'd sensed once before. It never came. The woman...the girl on the ground, was not as he had thought. She had the feel of something *Sidhe*, yet not, and a mind-numbing capacity for power that near blinded him. There was also present scarring of the soul...the remnants of a horrifying trauma. It faded even as he watched, sent into retreat by a steadily healing glow. Unfortunately, it didn't disappear completely. His Gift prodded him to go to her, but something held him back as if this were not his place. As, in fact, it wasn't. He didn't know enough of the situation; just the little his empathy could glean. The crucial thing he could not tell: Who was she, and what had happened to her?

"She is called Kara O'Keefe, a human with the blood o' the kin mingled in her veins, though in no way that we have ever seen before." Goibhniu's matter-of-fact explanation startled Aí. He had not even noticed the Smithgod move away from the girl to stand beside him. Not surprising as all his attention had been riveted on the unconscious Kara. It wasn't hard to notice that Goibhniu only answered half of his question and showed no intention of addressing the other half.

Aí looked back in time to see the unfamiliar *Sidhe* carry the girl in the direction of *Mór Halla*. Her face was pressed against the woman's shoulder, hidden by shadow, but her glorious red hair dazzled his eye. Somehow he knew her, knew something of what she had been through, and would face, but it was all vague feelings with no details behind it. He would have followed them if not for Goibhniu's hand upon his shoulder.

"A moment, *leanbh*."

It was no request. Aí turned to face the Smithgod, obedient and attentive, though the urge to follow the women pricked him. He sensed there was something he must do there.

It would have to wait. As guided, he sat down at the base of the shrine, waiting patiently for the Smithgod to speak what he would. Uncomfortably aware of the marble's unprecedented glow, Ai turned his gaze to the spot beneath the trees where earlier Agnieszka had rested. She was still between them. As was the girl, Kara...and the ill-fated Murna. They were distinct presences in both their thoughts, though none of the women were anywhere near. His rambling brought him back to the shrine. Were it not for the return of the joyous forest-sounds, the silence would have grown oppressive.

Curiosity won out again. "What happened here?"

"A miracle...a revelation..." Goibhniu's voice filled with wonder when he finally spoke. "That lass ye saw carried away has done something by all rights she shouldn't be able to do. Mortal an' almost entirely untrained, she called up the power to unleash the eternal flame, freeing Murna from her unnatural state."

Aí could not speak for gasping. Never had he heard of an untrained soul strong enough to call forth the flame. Few enough were the trained ones who could manage it: Goibhniu, the other *Sidhe* rulers, perhaps a handful of the older, stronger kin, no more. How had the girl survived? By all rights, she should have been left as a burnt cinder in its wake, even if her efforts were successful. How had she been able to do it at all? How had she even known it was the thing to do?!

"I can't say how, nor why, but what she has done here restores our hope. 'Tis the key, Aí, the answer to reclaiming those souls lost to us." Reaching down between them, Goibhniu's massive hand traced an inscription that had gone unnoticed for so long. That was impossible now: after what had taken place, the words glowed like the white-hot center of Goibhniu's own forge.

Aí read them but did not comprehend. He lifted questioning eyes to the Smithgod. The expression he discovered there was sobering and he kept silent as Goibhniu again spoke. "Do ye recall the tale of Anu and Danu, the Savior and the Mother? Then ye'll recall the very first time the faelings fled the *Namaid*...the Enemy. They have done so a second time Now.

"Though we didn't realize it, we harbored great evil in our midst. Here in the heart o' *Tír na nÓg*. By some means o' what they do, they have the power to shackle the souls o' their victims, denying them the cleansing flame that takes all our kind at the moment o' death. When Kara called it forth an' set Murna free, she broke their hold. Ye'll notice the faelings have returned.

"I've soulspoken with Lugh at Tir na mBan, an' already one o' their women quickens with child. I am sure this is the key. If we can but reclaim the bodies o' the fallen, I can do the same, an' children will once again bless the Hall o' *Tír na nÓg*; the *Daoine Maithé* will be nearly whole again."

Aí felt a surge of hope and joy well up within him. For a moment, he reveled in the sensation, only to have it crash in on him. Uncertainty crept into his thoughts and shadowed his eyes. "But how are we to find them? In all o' this time, Murna is the only one we've come upon."

"We have hidden Underhill long enough; thanks to Kara, we have learned something o' at least one o' the enemies we face, an' now a way to thwart them. 'Tis time we put that knowledge to use an' take the fight to their doorstep." The expression on Goibniu's face as he spoke was fierce and foreboding; the conviction in his words sent pride and confidence to straighten Aí's shoulders and banish the doubt in his heart. "Come, we will gather the *Sidhe Fianna* an' decide how this will come to pass."

Somber did not begin to describe the overpowering atmosphere in the chamber. Feeling out of place among the warriors, Aí stood to the side, watching the interplay of emotions among the Kin: disbelief, rage, determination...fear. Those were the strongest, though they ran the gambit of all the darker emotions. The girl from the clearing, recovered from her ordeal, sat as apart from everyone else as the close quarters allowed. He sensed her struggle to remain where she was, withdrawing neither to another room nor to some point deep inside her own thoughts. Of all gathered, her expression was the most determined, the most fierce. She almost seemed haunted...driven. The merciless strain she was under was apparent. Knowing at least part of it had abated in the clearing, he shuddered to think what she had suffered before she began to heal.

His Gift prodded him mercilessly to help. But it was not so simple. To use his Gift without it being asked would be a violation, no matter how well-meaning. He would have to watch for an opportunity to offer his aid. In the meantime, he had better look elsewhere or go slowly mad. That was when he noticed the other human among those gathered, a man. He watched the girl nearly as intently as Aí himself. It was not so easy to read him; his natural barriers were too solid to breach, particularly unbidden.

Who are they, Goibhniu? Aí allowed his gaze to move to the Smithgod, seated in the farthest corner of the room. He wasn't alone—all attention riveted upon Goibhniu as the company fanned out, waiting for his guidance. *This girl, Kara, an' the man?*

Waterkin...an' much more if what we've Seen so far proves true. He is her father, Patrick.

Aí examined the girl more closely. From the drape of her hair and the way she sat, he could not catch more than a glimpse of her face. That merely intrigued him, though. From what he had seen earlier and the little he had heard since returning to the Hall, this was one peculiar waterkin; a slap in the face, in fact, to all whom for longer than conscious memory had used the term to imply inferiority in any offspring produced by a mingling of *Sidhe* and human blood.

He set all musings aside when one final *Sidhe* slipped into the room and melded with the group already gathered. He recognized her as the one who had carried the girl earlier and so was not surprised that she settled near her now. As if that were an alert, all conversation ended, and nearly forty sets of eyes stared unblinking at the Smithgod. One would have thought there was a script or cue cards. Those who stood folded themselves down to kneel respectfully; those already upon the ground adjusted their posture from relaxed to attentive. And then Goibhniu spoke.

"Ye all know a bit o' what we've faced o' late, not only here in *Tír na nÓg*, but all across the *Sidhe* Lands.

"Both ancient an' unknown enemies have risen from the mists to try the strength o' the *Sidhe* once more. Between them, they have defiled the land around us, including our sacred places, torn our monuments in the mortal world to the ground, an' wreaked grievous harm to first the faelings, our Clans, an' then the Kin themselves."

"It shames me to think many o' the *Daoine Maithé* have grown weak in spirit. But how can I na? What else explains why the *Tuatha de Danaan* have been cowed by this shadow enemy, like frightened children, uncertain o' what lurks in the dark? It has fallen to a mortal lass to remind the Kin o' their courage an' strength." The pride and respect in Goibhniu's expression startled Ai. Rarely did he allow such things to show where all could see because to do so inspired jealousy and bitterness among the rank-conscious Kin. Rather than focus on its significance, Aí turned his attention back to the words Goibhniu spoke, just in time to feel a burst of pride as he and all the *Sidhe* around him received similar regard.

"All o' ye are here because ye don't number among those o' which I speak. Yer hearts are fierce an' strong an' ye don't turn a blind eye to what is wrong in the world—mortal or fey. Ye'll have need o' those traits aplenty with what

I'm about to ask o' ye." The Smithgod paused, allowing all to consider the gravity of what he implied. Very few among the *Sidhe* had a personal memory of anything more than petty conflict. No one there had any illusion that Goibhniu spoke of anything short of war.

A murmur went up from the gathering, all save the mortals. What had they seen that they did not even blink an eye at Goibhniu's words? If anything, as those around her grew curious and speculative, Kara O'Keefe seemed to stiffen even further with resolve. Only the subtle way in which her jaw flexed, its curve just visible around the wave of her hair, betrayed any hint of nerves.

"We've Kara to thank for helping to put a name to our foe an' for discovering how to return to the *Daoine Maithé* those souls that have been torn from us. Now all that remains is to seek out the one to find the other." The god's gaze was solemn as he caught every eye in the room in turn, including Aí's. His tone was loving but firm. Curiously, the girl did not look up at the praise; in fact, she seemed to avoid making eye contact with anyone in the room. "'Tisn't simple to battle the unknown, but I must ask it o' ye. We can't have another Anu to torment our hearts. Will each o' ye take up the charge I've laid before ye, or will ye take yerself from here never to return? A harsh choice, but I won't have a soul in *Tír na nÓg* that enjoys Her pleasure without answering the call when 'tis made. Not any o' ye, nor any out there. Yer moment to decide is now; theirs will come in time."

With his final statement, all trace of softness fled the Smithgod's expression. His eyes grew hard, and his mouth set unyielding. It was clear he didn't expect any of them to decline the charge, but he also left no doubt the reception they would receive if they did. This was no idle threat. It was a grave consequence for a deadly serious matter. Never before had such an ultimatum been issued to any of the Kin. It spoke of Goibhniu's disgust and the end of his tolerance for the infantile escapists that had flocked to this Hall since long before he assumed its throne. Aí suspected that those of such an inclination would no longer receive an open reception from here on out. Goibhniu made it very evident that it was time the Children of Danu grew up, and while he did not count those before him as the worst offenders, his attitude also made it clear he felt even they had not quite shrugged off the coils of their adolescence. For those gathered in this room, they would find their maturity in the crucible of war.

"The party's over then, is it?" someone muttered in the back, one of the *Fianna* who had recently returned from America, from the sound of it. The others chuckled uneasily, but no more comments were offered up. Aí nearly held his breath, waiting for Goibhniu to set down the wiseass. The reprimand never came. The comment had been made out of nerves and not insolence. Who could blame that, after all?

"Prepare yerselves to depart within the hour. Once ye leave this chamber, ye'll follow Cliodna, who answers to Maggie McCormick in the mortal realm. I could choose no better to lead ye. Maggie, stand yerself up."

The woman rose, and Aí was struck by the gravity of her expression and the firm set of her mouth; only her eyes betrayed that she was on familiar terms with laughter and smiling. Though something rested heavy upon her heart — perhaps something that would find its ease in the conflict they engaged? Aí felt the tug of this woman's sorrow; it called to him, begging for healing. Once again, he had to force himself to resist. If they didn't wrap this up soon so he could put some distance between himself and the raw emotions, he would be the one needing succor. As it was, until he had the chance to approach both women discretely, his own heart would suffer their pangs. He'd felt the same with Agnieszka and had yet to ease the pressure there. He wondered how much more he could bear before he would break. In all his years, he had never reached that point; he feared this conflict, if nothing else, would come close.

"Now that ye know who ye'll follow, a glimpse o' what ye may face…"

All of a sudden compact streams of pure thought, straight from Goibhniu's own mind, bombarded Aí — and most assuredly everyone else in the room. Within seconds, he knew much more than he could stand to about the recent assaults on the *Tuatha de Danaan*, from the very first warnings, right down to what Goibhniu had seen when the girl Kara called down the flame. Some of it he'd already known or heard about, just as he was sure others in the room had been privy to what he was not. But what frightened him the most was that the information wasn't nearly enough. What face did their enemy wear?

Not again! Maggie could not restrain her gut reaction. She stood before them and took note of the few faces she had not seen when their band was first formed. There were three who were new: Kara and her father, and a man of the *Sidhe* whom she did not recognize. So young he seemed, and untried. This was no elven warrior. Maggie felt ready to weep.

How can I bring them back safely when ye keep adding to my ranks those who aren't fighters? She could not withhold her frustration from Goibhniu any longer, soulspeaking what could not be uttered aloud before her *Fianna*.

Ye already have all the seasoned warriors left in Tír na nÓg. Besides, 'tis the heart that make a Sidhe warrior, Maggie-lass, not the training. The Smithgod answered sagely. *The training merely gives focus to what's already there.*

Platitudes won't serve me on the battlefield. Maggie felt like screaming but knew better than to press the point. She'd already lost one argument when Goibhniu insisted Kara must go with the *Sidhe Fianna* to free the souls of those who were missing; why did Maggie expect this would be any different?

Come now, leanbh, *ye're proof o' what I've said yerself.* As he had once before, Goibhniu flooded her with the pride and faith he had in her. It was a heady experience, one Maggie could not hope to resist. *Think, Maggie: what I send ye off to do will impact profoundly on the future o' the Daoine Maithé, for good or ill. Do ye truly think I'd send ye off to fail? Every person I place under yer command serves a purpose, has a skill. I trust ye to do yer best by yer people. Won't ye trust me to do the same?*

Maggie's doubt dissolved like a summer mist. Faith was more potent than doubt any day; she was ashamed to have had less in Goibhniu than he in her. Her confidence restored, the leader of the *Sidhe Fianna* turned to address her warriors.

"Ye heard him, one hour we leave. We won't return until we've tracked down what we're after, so bring what ye'll need…an' only what ye'll need. I will be inspecting yer gear before we go." Maggie took a firm stance as she continued. The only authority many of those before her were used to recognizing was Goibhniu himself. That changed now. "Leave behind anything ye can't bear to lose. Anything ye forget stays forgotten. The enemy is drawn to power; no magic will be worked once we leave *Tír na nÓg* unless I deem it vital. Remember, one hour, in the clearing in front of *Mór Halla*."

Turning abruptly on her heel, Maggie did not give anyone the opportunity to protest her instructions. She didn't believe that her forces would have a problem following her — they hadn't so far — but she could not afford to take that chance with their lives. She hoped her preemptive strike would head off any *Sidhe* with the mistaken idea that Maggie's commands were optional.

Chapter 13

As Jacko accompanied Granddame Rose to the market at Dublin's Moore Street, her quick, clawlike grip whipped out to snag his arm. "No running off. We are here for information, not so you can hie back to England when my back is turned."

He turned and glared at her. It was an effort to rein in his temper, but Jacko managed. It was too late now, anyway. The damage had undoubtedly been done, in regards to Agnieszka.

Rose turned away as if his obedience was a given. His grip on his temper slipped, and he ground his teeth behind the old woman's back, glaring at her with all the anger built up since she made Sveta steal away with him. There was no doubt they had slipped something in his drink to make him sleep. Otherwise, he would have never slept through the team being hitched up and driven halfway across Britain.

He followed as she made her way down the line of stalls, with no evident purpose, stopping here and there to examine what was on offer, chatting with a few of the women or young children in Romani before moving on again, her basket still empty.

With nothing to occupy him, Jacko's thoughts circled back to his precious Agnieszka. He was worried about her and felt a driving need to keep her safe. But no, instead, he followed the granddame around while somewhere in England, his friend surely cursed his name and justifiably thought him fickle.

"He is here." Almost as if of its own accord, Rose's hand crept up to clutch at a copper pendant she wore around her neck.

"I'm sorry, Granddame, what?"

"He is here, and we must find him; the confrontation will be soon. We must be ready."

Jacko shook his head, confused. Granddame Rose had always kept silent regarding her reasons for leaving New York, joining their caravan, and then rushing them to Ireland. They had always presumed she ran *from* something. They'd never considered she was tracking someone down. Who was this "he" she spoke of? And why did Jacko see fear mingled with the determination in her eyes when she did so?

"Who, Granddame? Who is here?"

She looked at him with venom and flapped her hands at him. All of a sudden, she hurried along the plethora of stalls, examining everything in minute detail and filling her basket—and his arms—with mounds of herbs and candles, not to mention two live chickens. Lunch, or fresh ingredients for some charm? So radical was the change in her behavior that the word "possessed" came to Jacko's mind. He nearly laughed at the absurdity.

With disturbing speed, she whirled on him, and the look in her eye was full of wrath...and just a touch of guilt. Shock stole the amused smile from Jacko's face, and he paled beneath his olive complexion as she swept forward and reached up a gnarled hand to grab his ear, yanking it down to where he would have no trouble hearing her low, menacing tone. "*Him*, not me. And I would not be so quick to laugh; your...friend will have a share of the danger if I cannot unseat the Evil One for good this time. I bought time in New York, but that time is running out."

The cryptic omen sent icy chills through Jacko's veins, and he fervently began to pray the copper pennies he had scattered back at Wicklow Cottage would be enough to safeguard Agnieszka. In the meantime, his eyes scanned the stalls for anything he knew was used for protection against evil. Despite his anger and inadvertent irreverence, he respected Granddame Rose; her words had done more than disturb him. Suddenly, he was relieved Agnieszka was safely far away in England.

To all appearances, the *Sidhe* were naught but a group of carefree backpackers on a hiking tour of the country. The glamory masked the intensity in their eyes, their determination to bring down evil. Kara shared the same, though with less pure intent. Her goal was the vengeance she would exact someday...soon. Then perhaps Tony would no longer leer at her from the face of every man she encountered.

Once in Dublin proper, the *Fianna* headed for the burnt-out husk of the pub she and Maggie had encountered on their first trip there. Standing before it, Kara shivered reflexively.

The aura had grown. It spread over the city like ivy, insidious tendrils creeping out to cover it entirely. She closed her eyes briefly and extended her other senses with an ease she had not been capable of only days ago. She sought the billowing black cloud tinged green with a lurking power that would have sent every man and woman fleeing from the city...if only they could see it, and not just its mundane effects. It was widespread and avaricious, absorbing as much magical power as it could draw away from the unsuspecting. Already two points were as dense as thunderclouds ready to spill. One was the site of the fire, behind them. The other was a beacon in the distance, taunting them, it seemed.

As a group, they followed the tendrils, soulspeaking their observations to one another as they moved closer to their goal. Kara fought not to flinch each time they did. The soulspeech was like having a radio headphone tucked permanently in her ear, buzzing away until she wanted to rip it off. She didn't want anyone in her head; she was no longer comfortable with such intimacy. It was even worse when one of the male *Sidhe* 'spoke; it overlapped with the poisonous digs Tony had made when she was his captive or the mental taunts he cast at her when he'd escaped. It happened over and over again until Kara wanted to scream. Only having her father by her side kept the urge subdued.

Things had improved since she'd called the fire down upon the tainted corpse. Now Tony's features merely superimposed themselves over those of whatever man she could not avoid looking at. Before, they had supplanted them completely. And when a man spoke, she could hear his voice, his words, beneath Tony's, rather than Tony's poison alone.

She told herself that was progress. Proof the curse could be broken. But for now, she had to remain strong or she would never gain the satisfaction of seeing Tony cower before her or the joy of silencing him forever.

Hot upon the trail of the foe, Maggie entered a care-worn pub and was immediately startled to encounter a *Sidhe*'s worried gaze where she only expected to see dissidents. Once it was apparent the pub was their goal, she had asked discreet questions and learned that the place was the headquarters of a particularly nasty splinter group of the IRA. It sounded right to her until she'd come face to face with one of the Kin.

Maggie sauntered up to the bar and called for a pint before turning and allowing her eyes to again run over the men occupying the tables and stools set up around the open room. She made sure to make eye contact with the strange *Sidhe* several times. When he realized he'd caught her gaze, the worry became overwhelming relief. She could not help but look on in puzzlement as she reached out a guarded tendril of thought to get the feel of him. There were such things as dark *Sidhe*, after all. When he noticed her mental touch, he reacted as a man about to drown does when a floating crate drifts by. So desperately, he mentally clung to her that she quickly pulled away and slammed down her shields. He grew shame-faced and moderated his reaction.

Please no! Do not go away. The tone was fraught. *'Tis Rory McIntyre they call me an' I need yer help something fierce. Please, will ye not listen?* He was so desperate Maggie felt as if he clung to her arm, though he sat clear across the pub, and they spoke only in their thoughts.

Go on then...

I'm here to spy upon this faction that we might stop them. We've had enough of the brutal, senseless killing that is tearing Eire an' our Rath apart, an' this group is the worst. Only something happened. A few weeks ago, there was an explosion at the original headquarters... Things got much worse after that.

All o' a sudden the leader, John McDubh, could do things he couldn't do before an' knew things he ought not... Maggie noticed how anxious Rory grew as he realized what he'd said and looked around him reflexively. She could tell it took him serious effort to both keep a sexy smile draped across his face and not run nervous fingers through his tawny locks. McDubh could not have been anywhere around because Rory relaxed just a little...very little, and continued. *He's gotten bolder, more ruthless. The potential for magic was always there, but dormant in the man. Now he seems to sense magic like he grew up in it, especially when 'tis active. I haven't seen him use a bit o' it, but I dare not contact anyone or try the simplest o' spells. I've seen what happened to those that did once McDubh got ahold o' them...Mindless husks they were, an' Himself as sleek as a cat fed on cream — at least, on the surface. 'Tis frightful an ye look at him with mage sight.*

Rory's mind quailed as he tried to go from showing her a mental image of how this McDubh appeared, to his true state. Maggie changed the topic, if ever so slightly, to something safer. It was enough that he had shown her the face the man displayed to the world; she could discover for herself what lay beneath the surface.

There's another we look for. Have ye spied among them a man o' Romani blood with ice-blue eyes? Maggie projected an image of Tony with her words. She was not reassured by the way the man went still and shrank in upon himself before responding. *Aye, That one's been around o' late, eyes as cold as hoarfrost.* Rory answered, struggling to keep his emotions from his face. *A bad patch, that one, even for this lot. He left no traces, but I know he's killed at least one wench in the area since he showed up a few days ago. I was there when the remains were found...they reeked o' ritual magic. She didn't die a natural death.* He shook his head and stared into his beer as if the world were on his shoulders *I've stayed clear o' that man ever since.*

Taking a deep, troubled breath, Maggie regretted setting him upon this path, but there was nothing for it now. Once Rory finished, she realized what must be done. If the terrorist group's plans went off as her new companion had outlined then Ireland would be thrown into chaos, and relations with Britain would be irreparably harmed. That would not be good for the humans or the *Sidhe*. The bombings and killings would never end and the lands both parties loved and depended on for their well-being would be devastated.

She could not allow it. Before leaving, Maggie was sure to get every bit of information Rory had regarding the terrorists' plot, their leader, and anything else that might prove useful. Rory McIntyre would be clear of this place and untraceable within moments of the *Fianna* leaving. Once she had everything, she wished the man well and turned her thoughts to her forces.

Mentally, she divided them into three separate teams, feeding them instructions gleaned from the specifics Rory had provided. They had three goals: disarm the traps at the convention center and the municipal building, track down the terrorist leader, and find the location of the missing *Sidhe*. Maggie and her group would see to the traps personally, as they held the most risk. The other groups would head for the rallies in the hopes of locating the leader and through him their missing kin. Her only dilemma was what to do with Kara. Tony would most likely be at one of the rallies. Which meant Kara would have to go with Maggie. Now the only problem was how to keep Kara from knowing he was around. For make no mistake, though the girl may have thought she'd hidden it well, Maggie had seen in her eyes the call for blood.

Jetlag did not begin to describe what Arn felt at that moment. He'd lost track of how many hours it had been since he had slept. Secretly, he doubted he would ever sleep again, not with the images and fears that now plagued him. He actually didn't care if he stayed up for the rest of his life, as long as it meant he could hold his sleeping wife as he did so.

Arn gave himself a mental shake. On the flight, looking down at the broad, endless expanse of the Atlantic, he had sworn to himself that he would not think of such things. Until he knew of Lynn's fate, it would only torture him to picture her in his arms or anywhere else, for that matter.

Instead, he waited anxiously for his turn to disembark the plane. He was intensely aware that Urias stood just behind him as patiently as if he had absolutely nowhere to be and no cares in the world. Must be nice.

Standing there half-dead, his carry-on once more slung over his shoulder, Arn rubbed absently at his hands. Why hadn't he thought to bring lotion? The prolonged time in the processed air of the plane had left them dry and chaffed. He could not help but rub at them, though he knew better. As he did, he caught himself lingering along the blades of his hands. His reddened skin made faint scars there as visible as a brand. Mostly he forgot about them, but in an odd way, if it hadn't been for those scars, he wouldn't be here today.

His mind wandered to that time long past. Over thirty-six years ago, he had been introduced to a young boy with nearly identical, though more recent scars. Patrick O'Keefe had been brought together with him in the hopes that Arn and his well-adjusted attitude would rub off on the young boy, who was having trouble adjusting to the concept of a five-fingered hand, though it was what he had longed for all of his short life. The difference was that Arn had had six years to get used to it; Patrick had only had days.

Funny how things turned out. If he hadn't met that young Irish boy, he wouldn't be here today, hunting desperately for his wife. But then, chances were that without Patrick, Arn would never have married Lynn, to begin with. Patrick's charm was what had drawn her to them in college, after all. Not that that mattered; even knowing what he knew now, Arn wouldn't have given up meeting his best friend in the world just to avoid this horror. He would be giving up the best parts of himself if he did.

God, he hated waiting! It left way too much time for uncomfortable thoughts...delving into memories...self-examination. Unable to take it any longer, he fidgeted until those in front of him stopped retrieving their bags and glared at him. Unable to bear the stress any longer, he gave up on politeness. Glaring back, he pushed past them and out into freedom, completely ignoring the protests that rose behind him as he stood for the first time on Irish soil, tarmac-covered though it was.

Withdrawn into her own little world, Kara trailed after Maggie and the rest of their group. As had become her habit, she kept her eyes down and her hands in her pockets. So what if she looked like a bored American? That could only add validity to their cover, right?

Even attempting to isolate herself as she did, she was intensely aware of the *Sidhe* surrounding her. They were both a comfort and an ordeal because over half of the *Sidhe Fianna* were male. Kara fought the same battle she had been fighting since her rescue. She was determined to overcome the curse. Someday soon, she would look at a man and not cringe because the eyes she saw looking back were not his. Someday, she would have a conversation without the urge to scream because she heard other words than were actually spoken. And someday...eventually, she would be touched by a man and not flinch away because the pleasure would be followed swiftly by the memory of pain.

Unfortunately, this was not someday.

All three groups still traveled in one loose mass, not needing to break off for their separate ways quite yet. They would reach St. Stephen's Green before they went off in different directions. In the meantime, she hovered on the fringes at the tail end of the group, several of what Maggie called her *Bean Fianna*—her women warriors—keeping an eye on her.

As they crossed the Green, Kara made the mistake of looking up into the gathering crowd; looking back at her was a sea of men with Tony's features translucently superimposed over their own. It nearly undid her. She had not seen so many people together at once since leaving New York, not even in *Tír na nÓg*. Worse yet, most of them were men. Biting back tortured moans, she focused everything she had to keep it together. As she struggled to tear her gaze away, she saw him. At first, she thought it was simply more evidence of her losing battle with the curse, for rather than looking like a thin, waxy mask, this Tony's face was solid, opaque, and quite real, with no hint of another's features beneath. Then his eyes met hers, and a nasty leer flowed across his face.

So, not the curse, but the demon himself.

Without thought or consideration, she dropped back further from the Sidhe. None noticed as the group was due to fracture here as it was; she was simply changing her part in the game. Her pulse quickened. Images of retribution flooded her mind. One way or the other, she would free herself from the curse this day. And if along the way she treated Tony to a taste of the creature he'd created, then that was only justice wasn't it?

With tangible tension, Kara began her slow, almost stately march across the crowded square. She moved with such rigid control, taut as a well-stretched bodhran. Those standing close by looked down at the weathered cobblestones rather than risk catching her smoldering gaze.

Kara barely noticed.

Before her stood the man...the thing...perhaps even the godling, as the *Sidhe* believed, responsible for completely overturning her world. It was this man's fault Kara was forced to leave behind the innocence of her humanity for the uncertainty of a world full of elves and magic, and the fear of assault every time a man approached her, all of them wearing his face. She had lost everything — her hope, her security, her confidence — and there he stood, arrogant and secure in his own power and ability to wear anyone like a suit of clothes, to do as he pleased with no one to stop him.

Well, it did not matter what face her adversary wore, she knew what sat behind those eyes, recognized the power-lust as the same hunger she brushed against for an eternal second on a rooftop beyond the ocean. She'd seen it again in a Dublin warehouse when the same lust coupled with violence to threaten her again. Maggie's tale of Carmán and her children had given Kara a name to go with that pure distillation of evil: Olcas. She had no doubt he was the ancient god returned, though he watched her through Tony's eyes, and Lucien's sneer twisted his stolen lips.

Tony...Lucien...Olcas...she didn't care which stood before her, or if it was all three seated in the young man's frame, she would have revenge for what they had done to her family, to her. And if all of that were set aside, then this was still a predator hunting innocents to dominate and destroy. Never again would she, or anyone else, be preyed upon by them or their kind while Kara stood by.

She was halfway to her objective. As she passed, some could hear her humming forcefully beneath her breath with the same intensity of angry wild bees. Several swore that after they saw wisps of light like foxfire gathering, twining all around her, though most brilliantly at her clenched fists and around her eyes. So absorbed was the crowd with the powerful presence of the

American girl that they gasped as a whole when a beautiful young Irishman dared to step forward, blocking her path.

Kara's teeth visibly clenched as the line of sight between her and her quarry was broken. One trembling hand reached out to thrust the man aside, the force of her gathered power barely held in check. It took her a moment to realize that, as she looked upon the stranger, she briefly saw him as he was before only a faint shadow of Tony cloaked him. She stumbled and momentarily stopped, her startled gaze drifting back to his face. Had she imagined his unclouded features? Perhaps. But it was more important to her to reach Tony, and this man was in her way.

"Kara," with a breath of a whisper, he spoke to her, "this isn't the way."

The muscles in her face quivered as she fought the compulsion of his brilliant blue eyes. Blue beneath the blue glittering in Technicolor. She was immediately put further off balance by a flash of recognition. Something told her she should know him, but further examination did not produce the memory in question. The only certain thing was that for the moment, he was an obstacle. At a glance, his shoulder-length, chestnut silk waves and lean build were startlingly at odds with the rest of the impression he gave: strong and unyielding. This man was like a pillar seated deep within bedrock. She crashed against his will, and he pinned her with a look, stern and inflexible beneath the compassion.

As she stared into his eyes, something loosened deep inside her. Something in his expression was sorrowful, as if she reminded him of a moment from his own past. Without realization, Kara's gaze broke away to sweep his face as if tracing a scar, recognizing it as a reflection of one she would bear if she continued on this path. At that moment, she could see herself clearly as he saw her, could see the darkness that gripped her, twisted her into a creature of its own purpose.

Out of nowhere, she suddenly remembered the children from the bus station, and she was grossly ashamed. She had thought the situation such a revelation; was certain she had learned so much from witnessing that brief encounter. How wrong she had been. This situation was glaring evidence of that—this was not about justice, but revenge. It slowly came to her that the man who had intervened echoed her very thoughts.

"Kara, do not confuse pride with honor," his low, soothing tone drew her back from the chasm, "nor revenge with justice." She looked to herself and saw how anger and a lust for vengeance had nearly accomplished what Lucien's seductive words had been unable to. Not wanting to face the pain, the irrational fear, Kara had closed off too much of her humanity and instead had clung to dreams of retribution.

"Nooo!" With a strangled moan, Kara came back to herself. What had she almost done? She would never be able to look upon Tony or one like him without seeing a shadow of herself, what she had nearly become. That realization rattled her to her core, her entire body quaking uncontrollably, loosening her grip on the power she had gathered. It flew through her like a wave of lightning rising up from the earth, jolting the closest onlookers, and raising the short hairs of the entire crowd, though they did not know why.

Being the nexus of all that aborted power was like throwing the switch on a fuse box. One moment she was totally charged, and the next, there was no juice to keep her going. As she drifted down into a gentler kind of darkness, the last thing Kara saw was the unshakable calm of immortal, electric-blue eyes.

Maggie McCormick cursed herself for not taking more care, for not showing the foresight she most assuredly should have. She didn't know how Kara had discovered Tony's presence at the rallies, but she had known the girl would be drawn by the lure of vengeance. They should have kept a better eye on her. By the time one of the others told Maggie what the girl had done, it had been too late. Now there was nothing she could do. With but an hour before the terrorist devices were due to go off, there was no time to go after Kara. Regardless of her Clan oath, Maggie knew that if it came down to the safety of one of her charges and the safety of all of Ireland, there was no choice to be made. She would mourn Kara should it come to that, and forever blame herself for letting it happen, but she could do no more until the threat to Eire had been averted.

Counting heads one last time in desperation, Maggie again came up with the same tally. Thank the Goddess she had put Patrick in the second group. She would not have been able to meet his eye and confess she put a country before his daughter. Not after all they had been through.

Enough. She had a duty to do, and time moved on without her. Gathering her force around her, she gave thanks for the glamory. She could marshal her warriors with none the wiser, and those passing by would see nothing more than a tour guide with her group.

"We've twenty-five minutes left to see to both the conference center an' the municipal building. To accommodate those with different interests, we'll split up an' meet back here in twenty, so use whatever tricks ye have up yer sleeves to get in everything ye just have to see." Maggie announced in her tour-guide voice but met each warrior's eyes with a significant look before sending them off with a final reminder. "Don't forget to grab yerselves a souvenir or two. An' remember, we're off to Kildare straight away once we're finished up. The other two groups will be meeting us here, so we can't be late."

Without a backward glance, the group divided itself yet again, half following Maggie and the others following the *Fear Fianna* she'd selected to lead them. Time was running out. She motioned for her chosen warriors to follow. Theirs was the touchiest part of the whole operation. Positioning three of them along the service corridor to guard their backs, she and the others continued toward their goal.

That was the moment everything went to hell. As they headed for the sub-ventilation system, a wall of well-muscled flesh spread out to block them, resolving itself into three burly men who looked like prime candidates for the Celtic Games.

"Lost, are ye?"

Without flinching, Maggie met the cold hard gaze of the one who spoke. "Actually, no. One o' the men on my tour is an engineer an' would dearly love to see the infrastructure o' this landmark building. We've special permission to visit the service areas. The superintendent is on his way."

What were they doing here? Rory had been quite clear: the terrorists were to deliver the package and be out by midnight. How much more of what he'd told her was inaccurate? She glanced at her watch, it was approaching noon. Things only got worse when she sensed more men come up from behind. There were at least five of them, unless she missed her guess.

"Is that so? Well, I'd advise ye to turn around an' satisfy yerself with some other...infrastructure today."

Taking in the subtle shifting in the men's posture, resignation settled in. This was not going to work. These men were shrewd and single-minded. Even if they bought Maggie's story, they weren't about to let them past. There was no time to be sneaky. With a subtle signal of her own, Maggie warned the *Fianna* their glamory was about to drop, their cue to raise their weapons.

More comfortable with a staff than a sword, Maggie had a stout walking stick strapped to her back. With inhuman speed and grace, she had it out in seconds and, in a continuation of her draw, immediately whirled on the leader. She was masterful with a staff, but he was no stranger to brawling. Only one of her three hits connected with any force. As he blocked the last one he pressed the attack. Maggie's superior reflexes kept her from being pummeled too horribly, but that was all. Falling back to a defensive stance, she took quick stock of the situation.

Though they outnumbered the men, if just barely, the close quarters more than evened the odds, and not in their favor. One of the *Fianna* was down, and several others showed evidence that they'd taken more abuse than they'd bargained on. Maggie did not have to look at her watch to know their final window was rapidly approaching. She made the only decision she could. Using far more magic than she thought wise given the caution Rory issued earlier, Maggie — without time to warn her own warriors — cast a binding spell on the terrorists.

She watched with horror and guilt as two of the mortal men received unintentional death blows the moment her spell bound them. The *Sidhe* warriors, already committed to their actions, felt similar pangs as they took the lives of men they would have rather left bound to face the justice of their own society. Five more of the terrorists went down until only one man was left standing. The leader's bulging veins showed how he fought the mage binding. The rage in his eyes spoke volumes of what treatment they would receive were he to succeed. Not that he had a chance against the spell, or against the next one Maggie cast.

"Speak to me true, human." Maggie's expression was harsh and unyielding, "Ye an' yer men were supposed to have gone from here by midnight, yet 'tis noon. Why are ye here?" Conscious of the dwindling time and the *Sidhe* clustered behind her, Maggie paused, her raised hand halting the man's forced answer a moment.

What are ye waiting on? Get yer arses where they should be, before 'tis too late. An anything else is wrong, I'll 'speak ye right away. Now hurry! The *Fianna* ran off down the hall to do her bidding. Not pausing to watch them, she turned back to her reluctantly cooperative prisoner. "Answer the question...now."

"'Twas a safeguard against the moles. The Black Vipers know that when McDubh orders something for midnight, he wants it the next noon, if he asks for it at noon, he wants the midnight before. Everything else is just as he says." A split second later, the man doubled over in agony as much as the binding spell allowed—virtually not at all—but Maggie got the idea. He had lied to her.

"Come now, m'boy," she purred. "Ye don't think I'd go to the trouble to spell ye an' not make sure ye had to tell me true, now do ye? Or did ye just think I was terrible at spells? Try it again now."

"The packages...they...they're always set to go off half an hour early." The sadistic triumph in his voice relieved Maggie of all traces of mercy. They had given themselves twenty minutes leeway...her people, and everyone in this building were about to die a horrible death unless Maggie could bring herself to be as ruthless as the men she was up against.

There really was no question. Brutally, Maggie tore the mental image of the package from her prisoner's mind, leaving behind a gaping hole in what would have been his memory...had there been anything left to remember. His mind was now a wasteland. He had left her no time for delicacy.

Focusing the image in her thoughts, she ripped away the package in much the same way she had done with the memory. Blessed Danu, she was glad this was an object and not a person. She propelled it harmlessly into the void, there to spend eternity endlessly drifting in the same moment of time. She could do that with an object.

She longed to collapse. She longed to scream. And she longed for the comfort of knowing that though three horrible men were dead, thousands continued to live for her actions here. But it was no comfort. Though it was by no means the first time she'd killed with justification, it was also not the first time she had felt the bite of this particular guilt. Numbly, she secured the remaining terrorists, leaving them to be found by the authorities. If nothing else, the activity took her mind off of the guilt. Well, for a moment, anyway. She would survive, and the pain would fade, though not the memory. And, should a similar situation arise again, there would be no difference in her decision.

That was when horror gripped her...*the packages were always set to go off half an hour early...*The other group...the bombs! And there was no convenient mind to pluck a location from this time.

Maggie did the best she could. *My brave Fianna, send the packages you have found to the void...now!*

She prayed she was in time. She prayed that they heard and understood her. She simply prayed, and as she did so, the *Fianna* in her group gathered around, quietly tending their wounds. Trying very hard not to look too confused.

With a sigh, Maggie brought the glamory back up around them, and they made their way to the rendezvous point. The bodies — living and otherwise — were left where they were. Just let the RUC try and figure it all out.

As they neared the main exit and the end of their mission, Maggie continued to pray. Then they walked out into the sunlight, and for a moment, she nearly went down to her knees. There they were: the rest of her warriors lounged on the curb, to all appearances enjoying the unseasonably warm weather.

Taking a mental note of the wounds they did not show the world, Maggie surmised they had had much the same reception as her group had. She didn't even have the strength to sigh as she led them to a more private spot. Weary beyond belief, she gripped the torc and willed them all back to *Tír na nÓg*. And just in case she thought to relax a little too much now that they were done, a haunting image of Kara wafted up to taunt her mind's eye.

Not again! She cannot get away from me again, Dubh! Why didn't it work? You promised she would be ours! Dubh directed a disgusted look across the square to where his brother barely held his position. Olcas's obsession twisted his handsome face into an ugly mask. With economic and outwardly unhurried steps, Dubh made his way to Olcas's side before he could go rushing off like an ill-trained hound.

Who said it hadn't worked? The trouble with his brother was that his single-mindedness limited his vision. Olcas might have slaked his urges back in that dirty alley days ago, but it hadn't deadened the hunger his prize inspired in him, and that would be his downfall, for it made him blind to all else. The purpose of the rally had not been to capture Olcas's elusive prey; the intent was to distract the RUC, so the little surprises that had been hidden would not be found in time. Little Kara was not his problem or concern, though any other time, he would gladly accept her as a diversion. He couldn't have been expected to know she would surface here. There were more important things than that tempting morsel, like the downfall of Celts, and then the *Sidhe*, to begin with.

Dubh sighed as the barest hiss slipped past Olcas's clenched teeth. His brother was so predictable. With a crushing grip, Dubh grabbed Olcas's arm before he could pursue the girl and her savior. "If you would stop your blustering, you would realize it worked better than you could have hoped," Dubh snarled aloud. Not depending on reason to cut through the remainder of Olcas's frenzy, he used a judicious touch of power to anchor his brother in place. If the petulant little sot could not see it for himself, Dubh certainly wasn't going to bother to explain it to him. "Now settle down; we've more to accomplish here today than to reclaim your admittedly tempting prize."

Diversion though this rally might be, it was an important one. With eminent social unrest brewing prominently in the city thanks to the mess caused by Brexit, the RUC was oblivious to the hidden threat right on their doorstep. And yet even as Dubh brought his brother to heel, he found himself tracking the swift progress of the "young man" hurrying from the square, unhindered by the burden he carried. This was no human coming to the aid of another; it was the ancient enemy claiming a prize that was rightfully theirs—one of the *Sidhe*, once again meddling where they had no right. Exerting self-discipline, Dubh yanked his thoughts away from the immortal before he forgot himself and lashed out, ruining centuries of planning by revealing himself too soon. He was getting as bad as his brother. Soon enough the loathsome *Sidhe* would be ground beneath the heel of Carmán's children; there was no call for it to be right now.

Now the girl in the *Sidhe*'s arms, she was another matter altogether. This was the same Kara they had discussed, the temptation that had nearly undone all their careful planning by refusing to be engulfed by his beguiling little brother, coming perilously close to destroying him in the process. Dubh could see the lure she represented, but it was no effort to resist it in the face of their more pressing agenda: revenge upon the blasted *Sidhe*, those responsible for the death of Carmán and the unseating of her sons from their corporeal shells.

But now was not the time. Better to ignore both girl and rescuer until the situation was more favorable. Revenge on a single *Sidhe* was scarcely worth the effort or the scuttling of all their plans for just a moment's satisfaction; by the time the brothers were done, their enemies would not even be a lingering myth. That thought was much more satisfying than seeing just this one gutted before him with the horrible realization of his executioner's identity dawning in his eyes as the light in them went out forever. Why, the daydream of it alone was enough to hold Dubh over until they could make it a reality on a much broader scale. For now, they must prepare...and wait for their eldest brother, Calma, to surface.

Turning back to a crowd that moments ago had verged on becoming a mob, Dubh drew on the power tendrils that made up the boundaries of the otherworld. Gathering the sullen energy to himself, he carefully fed it to the most receptive of the disgruntled mass that filled the square. He must draw them back in; repair the damage to this carefully nurtured potential riot.

Damn! It was too late. Too many in the crowd had been caught up in the quiet drama caused by the girl and her collapse. They had no idea that they'd almost been caught in the deadly tempest of a mage battle. They had no clue she would have brought them down to their deaths, had her rage not been diverted by the *Sidhe*. How contemptible!

Anyway, the cohesiveness of the mob had disintegrated too thoroughly to revive it. Drawing Olcas away with him, Dubh slipped from the crowd, seething at the disruption of their plans. There was no telling if the rally had in itself been enough of a diversion, without erupting into a full-blown riot. Most certainly, they had not garnered the amount of violent energy they had anticipated. What had been gathered had better be enough, or the two retreating figures would pay even more dearly in the end.

Kara was a comfortable mass cradled against his chest. Light and long of limb, there was a presence within her that would have betrayed her as waterkin, even had he not already known. If not for that, so vibrant was her being, he would have suspected he carried a full blood. Her fair skin glowed, faintly echoing the radiance of the *Sidhe*, and the deep red curtain of her hair was like burnished silk draping along his shoulder and nearly down to his knees. Of course, he could not help but recall her eyes, like molten amber, burning with hatred and brimming with vengeance, so intent on the object of her malice that she had been blind to the innocents nearby. Aye, that was a very *Sidhe* reaction, and a dark one at that. A reaction Aí was much too intimately familiar with. Seeing it in her had filled him with both fear and despair.

But he could not dwell on the transgressions of his own past. Kara needed his help. Aí knew her path was not a smooth one and that she would be...already had been severely tested along the way. The flash of recognition he'd experienced when he'd seen her carried from Anu's shrine had been resolved. He knew her from a vision. The moment she had undertaken her journey across the Great Water, his Sight had revealed her to him, though he had not been aware of her personally until he spied her in the clearing. His visions had not been comfortable ones. He wouldn't wish the hardship and torment destined for this young girl on anyone, the choices she would have to make...not even with a hint of the blessings at the end. Her situation very much reminded him of Agnieszka.

Anyway, now was not the time to dwell on what would be. He would serve her better to see her safely away. With a twist of thought, the mists of magic—the *Fe-Fiada*—descended upon them. Aí reached for the currents and prepared to draw them away to *Tír na nÓg*.

"Put me down...*now*."

The words were soft-spoken, but there was no mistaking the mettle beneath them, or the implicit threat. Slowly and with extreme care, Aí lowered his left arm until her feet were once again upon the ground. Part of him noticed how she swayed, reluctantly maintaining her grip on his shoulder for a moment so fleeting anyone else would have overlooked it. The rest of him was fully focused on the steel below the surface of her voice.

"Are ye alright, then?" he asked, his tone calm.

"I don't know who you are or what you intended, but since I'm grateful you brought me to my senses before I made a horrible mistake, I'll allow you to walk away before I defend myself." The look on the girl's face...Kara's face was harsh and unyielding. Only someone quite perceptive would be able to see how she paled and trembled. Despite his Gift, Aí nearly missed it, almost did not see the barely checked terror lurking deep below. Apparently, Kara was very good at hiding.

The magical currents he'd gathered earlier began to swirl about Kara's head, billowing like thunderclouds, dark and foreboding. The longer he watched her, the quicker the effect spread until they were encased on all sides.

How had she taken magic he'd summoned and turned it to her own will? The enormity of it was so awe-inspiring, Aí forgot about her frank warning.

"I will not ask you again, but I will see that you obey."

"No! No need for all o' that, Kara. My name is Aí...I'm o' the *Sidhe Fianna*, come to see ye safely home." He kept his voice even, not once betraying the tremors tripping along his spine. Perhaps she reminded him too much of Agnieszka, whom he now knew to be pure *Sidhe*. He had been assured by the Smithgod himself this one was without a doubt waterkin, albeit one of such potential as had never been seen before, but her anger kindled with the might and fervor of an immortal.

Aí caught a glimpse of the fear and guilt that burned through Kara at the mention of the *Fianna*. There was no doubt that she could imagine Maggie's anger and concern at her disobedience. After all that had happened, after all she had paid for her previous willfulness, she had once again defied the *Sidhe*. This time risking herself, those who had depended on her participation at the conference center, and those that were charged with bringing her back safely: namely, Aí himself.

"Come now, 'tis alright," Aí reasoned. "We'll both o' us return to *Tír na nÓg* an' no harm done." He soulspoke the *Fianna* searching the square for their quarry and informed them where they could find Tony. May they have the luck to find out where they could rescue their Kin. Meanwhile, he must get Kara away from here and see if something couldn't be done to heal the festering wounds she harbored on the inside. Gently and with such finesse that Kara did not notice in time to protest, Aí reclaimed his summoned power and completed the spell that would whisk them away to the Land of Youth.

"Nothing! Nothing?! All that careful planning and investment, and the result was...Nothing?!" Rage infused him. "Correction...nothing but loss!

"Would ye care to explain how the lot o' ye managed such a total cock-up?"

The man before him flinched, his expression taut. He ducked his head, and though he responded, it was but a mumble.

"Excuse me?"

"I don't know. All was going according to yer plan, and then..." The man's words trailed off, clearly at a loss for what to say.

Such incompetence!

Dubh's three best men were dead, and five others had been captured. The Celts were not beset by conflict; he did not have the *Sidhe* humbled before him, and his brother still obsessed over the girl. What had gone wrong? Mankind clearly was the inherent flaw! Or was betrayal the cause?

Every muscle of Dubh's assumed body flexed with the need to rend and destroy. Beneath the seeming of supple, unblemished skin, his fisted knuckles cracked, revealing red, inflamed tissue beneath. As his body tensed, the flood of agony from the tool's tortured flesh fed Dubh even more, like an addict pumped up on crack cocaine. He leaned in close until he was inches from the messenger. "Wrong. Answer."

With a satisfying roar, the frustrated godling unleashed a bolt of combined fury and energy upon the hapless Cell member who'd brought him the news. No damage at all marred the worn wooden floor of the flat. Such precision usually delighted him, unfortunately, watching the body twitch and flare until nothing but cinders were left only enflamed him further. The harvest from that death was a pittance compared to what he would have gained had his plans run as intended.

Someone would pay, and it would not be the quick, if agonizing, end this fool had faced. No, whoever had foiled his plot would dance and twitch and become intimate with suffering for centuries, if not all eternity.

"Where is Tony?" Dubh demanded of no one in particular as he left the bedroom. His eyes flashed, and those nearby flinched away. No one answered.

Not that he expected them to. He would have been shocked had any of them had an answer. Questing with his divine perception bore no results; the little blighter had run off to sulk somewhere, hiding away like a petulant child. He always had been incredibly self-absorbed. Well, once the Celts were beneath Dubh's thumb, Olcas could run off all he wanted, but for now…suffice it to say his little brother would pay dearly for this spoiled stunt. Perhaps Dubh would even pluck Kara from beneath Olcas's very grasp at the end, fitting retribution for abandonment. Yes, perhaps he would.

Olcas! the mental bellow tore through the ether. *Show yourself, brother, or you will have cause to regret it.* No matter how hidden he was, Olcas would hear that cry. Confident he would surface sooner than later, Dubh considered what needed to be done next. He hit the buzzer on the wall, triggering a specific light behind the bar below, and then moved to the diamond-paned window to wait. It was time to uncover some answers.

When countless minutes went by with no sign of Rory, the explanation was clear.

Maggie heaved a relieved sigh as she stepped into the chamber Goibhniu set aside for them. She was greeted by twelve pairs of immortal eyes…and one hopeful mortal gaze. The second group may have gotten here before hers, but from the look on Patrick's face, it did not seem the first had yet.

Damn! What was she to tell him now? It wasn't as if she had any reassurances she could offer, not when her own heart was sick with worry. This was to be a simply foray, information only. Instead, it had turned into a full-blown encounter for at least one group. They had come away reasonably unscathed considering. Only her own group—herself included—had any wounded to speak of, and that mostly bruises and contusions, except for the single *Fear Fianna* whose brains were rattled a bit. Still, they'd no idea how soon before they would be called to venture out again. Better to take a moment to bring them all back to top form.

Maggie cast her thoughts out to Goibhniu, too weary to seek him out. *We've a bit o' bruising that needs looking after, but Miach's still out an' about. Where should we direct the walking wounded?*

She had the unsettling sensation of a chuckle not her own rippling through her mind, followed by a warm healing glow. From the expression on the faces of the other wounded, she was not alone in this. She was left with a sense of intense well-being once the glow faded. Goibhniu had seen to them himself. Maggie thanked him in her thoughts before turning her attention back to the *Fianna*.

Waiting around to find out the fate of the other group was going to be torturous. Rather than bring all their spirits low by dwelling on it, she deftly avoided the conflict by summoning food and drink.

In short order, the food arrived, and on its heels was Goibhniu, a re-assuring smile on his face and a gleam in his eye that would have spoken of impishness in anyone of smaller stature. Before Maggie could wonder, the Smithgod stepped aside, revealing Kara, looking livelier than she had of late, less withdrawn.

Maggie's heart flooded with relief. Had the girl not gone after Tony, after all? There was no sign of injury, though there was something about the eyes, the way Kara winced as she entered and looked away from those waiting. She was also dragging her feet, giving Maggie the impression she would have run if it weren't for the fact that Aí, the newest of Maggie's *Fianna,* entered right behind her.

Who was he, this Aí, and how had he and Kara come together? Though they did not look at one another, there was a palpable but indefinable tension between the two. Maggie wondered what story there might be there to tell. Of course, perhaps she was just seeing a bit much into things. She wasn't familiar enough with the young *Sidhe* to know his normal behavior; as for Kara, she had no normal behavior of late. Right now, the girl held herself stiffly, tense as a caged tiger, with her fists clenching and her eyes darting glances back the way she had come. But Maggie did not get the impression it was the crowd of people, or even the man behind Kara, that had her so agitated. What had hap-pened back at that square? Kara looked raw and sensitive, like steam-burnt flesh drawn too near to a source of heat. Maggie sensed that one provocation was all it would take for her to explode out of her skin.

In their excitement at having the girl back safely, the others in the room were oblivious to her turmoil. Cheers rose up around them, but one cry rang louder than any other.

"Kara!" Patrick's voice was thick with both relief and concern. Prudently, Maggie stepped aside rather than learn the hard way whether he would barrel through her or give her time to move. Love and joy kindled within her when Kara stood firm and welcomed her father's embrace, though she kept her eyes averted.

This was the first time the girl had allowed him so close since she'd come back among them. It was a testament to Patrick's worry that he forgot. Maggie could not help but smile at the tender look upon his face once he realized the minor miracle that had just taken place; she could empathize with the hasty way in which he blinked tears from his eye as he gently swept his daughter into his arms.

"Lass, 'tis a wonder I've not gone all grey with worrying over ye. I've little enough time left, even with what I've gained back by healing, so I'll say it once...cut it out! Yer taking years off my life."

Though it was clear Patrick was at least partially earnest beneath his levity, healing laughter filled the chamber. Maggie herself sobered quickly,

though, as his comment fully registered. Little enough time? But what about...
Seeing her appalled look mirrored in Kara's stricken expression, Maggie
realized the awful truth. With all that had happened, they had yet to reveal to
Patrick the reason he'd been brought to *Tír na nÓg*. He had absolutely no idea
of his options or the weighty choice that stood before him. Worse yet, now was
not the time to tell him.

She never would have thought a bit more guilt would make a difference,
but this offense weighed heavier on Maggie's soul than anything that had
transpired of late. Without a word, she stepped forward and draped her arms
around father and daughter, a silent, unexplained apology...for everything. It
was hardly adequate but would have to do for now. Other matters demanded
their attention. Pressing matters: Like how to ensure they *all* survived.

Gently, Maggie guided the O'Keefes deeper into the room. Settling them
down together on a mound of cushions, she pushed food and drinks before
them and turned to address those gathered. Quickly scanning those in the
room, she noticed the rest of the *Fianna* had arrived.

"All right...we may have averted disaster for now, but that isn't the end o'
it. Those that have thrown themselves against us will be more determined than
ever. We must be ready for the next encounter. 'Tis time to report what each o'
us discovered in this little excursion." She started them off with the details
she'd been given by Rory and an accounting of her group's run-in with the
terrorists. As they continued around the room, she took careful note of each
new detail, where they conflicted or corroborated, searching desperately for
some continuity. What had happened so far, both in America and here in
Ireland, was a jumble of disjointed occurrences. They had to find the common
thread if they were to unravel the plot. It was disheartening. As each warrior
spoke his or her piece, things still did not come together. Finally, the *Sidhe*
who'd entered with Kara and Goibhniu cleared his throat and stepped
forward.

"Ye'll not know me, most o' ye. I'm called Aí, an' until recently, I was but
one o' Goibhniu's messengers." The young warrior paused as if to gather his
thoughts. Maggie did not miss the quick, furtive glance he sent toward
Goibhniu, almost as if he wasn't sure he wouldn't be silenced in short order.
He continued unhindered. "I've seen much an' have heard even more since
the trouble began, as I was sent out to both warn the People an' gather knowledge o' what was taking place outside our own domain.

"This is what I can tell ye: there isn't just one foe. It seems like we've more
a legion set against us. Today, as we *Fianna* tried to find out where our Kin had
been taken, I spied the faces o' two o' our adversaries." As he continued, his
words accompanied by mental images of what he had seen, Maggie felt dread
creep over her. With each descriptive account of deed and disaster, her
conviction grew. Carmán's children had indeed returned, but which of them?

Or was it all three? They had two faces so far, and both would haunt her, thanks to what Aí had shared. One was familiar; the other she didn't know. Was there a third one out there lurking in ambush? The *Tuatha de Danaan* had stood against them once, but could they do so again? Or had peaceful living dulled the edge of their battle skills and set them up for sure doom?

Suddenly a quiet, intent voice interrupted. It was Kara. She had not spoken once since entering the room, but it seemed she could not stay silent in this.

"It gets worse. There is something else there...something ancient and evil that I don't recognize. I have felt it more than once, though I didn't know it for what it was until I cleansed the body on the shrine. I have never heard of anything like it in the tales told by my Grandda." Maggie met her eyes and found them haunted. Her voice did not tremble, but it was taut as one of Quicksilver's strings, one that had been overtuned, at that. Still, it seemed that Kara had finally climbed from her nightmare enough that she spoke with quiet dignity and conviction. "But this, I know...It was ravenous and wicked. Something alien grew inside of her. And even unformed as it was, it wanted to kill me...no, it wanted to devour us all."

Maggie's heart raced at the girl's words, though she wasn't quite sure why. The *Tuatha de Danaan* had encountered evil before, but this seemed different, more personal. Somehow what Kara described did not seem as alien as it should be, as if an ancient memory struggled to surface, to no avail. Shivers danced down Maggie's spine, chased by dread.

Chapter 14

In the twilight hours, the caravan wended its way across the Irish countryside. There was no music or laughter to mark their progress, no children draped half out of windows, and no ragtag dogs trotted between the anachronistic wheels or taunted the dray horses by dodging in and cut around their hooves. They were quite the uncharacteristic image of rovers this day.

At the forefront of the wagon train, Jacko sat at the reins and continued to mourn his fate. Never again would he be welcome at Wicklow Cottage; he would not sit in Agnieszka's kitchen, playing the rascal to draw out her enigmatic little smile or her caustic wit. He tormented himself with daydreams of letting down her snowy braid and loosening the coil with his fingers until the hair spread like a rippling cape down her back. There was no chance he would see such a thing in this lifetime...not now when she could not possibly think anything but that he'd forsaken her. A rumble of thunder interrupted his musings, aptly mirroring his mood.

Jacko glanced up at the looming sky and wished he hadn't. Unless they reached their destination soon, he would get very wet. Clenching his teeth and expelling an explosive breath, he fingered the reins and longingly thought of turning the rig back around and going the way his heart demanded. But he knew full well there was no path for any of them, other than the one Granddame Rose dictated.

Rose herself sat beside him, her gaze intent as the landscape unfolded before them, speaking only enough to direct him. All in the caravan wondered what drove the woman, but none of them questioned the wisdom of following her. They had seen too much to doubt.

After long hours of travel since morning, they drew even with a stand of oak and hawthorn on a gentle rise. Rose suddenly laid a clawed hand upon his arm and uttered but one intent word, "Here."

Obediently, Jacko raised his whip to signal the rest of the caravan and reined in his team. "Do we set up camp, Granddame, or will we be moving on?"

She just grunted and climbed down unaided from the wagon. With a sigh, Jacko slid to the ground as well. Not knowing how long they would be here, he checked that the harness would not gall the ponies and gave them a nosebag of well-deserved grain, draping them with blankets in case it should rain while they were stopped. Looking back along the caravan, he noted the other drivers following his lead.

Having seen to the immediate needs of the animals, he grabbed the water bucket and headed into the trees to find the spring that was surely there. No reason to drink stale water from their supplies with a delightfully fresh source close at hand. It had seemed like an excellent idea, but the deeper he went into the tree line, the more on edge Jacko became. He had the intense conviction he was being watched and only hoped whoever...whatever...it was did not take offense at his presence. With each step, the feeling got worse, until he decided water from their casks would be absolutely delicious after all. That was when he realized where they must be. He had seen no signs of a mushroom ring or any of the other warnings, but there was no doubt in his mind this small grove was faerie-claimed. His empty bucket swung a bit wild as he pivoted around and headed briskly back out beneath the open sky. The reproachful look Granddame Rose gave him did nothing to improve his disposition.

She just stood there a moment, the two chickens she bought at the market in Dublin clutched in her hands and the pockets sewn to her full, patchwork skirt bulging. When she continued to stare at him as if she measured his worth, Jacko tensed and fought the overwhelming desire to flinch. On the outside, he kept his face impassive and stared back at her with veiled eyes. Abruptly she gave a sharp, satisfied nod and turned away from him, heading off around the hillside as if the fate of humanity were the weight in her pockets, ready to drag her down if she stopped her shuffling progress.

No longer interested in water, and now quite confident they would *not* be making camp here, he instead occupied himself with ensuring the wagon was in good repair and ready to move out with haste. Linchpins were tested, axels greased, the tack was checked for disrepair, and the teams' hooves for stray pebbles and muck. He didn't want any mishaps when they suddenly found themselves in a hurry to be away.

Traveling instantaneously from one point to another was no small feat, and doubtless, the benefits were near endless, but just the same, it was an experience Arn could have happily done without. His body's reaction was no better than the first time. Muscles twitched and sweat beaded his brow as he stepped from nowhere onto an Irish hillside. The sun was just setting and the breeze nipped at him with autumn's chill, making him shiver even more.

"Come, my friend, we're nearly there." Urias placed a supportive hand on his shoulder. It took extreme effort for Arn to resist shrugging it off. He did *not* like the surreal bend his life had taken or Urias's part in it, and he most definitely did not like the reason they were here. It was hard not to be surly with all of that to contend with, especially after a transatlantic flight and three days of little sleep. But still, this man was only here to help; being bad-tempered was hardly reasonable.

"Where is 'there'?" Arn could not help but ask acrimoniously, though he knew the answer would only add to his uneasiness. "And why are we going?"

"'Tis a place called *Tír na nÓg*," Urias answered with a good-natured smile. "I believe ye've heard o' it. An' we're going there so ye can see yer friend, Patrick, an' his family, while I've a few words with Maggie, o' whom we've spoken. 'Tis certain I am she'll know how to find yer wife."

As desperate as he was to find Lynn, Arn couldn't suppress a surge of eagerness to be reunited with his friend, after all the worry of the past days, to see him alive and well. The moment he realized his joy, guilt flooded his heart. Urias's understanding look only made Arn feel worse. What kind of husband was he?

Following his companion up the gentle surge of the hillside, Arn realized it didn't matter in the end. For now, he had no choice but to follow Urias. And if that meant he was able to reassure himself of his friend's well being, then so be it. Where they went was out of his control and thus did not reflect on his character as a husband or a human being. He could strike out on his own, now that he was here, but that would only reduce his chances of finding Lynn quickly, not increase them.

"Don't feel ye're placing yer friend before yer wife. I'd be taking ye here regardless, as we need a plan, not to mention assistance."

It unsettled him to hear his thoughts spoken out loud by another. Was he really that transparent? Or had the fey creature—Arn no longer doubted Urias was, as he claimed, a member of the race known as *Sidhe*—dipped into his mind? If he remembered the legends Conall O'Keefe used to tell, it was entirely possible. He was about to remind the *Sidhe* that invading his thoughts was not acceptable when suddenly Urias stopped short in front of him and reached back a hand to halt Arn's progress.

From out of nowhere, the smell of beeswax and blood were thick on the air, mingled with the subtler scent of crushed greenery of an indeterminable nature. Where was it coming from...and what did it mean? They were in the middle of the countryside, no cottages nearby. They were alone in the dark, without even the sounds of the nighttime wildlife to soften the harsh edge of the sudden silence.

Just then, Arn looked up and saw her. There on the rise above them stood a withered old woman, her glowing white hair and flamboyant clothing standing out against the muted backdrop of the twilight-darkened trees. Her mere presence was startling enough, but his astonishment did not stop there. In each hand, she clutched a chicken carcass by the feet, a diminishing flow of blood running from their slit throats. To either side of her feet burned a thick white candle...only the flame on each burned blue. What was more, when the chicken blood struck the flames, instead of going out, they flared a brilliant green.

"Good woman, what is it that ye do?" Though Urias's tone sounded mild and conversational, his body language—at least to Arn—spoke of battle-readiness and caution. The glow of the candle flames was not enough for Arn to read the woman's expression.

"I have closed this gateway to you and what trails you."

Arn didn't begin to understand what the woman had done, but the tension in Urias's shoulders suddenly increased, and the stance he took became a little more wide-set. Whatever it was, it could not be good. What was more, though it was hard to be sure, it seemed her gaze was not upon Urias as she spoke...that her words were for him and not the *Sidhe*. Once again, he began to wonder why lately everything and everyone seemed determined to stand in his way.

"An' why would ye be doing that, then?" Urias asked. "Have ye a reason for blocking my way home?"

"I couldn't hope to ever block you, nor have I reason to; you may pass through. But your companion cannot. Threat follows in his footsteps; Evil would find its way with ease where it has no right to be with the trail this one unknowingly leaves for it to follow."

"Are ye a Seer, then?"

"I don't know what will happen, I know only what must be done...or not done."

"Convenient, that. Seems to me what must an' must not be done is rather subjective. Anyway, the threat, 'tis there in either case. I need no manner o' Seeing to know that." Urias argued his jaw set and his brow drawn down. "I must go to *Tír na nÓg* an' I'll not leave my friend on the hillside to face danger alone."

As the *Sidhe* confronted the old woman, Arn surreptitiously looked around for any other threat. He saw nothing, even in the bright light of the full moon. Unfortunately, that didn't mean nothing was there.

"Would you risk bringing danger down on your people? That man cannot be allowed to cross into the Otherworld. His passage will leave the door open for great evil to follow behind him."

Great Evil? What in the world did she mean? It was gibberish, nonsense. He was not evil, had nothing to do with evil. He was a healer, in fact. His life was dedicated to the good of others.

There was nothing but silence as each of them stared at the other, and Arn wondered where things went from here.

Finally, his goal...and no one about to interfere. When he had first seen the waterkin Aí carried, Bran was consumed by resentment. First Sadb and now waterkin? There was no doubt Aí cared something for the repellent creature, more than he cared for Bran. Well, his adversary would soon learn to regret flaunting his feelings. The white-haired woman would serve well to both advance Bran's plans and punish Aí, all at the same time.

Muted light bathed the chamber before him, blending with the sound from the garden to create a magical tableau. With the women in the middle of this fantastic backdrop, it was all nauseatingly touching. Fortunately, it would not last long. As he lurked among the ferns to evaluate his best approach, Bran felt his lip lifting reflexively in distaste. He had no objection to the beauty of the landscape. It was a requirement actually; the velvet cushion against which to display his own dazzling splendor. Bran's problem was with the vermin in the chamber, waterkin and worse...a human settling in as if deserving. *Tír na nÓg* was for the Kin. All others were parasites, squatters, their only value in how they could serve him. He didn't know a thing about the woman...beyond the fact that she was mother to that other loathsome waterkin. The memory of his encounter with the creature rose up bitterly. He would deal with her more permanently later.

Anyway, he was not here to dwell on the past. No, today he'd strike a blow against loftier targets. Goibhniu, and more importantly, his lackey, the infernal...beautiful Aí. The Smithgod was a matter of ambition; Aí was something more. He would rue the way he repeatedly spurned Bran. And so would the woman in the other room, the white-haired waterkin. Bad enough for her she claimed some part of his love's heart, but there was also something scintillating about her, something that raised her above others of her kind.

Marveling at the injustice, Bran caressed the women with a tendril of awareness, taking note of the bounds of their individual potential, testing their presence for any defenses. As he expected, the human was beneath his consideration, barely a glow to catch his eye. But the other...He clenched his fists and bit down on a snarl before it could escape him. There were Kin who did not measure up to the potential of this white-haired witch. He was not one to whom that applied, but Bran hated her for it regardless.

That was what had decided him. As far as he was concerned, such potential in one not full-blooded *Sidhe* was reprehensible; by making her the focal point of his attack he would right more than one wrong. No longer would they—Goibhniu and his cretins—cast Bran aside, disrespected and discounted. He would have justice for those wrongs, the mistreatment he could not begin to dwell upon without his mind going blank with rage. Already his breath quickened with the memories. He must push them aside if he was to carry forth his plan. While he could not see the value in one such as this, he could see why Goibhniu and Aí prized the woman. Her beauty was perfect and her Gift nearly unrivaled, and, if the waterkin that came before her were any indication, she would be extremely malleable. Bran depended on it, in fact. And now was the time to act, while his enemies were distracted by their little intelligence-swapping session. The fools...they would never learn enough to save their sorry souls...at least, not before the end, and then much too late.

So gratifying was the thought that his eyes narrowed with sly satisfaction, and his lips quirked in a sinister smile that he wiped from his face just as he swept into the room. He savored the human woman's shock for but a moment before giving her a dismissive, sideways glance. He had to suppress the urge to smile once more as doubt crept into her eyes and settled in her heart with a sigh.

"You will leave now," he ordered.

That should have been it.

"I don't think so. Unless Goibhniu himself comes to claim her, she's my charge." The woman's voice held a subtle quaver; her expression, however, was rock-solid.

"You presume to defy me?" His eyes should have been a warning. He did not narrow them with anger; he threw them wide and allowed them to flash with righteous indignation. "Who exactly do you suppose sent me to fetch the woman?"

She did not back down beneath his heated gaze, though her certainty wavered. At that moment, he moved. Taking advantage of her doubt, he swooped down to gather his prize to his chest, all the while seething. He had intended to claim his victim quickly and without question, but this human was not going to accept his right to do so. The moment he walked away, she would raise the cry.

He could not allow that. He would have to squander precious power to wipe her thoughts. While it took but a thought and a whisper of power to accomplish, it was time and energy diverted from exacting his revenge. He resented that more than the effort itself.

As the woman crumbled, unconscious, to the ground, Bran sneered at her weakness, that a simple memory wipe sent her spiraling. Humans were such insipid creatures. Sparing her not another thought, he gathered up the white-haired woman and headed off. Making his way through the forest toward a stable gate he relaxed and let satisfaction take him. No one would know for quite some time that this waterkin was missing, and when they did, who was to say who took her, especially when he would have returned by then, his venture unnoticed. He laughed, reveling in the way the vermin in the forest scattered before him, rustling wings and jangling notes left in the faelings' wake. Abominations! They had better fear him. When he ruled in *Tír na nÓg*, they would flee for good. He would see to it.

Cold stone and echoing tunnels more than suited his current frame of mind. In no mood to suffer his brother's contempt, Olcas fled to his mountain retreat even as the rally dispersed. His prize had been within his grasp and yet slipped away once more. His craving for her was only amplified by the repeated influx of torment, telling him his curse worked quite splendidly; the sight of her intensified his obsession a hundredfold. He would not rest until Kara was back in his clutches. Surrounding himself with opulence amid this harsh and unforgiving landscape was not even enough to pacify his discontent.

Though he expected Kara had fled to the safety of the *Sidhe* lands, Olcas pulled out the girl's scarf anyway. Settling down with it across his knee, he opened himself to the void, sending out his awareness in search of the girl. He got no further than his preparations before a furious roar echoing through his mind aborted the effort.

Dubh's scream drove Olcas into a vicious growl of his own. He severed his connection. Open as he had been to search the ether, his brother's bellow ricocheted mercilessly through him.

So, darling Dubh was not pleased. Well, let him rage. Perhaps it would teach him how limited his control was. Olcas would surface in his own time, not at someone else's demand. Being sure to shield himself more carefully, he extended his awareness yet again.

Could it be?! Well then, his luck was not as fleeting as he had thought. With his inner eye and a good deal more focus, Olcas scanned the ether once more. Yes! Finally, the good doctor had surfaced. Olcas's eyes brightened with avarice and his pulse quickening with his own flavor of passion. A subtle probing with an ethereal touch confirmed his tag still anchored him firmly to Arn Barnert.

How to use this man to his advantage? He already knew where the girl was...completely inaccessible and likely to stay that way. But the man may still prove useful. It seemed he was accompanied by one of the *Sidhe*. Given the doctor's connection to Kara and her family, perhaps they traveled to join with them. How kind Fate deigned to be! A perfect plan formed in Olcas's tightly focused thoughts. But first, he would need a diversion, and—as infuriating as it was—there was but one place to go. It galled him that Dubh would attribute Olcas's sudden appearance to his presumptuous summons, but that could not be helped. He could think of no one better suited to drawing attention away from him than his brother—after all, it was his favorite pastime. Of course, Dubh couldn't know the reason for the attack. He would either find a way to reap the benefits for himself or become uncooperative. That was just the nature of their relationship.

It would have to be revenge, then. That was the only thing that would draw his brother forth at the moment...he burned for revenge.

Returning the scarf to a convenient pocket, Olcas rose and looked around him. What else would he need? Weapons were not his style, so there were none to gather. The woman Lynn served her purpose better here, and one demon would not be worth much against a host of *Sidhe*. It would be wiser to leave both behind. Olcas still wasn't sure what he would do with either one in the end, but for now, he had better see to their needs. No telling how long he would be away and returning to find both of them as withered corpses would be wasteful. He allowed his creature to feed briefly off the woman's terror, which would hold it for a considerable time, and then severed the link between the two. He then left food for the woman and charged the demon to see she didn't expire while he was gone.

With things as settled as they could be, Olcas located his brother with a thought and tore a rent in the void. His demeanor was deceptively casual, yet rampant anticipation set his eyes ablaze as he stepped through to stand beside Dubh, holding open the path through which he'd come.

It was so perfect he could not resist.

"He's here," was all he said, his voice laden with anticipation, as he looped an arm around his brother's and stepped them both through the void. It was short work from there to follow the tag with which he'd marked Arnold Barnert. All the while, he savored his brother's shocked outrage.

❁

Panic...fear...anger...despair... They bombarded Kara mercilessly. Every moment, waking and sleeping was a battle against destructive emotions. She had been doing well until this afternoon, though for days after her...encounter in Dublin—was it truly only days?!—she had forgotten what happiness and joy were and had pushed away love and concern. It had been a struggle to get back to the point where she could smile and chat and even touch another. The occasional flare-up still occurred, where it all came crashing down. Given this, it was hardly a surprise that she did not recognize the point at which those feelings started plaguing her from outside herself.

Running a trembling hand across her face, she shook her weary head like a dog, one on Prozac, true, but still like a dog. It was no use: it did not clear the insistent buzzing, the discordant hum. Rolling her neck, she tried to slip out from under the mounting tension that sent a frisson of dread through her entire body. Something was wrong...horribly wrong, and it seemed to come at her from every side. Her muscles bunched and her heart raced; before long, she furtively sought some escape. Was she going insane, or was she becoming intensely aware of all around her? Kara thought perhaps she wanted it to be the insanity. She didn't know if she could bear if this, and everything else that happened in the last week, were all for real.

When she noticed his eyes on her—Aí's damnable eyes—she shoved all the turmoil as far from her as she could, trying instead to focus on what was being said. In the end, she wished she hadn't.

"Are ye okay?" he whispered as a groan slipped free from her. Kara couldn't help but sigh but nodded anyway. Though he looked doubtful, Aí respected her response and turned his attention to the farce taking place in the chamber.

It was a lie, of course. When Kara realized half the people in the room still denied all of what she'd told them, then no, she was not okay. It had not been easy for her to face evil again so soon, especially one as intense and ancient as she had found in the dell. Sharing the experience with the others had been even harder. Yet they did not treat it with the serious consideration it deserved. What had been the point? She was both disgusted and discouraged by them. She could not bear to sit and listen any longer.

Kara had nearly slipped out unnoticed when a catapulted force struck her at knee level. A second and a third followed quickly after the first. The emotional bombardment increased exponentially, so much so that Kara nearly crumbled, but somehow she found the strength to remain standing. Reflexively holding her hands at her side, she marveled as three sprites—for once in their human-like forms—reached up their tiny hands to grasp her fingers and haul themselves up. It was difficult not to reel beneath the physical and emotional assault, but Kara found it cleansing to focus on the concerns of others in place of her own and so she opened herself to what was taking place.

Two of the sprites were unfamiliar, but the third one was Beag Scath. He looked up at her with beseeching eyes, crooning and moaning deep within his throat. Instantly, images flooded her brain with rapid-fire precision from three separate sources. Most of it blended together into a hodge-podge of disjointed visions, but two images reached out and drove her to clutch her chest.

"Quiet! The white-haired woman...who is she?" A small part of Kara noticed the relieved sighs heaved by Maggie and the other *Sidhe* from New York; Papa actually grinned. Apparently, they were so pleased that she'd come out of herself that every one of them ignored her question. Kara struggled not to lose her temper. As if in a reflection of her exasperation, the darker of the two strange sprites growled. "Who is she?" Kara demanded again.

"Her name is Agnieszka, an' she is the little one's friend, that bonny fellow there whose stripes are as black as his present temper."

Kara was surprised Aí was the one to answer. Was he in the middle of everything going on at the moment? No...unimportant, back to the point.

"This Agnieszka," Kara went slowly as to not mangle the pronunciation, "she has been taken. One of the *Sidhe* knocked out my mother, and then walked out with the woman."

More than one gasp rose from the *Fianna*, but all her attention was for Papa as he hurried from the room, rushing to Mathair; Maggie, Miach, and Aí were hard upon his heels. Aí was absolutely enraged. He muttered the name Bran through clenched teeth as he stalked out.

Except for Goibhniu, everyone else looked stunned. Kara herself was staggered. But the thought images had been quite clear. It had been one of the *Sidhe*, and what was more—now that she realized it—he was not unfamiliar to her. Given their earlier encounter, she could not say she was surprised. No one else in the room seemed to be either.

Turning from the *Fianna*, Kara went to join her family. If Mathair were harmed by whatever was done to her...well, Kara would have no mercy for this Bran, should that be the case.

The void was formless and cold. There was no sensation, no time. There was no chance of discovery. Olcas and Dubh hovered there, watching through the veil of the ether as the scene before them unfolded. Ready to tear the throat out of the unknown Romani woman even as she had the ridiculous chickens she clutched in each hand, Olcas fought the urge to leave his hiding place.

What now, little brother? The mental tone accompanying Dubh's thoughts was anything but endearing. Olcas snarled deep in his most private thoughts. The woman would die for this disruption of his plans.

Now, call your pets. With the Bás toying with this lot, the Fianna will come to their rescue. Olcas could feel his brother's dawning realization that his suggestion could work, and work quite well, at that. Encouraged, he egged him on further. *Then we will have our revenge before they even realize who has beset them.*

It seemed like forever before his brother complied. At last, Olcas could feel the change in the ether; sensed the summons of the *Bás*.

Peering out upon the hillside, he savored what was about to be unleashed. The sight was beautiful...stunning...feral. From out of nowhere, boiling from a fresh slash in the void, six deadly women surrounded the unwary on the verge of the hill. They were glorious, blood-red eyes glowing and razor-sharp teeth bared. Living proof that death could indeed be lovely.

Arn knew the Ruger had not been a mistake. Of course, he had figured it would be used defending Lynn's life, not his own, but by now, it ceased to surprise him when matters did not go as he expected. Three women spread out before him, like some Hollywood syndicate's wet dream. They were like the 'Real-Life' answer to 'Buffy' or 'Charmed': beautiful, haunting, deadly, and, to all appearances, well...real. He couldn't tell if they were naked, furred, or just wearing outrageous outfits more revealing than nothing at all, but the effect was literally mesmerizing. He kept his senses just enough to realize he definitely didn't want to find out if the daggers on their fingers were natural, or the latest thing in manicure tips.

Where had they come from? Out of nowhere just as he had, he supposed. At this stage in the game, he was more than ready to send them back there because, from the lethal look in their burning red eyes, they had every intention of freeing him from his own mortal coil unless he did so.

With a sidewise glance at Urias, he pulled the pistol from his waistband and charged it. The finality of the click as the round entered the chamber brought him out of a surreal, dreamlike state. He never gave it a thought during his hours on the target range, never considered that someday what he aimed at might stare back. A thick film of sweat raced like a wave across every inch of his body, but he pushed the doubt away. Life or death...if he had to choose right now, he chose life, except three haunting words surfaced in his mind..."Do no harm", he shoved them down until he could hear them no more. Hippocratic Oath or no, he...chose...life—his own. Releasing the safety, he brought his weapon to bear.

"What the hell are they, Urias?" Instead of any kind of answer from the *Sidhe*, an eerie, undulating cry spread across the hillside. It was a woman's voice in no language Arn had ever heard. Whirling to defend Urias's back, his gaze fell upon a startling vision—which was saying a lot after having three...make that six...snarling women materialize from thin air. There behind him, her hunched back straight as an iron rod, the Romani woman raised her voice defiantly again. Something in her gaze or her stance, or perhaps the alien words she screamed, held back the three attackers that had materialized unnoticed at their backs. The woman drew out two pendants suspended on what appeared to be leather thongs from somewhere in her full skirts. Without taking her eyes from the women, the old woman strolled effortlessly forward and quickly draped what he assumed was some sort of protective amulet over his head, somehow not interfering a bit with his line of sight. He noticed another such pendant swayed against her chest. She draped the last over Urias and then let loose with yet another piercing yell. Before Arn could wonder if it were part of some spell or a battle cry he saw a glorious sight rounding the base of the hill. The cavalry was here...and they were five brawny Romani men.

There was a scent on the breeze, one Jacko recognized from another uneasy time not long ago. "'Ware, lads; Something else is up there."

Then a shot rang out. Rose shrieked and crumbled to the ground. Jacko ran on, spurred to fly faster than the others. His heart wanted to scream, as with precision, the stranger again took aim.

"Down! Damn it! Down!" An unfamiliar voice cried from above.

What was going on? As he watched with a mixture of horror and relief, Granddame Rose crawled toward the man with the gun. If possible, Jacko ran faster, desperate to get there before it was too late.

"In Danu's name, will ye not get clear?"

Jacko stopped dead in confusion. Suddenly, the pistol-fire cracked again. This time, Jacko heard the bullet sizzle past.

Sweet baby Jesus! The gunman aimed for him now!

Jacko stood stock-still, confident in the next moment a bullet would lodge in his chest, but for some reason, he was unable to throw himself to the ground. The tableau before him was too gripping. Rose continued crawling forward, steadily making progress until she clung to the gunman's leg, huddled behind him as a frightened child would. Things just got more confused, more disjointed.

Yet another shot rang out, this time nowhere near any of them; it was fired up on the mound. Was the man mad? No one was there. Even as Jacko thought it, he was astounded, for again, the gunman took aim, but before he could send another brass casing flipping from his weapon, he cried out in pain, and the firearm went flying. Jacko was close enough to see the runnel of blood streaming down the man's arm.

His cousins caught up to him, close enough he felt their breath on his sweat-beaded neck. "What the hell?!" one of them murmured. Jacko felt the same. What had he just seen? Or not seen... How in the world did you fight what couldn't be seen?

"Oy!" The Irishman on the hilltop sought to gain Jacko's attention. Jacko simply lifted his chin, listening.

"For the life o' all o' us, get to the glade, man. Go, just entering will draw their attention an' gain us some aid."

Finally it dawned on Jacko who...or rather what...the stranger was. Not many knew the secret of this copse. None save a Druid, a Romani, or one of the *Sidhe* themselves. By the glimmer of beauty that was evident, Jacko figured he knew which he looked upon. Without another thought, he took off like the bullets were still flying, heading back into the woods, praying all the way someone noticed.

As he ran, he became aware that flickers of white trailed behind him, reaching for him with the hands of death. They spurred him on, as he had never run before. He never wanted to know what pursued him. In fact, he nearly crowed in triumph when they fell away the moment his shadow hit the drip-line of the trees. Whatever they were, they did not dare to follow him onto the faeries' land. Of course, that was when it occurred to him, he hadn't particularly cared to be there himself.

Arn felt both detached and yet focused at the same time. It was as if he did not face death but merely observed it. Quite disturbing, to say the least. He called over his shoulder to his companion. "Urias, I didn't miss. The bullets had no effect whatsoever."

"Aye, I was noticing."

"Mind telling me why it isn't working?"

"Well, near as I can figure from my short analysis, I'm thinking 'tis dimensional. Somehow, the ladies in question aren't entirely upon the same plane as we are." Urias sounded amazingly Spock-like, and Arn couldn't help laughing at the thought of an elven Trekkie. Of course, he'd just realized his friend did not have the pointed ears of the stereotypical elf, which blew the Spock image. Just as well. Arn never would have gotten through this with the image of Urias in a Star Fleet uniform, saying "Live long..." and all of that, dancing through his head.

A hiss and a swipe from one of his female admirers brought Arn out of his reverie. What was he thinking, letting himself get distracted like that? Finally, it happened; one of them found their mark, leaving a burning slash across his right arm. He lost sensation in his fingers and with it his grip on the useless Ruger. Too controlled at the moment to scream, Arn let out a hiss of his own.

So, to recap: they were huddled on a hillside, in the middle of Ireland, being attacked by dimensionally challenged madwomen...His gun was no good—not to mention no longer in his possession—an ancient and injured Romani woman hid behind his knees, oh, and the elf next to him was offering him a three-inch blade. And why was it he had no problem dealing with this?

"Take it, Arn. 'Tis much better than nothing." Urias did reasonable way too well. "B'sides, 'tis o' Goibhniu's own forging. If anything can help ye, this will."

"I was much more comfortable with this before you added the 'if,' you know."

People had crammed the room by the time Kara arrived. Wending her way none too gently through them, she drew a sharp breath. Mathair lay sprawled on the slate floor, her face deathly pale, but otherwise showing no harm. Pushing the others aside, Kara helped Papa lift her mother until she lay comfortably upon the cushions.

After checking her over to ensure there were no physical injuries, Kara did as she always had; she drew Quicksilver to her and began to play. It was challenging to keep her attention on the notes when she could sense the turmoil of those standing around her, but for her family, she forced herself to do so. Music had always been a balm for them.

She barely noticed when Maggie stooped beside her and laid a hand gently upon her shoulder. "I'm sorry, love. I didn't think any o' ye would come to harm here."

Kara ignored the regret in the *Sidhe*'s voice and continued playing as if Mathair's life depended on it.

"'Tisn't serious, Kara. She'll be fine when she wakes."

Kara wanted to rage at those words. Instead, she played furiously, the strings of her poor violin wailing with her own frustration. Her tune did not change until Maggie sighed and rose again.

As the *Sidhe* herded the others out the door, she stopped a moment. "We go to decide what to do about the one who did this. His name is Bran, but that is all I ken, other than that he is dark o' nature, an' actions such as this aren't beyond his nature.

"Without knowing where he's gone or what he intends, 'tis difficult to determine what steps to take. If ye wish it, I'll call for ye when we're ready to discuss where the *Fianna* go from here."

Maggie left when Kara neither accepted nor rejected the offer. As if her greatest concern was a stranger...Kara took a deep breath and settled herself before the anger crept into the music. That would not help her parents at all. She liked to think that she brought some measure of peace to them after that; Mathair's color did look much better, but it was hard to deny the worry in Papa's eyes. Kara was startled when he spoke.

"I always wondered what it was like for ye."

Her music faltered. "What?"

"This is how ye were before I found ye at Yesterday's Dreams." With a nod, he indicated her unconscious mother. "Maggie had made ye as comfortable as she could an' had talked ye out o' the shock, but ye were still shaken by the time I got to see ye. Demne...Demne explained to me later all about reaction shock...magical overload. He told me how the impact o' what had happened had shorted out yer ability to handle the energy. In defense, yer mind retreated into itself. That's what we're seeing here. We just have to give her time to come out o' it."

"I'm sorry I put both of you through all of this." It was all Kara could think to say. Quicksilver slid forgotten into her lap, and she huddled in on herself. She had not done well by her parents. Pretty ironic, considering that was how all this had started: pawn the violin to keep the house and relieve her parents' worries. Instead, she threw all of them into some sort of magical nightmare. Who knew how it would end?

"Hey! Now that's enough o' that then." Papa's voice rang with such strength and conviction that Kara's heart clenched. It had been so long since he'd the confidence or the energy to speak forcefully. Illness had robbed him of that long ago. She was so overjoyed to hear it back that her self-recrimination fell away.

"Now take up that fiddle an' show me all those lessons weren't wasted."

Obligingly, Kara threw herself into the music, playing tune upon tune with such passion and hope that the notes flooded the room and inevitably spilled out into the corridor. Perhaps even as far as the Court. When she stopped, she felt weary, but no longer trampled by the whirlwind of insanity life had become. Breathing deep to savor the feeling of serenity, Kara reveled in the renewed peace. After a long while, she opened eyes she hadn't realized she'd closed, surprised to meet Maggie's wondering gaze as she leaned in the doorway. Without a word, Kara watched the *Sidhe* woman blink and slowly shake her head, sighing a tranquil sigh. There was gratitude telegraphed by those immortal eyes, but Kara didn't think she wanted to pursue the reason why, not just yet.

"'Tis decided." The simple words brought reality back full force, but not the terror or heartache of it, just the memory. Kara was about to rise to go to Maggie, when she stopped dead at the question that rose from the corner.

"What's decided?" The words were low and throaty, but beautiful just the same to Kara's ears.

"Mathair?" Kara whirled and hurried to her mother's side, vying for space beside her father. "Are you okay?"

"What happened?" Kara and her father exchanged glances, not knowing how wise it would be to tell her if she didn't remember.

"Darlin' Bobbi, we aren't sure. We were hoping ye might tell us."

Slowly Mathair shook her head, a hand slowly going up to push aside the bangs dangling in her eyes. "No...no...I'm afraid I couldn't. I don't know."

Kara ground her teeth and struggled hard not to show her frustration. It was no surprise Mathair didn't know. The question was, were the memories stolen from her on purpose, or had the loss been caused by whatever had put her into overload? Irrelevant now, they already knew what had happened, thanks to the sprites. Whatever Mathair had to add would not change anything: a woman had been kidnapped from the very Halls of *Tír na nÓg*, and the culprit would answer for it in the end.

Maggie cleared her throat in the doorway. "We must wait to take action on Bran. Something dire has come up an' the *Fianna* are summoned back to Goibhniu's chamber, immediately. We must move quickly."

Running a gentle hand through her mother's golden curls, Kara kissed her forehead and started to rise.

"Um, Kara." Maggie's tone seemed suddenly uncomfortable. "Kara, I've come for Patrick...an' to ask that ye set a bit with yer mother an' make sure she's okay."

The silence returned thick and heavy in the air. "Excuse me?"

"Goibhiniu an' the *Fianna*, they wish ye to stay in *Tír na nÓg*. I wish ye to stay."

"*Excuse me?!*" Kara's voice continued to rise. She could not control it. "After everything, you want me to do what?"

Maggie came forward and took her hand. It was all Kara could do not to tear it away—as it was, every muscle in her body tensed, and her heart pounded in her chest. "Kara, listen to me... There is no denying ye're powerful, an' without doubt ye have a stake in what has happened, but something's come up an' we can't help but think ye'd be better off here."

This was unbelievable. When Kara would have protested, Maggie stopped her with a raised hand. "In the end, love, ye aren't *Fianna*...ye aren't a warrior... ye're not even trained as a mage. An' after all that has happened, ye'd only distract us when we need to be worrying about the foe we're off to face."

"What do you mean?" She could not bring herself to admit she knew what Maggie meant. No, some determined, perverse part of her would force the words from the *Sidhe*. No more evasion; it was not real until the *Sidhe* said it. Kara hardened herself to the regret in Maggie's eyes and stood her ground.

"Must I really say it, then?" It was not a question expecting an answer. Kara recognized that and waited for Maggie to continue. "Fine... We don't want ye to join us because each time ye've had the chance, ye've run off on yer own an' immediately gotten yerself neck-deep in trouble. We'll not have ye in a position to need rescuing again, not when we must look to our own skins. I care for ye greatly, an' I certainly understand, but ye just aren't ready."

The words were harsh and unyielding, and the look in Maggie's eyes no longer spoke of regret. No, it was full of resolve and Kara found herself tensing beneath the unyielding gaze. She wanted to deny all of it, but she could not. Each time she'd gone off on her own had been an unmitigated disaster. There was no doubt in her mind that she could stand against her enemy, and certainly she needed to, but how to do so without her emotions getting in the way and tripping her up? Clutching the violin until her knuckles ached, Kara stood her ground. "I must face him!"

"'Tisn't him, 'tis another threat at our door. *We* will take care o' it an' then the rest can be discussed when the *Fianna* return. An ye want it that badly, we'll make ye ready to join us the next time 'tis Tony we face, but for now there is no discussion. Ye're staying if Goibhniu himself must put the sleep on ye."

Kara stood there, stunned, as Maggie and her father hurried from the room, neither giving her another glance. Rage and despair battled in her heart until she barely heard the soft sigh from the corner of the room.

"Don't do it."

Fighting hard against lashing out, Kara turned her head to look where Mathair now sat up against her cushions. "I mean it. You will come into this room and sit down, young lady. I will not have you put yourself and the rest of them at risk just because you don't have the sense to know when you are in over your head."

If the words had not shocked her, the uncompromising tone would have. Kara pivoted to face her mother, newfound respect joining the love in her eyes. "Mathair, it eats at me. How can I sit here, knowing that those I care for are out there facing an evil I let get by me more than once?"

"You heard her, Kara. They don't even go to face this Tony." Kara felt a flood of guilt as Mathair shivered violently at just the mention of the man who had so hurt her daughter. But when she saw her mother's eyes, she was shocked to realize that ferocious hatred had set off the tremors, not fear. "If you want an opportunity to make up for however you feel you have failed, then sit your ass down and wait. When they get back, you can talk to them about how to prepare, so you aren't caught short again."

Kara groaned as she did as she was bid, but she did not merely sit beside her mother. She practically curled up in her lap, unafraid to admit she needed the reassurance and safety of that haven. Shaking with reaction, she closed her eyes and allowed the soothing comfort of her mother's caresses to wash over her.

No! No! The *Sidhe* were supposed to come, not the Rom. The sounds of gnashing teeth echoed through the ether. Dubh wanted revenge with such intensity he was ready to rip the void to shreds with his bare hands trying to get through to *Tír na nÓg*. The *Sidhe* and that blasted Rory had totally disrupted his plans. Time to collect what he could in immortal flesh, but only if he could get them to come out of their blasted hole!

Recklessly spending power, Dubh summoned the remainder of the *Bás*, calling them to him and feeding them on the rage and fury that coursed through his stolen veins. The frenzy it set loose in their primal hearts was glorious. Thrilling in their hunger, he nearly joined them in their mindless state, that is, until Olcas reached out a steadying touch and brought him back to reality. "Do you truly intend to slaughter them before anyone else comes out to play?" Olcas's words were not heated or brutal, as Dubh would have expected. Rather they were like a bucket of cold water, waking up his common sense.

Amazed his brother found the restraint to use just the right approach rather than pummel him senseless for jeopardizing their plot, Dubh found the strength to ground himself in the rationale before he aided the *Sidhe* to thwart his own plan. That didn't mean he didn't have urges to grind Olcas beneath his heel as well, but that was something to consider for another time.

No, baby brother was right: if he sent all of his pets to the hillside in this state, they would slaughter the bait before it had a chance to draw his true targets out of safety. Centering himself and reining in his murderous wrath, he released the *Conairt* into the conflict, instructing them to toy with their prey, not slaughter it. Familiar as they were with the concept of bait, they were only too happy to play with their food first.

❈

They came streaming from the very depths of the forest so quickly and forcefully that Jacko almost forgot he had been sent after them. Sliding to a halt, he scrambled for footing and prepared to defend himself.

They continued past him as if he were not there.

Shaking his head in confusion, he stared after the terrifying beauty that was the *Sidhe*. Their faces were fierce, and their loping strides commanding. He watched them go, wondering what he should do. There he was, in the middle of a faerie forest as the Kindly Ones rushed off to...battle. At least, he thought it was battle; all he had seen was a man with a gun and one of the *Sidhe* back to back, their stances wary and their faces grim. He thought Granddame Rose had been shot, but since she crawled to the one he'd thought had shot her and crouched between the men for safety, well, Jacko had no idea what was going on now. He had sensed something familiar, something unsettling, but what?

As he stood there lost in doubt, a firm grip took his arm and propelled him after the departing *Sidhe*. Startled, he set his heels and tried to draw back, but the hold was like being caught in solid stone. Looking up, he met a pair of flashing green eyes in a face framed by a multitude of reddish-blonde braids and could only marvel that such beauty was capable of looking so ferocious.

"Come on then, or were ye wanting to find out how we guard our sacred forests?"

"Who..." He couldn't finish. Her gaze pinned him until he despaired of uttering another word.

"Snap out o' it, Romani. Yer acting like a silly boy." Her gaze held just enough contempt to draw him out of his daze. "I'm called Maggie McCormick an' I lead the *Sidhe Fianna*. 'Tis us ye were looking for, was it na?"

With a deep breath, Jacko shook his head to clear the uncharacteristic fog. This was not the first time in his life he'd seen something magical. Yet she was right; so much had happened at once that he was behaving foolishly. The Rom did not frighten so easily, particularly for no reason. Giving Maggie McCormick an abrupt nod, Jacko set off after the others, the immortal keeping pace at his side.

The *Sidhe* had paused at the edge of the woods. One or two looked back into the forest, obviously wondering what kept them; while the rest scanned the hillside, their expressions grim and their bodies taut as if they would cast themselves upon the scene below like avenging archangels. One towered above all the others and, when he turned to look their way,

Jacko quaked with righteous terror. He put his hand out to Maggie beside him.

"Who..." Again he could not speak, but he didn't need to.

Watching him with understanding, this time, Maggie gave a quirking little smile. "I lead the *Fianna*...he leads me. 'Tis Goibhniu the Smith."

Jacko's heart raced, and his mouth went instantly dry. While he was not of Ireland, he had wandered here for quite a spell. He knew the myth—and something of the reality—of the *Sidhe*. Goibhniu was not just an immortal: he was a god. And he was looking straight at Jacko himself.

"Come closer, child o' Rom."

The voice rumbled deeply, the eyes burned like live coals. Jacko eyed the bulging muscles, evidence of the effort Goibhniu put into his craft, and wasn't so sure he wanted to move closer. He wanted to run back into the forest...fast. He didn't, though. Even as the thought formed in his mind, he was already halfway to where the Smithgod stood.

By all that was holy in any land, he was a tall one. Once again feeling insignificant, Jacko struggled to hold his ground. This would not do. Rom did not grovel or cower. They were strong and courageous. Standing tall, with dignity, he reminded himself he was of the Rom.

Perhaps that was why the chuckle took him by surprise.

"Very good, very good." The Smithgod beamed with approval a fleet moment before becoming grave again. "Ye will fight well beside us an ye chose to. Do ye?"

"My family is down there. I will fight, with or without you."

That only caused Goibhniu to laugh full out this time. Not only was it an offense, but it drew unwanted attention from whatever awaited them below. Maybe a god had no concerns about surprise and strategy, but mere mortals had to take care with their skin. He was ready to protest when Goibhniu reached into a pouch at his side and pulled out a small vial of clear liquid. It sparkled in the moonlight and danced like quicksilver as the god pulled out the tight stopper. Jacko was so absorbed by the movement of the fluid he was not prepared for what came next. Before he could protest or pull back, Goibhniu moistened his finger and drew it down across Jacko's right eye.

With a startled oath, Jacko threw himself backward, but not in time. He could feel the icy touch of moisture clinging to his lashes as he blinked furiously. Quickly, his hand flew up to rub the substance away, only to be caught inches from his eye by a familiar grip. Bellowing furiously, Jacko turned upon Maggie, ready to free himself by any means, only to stop dead, dumbfounded by what he saw.

Shimmering beauty. Shimmering beauty and utter perfection bathed in brilliant light, though they were yet beneath the shadow of the trees. He would not have given credence to anyone claiming this woman could be any more beautiful than the first moment he saw her. How wrong he would have been.

"What the..." Confusion reigned as his eyes darted all about, trying to take in what had happened. Somehow he could see the entire world, not just this Maggie, as he never had before. Where the *Sidhe* had been intensely beautiful, now they were glorious and divine. The forest, primal and powerful just moments ago, was now the very presence of Eden, unspoiled and perfect. Rage drained from him as quickly as water from a bottomless bag. It was miraculous, a gift, but that thought sobered him. Seldom were fey gifts pure. There was always a downside.

As if reading his thoughts, Maggie leaned forward. "'Twon't leave ye blind or drive ye mad, though perhaps ye'll be seeing things ye wouldn't wish to see."

Looking from her to Goibhniu, he could understand the wisdom of what she said. With a deep breath, he voiced the most important questions. "How long will it last? And why only the one eye?"

"But a few hours...long enough for ye to take part in the battle an' stand a chance o' surviving. If I'd given ye the Sight in both, ye wouldn't be able to see aught o' the mortal realm." Goibhniu answered him, and as he did so, he held out a blade handed to him by one of the others. "Here, take this. 'Tis only on loan, ye understand, but 'twill serve ye in good stead below."

Almost unconsciously, Jacko's hand reached out to grasp the extended hilt. The craftsmanship was splendid—perfection, in fact. He was not in the habit of using swords, though knives were familiar in his hand, but he would not refuse the offer. "What about the others?"

"If we are able, I will ensure they receive the same treatment as yerself."

Jacko waited for the "but" that was so obviously a part of that statement.

"If na, ye'll need to either work with them or get them to safety, for they won't survive unaided once the enemy unstays its hand."

Not for the first time that night, Jacko wondered what he was getting into. Perhaps he should just hand back the sword, turn around, and walk himself down the other side of the knoll, get into his wagon and do what Rom do best...travel far. Even with the aid he had been given, he was not sure that he was up to what they would face. But then it struck him, the worst oversight they had made: the women and children were alone at the wagons. What chance did they stand if there were two groups of attackers? Or what if some of those below broke away to attack the caravans during the fight? Indecision wracked him.

Yet again, it was as if they read his mind, as perhaps they did, but as he was tearing himself apart trying to decide what he should do, the one called Maggie spoke gently by his ear. "We know o' the women an' children. Others have been sent to see them to safety."

Relief flooded through him. He did not have to choose between his kin. With that dilemma solved, he could focus on this side of the hill. This was a good thing because the horrifying scene that met his gaze demanded his complete focus.

On the hillside below were those he had left when he had been sent to find the *Sidhe*. The Rom formed a circle around Granddame Rose, and the *Sidhe* and the gunman, with nothing but tiny knives in their hands, desperately tried to shield them. But that was not what horrified him. His new Sight revealed forty or so fiery-haired women circling and stalking the defenders. He thought they were not armed until he noticed these women had razor-sharp teeth and dagger-like claws on each finger.

What were they? There was no sign of them earlier. Or was there? An image of the raised gun filled his memory, then a bright line of red across the wielder's arm and the weapon falling away. Those claws looked sufficient to leave behind a bloody slash such as he remembered. In that instant, he prayed for all he was worth that those below could hold out just a little longer.

When a cry went up from the *Sidhe* surrounding him, Jacko brandished the unfamiliar sword as well as he was able and added his voice to their outcry. As a whole, they charged down from the shelter of the trees to engage the horror below them.

Chapter 15

Arn was not an overly religious man. As he waited for help to arrive, he had cause to regret that fact. He had thought the Rom's arrival would even the odds. That was before he realized they could not, for some unfathomable reason, even *see* the women attacking them. Now he had not only himself to be concerned with, but all of them as well. He and Urias had their hands full.

Adjusting his grip on the puny elven blade, he thought longingly of his Ruger, lost somewhereon the ground. It hadn't done him a bit of good, but damn, the familiar weight of it had been reassuring. He was marking them with the knife, which was more than could be said for the gun, but for each score he managed, they got in at least five among him and the others in the huddle.

"We can't hold out like this, Urias." Arn flinched as someone in the group hissed with new pain. The sickly sweet odor of fresh-drawn blood made his stomach churn. He had learned early on in the encounter not to look their attackers in the face. Seeing such voracious, animal-like hunger on faces so nearly human was bad enough, but knowing it was his flesh they craved drove him mad.

"Aye, but we can, my friend," Urias answered, his tone grim. "Don't ye realize they toy with us? We aren't the prey they seek, we're the lure."

Arn didn't think there was any blood left in his face to drain away. He must have been wrong, because as the sense of what Urias said sank in, Arn went lightheaded with the enormity of it all. Taking a firm grip upon himself, he realized the freedom—no, the invulnerability the revelation gave him. If he did not have to fear for their lives—right now, at least—there was no need for caution. He didn't know what he would do yet, but he would choose his time well so that his blow was sure to count.

Of course, that was all well and good, but boy, did he have trouble keeping his resolve when suddenly red-hot fire burned along his side and a thin trail of blood trickled down to pool inside his shoe. Whirling, Arn stared into blood-red eyes filled intense hunger and unholy glee. The woman slinked closer. There was no other word for it; she slinked as if the conclusion were forgone, and she had only to savor the moment. Behind her, he could see two others, as alike enough to the first to be mistaken for her reflection. All three played the game, slinking forward and drawing back. Was he really so confident they were only baiting the defenders?

Keeping his knife hand up, Arn reached down with his other to assess the wound. The skin over his ribs was barely parted, though the groove deepened slightly as it descended. All in all, it was more a bloody mess than anything serious. He was amazed he still stood, for the blow had been precise, and he knew that if they had wanted him dead, he would be.

So far, his injuries were superficial. Even together, they were scarcely life-threatening, but that did not dampen the frantic instinct within him that screamed for escape, for survival.

As the assault went on, Arn began to wonder if the gypsy had run for help...or if he had just run. Just as his cynicism began to rise, a glorious sight appeared from the top of the hill. Too beautiful for words and too terrifying to imagine, a host of *Sidhe* charged down the slope with a giant of a man in the forefront and the gypsy man in the middle of the ranks. They, Arn noticed, had wisely brought swords.

Too bad they were too late.

In his moment of distraction, one of the beast women darted forward and slashed his wound deeper yet, and Arn went down.

It had worked. Olcas's little plot had worked. Scanning the battle through the mists of the void, Dubh had a moment's concern. Already, scarcely anyone on the battlefield remained unscathed, on either side, but should it go much further, he would lose everything! He had worked hard to gain the *Bás*'s trust and even harder to build their numbers up to even the paltry few they were today. He would not allow them to be squandered before they served his purpose. Quickly, he called off all but the worst wounded — in the mentality of their race, they were already dead anyway, so what would be the point in recalling them? No, let them fight to the end. Even wounded the *Bás* were formidable; he would allow those injured to avenge themselves before they went off to complete the process of dying.

He would not leave it at that, though. He would exact retribution for the Pack members lost this day. And he would see that those responsible fostered their replacements. Tearing a rent in the void, he and Olcas climbed through. The moment they landed on Irish soil, Dubh felt his brother tense, even as he did himself. Immediately, they each reached for the mage currents at hand, tearing them from their anchors and letting the energy build until it visibly crackled in the air around them. When he could take in no more, Dubh cast it forth, blasting a group of *Sidhe* too focused on the *Conairt* to see it coming. Unfortunately, someone else did see, and a hasty shield sprang up before the blast could impact. It was not enough to deflect the force altogether, but it drained away enough that his targets were only singed.

A curse rose from Dubh's lips until he noticed his brother. Olcas stood on a massive boulder slightly to the side of the fracas, and, from the look of it, he did not depend on sheer force to cut down their foe. Instead, he executed a complicated weaving intended to plague them more thoroughly. First, he gathered an amazing quantity of power and held it in check. Once that was prepared, he muttered a few words until the aspect of the clouds above changed. They became heavy and ominous, and in the dawning light, they were limned in an angry red glow that had nothing to do with being backlit by the sun. It was masterful, really. Dubh was quite impressed when the spell was cast. Looking above, he swiftly gauged the area of impact and made sure to step out of its bounds. As Olcas was the caster, he was already in the clear. Now they but had to watch. For a moment, Dubh felt a flash of concern for the *Conairt*, but even if they weren't already, in essence, dead, their very nature should exclude them from harm.

He couldn't help a snigger of glee when the rain came down, sizzling and burning whatever got in the way of its acid touch. Well, they had made their entrance, and it had turned out pretty spectacular at that. Now it was time for business.

As Olcas prepared another attack, Dubh held back. At first, it was out of awe, which did not sit easy with him, but then he realized the added benefits of allowing his brother to wear himself down while Dubh conserved his power. Still, he could not deny the grudging respect beginning to form. Always before, from the time when they'd worn their own faces right up to now, his youngest brother had been inferior in all ways. His control of the feral mage currents had been weak, his grasp of mental manipulation only basic. But now he had happened upon something outside of Dubh's realm of understanding... mundane magic. And like it or not, Olcas was masterful in its use.

Of course, that only sealed Olcas's doom. Inept, he could be tolerated for those moments in which he was useful, but with his increased abilities, he was too much of a threat. Dubh would ensure he spent himself in this battle, and when he was weak and vulnerable...well, when Carmán's children divided the power gleaned from Ireland, it would be split only two ways, assuming Calma ever deigned to show up.

So caught up was he in his scheming, Dubh barely noticed in time when their quarry gathered itself for a strategic retreat. The worst of the wounded were already whisked away before he realized it. With a scream of rage, he hurried to pursue them.

As they sat there together in the muted light of *Tír na nÓg*, soothed by the song of either birds or faelings — it was hard to tell the two apart out of sight — Kara's mother drifted off into a peaceful slumber. Apparently, her earlier ordeal had cost her more than she had realized. Kara wished she could rest so easily, but thoughts of the conflict in the mortal world would not release her. Papa was out there, and Maggie, and Miach, and half a dozen others whom she didn't even have names for but who she owed a great deal. Even Goibhniu was out there, though she hadn't expected that. Did they face danger because of her, or would it have come to their threshold regardless?

Like it made a difference. It ate at her, knowing the risks they took...and that they had not wanted her among them. Maggie claimed it was not Tony they faced. Had she lied? Kara would not go against her implicit promise to Mathair, but she had to know. Here, alone in silence, with nothing but her concerns to occupy her, Kara felt her gut twisting in knots. Carefully sliding from where she nestled against her mother, Kara grabbed the case holding Quicksilver and went out to ease her troubled thoughts.

The halls of *Tír na nÓg* were virtually empty. Surely not everyone was off to war. For most of them, the closest they came to battle was squabbling amongst themselves. Kara took a deep breath and tried not to look as if she were sneaking out, then did precisely that. Making her way through the forest, she prayed this was not something she would come to regret. But she had to know!

As she approached the gate, she wondered what to do. She had as much as promised not to leave again. Mathair would be crushed if she did. The thought of the censure on her mother's face was enough alone to ensure Kara stayed, but how was she to know what was going on? It was like having chickenpox in some impossible place that couldn't possibly be scratched...like deep in the ear or under a nail. She felt she would scream with not knowing. Like a caged tiger, she stalked around the gate, wondering if it were possible to open it like a door, to *look* through but not *go* through. Edging closer, she tested the bounds; she could get within a foot of the thing before she started to tingle, six inches before she began to feel as if she were in two places at once. And still, all she saw before her were the trees of *Tír na nÓg*.

It was so tempting. Would she really be disobeying if she slipped through and then back again? What if she left only to see what happened and then returned? That was really tempting.

She'd almost stepped forward when she thought she saw a movement in the forest. Her heart pounded and her eyes went wide. She scrambled back away from the gate and wondered if there was any point in hiding. Or was it even necessary? Perhaps her guilty mind simply played tricks on her. Several long moments later, she still thought she'd seen something, yet no one drew near. It was possible she saw a flash of sunlight off something like aged gold, but had she truly seen movement? She scanned the trees around her, but there was nothing there. It was a faerie, perhaps, or some other of the kin-cousins. Putting it from her mind, she focused all of her attention back on the gate. There had to be a way.

Kara stood before the portal, close enough to sense it, but far enough away to not give in to temptation. She bent her will upon it, confident, thanks to Grandda's tales, that all she had to do to see through to the other side was want it badly enough. And she was right. It was like looking through a heavy veil, but better than nothing when she fretted about the safety of her friends.

What was she doing?! Damn her to the Cursed Land! Bran had slipped back into the Land of Youth expecting to settle back into his indulgent patterns completely unsuspected. Instead, he found that the blasted sprites had betrayed him, and he dared not show his face. Now, as he desired to make his final escape before someone discovered his return, the girl Kara blocked his way. The only thing he hated more than a faeling was a waterkin, and this particular one seemed set on serving as his bane.

In the cover of the underbrush, he waited with what was for him extreme patience. When he had heard of the battle, the...*Fianna*—in his own thoughts, he twisted the word into an insult—set out to fight, he knew what he would do. It was perfect, flawless. Wending his way among the secret paths he by all rights should not have known—discovered long ago to avoid the torment of seeing the object of his love absorbed with another—Bran claimed the hidden treasure that would ensure his ascension...a blade beyond the scope of all others...a blade even Goibhniu had cause to fear. One thrust would take the god out of the way; then none would gainsay Bran.

If only the blasted waterkin would move! Bran looked for a way to access the gate around her, but there was no approach that she would not see. The plan would not work if she had time to warn the others.

What would entice her to move? He'd watched her from secret since she'd first arrived in *Tír na nÓg*. Dear little Kara had connected with a handful of the Kin, but they were all on the other side of the gate, and she knew it. The vermin faelings flocked to her for some reason, but they avoided him, so there was no help there. The only thing he could think of was family. There was nothing she cared about more than family, from what he had seen. And thus, the plan sprang into his thoughts full-blown.

Reaching into his memory for the voice of the girl's mother, he called out, "Kara? Kara? Where are you?" He carefully injected a thread of fear into the words as he threw his voice, making it sound as if it came from the vicinity of *Mór Halla*. All the while, he watched the girl intently, enjoying the internal struggle in her every move. First her gaze darted toward the gate, then toward the direction of the voice. Her guilt showed plainly on her face, though he did not know, or even care, why. She was on the edge of decision. So close...Bran sent up the cry once more, adding a little more urgency, lacing it with concern.

It was too much for the girl. As she slipped away through the forest, Bran hurried forward to steal through the gate.

Maggie could see how difficult it was for Goibhniu to stay his hand. The sounds of his people's suffering had turned his face into a mask of ferocity. She knew that any blade forged by his hand, no matter who drew it, would not fail to find its mark, the wound inevitably fatal. When the blade in question was also *wielded* in Goibhniu's own hand, the results were too dire to contemplate. Though his sword rose and fell in essence in her defense, she found she could not look on him for long.

It was just as well, for if she did not look to herself, he would have to avenge her, not defend her. Gripping her hilt more firmly, Maggie fought with skill and determination. The Smithgod's blades may always strike a fatal blow, but that was a bit too vague for her. Yes, whatever she hit would die of the wound—she had seen this too many times to dispute it—however, there was no time frame attached to that assurance. Maggie would just as soon make sure that the deed took place now and aimed accordingly.

Lashing out with a vengeance, she came beside one of the Kin she did not expect to see. Urias was in somewhat worse shape than when she had last seen him in New York, but the look of fierce determination he wore bordered on glee. His golden eyes flashed like the sun, and his smile had more of the feral beast in it than anything else. Maggie spared him an appraising look as he engaged the foe. He was smeared with blood from neck to torso and the angry slashes across his sword arm, back, and chest spoke tellingly of his dedication to the fight. Each move he made was as sure and powerful as if his flesh was unmarked, and the look in his eye would have daunted any but the inhuman women they faced. But as he lunged forth against a trio of them, Maggie was aghast to notice he faced off against them with nothing more than a dagger, not the sword she'd assumed. Urias himself was driven enough not to care what he held. Maggie would have to have care for him.

Quickly dispatching her current adversary, she made her way to the edge of the battle where those most wounded had been dragged to receive Miach's attention. She scanned the healing zone, protected by several of the fiercest of her *Fianna*, searching for a suitable blade among those cast aside, forgotten for the moment. As she scooped one up, she made sure it bore Goibhniu's maker's mark before dashing back into the fray.

Now where has the blasted youngling gotten to? she thought furiously. He was gone from where she remembered him being. Damn him if he got himself killed before she could get a suitable weapon into his hands. *Urias?*

I'm a bit busy...at the moment...an ye don't mind. Leave him alone...ye harpy! The last thought was vicious and lethal and clearly aimed at another, though it shocked Maggie to no end. Her young friend's thoughts betrayed the toll of this battle upon him. It was enough to give her a feel for his location, though. She scanned the area where she sensed him and hurried forward when she spied his spiky blue crest. She barreled past those fighting, too quickly to be engaged, clearing the way with a violent howl when the mere sight of her didn't hasten all out of her way.

Her heart clenched as she examined Urias more closely: he sported a new slash across his face and he was surrounded on all sides by deadly, stalking creatures, their velvety white pelts smeared with blood. Maggie saw little sign that any of it was theirs. That was about to change. Diving among them, she struck like a viper with her blade while tossing Urias the one she had fetched for him. She had not noticed before, but there was a fallen human at her kinsman's feet, one he straddled with care. How curious...and what was the story there? Maggie put the thought from her mind and turned a challenging look at their foe.

The *Sidhe* made a formidable pair, and the enemy fled rather than confront their joint wrath. There was no time for triumph, though. The demon women did not flee the battlefield; they merely sought out easier prey. Immediately, Urias gathered up the fallen man and moved on with purpose and renewed vigor toward Miach's little neutral zone, sparing Maggie not even a moment's thought or thanks. Of course, from the looks of the unconscious human, there wasn't time for that, either.

"Arn, ye must be all right, man, ye must...'tis so close we are." Urias kept up a steady stream of pleas, tugging at Maggie's heart long after she could see them no more.

Wishing them godspeed, Maggie turned her eye on the others fighting around her when it struck her the man had been human, but not Romani. Where had he come from? And why had he joined forces with them? Of the Rom here when they'd arrived, including the one in the woods, only three had chosen to join them in battle; the others had fought their way free and then headed off to see to their families and their wagons. He was not one of them. But this was not a puzzle for battle. She brought her focus back to bear, looking for the encounter where her aid would be most welcome.

One of the Rom who stayed was now beside her, fighting as fearlessly as any of the *Fianna*. No amount of courage could make up for horrible odds, though. As he blocked and parried two of the wild women, a third darted in for the kill. Well, that one had a surprise coming because Maggie was not about to stand by and let it happen.

She was a little too far off, but with an undulating yell, she lunged forward just as the claws began their swipe. Bringing her blade up sharply, she sliced through what could only be described as a natural growth of daggers, cutting them to the quick, and continued her downward slash to cleave through the woman's torso. Maggie had only a moment to dwell on that before she discovered the flaw in her plan: While it allowed the man to scurry free to a better fighting position, it left Maggie horribly extended and even with the grace, flexibility, and reflexes of the *Sidhe*, she could not recover quickly enough to avoid the slightest of claw tips wielded by one of her victim's sisters. It opened Maggie's back from nape to rear.

"Auuuugh!" The scream tore from her, leaving her throat raw and her teeth clenched. It was a superficial slash, but it hurt like hell with the slightest motion. Gritting her teeth, she whirled reflexively, and with one swing, she took off the head of the attacker responsible for the wound. Growling and snarling as much as they, Maggie dared any others to try her.

Suddenly the women stopped...alert and intent upon something. With reluctant growls, they lashed out a final, rebellious time before fleeing away through the ether. Reluctance was evident in the taut line of their muscles as they disappeared. The *Sidhe* and the humans were left alone and confused on the battlefield, milling about, trying to find some reason for what had just occurred. It was then Maggie noticed Goibhniu and, to her greatest horror, found herself too far removed to do a thing.

Kara couldn't say what made her turn around. Was it a sound? Was it the intense feeling of dread that tripped down her spine? Had that flicker of movement teased at the corner of her eye yet again? Regardless of what it was, Kara turned just in time to see someone duck through the gate...someone with hair the color of old gold that matched the hilt of the sword she could not miss, strapped across his back as it was. She knew that sword: it was the one Maggie brought from New York. Kara had seen it when they prepared to leave, and Maggie had told her its greatest strength and why it must be guarded. Goibhniu had to be warned! But what of her promise to Mathair? Surely, this was different. Wasn't it?

The dread revved up full force. It was too much for her; before she could think, Kara dashed to the gate on the heels of Bran, Quicksilver still clutched tightly in her grasp.

By the time she reached the telltale shimmer, the *Sidhe* had already passed through. What was going on? Standing by the gate gripped with indecision, Kara weighed what she knew. Bran was bad; he had stolen a woman from the safety of *Tír na nÓg* and run off. He did not like waterkin or very much else that wasn't directly related to him. Right now there was a battle on the far side of that gate, and the *Sidhe* he hated most were in the middle of it. And finally, Kara was the only one who knew all of this. Oh yeah, and the sword casually slung across his back, the one he should never have been able to find, was a god-killer.

With no more second thoughts, Kara plunged through the gate in time to see Bran disappear through the trees. What was she to do now? If she hadn't come, Goibhniu would be at risk; now that she had, she was at risk. Suddenly she thought with longing of all the magical training she could have had if she hadn't foolishly moved from one self-caused crisis to another.

There was nothing to be done for it now. Taking a firmer grasp on Quicksilver, she crept forward to the edge of the tree line. Perhaps she could find a way to do this without exposing herself. Kara sighed, thinking, *Yeah, and maybe I can walk on water, too.* Wishing she had brought someone with better decision-making skills along, or at least someone with a better track record with the results, she looked out onto the carnage of the battlefield. It was so much different that at Yesterday's Dreams, so much more visceral. There was blood and fury and suffering on a scale she had never before seen up close. And, as she watched a dark golden head wend its way through the fighters, she recognized there was more treachery, as well.

Did she have the courage to make it across that field? Did she even need to? With a focus fine-tuned by desperation, Kara reached out to Goibhniu with her thoughts only to fine a roiling mass of intensity that set her head spinning. *Okay,* she thought, *perhaps trying to contact him with my mind in the middle of a battle was not a good idea.* Maggie? She tried again, this time finding a scintillating shield, through which she could not pass.

Her jaw clenched. Kara forced herself to breathe deeply, gearing herself up to plunge through the fighting.

Was she really doing this? Again? No...she could not panic, she could not put herself and others in danger again, or she would only prove their earlier claims. She had not chosen to disobey; her hand had been forced. That did not mean she had to repeat her past mistakes. How could she foil Bran without placing herself in harm's way? As she turned her mind to the problem, a faint strand of music flitted across her thoughts.

She had her answer.

Perched on a boulder at the edge of the woods, Kara brought out Quicksilver, grateful the instrument was already tuned. She positioned the violin beneath her chin and set her bow to the strings. At first, she gave no thought to the tune or the melody. She just let the notes flow where they would. She was mesmerized by the growing cloud of energy that crackled around her, cradling her in its coils, caressing her with charged fingers, but as the pressure increased, so did the attention she drew. She could hear vague exclamations from below and knew she must act quickly. Taking stock of Bran's progress, she was aghast to realize how close he had drawn to Goibhniu while she had lost herself to the siren's call of the music.

"Stop!" Her cry echoed across the hillside, her voice compelling beyond recognition. "You will not harm him."

Her command shaped the magic she had gathered, her focus gave it direction. As Bran prepared to strike, Kara unleashed the summoned power. In a supreme display of overkill, she used the energies to block the attack, locking the blade in a coil of power and jerking it away before Bran could bring Goibhniu down. The sword only flew a foot or so. She did not have the control or strength to draw it away farther. Her cry had alerted the others, however, and they moved in to claim both sword and villain.

Bran's face locked in a rictus of rage. Rooted in place, Kara watched the eerie, bone-colored eyes rise to meet hers. His gaze held a sickening promise. She suppressed a shiver of tension, forced her own expression to remain blank. She fought not to flinch as Bran snarled and lashed out. She expected to die, but his strike arrowed past her. Brutally, he ripped power from the very fabric of *Tír na nÓg*. Kara could do nothing but gasp in protest as he vanished from sight.

His disappearance freed her from her paralysis. Cursing, Kara stared in frustration at the spot where he had stood. There was nothing to be done. He would not face justice today. That was when she realized she better get herself back to *Tír na nÓg* before Maggie or someone else caught her out on the hilltop. Carefully stowing Quicksilver back in her case, Kara turned to leave, only to freeze in place once more.

"Hello, Kara."

Swallowing hard, Kara prayed for the hazy shimmer that would reassure her that what she saw was a product of her curse. She prayed for it desperately...in vain.

"Come now, no 'hello' for an old *intimate*?"

Kara shivered in distaste at his implication and felt a twinge in her chest, though the wounds were gone as if they'd never existed. Gone on the outside, at least. She did not try to pick up Quicksilver. It would do her no good. He'd likely strike her down before she could even open the case. Instead, she used her foot to push her precious violin behind her where it was less likely to fall victim to anything that transpired in the next few moments.

"How touching. Why do you bother? You know you are powerless against me. You cannot even rid yourself of my parting gift, how do you think you could possibly stand against me in person?" The look on Tony's face was lecherous and hungry. Kara struggled just to keep her breathing even as she bore the full brunt of his stare. She wanted to stand up to him, desperately needed to, in fact, but the harder she tried, the more she slid into the flashbacks of her capture. Would she never be free of him? Was he right—had she no hope?

The very possibility infuriated her. Tony would never be right in this. Her breath quickened, this time with righteous wrath. Without the aid of Quicksilver, Kara captured the magic around her, both the remnants of what she had called previously and the feral lines she sensed flowing nearby. This time she did not sit quietly. This time he would feel her teeth at his throat. More than anything, she wished she had the blade Bran had wielded against

Goibhniu. If Maggie were to be believed, this was not Tony before her, or at least not him alone, but also one of the sons of the goddess Carmán. Kara thought it would have been nice to hold a god-killing blade to his throat. Instead she visualized a spear of pure light, crackling with energy as it pierced Tony's heart.

"I don't think so, precious."

Kara was torn between not presenting her back to Tony and whirling to see who had crept up behind her. The voice sounded hoarse and tight, almost gravelly like a chronic smoker's, and it was too close at her back. Compromising, she angled herself slightly until she could watch both men. She paled at her first glimpse of Tony's accomplice. She should have known, but with everything else that had happened, the memory had fallen away, buried beneath her terrible experiences after. Not four feet away was the walking corpse from the bus station, the burned man who'd tormented her by chewing strips of his own flesh.

She had done it again. Despite all of her good intentions, she had done it again. Deep inside, she wanted to cry; on the surface, she managed to wreathe her face in contempt. Confidently flexing her fingers, as if ready to tear the two of them apart with nothing more, she diverted some of her harvested energy, settling it like a bubble around her. Safe, for the moment, she tried to call for Maggie, for anyone.

The brothers only laughed sadistically, making it quite clear their opinion of her efforts, so easily blocked by their own. Kara did not allow herself to give in to the anger she felt toward them. Anger made her sloppy. Linking herself to the mage energy, she quested the area around her, looking for a connection to the land, hoping desperately to find one that she could manipulate across the gate, pulling herself to *Tír na nÓg*. She never got the chance. There was a thud behind her like a man jumping to the ground. Kara nearly lost her battle with despair. Fate was a cruel bitch; she thought she stood a chance against two, but three...that would be much trickier. With a quavering breath, she made it seem like she had dropped her makeshift shield and released the mage energy she'd gathered harmlessly into the ground. She allowed her jaw to tremble as if she struggled not to cry. She had to let them think she was giving up.

"I believe this little treasure was on yer mind, was it na?" Amazement flooded her as a gentle, familiar voice spoke smoothly in her ear, and a hilt extended past her shoulder. "So an' who might these *gentlemen* be?"

Kara nearly went weak at the sound of his voice, relief flooding through her, stealing the taut strain that was the only thing keeping her upright at the moment. So, not another foe...but Aí. She fought hard to resist the impulse to relax. The danger they were in was still quite real, just because she did not stand alone, that did not mean the day was hers. A thrill of triumph shot through her as she reached up to grasp the hilt he offered, her stance automatically shifting to compensate, thanks to her years of sword training. And even still, for a moment, the weight of the blade startled her. It was much heavier than anything she'd wielded before. It bore her arm down like a lead weight until she thought it would anchor her to the ground—but only for a moment. As she got a feel for the weapon in her hands, it was as if it did the same with her, testing and compensating, adjusting its own balance according to her ability to hold it aloft. By the time she brought it to the fore, she would have sworn the sword had been crafted with her hand in mind to wield it. Kara O'Keefe, who never before had raised anything heftier than a light sword, felt like a match for Conan or Lancelot or mighty Cúchulainn himself.

Empowered by the feeling, she turned toward her immortal enemy, her expression formidable as she brandished the god-killing blade. The response was gratifying.

Tony went pale beyond any degree she had ever seen for someone of his complexion, and his burnt-cinder companion quivered violently. But those reactions were unconscious, uncontrolled, and the rampant brutality in their eyes gave lie to them. What struck her most was the way their gazes burned with recognition and did not leave the sword, as if it wielded itself, and there was nothing to concern them but the weapon alone.

Suddenly, she had no doubt of who stood before her. These were Carmán's sons, or two of them, anyway. Of course, they recognized the sword...it was the god-killer...and without a doubt, they had felt its bite before. Terrible memories seemed to play across their features, too fast and fleeting for Kara to grasp even a glimmer of them, but having heard the tale of their demise, understanding took her breath away.

She forgot about Aí, forgot about the battlefield, forgot, even, about vengeance. With extreme reluctance, Kara experienced a wave of compassion for the obvious terror these two had for what she held in her hands. The realization dawned on her that with the merest touch of this blade, the two beings in front of her would be no more. No doubt a necessary thing, as far as those who had suffered their attentions would agree, but was it something she could bring herself to do? There was no pulling punches here, just a scratch, and it was done, but what scars would that add to her already battered heart, to take lives, no matter how reprehensible?

Her struggle lasted but a moment. What scars would it leave if she *didn't*? That was the better question. Who would she irreparably harm if she walked away from Carmán's children this day? How many would suffer their attention until someone with more resolve than she had was again in a position to stop them? What sins would blacken her soul as surely as if she'd committed them herself? No, there was no choice, no mercy, no leniency...the harm such creatures would let loose upon the world was without measure. Adjusting her grip and finding her balance, Kara advanced upon them, eyes flashing and jaw set, a subtle sheen of sweat across her brow the only betrayal of her internal conflict. Immediately, the brothers darted away from each other, putting distance between them and her, as well. Their movements were cagey, and their expressions went flat and cold, revealing nothing. And then the assault began, subtle and unexpected. Creeping across her awareness, Kara felt an intimate touch, invasive and threatening, brutal and ruthless. The muscle just below her right eye twitched, and her teeth ground viciously. A dark, reddish haze settled over her thoughts, slicing at her heart, and bands of misty power wrapped around her wrists and ankles, tugging tight enough to make her wince, though nothing physical was there.

No! She would not descend into that madness again. They would not do that to her, she would not allow it. With a feral growl, she twisted her wrist, sending the sword weaving and slashing through the gloaming, flashes of starlight sparkling along the deadly edge. A smile danced across her lips, one with not even a passing acquaintance with joy or simple pleasures. She slashed decisively at her blackened adversary, the one closest to her lunge. He hissed and leapt back, eyes flashing like neon-green flames, his mouth a permanent and ferocious grimace. The expression on his face nearly mesmerized Kara, keeping her in place too long. But somewhere beyond her single-minded focus, there was a more observant Kara, one who noticed things she had no call to see; things like magical currents and mythical beings, deities and devils. Right now, that part of her marked the growing aura of intense acid-green light gathering at the burned man's hands. Her perceptive self struggled to overcome her warrior self, winning the battle just in time for her to jump away from the spot she had been standing. The spot where freshly charred earth spoke of the close call she had just barely missed.

As Kara focused even more keenly on the godling, she barely noticed that Aí closed with Tony, keeping him occupied and away from her back. She heard other sounds of battle draw closer, climbing the hillside. Like a wounded and cornered beast, the man she faced became more dangerous than before. Pushing her assault, she rushed him, slashing and thrusting with a skill she would not have possessed with any other blade.

She flinched as a spear of mage energy slashed across her cheek, leaving a long, raw burn that glowed like unhealthy foxfire. With a curse, she tried to draw hasty shields about her, but the results were crude and faulty, her attention too divided to allow her both to fight and protect herself. If she had brought the shields up first, perhaps, but she had not learned the automatic control that would allow her to do it with anything less than complete concentration.

With unwavering fervor, Kara pressed on, ignoring the frantic blows that struck her, caring not for herself but that she put an end to such evil. She felt a strong, punishing grip lock on her arm—the one without the sword. It was a familiar touch, too familiar, and Kara snarled and spat like a wildcat. Swinging around, she found herself face to face with Tony. From behind, she could hear Aí's warning yell, followed by the sounds of battle as he engaged her former combatant, but she could not spare a thought for him. Her attention was all for the man before her.

They stood there, trapped by each other's gaze, pulsing with an electric charge that had nothing to do with battle. Kara was disoriented by the shifting features on the face staring back at her. Suddenly, Tony's face was superimposed with...well, Tony's face. She shook her head and drew heavy, raking breaths through clenched teeth. One face had brown eyes, the other blue. A memory of the last time that had happened washed over her. On the heels of the memory followed a flood of fury. Her sword arm came up and drew back, and she readied a deathblow with all of her strength behind it. A yell exploded from her. Breathing came in rapid pants, and there was no more remorse in her heart as the sword began to quiver, eager to descend. Tony's...no, not Tony's...Lucien's eyes? Olcas's eyes? Evil's eyes stared at her from what she now realized was a stolen face. The gaze filled with hatred and enmity. It was a gaze wreathed in both murderous intent and avarice. Its memory would stay with Kara forever, even should the curse fade away.

"You will not harm another, you will not poison them with your pain and twisted pleasure, you will not steal their peace and their power. You will be no more and I will send you there...as promised."

Tony laughed a contemptuous and dismissive laugh. "Really, little girl? Go ahead. You will only take my place as the monster." His gaze grew considering, his eyes leered. "If you can even bring yourself to do it. Can you murder me, really? Have you got it in you? If you do, I've won, for you are as I am. And if you don't, still I've won, because you are mine." His calm, matter-of-fact tone infuriated her.

"Shut up!"

"So tell me...do you have what it takes to murder a god?"

"Shut up! You are no god...you are a devil, and if killing you will mean the world is that much safer, I will gladly go to hell for it!" Kara spat the words at him and drew down the sword once more, eager for it now, all restraint burned away by her rage.

Her focus was so complete she nearly missed the flutter of movement darting forward, interposing itself between her and her target. Only the stunned look on Tony's face brought Kara around, clearing her obsession sufficiently for her to see the Romani woman suddenly between them, right in the path of the strike, her face wrinkled and ancient and her eyes practically hidden in the folds of age. Blood already streaked her silver-white hair and a shallow, slashing wound opened her from shoulder to breastbone. Diminutive though she was, her stance was commanding.

There was a crackle in the air, currents as supercharged as ball lightning washing over Kara in waves. The sword halted yet again and she shook her head in a desperate attempt to clear it, to restore some sense...some focus...some sanity. It didn't work. Before her stood a gnarled Romani woman, her eyes tired, but determined, one hand gripping the pendant around Tony's neck—Kara vaguely remembered it from her time in his clutches—the other hand braced against Kara's sword arm. Her gaze wandered from the woman up to Tony's face, and she nearly staggered. He watched her with terror and confusion. Fear glinted in his now chocolate-brown eyes. What was going on?

"No...not this way. You will not take both to be free of the one; I cannot allow it. Family before all others." The woman spoke in cryptic words, except Kara knew precisely what she meant. The woman would not allow Tony to be sacrificed so that Olcas...or whichever brother wore him like a suit...could be banished. She watched with detached wonder as the woman took a tiny blade from somewhere in her skirts, a blade vaguely reminiscent of the sword Kara still raised above her head. It puzzled her when the woman muttered a few words in what could only be her native language and drew the blade in a precise slashing motion across the space between Tony and Kara herself. The act seemed like nothing more than a showy display, meant to impress and dazzle, but to no more end than that. Only it was not so simple. Kara felt a tearing agony ripple across her chest and over her brain, as if something deep-rooted was torn free from her. With a snap that nearly brought her to her knees, a binding, restrictive agony lifted from her, and suddenly, she knew what the woman had done. A sob erupted from her throat, and Kara kept her feet by sheer will alone. She did not even protest when the woman released her hold on the pendant, and Tony became not-Tony once again, wrath flooding his face and caution winning out over the thirst for retribution as Kara found the strength to raise her blade in warning. With a snarled curse, he backed away, muttering harsh, biting syllables that were vaguely familiar to Kara's ears. Sparing them both the barest of bows that had nothing to do with respect and everything to do with a silent promise of revenge, Tony once again tore a gaping hole in the fabric of reality and sped away through it. Kara was too spent to try and stop him.

Another oath, this time from behind, and Kara whirled in time to see the burnt one pull the same trick, leaving Aí clutching empty air until he landed heavily upon the ground, with soot marks all that remained of his opponent. Kara looked from him to where the Romani stood. The woman stared back, worry, regret, and defiance in her gaze.

A wave of trembling shook Kara from top to toes, and while she said nothing, her heart ached even as she snarled. She had betrayed her promise. And for what? Thanks to this woman, Bran had fled, Tony and his ally escaped once more, and Kara had again just barely avoided complete disaster. She didn't know who she was more furious at: herself or the Romani.

She turned with dread in her eyes to meet Aí's steady gaze. She was so drained she hardly registered what she saw, except that there was no anger, no rebuke or disappointment, only Aí's reassuring smile, more evident in his brilliant blue eyes than on his tired mouth. Startled...self-conscious, Kara looked away, her gaze trailing across the now empty battlefield.

She had to look closely for signs of battle, all the wounded were gone, and the thirsty ground had absorbed any mortal blood. A shudder shook her at the thought. The evidence of suffering should not vanish so readily.

Kara flinched as gentle fingers brushed across her brow in understanding, and Aí puzzled her by tucking her hair behind her ear before his hand traveled down her cheek to settle beneath her chin. She puzzled herself by letting him. Lightly he pressed up, lifting her face so they looked into each other's eyes.

"What's wrong, *Lhiannon*?"

Kara could not suppress a shudder as she mentally prepared herself to see Tony's features superimposed over another's. Her breaths drew shallow and she found it difficult to force her eyes to focus when she didn't want to see, but she must, or Tony won yet again. Breathing deeply, she nodded and offered Aí a weary smile, a smile that fled before her sudden overwhelming confusion. Aí stared at her, puzzlement and concern written in his gaze. With frightened wonder, she raised her hand and ran it across his brow, down over his cheeks, lingering over his lips, savoring the joy of seeing exactly what she touched, with no nightmares to envelope it.

"It's gone," she said in a hoarse whisper. "It's gone!"

Her laugh, when it came, bordered on hysterical, and she trembled uncontrollably. The curse...she had not dared to believe, though she had suspected. The Romani woman severed the curse linking her to Tony. Tears streamed down her cheeks, but her smile was dazzling as she looked from Aí to the Romani and back again. Of course, there was still a thick ribbon of dread within her as they all turned toward the gate to *Tír na nÓg*.

Chapter 16

and leaving behind the pointless debate going on around her, as many of the *Sidhe* waited for the rulers of the Lands to come out and make their decree in the matter of the one known as Bran. It was clear that most of them would have stormed the chamber by now if it weren't for the shimmering curtain of energy shielding the doors and the lace-like walls from both entry and view. She watched the goings-on from the other side of the clearing that led to the gates of Goibhniu's rath, too hypersensitive at the moment to get any closer to the emotional maelstrom. (Besides which, she had no intention of making herself a target for the disgruntled crowd.) Things were tense enough.

She turned away from the Court. Their angry intensity only agitated her more. Breathing deeply, she tried for a bit of Zen herself. The battle...the healing...the arguing...most of it was over for now. Even if they couldn't, she needed to let it go, so she'd be able to act rather than react. There were, after all, several enemies still out there somewhere.

Suddenly, the barrier dropped, and the doors to *Mór Halla* flew open. Within, attendants stepped back sharply, and there was a whirl of activity in the entranceway.

*Oh no, not again...*Kara closed her eyes a moment, willing herself calm as she gathered her strength for whatever was about to hit. Meeting with some success, she slowly opened her eyes. The first thing she saw was Goibhniu striding forward like an angry Titan, the rulers of the other *Sidhe* Lands close behind him.

By now, Kara thought she was familiar with rage and anger, that she knew the feel of fury intimately. But anything she had experienced paled in comparison to what she read beneath the surface of Goibhniu's neutral expression. What she had sensed earlier in the glade was as nothing next to this primal force, all the more frightening for his deft control of it.

"We have long overlooked the Bone Raven's dark ways. They were aspects o' his nature that he seemingly kept in check." Even Goibhniu's tone remained controlled and neutral, his voice like steel, regret and anger tempered with resolve. "But there are boundaries that must never be breached. In his actions today, he violated them. From this moment forth, Bran is no longer of the *Tuatha de Danaan*, he is cast out from the *Daoine Maithé*. Let it be as if he never was. His spirit forfeits the right to mingle with the Kin."

It seemed to Kara that that final bit echoed both in her mind and her ears as if it were broadcast far and wide. By the gasps that escaped the group as Goibhniu spoke, and the horror and sorrow shadowing every eye in the Court when he was done, Kara gathered that this was the worst proclamation that could be made. There was movement all around as those who had remained away or had left the vicinity of *Mór Halla* arrived.

Kara felt like a rock in the river, with immortals streaming past to either side of her. Something within her urged her forward. Unsure of what it was or why, she hesitated.

A shuddering breath sounded by her shoulder, and Kara looked up to find Maggie beside her. This was the first she had seen of her friend and mentor since before the attack. The *Sidhe*'s expression was veiled, and her arms wrapped tightly, almost protectively about her stomach, as if she might be ill.

"What does it mean?" Kara asked after a moment when she was sure Maggie would not just move past her. The *Sidhe* did not seem to hear. Trying to be patient, Kara moved her arm with only a moment's hesitation to rest across Maggie's shoulders, offering comfort. Something told Kara what was happening was important. She asked again, "Please, Maggie, what does it mean?"

Maggie swallowed hard and seemed to pale, her jaw flexing as she struggled to voice the words. "What it means is all places o' the *Sidhe* are closed to him. He will never be recognized again as a *Tuatha de Danaan*, an' his very pattern will be excised from the Great Wall as if he never existed. Bran not only is no more in the eyes o' his Kin, he never was. We do not kill our own kind in the name o' justice, but many would claim this to be even worse. It hasn't been done in living memory, excepting perhaps that o' the rulers o' the Lands."

"If thine eye offends thee, pluck it out," Kara could not help but murmur in response. She regretted the words the moment they left her lips, but Maggie merely quirked her mouth in a brief, grim smile. The reality of what the banishment represented settled in. Kara drew a sharp breath at the enormity of it and hugged Maggie closer as the *Sidhe* trembled and shook, still clutching her belly protectively.

"Thank ye, love." Maggie managed before she continued. "What is worse, 'tis forever. Should he die, even his soul won't rejoin the *Daoine Maithé*. With his evil act, he has diminished us all in a way that can't be repaired."

Kara felt Maggie shudder one last time before getting herself back under control. Breathing deep and regaining her composure, she offered Kara an apologetic smile. "Excuse me, love, I must leave ye for now. The

Kin are summoned to take part in the ritual striking the abomination from the Wall."

All of pure *blood you mean,* Kara thought, though she felt a tugging drawing her back to the Court. She followed though she knew many there would protest her presence.

Silence filled the air as Kara wandered *Tír na nÓg* alone. Even the faelings were subdued by what had happened...on the battlefield and in *Mór Halla*. Ever since the deed was done, everyone dispersed, going off on their own to try and rediscover a bit of the peace they had lost. *Tír na nÓg* had been somber ever since. For the first time in their personal experience, one of the Kin had been stricken from the Wall, condemned by his own dark deeds. The Court knew of the ritual, the long-faded history of its use, but few of them had had the ill fortune to participate...before now.

Sighing softly, Kara was stunned by the tranquility she found when she looked within her heart. There had been such turmoil lately, such doubt and fear. But she had faced her demons, and they no longer had power over her. Settling on a tiny hummock, overlooking a still pond whose edge was softened by plumy reed and lush cats-tails, Kara allowed her mind to wander carefully over what had happened after the battle.

When she and Aí had returned, they were met by rejoicing and concern, though Kara picked up on the threads of disappointment that were for her alone. It was a small thing, and perhaps she could make Maggie understand eventually, but for now, they kept their distance, each rediscovering their balance with the other. The most startling reception was when the wrinkled little Romani woman had come up to her after the cleansing. Kara knew the Rom had somehow gotten drawn into the fighting but did not realize they'd been brought into the hospitality of *Tír na nÓg*. Not knowing—or caring—what the woman who'd thwarted her justice wanted, or quite how to respond, she'd stood there and just listened to the clear, intense voice with the startling trace of Brooklyn in her accent. She could still hear the woman's words; they were ingrained in her memory:

"I want you to know I didn't understand what was happening, not until it was too late." The Romani woman said, coming upon her out of nowhere and placing herself squarely in Kara's path. They faced off in a narrow entranceway, so there was no going around her. Kara just stood and listened, trying to keep her resentment and confusion from her face.

"I'm sorry?"

"I was too late to stop it, and you have suffered because of my stubborn, blind pride. I had imagined it could not be, that I had protected him and raised him well. You can see how wrong I was."

"I'm not interested in apologies. What do you want?" Kara's jaw flexed and she drew herself up, tense and full of wrath that she could not vent because she knew it was irrational. That did not mean the force with which it pressed upon her heart was any less potent.

"I need you to listen. My grandson has fallen, his soul captured by ultimate Evil. I allowed that to happen, did not take sufficient action to prevent him from becoming as he is, and for that, I owe you a debt of honor.

"Whenever you call on me, I shall stand by your side, no matter what, until I have paid my penance. I will leave you now and only hope you will consider talking more to me later."

Kara drew a startled breath, her hand clutching her shirt above her breastbone where the knife scar had been. She knew who this woman meant and who she claimed to be. The realization was most unsettling. Before, she could picture Tony as some beast, some monster, not a regular guy, not much younger than herself, with a family who cared for him deeply. What had happened to him was a mystery, but the Romani woman implied that he was as much victim as she was...well, not quite, but far from the monster she envisioned. Once again, a memory surfaced of cold, hateful blue eyes that darkened to brown eyes filled with confusion...and fear.

The old woman stayed in *Tír na nÓg*, along with one of the Romani men who refused to leave. All the rest had gone back to their wagons and headed off, encouraged by the two left behind. They both looked haunted, Gypsy Rose and the one called Jacko, and Kara could not help but wonder how they were tied to her own fate. What would the battle with their private demons mean for her?

No. Kara pushed the thoughts away, along with the memories, suppressing it all for now. There was no doubt they were significant, but she could not deal with it for the moment. Now was the time for healing, not worry. Her thoughts returned instead to her loved ones.

Kara had yet to meet with Goibhniu...or her parents. She was still too raw, too uncertain. She needed to explore who *Kara* was before she could stand her ground against them. The Smithgod was too overwhelming. And her parents were too frustrating. They would not accept that their little girl was gone...grown into something they could never understand. How could they, when she barely did herself?

As she sat there contemplating the faerie mist swathing her own little bit of Eden, Kara had the conviction that whatever she found within herself, she would be okay with it...but not until another day.

Epilogue

 without heart, as many claimed. Appropriately done, revenge was passionate and heated; otherwise, it was not worth the effort. One took care with revenge to ensure it was fitting and thorough in every detail. At least, that was his philosophy. Cast out from his legacy, dead to his Kin in all regards, his eternal pattern stricken painfully from the Great Wall until no sign remained, Bran had nothing left but vengeance...well, vengeance and ambition, then. But in his case, they went hand in hand.

In a boggy wasteland, he constructed an oasis, dry and warm, secluded and secure. The denizens of the swamp, sinister and venomous, were his guardians, the pitfalls his security. He draped his hidden haven with silk and gauze, furnished it with every luxury at his hand. All the while he tried to blank out the wretched pain gnawing at his chest. It was difficult, and he roared when his efforts failed, but still, he worked on. If he shared eternity with this agony, he would do so in comfort.

When he was finally done, the Bone Raven filled his nest, a bower worthy of a king—or deity—with his most precious jewel: a white-haired elven beauty. And, thanks to Goibhniu, she was doomed to sleep forevermore...or at least until the time of sacrifice, when she would be the key to bringing down the Kin who forsook them both. This was the seed of Bran's revenge.

He didn't know how he had missed it at first, but the moment he sought to plunder her for her mage power, he uncovered her true nature (along with her power-granting name). It was difficult to not chortle with undignified glee. This little discovery increased the sting of his vengeance one-hundred-fold; not only did he steal Goibhniu's precious Agnieszka—so ill-fitting a name to one of such beauty, so awkward and harsh to his ears when compared to elven names, though uniquely beautiful for something mortal, he supposed—but she was so much more than he anticipated. Not waterkin, but Kin. With that realization, he could no longer simply claim her potential—no, he could do so much more. Now was the time to destroy Goibhniu and subjugate the *Daoine Maithé*, and lovely Agnieszka would summon the weapon he would use to do it. By the time he was done, he, Bran, would be the Bone Raven no more. Gone would be the cursed epitaph given to him by Aí and his ilk, supplanted by a name worthy of a god: He would be Valiant, and none would stand against him.

GLOSSARY

A chuisle mo chroí!: Irish Gaelic, a term of endearment meaning "o pulse of my heart".

Áes Sidhe: The people of the hills. It was one of the names given to the old Irish gods, the *Tuatha de Danaan*, when they retreated under the hills (*Sidhe*) after their defeat by the Milesians.

A ghrá!: Irish Gaelic for "O love!"

Anu: In Celtic lore, an alternate name for the goddess Danu, from whom the *Tuatha de Danaan* took their name. The names are used interchangeably throughout the mythology, though there is some debate as to whether these were one and the same goddess, or two separate. In the author's fabricated legend of Danu's time before arriving in Ireland Anu is not a variant on the name Danu but a person in her own right, Danu's older twin. For the purpose of this fiction Anu sacrifices herself to allow Danu to escape the clutches of the *Namhaid*, the enemy. In reverence Danu uses both names after the crossing to Ireland, ensuring that her beloved sister will ever be remembered (thus explaining the presence of both names in the actual Celtic mythology and Irish place-names).

Ard Namhaid: a combination of the Irish Gaelic words for High (*Ard*) and enemy (*Namhaid*). These are a fictitious caste of a race created by the author to explain several key points in Celtic myth of which no details are known. The Ard are all male and dominate the *Namhaid*. In appearance they are similar to the *Namhaid Conairt*(the female of the species), with a fine, velvety white pelt and dagger-like teeth in a blood-red mouth, however, their hair and eyes are deepest black, whereas the females' hair and eyes are red. Also, though their hands are likewise clawed, they are nowhere as pronounced as those of the *Namhaid Conairt*. (*See also Bás; Namhaid Conairt.*)

Ar Carmán...Scrios...Tógail...Díoltas...: Irish Gaelic for "For Carmán...Havoc... Destruction...Revenge." For the purpose of this story, the battle cry of Carmán's children.

Ard Ri: Irish Gaelic for High King.

Bás: Irish Gaelic for Death. In the author's created mythology, this is the name the *Namhaid*, the ancient enemy race of the *Sidhe*, have for themselves.

Beag Scath: A combination of the Irish Gaelic words meaning Little (beag) and Shadow (scath). The name Maggie gave the sprite that became emotionally attached to her long ago in Eire.

Bean Fianna: For the purpose of this story, the women warriors of the *Sidhe Fianna*.

Bean Sidhe: translating into woman of the hills, the bean *sidhe*, or banshee, is a faerie harbinger of death. Appearing as a woman in a green dress and grey cloak, with eyes fiery red from weeping, she is seen scrubbing bloody garments in a stream, or heard wailing outside a household where a family member is doomed to die. If the bean *sidhe* is caught, she must relinquish the name of the doomed. When multiple bean *sidhe* wail together they are heralding the death of a great or holy person. Cliodna, the goddess of beauty, is Bean *Sidhe* to the Clan O'Keefe.

Beyond the Veil: a Celtic euphemism for dying.

Bodhran: Pronounced bow-rawn, a Celtic frame drum made of cured goatskin stretched taut over a wooden frame, played either by the tapping of the fingers or with a double-headed stick called a cipín, tipper, or beater.

Brian Boru: (960-1014) The last High King, or Ard Ri, of Ireland. He defended Ireland against the attacks of the Vikings and ended that race's hopes of ever taking the island.

Brownie: In Scottish Celtic Mythology a domestic faerie known for doing nightly deeds for those who treat them kindly. Their coloring is representative of their name. They are commonly left offerings of milk in thanks.

Carmán: An Athenian goddess (possibly rooted in the Greek goddess Demeter) who, with her three sons: Calma (Valiant), Dubh (Black), and Olcas (Evil), terrorized early Ireland. They were eventually defeated by the *Tuatha de Danaan*. She was bound in chains and her three sons destroyed. It is said Carmán died of grief. Carmán is also portrayed as a goddess of black magick, destroying anything by chanting a spell three times.

The Cosaint: Irish Gaelic for safeguard. A legend of the author's creation, developed to support her extrapolation of why the *Sidhe* are called *Tuatha de Danaan* (The Children of Danu). The *Cosaint* is a *Sidhe* woman hidden at birth so that not even she knows what she is. Raised as a human, she is meant to be a safeguard against the *Sidhe* race being destroyed without a means of the souls returning to the earth, as nearly happened in the author's fabricated tale when

Danu herself was the last of her kind and had to hide from the *Namhaid.*

Cúchulainn (the Hound of Culann): One of the most famous heroes in Irish mythology. Originally called Sétanta, Cúchulainn got his name from defending himself and slaying the hound that defended the fortress of Culann, after which he vowed to defend the fortress himself until a new hound could be found and trained, thus becoming known as the Hound of Culann. Though his achievements are many, he is chiefly known for his single-handed defense of Ulster during the war of the Táin.

Cuimhnigh: Irish Gaelic for "remember". For the purpose of this story Goibhniu, the Smithgod, has used this word, along with a touch at three key points on the *Cosaint's* person, to release the hidden memories of her true nature.

Curragh of Kildare: The place where Earl Gerald is said to ride his horse around every seven years. To this day the region is known for the horse racing that takes place there.

Danu: In Irish Celtic mythology, the goddess from whom the *Tuatha de Danaan* took their name; for the purpose of this story, the birth mother of every *Sidhe* born in Ireland. The sole survivor of a concerted attack on the *Sidhe* in their homelands, she alone remained to give birth to the *Sidhe* souls returning for their next incarnation.

Daoine Maithé: Irish Gaelic for "Good People", one of the names by which the *Sidhe* are called. In the author's created mythology, this is also the name by which the *Sidhe* originally called themselves, before coming to Ireland and becoming the *Tuatha de Danaan.*

Díoltas: Irish Gaelic for "Revenge".

Eire: The original name for Ireland.

Falias, Finias, Gorias, and Murias: Four great cities said to be the former home of the *Tuatha de Danaan,* before they arrived in Ireland. Nothing more specific is mentioned of their original homeland. Each city contained a magical artifact that the *Tuatha de Danaan* carried with them to Ireland.

Fear Fianna: For the purpose of this story, the men warriors of the *Sidhe Fianna.*

The Fe-Fiada: In Irish Celtic mythology, a supernatural mist or fog.

Fianna: In Ireland's far past these were the warriors who were the royal bodyguard for the Ard Ri, the High King. (*Also See, Sidhe Fianna*)

Fionn Mac Cumhail (Finn Mac Cool): One of the most celebrated heroes in Irish myth. Born Demna, he gained the name of Fionn (the Fair One) when he burnt his finger on the flesh of the Salmon of Knowledge, which he was cooking for his master. Sucking his thumb to cool it, he obtained wisdom from the magical fish. He went on to become the leader of the *Fianna*, the royal bodyguard. His wife was the goddess Sadb, who was originally transformed into a fawn by a spurned Druid, who eventually whisks away and transforms her back into a fawn again while she is pregnant with Fionn's son. Fionn never found his wife, but his son, whom he named Oisín (fawn), eventually was discovered and came to be with him.

Fleadh Ghoibhnenn: The Otherworld feast held by the Smithgod Goibhniu. Any mortal to take part in the feast and the drink served becomes immortal.

Garda Faoi Rún: A combination of the Irish Gaelic words Garda (guard) and Faoi Rún (in secret). The name given to the sprite answering to Aí, left with Agnieszka to look over her until she could be brought to safety. Also called Rex by Agnieszka.

Geal leanbh: Irish Gaelic for cherished child.

Geal leannán: Irish Gaelic for cherished lover.

Gearoidh Iarla (Earl Gerard): A great man of the Fitzgeralds, he had a rath (fortress) at Mullaghmast. He was known for standing against injustice and for his abilities to transform himself into any form. It is said that he and his warriors now sleep in a long cavern under the Rath of Mullaghmast. Every seven years the Earl rides around the Curragh of Kildare on a steed with silver hooves. At a time when those hooves are worn thin as a cat's ear, the miller's son with six fingers to each hand will blow his trumpet to wake the warriors and Gearoidh Iarla will return to the land of the living. He will defend Ireland against the English, and reign as Ireland's king for two-score years.

Glamory: A spell to make whatever the caster wishes—himself, an object, or another person—appear other than it really is.

Goibhniu the Smith: An Irish/Celtic blacksmith god. Son of the goddess Danu. He manufactures swords that always strike true, and he possesses the mead (ale) of eternal life. He is also considered the god of healing due to the role of iron in Celtic life and the magical properties it is said to have. Goibhniu presides over an Otherworld feast (Fleadh Ghoibhnenn) where any mortal to take part becomes immortal; exempt from common death and disease. In some accounts this is attributed to the food, and in most others it is attributed to the ale or mead given to drink at the Feast.

Gorgio: In England, the term the Romani use for other folk.

Imeacht gan teacht ort: An Irish Gaelic curse meaning "may you leave without returning".

Lamai/lamiai: In Greek myth, this is a vampiric woman, half woman and half serpent. She lives in caves and gets sustenance from drinking the blood of children.

Leanbh: Irish Gaelic for "child".

Leprechaun: In Irish Celtic Mythology a diminutive member of the faerie folk known for making shoes, but only one at a time, never in pairs.

Lhiannon: Irish Gaelic for "Sweetheart".

Mamó: Irish Gaelic for "Grandma".

Manannan Mac Lir: Ruler of *Tír Tairnigiri* (The Land of Promise) A shape-changer, he is depicted with a mantle and helmet of invisibility (or flames), and an unfailing sword. He was also attributed with bring fertility and prosperity and was associated with the cauldron of regeneration.

Mathair: Irish Gaelic for "Mother".

The Miller's Son: It is said in the legend of Gearoidh Iarla, that the miller's son, who will be born with six fingers on each hand, will blow his trumpet and wake those who sleep beneath the Rath of Mullaghmast.

Namhaid: Irish Gaelic for "enemy". A fictitious race created by the author, they are the reason why the people who would come to be known as the *Sidhe* flee their original homes in Falias, Finias, Gorias, and Murias. The Enemy slays all but one of the *Sidhe*, a young elf named Danu. She escapes and flees to Ireland, there to bear her children, who from that day forward are known by the name *Tuatha de Danaan,* or the Children (People) of Danu.

The Namhaid Conairt: a combination of the Irish Gaelic words for "enemy" (*Namhaid*) and "pack" (*Conairt*). As created by the author, these are the hunter caste of the *Namhaid,* (or the *Bás,* as they call themselves) responsible for hunting down the elves and either capturing or killing them. They are all female, with a fine, velvety white pelt and flowing dark red hair. Their eyes are likewise red, and their teeth like dainty daggers in their blood-red mouths. Each hand is clawed with dagger-like nails, while those on the feet are blunted from running and capable of gouging, not slicing. The *Conairt* do not eat when they are breeding and they do not bear their own young. When they mate the sperm and eggs are stored in a sack at the base of the spine. Once a suitable host is found, the eggs are extruded through a barb that extends like a retractable tail from the female. Jabbed into the body of the victim, the eggs are seated in the abdomen. The individual so implanted is for all intents and purposes dead as a chemical injected with the sack inhibits the thought centers of the brain, allowing only the autonomous impulses to operate, and those only barely.

Olcas: Irish Gaelic for "evil". This is also the name of one of the three sons of the Athenian goddess Carmán.

Oisín (fawn): Son of Fionn Mac Cumhail and the goddess Sadb. Oisín's mother was transformed into a fawn and spirited away from her husband while she was pregnant with him. She bore him as a human child and raised him in her deer shape until he was a young boy. Found by his father, Oisín grew up amid the *Fianna* and became one of their leading champions.

Pixie: In Irish Celtic Mythology a cheerful and mischievous faerie that adores music and dancing.

Pucá (Pooka): in Irish Celtic mythology, a fey creature that leads travelers astray and performed other mischievous deeds. By some accounts it appears in the likeness of a fierce black steed that will pull the unwary onto his back run away with them through river and fen, not shaking them off until the grey of dawn.

Rath: A fortress or earthwork, usually circular, surrounding a chieftain's house. This has also come to mean the hills where the *Tuatha de Danaan* retreated beneath after their defeat by the Milesians.

Rath o' Mullaghmast: The fortress of Gearoidh Iarla (Earl Gerald). This is where legend says the miller's son will blow his trumpet.

Redcap: in Irish Celtic mythology, a faerie known by his red hat and blood-thirsty ways.

The Rom, The Romani: These are the nomadic Rom most common in Europe but found in one form or another all around the world. They are known occasionally to settle, though they do not lose their Romani ways.

The Royal Ulster Constabulary(RUC): the police force in Northern Ireland. Originally over 90% Protestant, this has been a major focus of reform.

Saints Catherine, Florian, Francis, and Lawrence: All said to be saints attributed with protecting against fire.

Scrios: Irish Gaelic for "Havoc".

The Sidhe: Pronounced "shee," the Fair Folk, Otherworldly beings that came to live in Ireland in the time before it was invaded by the Milesians. After their defeat they were banished underground, living in Mounds, also called *Sidhe*. They were said to be very long-lived, if not immortal, and possessing of mystical powers. (*See* Áes *Sidhe, Daoine Maithé,* The Gentry, *Tuatha de Danaan*)

The Sidhe Fianna: The author's creation for the purpose of this book. A group of warriors selected by Goibhniu the Smithgod to combat the assaults being perpetrated against the *Sidhe* in this novel. There are two groups of the *Sidhe Fianna*: the *Bean Fianna,* or warrior women, and the *Fear Fianna,* the warrior men.

Sowlth/Somhlth: In Irish Celtic mythology, a supernatural being without shape. Refers—for this series only—to Carmán's sons, who, for the author's purposes, were not destroyed but merely disembodied.

Sprite: Spirit faerie. Very creative, sprites are often depicted as muses, artists, and poets. They are some of the most creative faeries and may even decide to bond with a human or *Sidhe* and stay with them their whole lives.

Tír na mBan (The Land of Women/Land of the Maidens): Part of the Irish Celtic Otherworld, the land ruled by Balor of the Fomorian giants.

Tír na nÓg (The Land of Youth): Part of the Irish Celtic Otherworld, this is where Goibhniu presides over the Fleadh Ghoibhnenn.

Tír Tairnigiri (The Land of Promise): Part of the Irish Celtic Otherworld, this is where Manannan Mac Lir, the major sea-god, held his seat of power.

Tógail: Irish Gaelic for "Destruction".

Tuatha de Danaan: The Children of Danu, also translated in other texts as the People of Danu, another name for the *Sidhe*, said to be blessed by the goddess Danu, also called Anu or Danaa.

Undine: an elemental creature affiliated with water.

Waterkin: a term originating with the author to describe those of mixed blood, with both a *Sidhe* and human parent. It is originally a condescending term referring to the fact that the *Sidhe* blood has been diluted...watered down, thus less than the original, though repeated use has reduced it to merely an identifier.

Sources

Print Resources:

Ellis, Peter Berresford, *A Dictionary of Irish Mythology* (Santa Barbara, CA: ABC-CLIO, Inc, 1987.)

Ireland: The Complete Guide and Road Atlas, Seventh Edition (Guilford, CT: The Globe Pequot Press, 2002.)

Kelly, Sean, and Rosemary Rogers, *Saint Preserve Us!* (New York: Random House, 1993.)

Mac Mathúna, Séamus, and Ailbhe Ó Curráin, *Collins Gem: Irish Dictionary* (New York: HarperCollins Publishers, 1995).

Rolleston, T. W., *Celtic Myths and Legends* (Mineola, NY: Dover, 1990.)

Tong, Diane, *Gypsy Folk Tales* (New York: MJF Books, 1989.)

Yeats, W. B., *Irish Fairy & Folk Tales* (New York: Barnes & Noble Books, 1993.)

Internet Resources:

Celtic Myth

http://www.alia.ie/tirnanog/myth1.html

http://www.livingmyths.com/Celticmyth.htm

http://www.celticattic.com/olde_world/myths/fairy.htm

http://www.ladywoods.org/roots4.htm

http://www.seanachaidh.com/godcelt.html

http://magickwell.20m.com/danu.htm

http://www.danann.org/library/herb/cup2.html

http://joellessacredgrove.com/Celtic/deitiesg-h-i.html

http://www.deoxy.org/h_mounds.htm

Romani

http://www.romani.org/

http://www.christusrex.org/www2/Rom.net/

http://www.herts.ac.uk/UHPress/Rom.html

Miscellaneous

http://www.peevish.co.uk/slang/search.htm

About the Author

Award-winning author, editor and publisher Danielle Ackley-McPhail has worked both sides of the publishing industry for longer than she cares to admit. In 2014 she joined forces with husband Mike McPhail and friend Greg Schauer to form her own publishing house, eSpec Books.

Her works include six novels, *Yesterday's Dreams, Tomorrow's Memories, Today's Promise, The Halfling's Court, The Redcaps' Queen*, and *Baba Ali and the Clockwork Djinn*, written with Day Al-Mohamed. She is also the author of the solo collections *A Legacy of Stars, Consigned to the Sea, Flash in the Can*, and *Transcendence*, the non-fiction writers' guide, *The Literary Handyman, The Ginger KICK! Cookbook*, and is the senior editor of the *Bad-Ass Faeries* anthology series. Her short stories are included in numerous other anthologies and collections.

She is a member of Broad Universe, a writer's organization focusing on promoting the works of women authors in the speculative genres.

Danielle lives in New Jersey with husband and fellow writer, Mike McPhail and three extremely spoiled cats. She can be found on Facebook (Danielle Ackley-McPhail) and Twitter (DMcPhail, eSpecBooks).

To learn more about her work, visit www.*sidhe*nadaire.com and www.especbooks.com

www.ingramcontent.com/pod-product-compliance
Lightning Source LLC
Chambersburg PA
CBHW060905190726
48286CB00002B/380